STORIES
TO LIVE BY

Books by Marjorie Vetter

CHAMPLAIN SUMMER
CARGO FOR JENNIFER

Books edited by Marjorie Vetter

STORIES TO LIVE BY
CHRISTMAS ALL YEAR 'ROUND
ON MY HONOR
AMERICAN GIRL FAVORITE STORIES

Coauthor (with Laura Vitray)

THE QUESTIONS GIRLS ASK

STORIES
TO LIVE BY

A TREASURY OF FICTION
FROM THE AMERICAN GIRL

THIRTY STORIES
SELECTED AND EDITED BY
MARJORIE VETTER

PLATT & MUNK, Publishers
NEW YORK

PREFACE

We all want to have confidence in ourselves, to lead rich, full lives, to be respected and admired by those around us, to love and to be loved. We are sometimes mistaken in the things we think will give us all this. Often it takes years of living to make us realize that, by themselves, beauty, wealth, social position, fame—or even a combination of all of them—will not automatically make us successful persons, or guarantee our happiness.

Sometimes we go about achieving our aims in the wrong way and then blame others, our circumstances, or our bad luck when we fail.

As a girl in your teens, you are beginning to think about these things, groping to explore your own personality and to understand those around you. Bit by bit the direction of your life is passing from your parents into your own hands. What are you going to do with it?

Of course you are thinking about the future. You are beginning to plan your personal goals, forming values, setting standards that will guide your life and be passed on by you to your children.

Do you ever think that your dream of the kind of woman you would like to be someday is directly influencing your thoughts and actions now, and that the decisions you are making today will affect the woman you will be tomorrow?

There is bound to be uncertainty and confusion as you strive to know yourself and to take your place in a new grown-up world. Sometimes you need help in making up your mind how you really feel, what you really want to do and to be. Stories which present problems you meet in your own day-to-day living, can often help you see things in a fresh light or clarify your own ideas. Questions of ethics, values, standards can be forcefully, dramatically and unforgettably presented in fiction. Good stories have power to help us in our everyday thinking and living; great ones can change our lives.

5

We call the thirty stories in this collection *Stories To Live By* because hundreds of girls have told us, by letter and in person, that they have found these stories not only absorbing and entertaining, but thought-provoking and of direct help in this matter of making the most of life.

More than seven hundred thousand girls subscribe to *The American Girl,* the national Girl Scout magazine. We know that each copy of the magazine is read by at least four girls beside the subscriber; thus, well over two million girls read each issue. The editors of the magazine receive thousands of letters every year from all over the United States and from the far corners of the world. Every now and then in the letters there will be mentioned, over and over again, one story that has especially touched the hearts of our readers. Affectionate tribute to these stories keeps popping up in our mail for months, even for years.

Each of the thirty tales here is such a story. We rejoice, and so will girls everywhere, that these stories have been given a new and longer life between book covers. We hope they will bring pleasure, comfort and inspiration to both old and new readers.

MARJORIE VETTER

CONTENTS

CONTENTS—continued

STORIES
TO LIVE BY

*When it came to going steady, Laurie had
to choose between security and freedom*

There's Always
a Price Tag

Laura Nelson Baker

Laurie's mother was having a cup of coffee by herself when Laurie
came downstairs. It was Saturday, when Mr. Geddes, Laurie's
father, slept late.

"Morning, honey," her mother said, as Laurie came into the
kitchen in her pink brunch coat. "Do you want an egg?"

"I'll have cereal and toast this morning, I think." Laurie glanced
out the window as she took a slice of bread out of the wrapper and
dropped it into the toaster. It looked cold outside. She pushed the
toaster lever down. "Mom . . ."

"Yes, Laurie."

"Boyd Harris called me last night."

"Really?" her mother said. "But what about Tom?"

Tom Castles was the redheaded junior with whom Laurie was
going steady.

The toast popped up and Laurie carried the hot slice to the
place opposite her mother, where a glass of orange juice stood.
She drank the juice and said, "Oh, I told Boyd I had a date."

"Are you going out with him if he calls again?"

"Of course not." Laurie buttered her toast carefully, spreading
the butter to the edges.

There was silence in the kitchen as Laurie munched toast and
her mother set a bowl of hot cereal down in front of her. Then

11

Mrs. Geddes said, "The Harrises are joining our church; did you know that?"

"I knew they came to services sometimes," Laurie said. "I saw Mr. and Mrs. Harris there twice, and Boyd once."

The Harrises were newcomers to Manley Park, and Boyd, seventeen and a senior, had most of the high school watching eagerly to discover his taste in girls. His hair was brown and curly and he had an attractive smile. He was also shaping up as a track star and an honor student. Laurie knew what her mother was thinking. The Young People's League of the church had a sleigh ride planned for a week from tomorrow night. Tom didn't belong to their church, but as each League member could bring a guest, Laurie was taking Tom. Would Boyd go, she wondered, and would he invite a girl?

Laurie saw Boyd Harris a couple of times during the first part of the week. He passed her with Tom once in the hall; he was studying in the library on Tuesday afternoon when she went there to get a book. He looked up and gave her a friendly smile, but she was on her way to a meeting of the arrangements committee for the Sock Hop and had to hurry. Boyd lived only a few blocks from Laurie, but she never ran into him on the way to school because she and her chum Polly and Polly's boy friend George generally rode to school with Tom in his car.

The Sock Hop was going to be fun, Laurie thought, when she came out of the committee meeting. Everybody in the whole school was invited. There would be prizes for the funniest costumes. Her mother didn't approve of dancing in stocking feet in the middle of winter but the floor would be warm and they would wear wool socks.

When Tom came over to her house after supper on Wednesday evening, he and Laurie discussed their costumes.

"I'm pretty good at forgery," Tom said. "Why don't I fix up a couple of pairs of socks with autographs? You know, like from the President and Jayne Mansfield."

"Jayne Mansfield!" Laurie tossed the newspaper at him. "Make mine Pat Boone, thank you ever so much!"

Laurie's father came in from the kitchen. "Make mine Greta Garbo," he said.

"Greta Garbo . . ." Laurie stared at him. "Isn't she dead or something?"

Tom held out a hand to Laurie. "Say, we'd better get at that math. It's after eight already. The exam is first hour tomorrow, remember?"

"I know it," Laurie said guiltily, "and I've hardly looked at the review section."

They settled down together at the dining-room table, dark hair next to red. Laurie thought, as she had many times before, how much more fun it was to study when she could study with Tom. They earned better grades, too, than either of them used to get.

On Tuesday of the next week, Tom called at a quarter to seven in the morning to say he had to take his father to work because the family car was at the garage. "I won't have time to stop for you and Polly and George," he said.

"See you after first hour, then," Laurie said sleepily into the mouthpiece. Looking out the window, she saw it was snowing— not a blizzardy kind of snow, just the soft gentle kind she liked. It would be nice to walk to school. She would never want to live anywhere but Minnesota, because of its exciting weather.

The trees in the front yard were already trimmed with white when she stepped out the front door at a quarter to eight. It wasn't really cold though, just zesty.

The high school was about three quarters of a mile from the Geddes' house. Laurie had covered only about a quarter of the way when a voice said, "Are you the Snow Queen?"

Laurie blew a snowflake off her eyelashes and turned around. "Hi, Boyd," she said, "isn't it wonderful? I just love snow."

He had his storm coat on with the collar turned up around his face, but no hat, the crazy guy. It seemed to Laurie that all boys must hate to wear anything on their heads, summer or winter.

"It's great," Boyd said, "but it's sure wet. We'll be soaked by the time we get to school." He seemed pleased at the idea. He slogged along beside her, talking about the basketball game of the Saturday before and asking her about the student council advisers.

Boyd tried to brush the worst of the snow off Laurie as they hurried, snow-covered and breathless, down the wide walk that led into the high school building. Laurie felt a swift surge of relief that she was not going to meet Tom until after the first class. If he saw her with Boyd like this he might wonder, and she wouldn't be able to explain in front of Boyd that their meeting was accidental. She would tell Tom how it happened as soon as she saw him.

Unfortunately, she didn't have a chance to tell Tom—not until half the school had told him first. When Laurie met him at their favorite place beside the telephone booth in the lower hall, she had only to see his face—sober, almost glowering—to know that Tom was angry.

"Well, goodness," Laurie said, trying to laugh him out of it, "a girl walks to school with a boy in a snowstorm and that's something to be unhappy about? Let's not fight about anything so silly, Tom." She held his arm with her fingertips, lightly, coaxingly. Tom wasn't just her steady, he was her friend. They talked to each other about everything under the sun, things she didn't talk about with Polly, or even with her parents.

"I called your house at ten to eight," he said. "You'd already gone. You went early, hoping Boyd would come along." His blue eyes looked stormily down into Laurie's face. "He's got a crush on you, that guy. Everybody in school knows it. You told me yourself he called up and asked you for a date once. Laurie, you have to tell him we're going steady."

Laurie's fingers dropped from Tom's sleeve and she stood up a little straighter. "I *have* to, Tom?" she asked quietly. "You can't order me around, you know. I don't think Boyd Harris has a crush on me or any other girl in school—he's just friendly. But whether he has or not, I am not going to go up to him and say, 'Please don't smile at me, Mr. Harris, because it makes my boy friend mad.'"

She knew she shouldn't have said it as soon as she saw the red come up in Tom's cheeks. But she was angry herself by then and wouldn't yield. She hadn't done anything wrong and she wasn't going to pretend she had. Tom had no business tearing into her that way, without waiting for her to explain. Of course she had left the house early—walking took time. Maybe she need not have left quite so early as she had, but still, why should Tom decide just how long it would take her to get to school?

The bell rang for the next hour. Tom and Laurie stood there

glaring at each other while the rest of the students thronged past them. At last Tom said, "Oh, Laurie—"

The way he said it made all the anger slide out of Laurie. She took his arm. "Want to walk to two-o-one with me?" she asked.

By Sunday, the snow which had fallen earlier in the week had packed down and provided a smooth, hard surface perfect for sleighing. "Usually when we plan a sleigh ride," Laurie said to Tom when he came to take her to the church where the party was to gather, "the weatherman sends a good thaw and the snow disappears. This time he didn't and it didn't. I just love sleigh rides."

Tom held her jacket while she slipped her arms into it. *"I just love,"* he mocked her good-naturedly. "You just love new moons, and canoeing, and cheeseburgers, and skating, and sock hops, and sleigh rides—"

Laurie buttoned her jacket to the chin and flung the red hood over her hair, leaving only her bangs uncovered. She lifted her chin.

"What's wrong with being happy?" she asked. "I do love all those things, so why shouldn't I say so?"

"You should," Tom agreed. "It's because you're so happy all the time that everybody loves you. Didn't you know that?"

Laurie's fingers, which had been busy buttoning the hood around her throat, stopped suddenly. What a charming thing for Tom to say! Did everyone love her? No, of course they didn't, but it was nice that Tom thought so. Suddenly shy, she began to hunt for her wool mittens, keeping her face averted from Tom for a second or two.

Most of the Leaguers were at the church when Tom and Laurie reached it, but the sleigh hadn't come yet. Mr. Webb, the assistant minister who had arranged the outing, urged them to wait inside the church because of the cold.

Boyd Harris hadn't come, Laurie noted with a quick glance around. The Harrises were church members now, but maybe Boyd didn't feel sufficiently at home yet to join the Leaguers.

"Here's the sleigh!" somebody shouted, and the wool-clad crowd began to pile out of the vestibule into the crisp air.

Tom leaped into the sleigh and held out his hand to Laurie. "Up you come!" he said.

"Up you go, Elaine!" a voice behind Laurie said. "I'm a firm believer in the push system."

Laurie turned to look into the smiling face of Boyd Harris. He was pretending to push his sister into the sleigh.

"Hello," he said. "Do you know Elaine, Laurie? Elaine, this is Laurie Geddes."

"Hi," said Elaine. She was younger than Boyd and very pretty in a blue parka and ski outfit.

"Hi," Laurie said to both of them. "I'm glad you came." She took Tom's outstretched hand and swung herself up. "Tom, do you know Elaine and Boyd Harris?"

"How are you, Harris?" Tom said, not very cordially. "Hi, Elaine." He thrust an arm down to Elaine. "Here," he said, "this is how it's done. Grab."

Elaine grabbed. At the same moment Boyd boosted her from behind and she arrived on the sleigh with such momentum that she almost knocked Laurie over. They all laughed, including Tom.

The sleigh party was fun all right, Laurie thought later, when Tom had brought her home and she was in her own room getting ready for bed. Boyd was friendly but no more so to her than to the other girls. He was very sweet to his sister. I wish I had a brother, Laurie thought as she pinned her hair up in big curls to make soft waves. But of course all brothers weren't like Boyd.

"You make me furious," Polly Kent said to Laurie when they were on their way home from the skating rink late one afternoon. "You let me go on and on about Boyd Harris without ever saying a word."

"A word about what?"

"About how everybody knows he's crazy about you," Polly said indignantly. "Has he asked you for a date, Laurie?"

"Once," Laurie said. "But I didn't go, naturally."

"You mean because of Tom." Polly sighed. "Some girls have it and some don't. Two of the most attractive boys in Manley Park, and they both want to go out with you. I should think your head would burst."

"Oh, Polly, you exaggerate," Laurie said.

She parted from her friend on the corner and walked slowly along the street to her home. She didn't feel particularly puffed up about Boyd Harris' interest in her; in fact, it worried her. That was what Polly didn't realize—that even though it was exciting to have two boys wanting to date you, it was also a problem. The solution would be simple if she didn't happen to like *both* Tom and Boyd. It was not just a casual thing, either—she liked them both very much. A junco flew down from the bare branch of an oak to one of the barberry bushes which hedged the Geddes' lawn. Laurie stared at the bird without seeing it. The truth was, she wanted to go out with Boyd. But she didn't want to break up with Tom.

Mrs. Geddes was in the basement taking clothes out of the drier when Laurie entered the house. "Boyd Harris just phoned," Mrs. Geddes called up the stair well. "He said he'd try again in an hour."

An hour! Laurie leaned against the door casing, feeling panicked. "Mother," she asked, "are you coming upstairs soon? I have to talk to you before Boyd calls."

It was really very queer, Laurie thought as she walked up the stairs to her fourth-hour class the next Monday, not to meet Tom between classes, not to ride to school with him and Polly and George, not to study with him in the dining room in the evenings. She blinked suddenly misty eyes and climbed a little faster. Of course she missed Tom. You couldn't see so much of someone as she had of Tom for nearly two years without feeling lonely when he wasn't around any more.

"Nothing doing, Laurie," he had said that night after she and her mother had talked together, and Laurie had suggested to Tom that they still continue to be friends and go out with each other, but that they date others occasionally too. "Either you're my girl or you aren't."

Laurie had been annoyed by his dictatorial manner. She hadn't liked the stormy look in his eyes, either, or the way he had stood like a—like a big mule in the middle of the living-room floor.

"Well, then, I guess I'm not," she had said, and then, feeling pretty stormy herself, she had added, "You had better ask another girl to the Hop, Tom, before it's too late."

Why did I have to say that? Laurie asked herself now as she reached the landing and stared out at the gray March skies. There had been no need to mention the Hop at all, and maybe she and

Tom could have talked things over more calmly later. Perhaps they might have been able to work it out enough so that at least they could go to the Hop together. But of course it was too late now. Polly had told her that Tom had rushed right out and asked Julie Snow to go with him.

Laurie shrugged her shoulders. And she had turned Boyd down! It had seemed wrong to go to the Hop with Boyd after she and Tom had planned for so long to go together. She hadn't dreamed then that Tom had already asked another girl.

Boyd was waiting for her at the top of the stairs. "I have only a minute," he said, "but I wanted to ask you to a sort of party with me and my folks Sunday night. It's a kind of supper club for people with different national backgrounds—my Dad came from England, you know—which Dad belongs to in the city. They call it the Potpourri Club. It's kind of fun."

"I'd love to go," Laurie said. The Hop was on Friday night; by Sunday it would be past—and forgotten, she hoped—and she would feel better. She wished she dared to ask Boyd if he had found someone else to take to the Hop, but she was too proud. She smiled at him. "It sounds interesting," she said, and went on to her class.

Laurie remembered the talk she had had with her mother on that afternoon when she had come home and her mother told her Boyd had phoned. Going steady with a nice boy is a kind of security, her mother had reminded her, a security against loneliness and no dates and missing things. But, Laurie thought, a person missed things by going steady, too, things like going to various kinds of parties, meeting new people, getting to know different boys. Her head ached a little as she took her seat in her physics class. Her mother had told her no one could decide for her what to do; but she hadn't really decided for herself either, Laurie thought. She had just flared up at Tom and broken off with him out of temper, not because she had made up her mind objectively.

Laurie was doing the dishes the evening before the Sock Hop when the front doorbell rang. Her mother answered it. It was probably the paper boy, Laurie thought, come to collect.

"Laurie," her mother called, "Tom's here."

Tom! Laurie's heart gave a great big leap right up into her

mouth. Then it jumped back again. He was probably returning something she had left in his car, wanting to get rid of anything that even reminded him of her.

"Tell him to come on in here," she called back.

He came into the kitchen through the door from the dining room, looking just as big and comforting and dear as ever, Laurie thought with a gulp, as she dried her hands. In one hand he carried a paper bag.

"I brought over the socks," he said, when she had asked him to sit down.

"What socks?"

He drew them out of the bag, two pairs of white wool socks covered with autographs. The signature "Pat Boone" winked up at Laurie from the smaller pair.

"Why didn't you take them to Julie?"

"I'm not going to the Hop with Julie," he said sheepishly. "I never even asked her. I just told Polly that so she'd tell you. I was hurt and I wanted to hurt you back. But I didn't ask anybody. I couldn't, Laurie, not to the Sock Hop, not after we'd planned on it together nearly all winter."

Laurie felt like crying, and she felt like smiling, all mixed up together. "I know," she said. "I'm not going, either."

Tom leaned across the table and took hold of her hand. "Let's both go, Laurie, together."

Laurie caught her breath. To go to the Sock Hop after all, to make up with Tom, to feel sure and protected and happy again . . .

"Let's make up," Tom went on. "Let's go steady again, starting tonight." The blue eyes weren't stormy now; they were gentle and coaxing.

Stars danced inside Laurie. She would call Boyd tomorrow and tell him she couldn't go to his Potpourri supper party after all. She would tell him—a vision of Boyd's nice friendly face came into her mind.

"Oh, Tom—" she began, and stopped.

You can't have it both ways, Laurie, her mother had said. You can't have security and independence, too. You have to choose.

Slowly, reluctantly, Laurie pulled her fingers out of Tom's warm grasp. She shook her head, holding back the tears she felt pricking her eyelids. "I can't, Tom," she said. "I'd love to go to the Hop with you, but not on those terms. Not if it means going steady and not ever dating anyone else." She gave him a tremulous smile. "I like you better than any boy I know," she said truthfully, "but I'm not going to go steady with anyone. Not while I'm in high school, anyway."

"Well, you can't be my girl and somebody else's too," Tom insisted stubbornly. They got up and stood looking at each other, not angry any more, just unhappy. Then Tom said, "Well, see you around," and went back to the living room to get his rubbers and coat and let himself out the front door.

When he was gone, Laurie picked up the socks. I'll put them away somewhere, she thought, I'll keep them for a kind of symbol. "Love from Jayne." The words winked before her misty eyes. She felt a queer pain in her chest when her fingers touched the soft wool.

Sophomore Class dared to try
what their elders could not do

Operation Snow Lift

Skulda V. Baner

With the training that all her upper-Michigan winters had given her, Lindas Kallander leaped upon a snowbank out of reach of the heavy truck screeching over the ice. She balanced there, watching the street full of cars below her, the drivers all but holding their breaths and biting their tongues to keep right side up. Above her the sky was blue, nearly as blue as summer—Lindas thought —except that it was clearer, surer, than summer's hazy blue.

You'd never think, looking at it, she reflected, steadying her feet in stadium boots, that just yesterday it was all ragged and gray with blizzard!

She flipped the tail of her stocking cap back over her shoulder and started to slip down into a hole in the home-going traffic. Just at that instant she saw Mrs. Torrell. Mrs. Torrell was eighty, brisk as any good Iron Valley Swedish lady could be. But Mrs. Torrell's trim heel had caught on an ice bubble. She was teetering now, about to go down on her sealskin rear right in the path of a station wagon, which, with screaming brakes and scorching rubber, was trying to stop.

Lindas ran along the high bank and caught Mrs. Torrell just in time, held her until the old lady could find her own feet. Mrs. Torrell righted her smart little hat. "Goodness! Iron Valley is no place for a pedestrian in winter, is it?" she panted.

Lindas went with her to the corner where you could walk on

21

the sidewalk. Downtown, the walks had to be shoveled. And the great snow-eating plow that cleared the streets had to leave them that way. But outside of the business district, from October to May the sidewalks were buried under mounds of ice and snow, and pedestrians had to struggle along, competing with automobiles for a share of the middle of the street. It's disgraceful, Lindas thought, it's dangerous! Where was Iron Valley's civic pride? Something should be done about it. But what? People grew tired of shoveling their sidewalks only to have the plow come by and mound them up again.

Later, at supper, Lindas told Mom and Dad about Mrs. Torrell. Mom sputtered, as usual, her green eyes sparkling.

"It's a sin and a shame! Sidewalks all mounded with snow from October to May. Folks having to risk their necks in the middle of the slippery streets."

Dad sighed. "We've tried to put in the right people, petitions—voting." He shook his head. "When we get mad enough, we each go shovel our own place up to the neighbor's. But—"

"But along comes that great plow and there go our sidewalks!" Mom snapped. "Remember how it used to be, Papa? Even when times were poor, remember? The city could always get a horse to pull the sidewalk plow. And remember Washington's Birthday? School dismissed—and the dog races on? We had sidewalks to stand on then, indeed we had!"

Lindas laid down her fork. "Dog races?" Her gray eyes went from Mom to Dad. "I can almost remember dog races!"

"Not any more!" Mom sputtered indignantly. "Where would we stand to watch? Where would the dogs run—in and out of the tires? Along the drifts?"

Next morning, Lindas was still thinking about last night's conversation when Red Carleton joined her on the way to school.

"Imagine dog races up and down the street!" Lindas panted, keeping pace. "Bright sleds, and runners squealing, and dogs barking—races! Mom and Dad were talking about them last night!"

Red Carleton turned toward her, his bright hair starred with snow. "At your house, too? My mother took a nasty spill last night! And Dad came home looking like a snowman from a tumble. All

I had for supper, just about, was Dewey and his black-and-white dog winning the races!"

"Dewey?" Lindas felt something coming to a boil inside her. "You mean, the man who goes to work in a wheel chair, because his legs—"

"The same!"

They were not aware, either of them, that they had stopped spang in the narrow shoveled trail from street to school grounds, until a lusty chorus roused them.

"Races!" Red Carleton said slowly. "All my life I've heard about dog races!"

Lindas's gray eyes flashed eagerly. "Why not?"

Red Carleton's enthusiasm began to simmer down. "But how, Lindas? Where? After all we're just kids."

"There's Dewey!" Lindas stated firmly. "He can help us!"

"We could get an old nag. But—the plow? Where could we find a cutter plow to clear a way for the dogs to run and for the people to stand?"

"We'll find one!" Lindas tried to sound sure. "There are a million dogs! About every kid in sophomore class has a dog! As for sleds—who hasn't a sled in this snow country?"

Red's face was brightening. "We could make it a class project. Like the winter we had the museum of snow sculpture."

"This noon!" Lindas all but danced on her clumsy stadium-booted feet. "This very noon!"

In the school cafeteria, those who did not live near enough to go home for lunch settled together over sandwiches and hot chocolate. And first Red—who was sophomore class president—and then Lindas outlined the idea. Dog races. Dog races again. The idea caught fire slowly. Everyone had the same question. Where? The middle of the streets were full of cars now. Where could dogs run? Or people stand?

"That's the point," Lindas began deliberately. "All the old folks, all the parents remember the dog races. They'll say, let the kids have them again! But we can't have them without a place to run. So we'll have to get the walks shoveled. Then folks will be able to walk on the sidewalks instead of in the middle of the street.

After a while, everybody'll realize how much safer and better it would be to keep the sidewalks clear.

"Dad says petitioning, voting, does no good. You just get promises. Even the editorials he wrote in his paper didn't accomplish anything. But maybe, if we show them this way—" Lindas, almost trembling in her excitement, looked from one to the other of her fellow sophomores.

"Maybe we could even get Dewey! To lead—"

"Maybe we could get another Brutus! Like the one Dad said used to pull him to school."

"The Bergmans have a big St. Bernard," Red Carleton said. "I know they'd let Dewey have him."

Lindas watched doubt, uncertainty, slow-kindling enthusiasm ride the faces in front of her.

"I think perhaps we could," Aare Lehto said, with the caution of his North European ancestry.

"I *know* we could!" Mary Cavallo cried, excited and inflammable as her Italian-American parents.

And as they talked, it grew easier and easier to clear Iron Valley streets for the dog races—and the pedestrians. Walking home, most of sophomore class in a gesticulating, shouting huddle, Lindas and Red and the rest saw the whole plan as so ridiculously easy they wondered no one had thought of it all these years.

Dewey, too, when they went to see him, kindled with the idea. "Sure, kids! It'd, be fun, riding in a dog train again!"

And among all his fine cars Mr. Johnson had one old horse left from his livery-stable days.

"You just find the plow, kids," he told them, "you just find the plow, the old Tim horse is yours! Only—"

"*Only*—?" Lindas shook back her dark hair, as she stood there heading the committee.

"Far's I know," Mr. Johnson said regretfully, "the last of them old one-horse plows was junked more'n ten years ago!"

Every member of sophomore class scouted far out into the farm country, nearly to Lake Superior. Not a single sidewalk plow remained in all Iron Valley—in all Michigan, it seemed!

That called for a council of war. Red Carleton ably presided, Lindas in her elected place as vice-president beside him.

"So now, what do we do?" Sigrid Liimakka asked. "Dog races would have been so much fun!"

"Would have been!" Red Carleton snorted. "We've just got to figure something else!"

"If we all shoveled—" Annie Schwartz suggested timidly from a rear seat.

"We could, you know!" Lindas cried and Red Carleton echoed, "We could!"

Right then and there they blocked off Iron Valley into areas. A captain who lived within that space was briskly elected for each. The captains were to choose their own teams.

"Man, woman, and child of us," Red Carleton announced with a twinkle in his green eyes, "out we go and bare our walks."

A committee was appointed to track down the dogs, assign them. Another to find equipment—sleds and such. Another to plan the route of the proud procession that Dewey and a fresh "Brutus" should lead.

It began on a Saturday, this concentrated clearing of Iron Valley's walks. Lindas, shoveling until her breath was gone, took time to glance at the high blue sky that looked as if not a single snowflake could emerge from it again, ever. She shook away doubt, remembering temperamental Michigan weather.

"It's just *got* to stay clear!"

That evening over malted milks, the committee members of sophomore class breathed relief over their aching muscles. Iron Valley was clear in the whole area of the triumphal dog procession. And stars shone, sharp and white. Who cared about bent backs and blistered hands? Sunday, too, trudging to and from Sunday school and church, Lindas met first one and then another classmate who was bubbling over with the coming event.

In the afternoon, Dad showed Lindas his Iron Valley *Times,* and she saw the very headline that she herself had bubbled at him in the paper that would be on the street at dawn tomorrow:

KIDS AND DOGS ACCOMPLISH OPERATION SNOW LIFT

She took the advance copy to bed with her to read again all that stuff Dad had written about how it took kids to accomplish what their parents just talked about. She lay luxuriously reading, chewing on a nougat. A sudden gust fanned her curtains out straight into the room. As she rushed to shut the window, a handful of wet chill slapped her face.

"Snow!" She stood there shivering, sick, hardly able to make her mouth say it. *"Snow!"*

Iron Valley looked like an uncut wedding cake next morning. At school, sophomore class looked at one another helplessly. They were in the cafeteria when there fell the deadliest blow of all. Roaring, blowing, the great street plow sucked in huge drifts and spat them out, burying the sidewalks again.

After school, sophomore class stepped out into the unkindest cut of all. The blaring, needling blizzard was gone. Snow lay bland and sparkling under a fire-red sunset.

"Wouldn't you know!" Lollie mourned.

"We could have drawn a mob," Red groaned, "if tomorrow is like this." He made a snowball, slammed it against a white-hatted fence. "Almost hope it blizzards!"

Lindas was staring at the whipped-cream drifts that covered the sidewalks as they walked in the plow-bared middle of the street.

"If we could just ride on top of the drifts—"

They had to escape to the top of a snowbank, the lot of them, or block the traffic as they stood wildly talking a dream into reality. Somebody said, "With that big old Bergman hound up front!" Somebody said, "And Dewey. He's heavy enough for ballast!" Somebody said, "If there was just a way to drag the snow—" And somebody said, "A plow! A real old-time farmer's plow!"

Lindas never knew, in the frantic hours that followed, just what was done or how. She only remembered that the boys worked in Dad's toolshop in the woodshed, after that drive out to Petersons' on always-open highways for the rusted, discarded, old plow.

She didn't go to sleep, Lindas thought, she died. Not even the dread of another storm for tomorrow could keep her awake to worry.

The day was like a Christmas card—all glittering soapsuds, white and brilliant blue. They all met at the road which returned veterans had christened Burma Road. Dewey was late. For a desperate few minutes, Lindas and the others thought their wild plan had gone up in smoke. Then Dewey and his wheel chair came out of someone's car. And behind, big as a young bear, the great St.

Bernard that was so nearly like the photographs of Dewey's Brutus. Lindas watched Red and Aare and the rest strap and hook and hitch the animal to the crazy thing of fresh-polished steel and wood. It looked, Lindas thought, like something sent down from a flying saucer, with its sharp nose, its steel fins, and its flat body on low runners.

Just in time, she remembered her own roost on the low sled behind the big black Labrador, Ebony. She settled herself on the knees of her ski pants, grasped the leather reins firmly, sat back on her heels and waited for the starting signal.

There was a sharp, cap-pistol shot, the flail of a starting flag. A wild torrent of barks joined lustily. *Would* it work? They had had no time to rehearse, no time for anything but theory, really. *Would* it work? At first she thought, *No!* Dewey's dog just stood there, flank-deep in the snow.

"Get going!" Dewey ordered in his deep rumble. " 'Brutus,' whatever your name is, git!" Brutus just stood there. Then, like a shot, he was off, clumsy makeshift plow and heavy Dewey like feathers behind him. The steel plow knifed through the snow.

It was a kaleidoscope of color, motion, sound—the crazy ride, up one street, down the next, through the driftings, over residential walks, skidding this way and that along plowed ways. People crowded both sides of the streets as dogs and riders tugged forward in the trail that "Brutus" and his driver had cut. A mountain of snow would loom directly ahead, as Lindas' unblinking eyes stared into wind and glare. Then—the mountain was parted neatly as if before a Moses.

And then it was all over. Amid all the shouting and cheering, Dewey and his dog won the prize. The grinning Dewey accepted the gift that sophomore class had joined to buy.

"Makes me feel like a kid again!" he said.

Next day at school, everyone was bubbling with triumph. Even the teachers relaxed discipline a bit. Until assembly Mr. Watson stepped to the stage and ordered quiet. Mr. Watson held up a newspaper, spread out so they could see. It was the big Duluth daily, the front page filled with photographs.

The great black headline clinched the identification.

IRON VALLEY KIDS REVOLT

And below, a mite less black and towering:

LOOK WHAT HAPPENS TO SNOW WHEN
THE KIDS TAKE HOLD

Those strangers clicking cameras from the light poles must have been reporters. Lindas' frown deepened. She hadn't realized how this flaunt of dog racers to clear the walks might look to outsiders!

"It's as if we kids meant to show up the old home town!" Lindas groaned inwardly.

The others understood too, from Mr. Watson's silence over the newspaper, which he finally folded and pushed into his pocket.

"What'll we do," they asked a little helplessly, in cafeteria that noon, "so folks'll know we were not just poking fun! So just about all America won't think . . ."

The question plagued Lindas, as she knew it plagued the rest of her classmates all afternoon. There was the fun and excitement of dog races in the snow. There was the feat of showing the town folks how good it could be to have their walks to use again. But—beyond Iron Valley?

Uneasy, uncertain guilt had apparently kept all sophomore class awake, Lindas saw next morning. This thing they had so happily and proudly built had become a—what did you call it?—boomerang! It had hit them smack in their own community pride. It was a troubled Lindas who followed Red Carleton and the rest of the class, gravely ordered into Mr. Watson's private office. When she saw who sat there, too, Lindas' eyes raced to the door and retreat. But there was no retreat. She sat down, as did the rest.

Mayor Wood had the Duluth paper, too, and others from elsewhere along the peninsula. He passed them silently around.

"We've really got the limelight," he said, the corners of his mouth dipping just a bit.

Lindas could bear it no longer. "It was all my fault! It was all my idea! I saw Mrs. Torrell almost fall and I thought how dangerous it was and that maybe we could have the races just to get the sidewalks clean again as they used to be. And—"

What else she said, she never quite remembered. Nor what the others said, rising to defend, explain. But after that—after Mr. Watson had silenced the clamor so that Mayor Woods finally could talk, after that . . .

Still incredulous, Lindas tried to tell Dad that evening after supper.

"They're not mad!" she said, still unbelieving. "The Mayor, the City Council—they're not mad at all! They said all the pictures and publicity and stuff—why, the winter carnival we've always wanted is coming to Iron Valley! Just because we kids—just because dog races are news—just because—" She stood there shaking her head, wondering.

Dad reached for a fresh sheet of paper for his typewriter, rolled it into place.

"If you'll dictate, Lindas," he said, fingers poised, "if you'll simmer down and tell me, we'll do a real story for the *Times*. Front page."

"Oh, Dad!" Lindas hugged him, gray eyes shining.

"Well?" Dad grinned. "How do we begin?"

Lindas stared out into the lamplight, seeing how the words would look tomorrow on the *Times* first page.

"How about," she began, "how about—"

"IT'S OUR TOWN BECAUSE WE HELP RUN IT!" SAY IRON VALLEY KIDS

The Girl Who Had
Everything

Betty Cavanna

Diane paused at the steep steps leading from the house on the
bluff down to the beach and drew a long breath of delight. The
water of Pleasant Bay sparkled in the sunshine, a trio of tiny sails
scooted toward the Outer Bar, and at the tideline a group of sun-
burned children played around an overturned skiff.

It was a perfect summer picture. It included everything, even
what Diane mentally termed "cheesecake" in the form of her cousin,
Henrietta Harper, who was stretched, stomach down, upon a green
beach towel. Her bright bathing suit contrasted sharply with her
pale gold hair; her slim legs and arms were brown, and her finger-
nails and toenails were painted a clear orange-red. She could have
posed, with no change of position, for a travel ad.

Only her expression would have to be altered, decided Diane
as she ran down the steps to join her. Because Henrietta was
frowning in a really desperate manner as she chewed the end of a
pencil and surveyed a small notebook perched on a dollop of sand.

"What's the matter, Holly?" Diane asked.

"Everything," Henrietta sighed. "In other words, I'm broke."

"With *your* clothes allowance?" Diane sounded incredulous,
because she was acquainted with the really munificent sum assigned
to Holly every quarter. "But I thought it was—"

30

"That's just the trouble. It *was!*" Henrietta interrupted as Diane dropped down beside her. She groaned descriptively. "Do you know how much I have left to last until September first? Exactly sixteen dollars and eighty-five cents."

"Well, you don't really need anything, do you?" Diana offered comfortingly, "I mean you have lots of clothes—"

Henrietta sat up with a shriek, and the breeze riffled the pages of the little notebook, so that the higgledy-piggledy figures of her accounting danced in the sun. "Why, I haven't a thing to wear to the yacht-club dance Saturday. Not a single solitary thing!"

"Your flowered linen—" protested Diane.

"That old rag?" Henrietta's tone changed the linen into flowered sackcloth. "I've already worn it half a dozen times!"

Diane clasped her knees a little tighter but said nothing. She was thinking of her own blue embroidered cotton, tired from frequent and repeated laundering, but still considered "good enough to take along to Cape Cod." By Cranford standards it was, actually, quite all right, but Diane was beginning to realize that Holly would probably consider it disreputable. She almost wished that she wouldn't have to appear at the Saturday dance.

Of course there was the chance that nobody would ask her. Having been here only a week, she didn't know anyone in Henrietta's crowd of summer acquaintances really well. And because they were still strange, the group of young people seemed especially glamorous—cut from a different pattern from the crowd back home, geared to a quicker pace, possessed of a line of chatter which she envied but had not yet learned to imitate.

Still, she was enjoying herself hugely. The house which Holly's parents had taken for August was spacious and weather-beaten and filled with a collection of summer-cottage furniture and mellow antiques which made it especially hospitable. The fact that it looked directly over the bay, to the sweep of the ocean beyond the bar, brought summer right to the doorstep, and the added fact that Aunt Hope and Uncle Mark had rented a little Woodpussy for the girls' use made the vacation little short of perfect in Diane's eyes.

Henrietta, to her visiting cousin's surprise, was a creditable sailor, although she was continually disparaging the single-sail craft which was hers for the month and yearned for a bigger boat. But then, from Diane's point of view, Holly was always wishing for the moon. The fact that she frequently got it, served up in a star-studded sky with a good-looking boy thrown in for good measure, became less remarkable year by year, while it filled Diane with the desire to become as much like her glamorous cousin as possible.

"Sixteen dollars and eighty-five cents." Henrietta bit her pencil savagely. Then, oblivious to the sunlight twinkling on the water, she stretched out moodily on her back so that she could toast her throat and the insides of her arms, and described a dress she had seen in a Chatham show window.

She was still singing its praises when her mother and Diane's came down the steps and walked across the beach toward them, carrying back rests and magazines. With unusual alacrity she tucked the small notebook into her beach bag and jumped to her feet. "Hi, Mummy! Hello, Aunt Marcia! Isn't it a beautiful day?"

"Beautiful!" chorused the two women. They looked happy and attractively youthful in their trim swimming suits.

Henrietta arranged the back rest for her mother as Mrs. Graham asked, with a twinkle in her eye, "All *alone?*"

"For the moment, yes. I have problems," Henrietta admitted.

"Problems?" Mrs. Harper murmured conversationally.

Holly nodded. "I've torn my flowered linen—badly," she explained glibly, not the least disconcerted by Diane's surprised expression. "So I've just got to have a new dress for the yacht club dance," she added, as though she were making the most reasonable statement in the world.

"Oh," said her mother, settling herself and polishing her sunglasses, "I didn't know you'd been asked."

"I haven't yet, but I will be." Henrietta sounded very sure of herself. With a slight grimace of annoyance, she added, "Tom Ristine is bound to invite me, today or tomorrow."

Diane squirmed, although she had long since learned to be respectful concerning her cousin's boasts. Henrietta undoubtedly had a way with the boys. If only Jim were here, she found herself wishing, and the first flaw in an otherwise perfect vacation appeared in her glance as she caught her mother's eye. Which would be preferable, to remain at home, abandoned, on Saturday night, or to tag along at Holly's heels with a second-rate date which had somehow been "arranged"?

"Fortunately," she roused to hear Henrietta saying brightly, "there's a really sweet white piqué in the Deb Shop window, and it's terribly cheap, only about twelve dollars." She was talking faster now, leaning forward, her pretty knees drawn up under her chin.

"How much?"

Suddenly Diane remembered that their mothers had been down-town yesterday, and she saw the same awarenesss flash into Holly's big brown eyes.

"I forgot exactly, but it was around that, anyway."

"It was fourteen ninety-eight," said Mrs. Harper flatly. "I noticed it myself."

"Was it that much?" Holly asked innocently. "Well, it's beautiful, anyway, isn't it?"

"It's very pretty," admitted Diane's aunt, "but so is the linen. I'll take a look at it."

Diane could see alarm in her cousin's eyes as Henrietta changed her tactics. "Mummy, when you and Daddy gave me a clothes allowance, you said I could spend it my way. Well, if I have enough money left and want to get the dress and do without something else, I can, can't I?"

Mrs. Harper hesitated a minute. "You may," she said finally, "but remember, money doesn't stretch. And," she added firmly, "there will be no advance on your allowance. September is over three weeks off, and there will probably be many things you will want more than the piqué dress. Bertha told me when she did the wash this week that your slips are in a disgraceful condition."

Holly smiled brightly, a smile which conjured legions of popular boys—all begging for a dance with her. "Pooh," she shrugged, and leaned over to kiss her mother behind the ear.

Diane had been scooping up handfuls of sand to let the grains drift through her fingers. Embarrassed by this interplay, she rose abruptly. "I'm going for a walk. Want to come, Holly?"

Anticipating her cousin's refusal, she started down the beach. Holly s behavior disturbed her. But then, perhaps she was just being jealous, because Holly always seemed able to get what she wanted. It was probably stuffy to be upset by a few fibs and a bit of deceit. She could undoubtedly profit by learning some of Holly's tricks. "Spoilsport," she said aloud, kicking a pebble with her toe.

"Don't you know there's a fine for talking to yourself?"

Abashed, Diane looked up into Tom Ristine's amused green eyes. "Oh—hi!" she said with a slight gasp, because in the intervening second she realized that he was not alone. Beside him stood a lad who shone with a glow as bright as Henrietta Harper's. He was tall, blond, and so vital that he looked positively shiny.

"This is Scott Cunningham," Tom said.

As Diane put out her hand she wished that her nose didn't freckle and that she had lashes as long as Henrietta's. She wished that her hair were curly, that she were two inches taller, and that she had taken pains to develop a "line." "Hello," she breathed, and thought, Wait till Holly sees this! But at the moment they were hidden by the outcropping bluff from the group on the beach. If only she knew how to make that moment count!

But she only murmured. "You're new, aren't you?" as she tried to smile.

"Brand new," Tom answered for his friend. "He just got in last night."

"We go to school together, winters," Scott explained. His voice was deep and vigorous, and his grin was unstudied. Diane's heart flipped.

Then, having scarcely begun, her moment was over. "Where's Holly?" Tom asked. "We were just on the way to look you two up."

Grateful for the "you two," Diane glanced over her shoulder. "Holly's right around the bend, with our mothers."

Scott took her elbow and turned her around. "Come on, then. What are we waiting for?"

There was a brief satisfaction in walking the short distance between the two attractive boys, and in being the one who introduced Scott Cunningham. But then Holly began to take over, while Diane felt as though she were evaporating in front of everybody's eyes.

Scott was courteous and easy. He dropped to his knees in the sand and divided his attention between the girls and their mothers.

After about ten minutes the boys got to their feet. "I have to run over to Stage Harbor for a sec," Scott said casually. Then to the girls, "Want to come along?"

"May we?" Holly asked unnecessarily.

Mrs. Harper nodded. "If you'll pick up my grocery order on the way back."

Henrietta agreed with a sigh. "Mother's car is in the shop," she explained as they started off across the sand. There was an unspoken implication that the Harpers were a two-car family, instead of a one-and-only.

Minutes later, a sense of well-being returned to Diane. There was something definitely exciting about climbing into the sports convertible to which Scott Cunningham led them, even if Holly managed to appropriate the seat next to the driver. Settling back against the warm red leather, she smiled happily and said, "Golly, this is quite a car!"

Holly's profile told her that the remark was childish, but Scott turned to give her a quick grin. "Dad and I like it, but Mother thinks it's too flashy."

The ride from Chatham to Stage Harbor was much too short, and Diane, her hair blowing out straight behind her, pretended she was as sophisticated as she felt they all looked. With one ear she listened to the conversation, which included a description by Scott of marlin fishing in Florida. He parked facing the dock. "I'll just be a minute," he promised as he pulled on the brake and swung his long legs out the door.

After he disappeared inside a boathouse, the others talked in a desultory fashion. It was as though the sun had gone under a cloud. Then Holly, with no by-your-leave at all, said, "I think I'll walk down to the dock," and Diane was left alone with Tom.

She wished she were more like her cousin as she sat there, waiting. She yearned to say something bright and provocative. But she was silent, watching the bobbing sailboats—mostly Cape Cod knockabouts and Whistlers—and found Holly's little Woodpussy among them. Too bad it accommodated only two.

In the mooring quite far offshore was a craft new to the picture, a sloop-rigged white Weanno Senior which looked as though she would sail like a bird. "Let's walk down to the dock, too," Diane suggested. "I want a better look at that beautiful boat."

They had no sooner joined Holly, than Scott strolled up. "D'you have a sailboat here?" he asked.

Henrietta was so obviously in the middle of a daydream that Diane could almost see it crumble, but she recovered herself to smile and nod.

"Which one?"

Holly's eyes flew from the Woodpussy to the Weanno, with the name *Skylark* on the bow. Her forefinger, starting to point toward the Woodpussy, kept on until it reached the *Skylark*. Diane stifled a gasp.

"Which?" Scott was prodding.

"The—the *Skylark*."

What is she thinking of? Tom knows better, Diane thought, glancing at him out of the corner of her eye. He was staring at Holly with his mouth open.

Scott turned, squinting against the sun. "Some boat!" he said heartily.

"She is pretty nice," Holly admitted with apparent modesty. Diane was completely aghast. Of course there was only one thing for Holly to do now—laugh and admit it was just wishful thinking, but either Holly was too flustered to backtrack, or she thought she could actually get away with the fib.

"Say, I'd like to look her over," Scott said enthusiastically. "Let's go on board." For the first time, Diane noticed a dory with the same name tied up at the dock.

Henrietta jumped. "Oh, not now. I have to get back. Mother will be waiting for her groceries."

"But it's early," Scott insisted.

"Some other time," Holly demurred.

"Now!" Scott grabbed Henrietta's hand and helped her into the rowboat. "It won't take ten minutes. Come on, kids!"

Wretchedly, Diane allowed Tom to hand her into the dory. Suppose there were people on board. How would they explain? She sat with clenched hands as Scott unhitched the rope and pushed off. Facing her from the bow, Holly kept her chin in the air but refused to meet Diane's eyes. Diane felt almost sorry for her.

As the *Skylark* grew larger, the cavity in Diane's stomach began to yawn more uncomfortably. Suppose they were arrested for breaking and entering? Suppose?

She scarcely heard Scott, with complete good humor, saying to Holly, "*Skylark*. That's a pretty name."

Henrietta nodded. Rather miserably, Diane thought.

"Did you name her yourself?"

"Daddy named it—her, I mean. When he and Mother go off on a big evening he always calls it 'going skylarking.' "

That much is true, Diane told herself.

"Quaint," Scott chuckled. "Here we are."

Diane climbed aboard with the furtive air of a trespasser, scarcely daring to look around. The boat was larger than it had looked from a distance, and everything was very shipshape—the ropes coiled just so, the sail covered neatly.

Scott was wandering around, adjusting a coil of rope, examining the auxiliary engine. "Jeepers," he sighed, "I wish we had time to take her out."

"That's impossible," cried Holly sharply. "I must go home at once. Come on."

"Okay," Scott agreed amiably. Suddenly he seemed tired of the excursion. On the trip back to the dock, although Holly burst into nervous chatter, he rowed silently. When they had docked and were safely out of the strange dory, Diane heaved a sigh of relief. Her cousin's luck was holding.

Somehow, riding toward town, she found herself in the front seat beside Scott. It didn't seem premeditated. It just happened. So it was Tom who went into the grocery store with Holly to collect the order. As soon as they were alone Scott turned to Diane.

"Say," he said. "I'm new around here—and I gather you are too. Could I be lucky enough to get a date for the yacht club dance Saturday night?"

The question was so unexpected that Diane fumbled uncertainly, "With—with my cousin, you mean?"

"Gosh, no!" Scott said. "With you."

"Why—why—"

He was grinning down at her. "Do I have to list three convincing reasons? Couldn't you just say yes?"

"Yes." Diane laughed, and added primly, "I'd like it very much."

Then the other two were returning, Holly moving, as she always did, with the grace of complete assurance. She's recovered, Diane thought, as Holly, gay and laughing, turned all her charm on Scott. She brought up the Saturday night yacht club dance, hinting at her availability, and waiting expectantly for Scott's response. Diane thought unhappily, oh, dear, he's probably regretting his impulsiveness. He'll know now what a mistake he made.

But there was no regret in Scott's voice as he answered, "I am certainly looking forward to that dance! Diane has just agreed to go with me."

Uncomfortably trying not to notice Holly's chagrin, Diane kept her eyes fixed straight forward. To break the awkward silence, Tom began to talk about fishing.

When they reached the Harpers', Tom picked up the box of groceries. Diane saw Scott tuck a yacht club program between the coffee and the cereal. She said nothing, but when the boys had left, she went out to the kitchen and unearthed it, then let her eyes travel down the list of entries for the week-end races. There in unmistakable black type was the item for which she had been searching instinctively: "*Skylark*, owned and operated by Scott Cunningham and Scott Cunningham, Jr."

"Well, score one for the country cousin," Holly said, following her into the kitchen. "How did you manage it?"

Diane looked up and shook her head. "I don't know," she said. "He just asked me—while you were in the store with Tom."

Holly seemed honestly bewildered by Scott's stupidity in preferring the simple Diane to her own more arresting personality. Then she noticed the program in Diane's hand. "What's that?" she asked.

Silently Diane handed it to her and watched the hot flush redden her cousin's lovely face.

"What beastly luck!" Holly said at last. "It would have to be his boat! Now I've made a fool of myself in front of both boys." She dropped the program and turned to walk out of the kitchen. "Well, Mother will be relieved that I have the money for those new slips she thinks I ought to buy. I won't need the piqué dress. Tom didn't ask me either!"

She looked so like a puzzled spoiled child who does not understand why she suddenly has been slapped that Diane felt honestly sorry for her. "Maybe he'll call tonight," she offered in comfort.

Holly shook her head. "I guess good old Tom is fed up at last with my silly airs and graces," she said slowly, and went out the door.

Diane stood looking thoughtfully after her. Slowly she was coming to the realization that she wouldn't change places with Holly for all her beauty and glamour. It wasn't too bad to be plain Diane Graham with freckles on her nose. She would press her blue dress and wear it without regret. The yacht club dance, with Scott as escort, should be fun.

When the suave Toby came to dinner,
Diane almost made a mistake

Mr. Lincoln Lends a Hand

Betty Cavanna

Diane sat at the dinner table keeping her gaze deliberately turned away from Granny Graham, who was engaged in buttering a large, unbroken slice of bread. Diane's great-grandmother was quite unconscious that her table manners were offending any member of the Graham household. Here on her annual visit, she smiled happily to herself as she bit into the corner of the buttered square.

Diane's father, meanwhile, was blinking in the wavering light of the candles. He hated to eat dinner in the dark, and he intended to say so. "I'd like some more light in this room!" he remarked belligerently. "I can't even see whether this roast beef's red or gray."

He pushed back his chair, marched to the light switch, and clicked it on. Granny nodded, Mrs. Graham looked up in mild concern, and Diane frowned.

"Oh, Daddy," she objected in dismay. "Can't we at least have dinner like civilized people?"

"Civilized!" snorted Mr. Graham. "Civilized!" He narrowed his eyes and peered intently at his daughter. "For sixteen years your mother and I have got along without candles. I consider them darned uncivilized!"

"*Everybody* uses candles at dinner," Diane insisted. Her dark lashes dropped over stormy blue-gray eyes, and she cut a piece of roast beef with furious concentration.

"Who is everybody, I'd like to know?"

"Gordon," murmured his wife, shaking her head in a signal he did not choose to understand.

"Well, who *is* everybody?" Mr. Graham repeated. "It seems to me, Diane, you've acquired some pretty highfalutin' ideas lately."

Granny Graham nodded her head again, more vigorously, and Diane bit her lips. Why couldn't her father see that candles—were a sort of symbol—a symbol of gracious living? Why did he have to be so old-fashioned and—and plain?

It seemed that when Granny was visiting he became even worse than usual, more obdurate, as though he wanted to prove to his grandmother that he hadn't forgotten he had been brought up on a farm. It was infuriating, to say the least. Suddenly Diane decided to take issue. Pushing back her chair she faced her father. "Dad—"

"Will you pass the butter, please, Gordon?" asked Mrs. Graham quietly.

Diane broke in. "I'm working on a term paper on Lincoln. He was a farm boy, too."

Mr. Graham raised his eyebrows quizzically. "What's that got to do with candles?" he wanted to know.

"Just this," Diane raced on. "He came from a dirt-floor cabin in Kentucky, and when his family had to sell out and move to Indiana, there were pretty pinching times. He never had much, but he learned fast. By the time he became President he'd learned to accept candles on the table along with high silk hats, I'll bet."

Mr. Graham seemed to consider. "Are you aiming to be first lady President of these United States?" he asked with a twinkle in his eye.

"Oh, Daddy!" Annoyance colored Diane's tone. "I'm just drawing a parallel, don't you see? There's no such thing as standing still. We've got to move forward. Candles just represent a more gracious way of living, that's all. Why can't you be like Lincoln and *accept* things?"

Gordon Graham snapped his fingers and smiled at his wife. "Thought for the week!" he said in a stage whisper.

"Funny thing," mused Granny in her thin, singsong voice. "When electric lights came in, gas went out, just as oil lamps finished candles. Now here we are back to candles again. Funny thing." She peered over her spectacles without malice, and even Diane had to laugh.

But just the same she didn't intend to give up the crusade on which she had launched just after Christmas. It wasn't that she was trying to belittle her family's way of living. It was just that it should be so easy to make them over—to make them more like Toby's family, for instance. Toby Cook was the boy on whom she was presently trying to make an impression. She was sure the Cooks used candles every night and service plates, too. Of course, servants made a difference, but not *that* much difference. It was more an attitude of mind.

Anxious to change the subject, Mrs. Graham said, "I left the car in the shop, Gordon. There's something wrong with the ignition." Then she turned to her daughter. "By the way, Toby drove me home. And since he mentioned he was taking you to the Glee Club concert Saturday night. I suggested he come by for supper."

Diane looked up, abashed. "What did he say?"

"He seemed very much pleased."

"You mean he's *coming?*"

"Why, yes." Mrs. Graham nodded.

Diane was speechless with dismay, but she made no comment during dinner. As she was carrying dishes out to the kitchen later, however, she asked in a gloomy voice, "Golly, Mother, why did you have to do that?"

"Do what?"

"Ask Toby for dinner. With Granny here."

"What possible difference does that make?" Mrs. Graham sounded nonplused.

Diane groaned. "You know what Daddy's like when Granny's here. Look at tonight. He always slips right back to being a hayseed, just as though he'd never left the farm at all."

Mrs. Graham smiled. "He loved that farm," she said. "I think the years he spent there were the happiest ones in his childhood. He loves Granny, too. We both do."

"Of course," Diane murmured. "So do I." But privately she wondered if this were true. Sometimes her great-grandmother seemed more like a museum piece than a person, a relic from another time and another way of life. Diane wasn't of an age to appreciate the sterling quality of her great-grandmother's character, carried so gallantly in her bent, rickety frame. She couldn't know,

as her father knew so well, the hours and years of never-ending labor
that meant decent schooling for her beloved only son, Gordon's
father. Of course, Diane had heard Granny's story, but hearing and
knowing are two different things. Diane only knew Granny as she
was today—a pinched, withered old lady, her eyes pink from over-
strain, her hair in an unfashionable topknot, her inevitable apron.
Granny didn't seem very bright to Diane. When spoken to she was
apt to say "Hey?" very shrilly several times as if jerking herself back
to the present by the sound of her own voice. With Granny in the
house, it was hard to make much progress toward gracious living.

Day in and day out, the little old lady sat in the corner of the
living room, in an ancient bentwood rocker Mr. Graham always
hauled down from the attic just prior to her annual visit. She
neither read nor knitted; her eyes were too bad. She just sat and
rocked and talked about the past to anyone who would listen.

People did listen—Jim Roberts, the boy next door, among them.
Jim adored Granny, for some reason Diane couldn't quite fathom.
One day—after she found him sprawled at Granny's feet, massaging
Diane's dog Honeypot's left ear, which had developed a tendency
to stand up straight—she asked him about this strange attraction.
Jim's answer was noncommittal. He liked old people, he said. Old
people and dogs. He found them soothing.

For her own part, Diane was too busy to spend much time with
Granny. Exams were coming next week, her term paper was due
Monday, and what with Honey's Obedience Class, play tryouts, and
a dozen and one things, every hour seemed to be full.

On Saturday morning she opened her eyes reluctantly to a cold,
gray February day. Instead of anticipating the week end, she felt
let down and annoyed, because the term paper could be postponed
no longer. She would have to finish it by tomorrow night.

Yet when she had dutifully hurried through her breakfast and
sharpened three pencils and spread the library books, from which
she was collecting material, around her desk like fans, she sat with
her chin in her hands staring aimlessly and wishing that something
could be done about Granny, just for tonight.

Remembering the Spode china and the beautiful silver on which
refreshments had been served Christmas Eve at the Cooks', Diane
just couldn't reconcile her great-grandmother and Toby. Toby's

family lived with a certain elegance she both admired and envied. It made her own comparatively simple family living, which she had hitherto accepted without question, seem not quite good enough.

It wasn't that she was exactly ashamed of the way her mother and father did things. It was just that she wanted them to show up well. It was just that she didn't want Toby to think they were— well, *peasants*. But none of this did she seem able to explain.

Wandering into her daughter's room with an armful of clean laundry, Mrs. Graham stopped and smiled gently. "Thinking or just dreaming, dear?"

"A little of both, I guess."

" 'Lincoln and the Transcendentalists'!" Her mother read the title over Diane's shoulder. "Goodness! The words they use in high school these days," she murmured, stroking her daughter's bent head. "In my day that was college talk."

"Mommy—" Diane turned to slide an arm around her mother's neat waist. "Do you think Granny might like to have her dinner on a tray, just for tonight?"

Mrs. Graham looked surprised, then shocked and almost hurt. "You—you mean you're *ashamed* of Granny, Diane?"

"Not ashamed, exactly," Diane hastened to reply. "But you know what her table manners are like, and Toby's accustomed to things a little—oh, well, they live differently than we do, that's all."

"You mean with more pomp and ceremony?"

"Well, sort of."

Mrs. Graham smiled. "Then maybe we'll be a relief for Toby. That sort of living can be rather hard on a boy."

"But about Granny—"

Shaking her head, Mrs. Graham broke in, "Granny loves having her meals with us. It's no fun to eat alone."

"Then at least," worried Diane, "make Daddy promise not to make a fuss about the candles! If he gets up and switches on that dreadful overhead light I'll just die!"

At this, Marcia Graham laughed out loud. "I'll do my best," she told her daughter. "But try to take things more easily, darling. Goodness, I wouldn't be your age again, and in your frame of mind, for anything under the sun—even a baby-blue Cadillac with white-wall tires!"

Diane worked on her essay until midafternoon, then knocked off in order to help prepare for Toby. At least, to the best of her ability, she could make certain that everything was just right.

"I'll set the table," she told her mother, and on this operation she spent an hour. She polished the four-branch silver candelabra, put in new candles, then burned each down for half an inch so that they would look "used." Each fork, salad fork, knife, and spoon, she polished carefully. Each butter knife was placed at precisely the same angle and arranged meticulously. From the top of the kitchen cabinet she brought the old flint-glass goblets which were used only for parties. After a bath in hot suds she polished them until they glistened. Placed at the point of each knife they shone resplendently.

Next she attacked the living room, although it had been cleaned only yesterday morning. It was strange that last night it had looked especially warm and inviting, while this afternoon it looked decidedly seedy. Diane dusted all the wood surfaces with an oiled cloth and adjusted an ornament here, a lamp there, to her better liking, while Honey lay on the hearth rug and watched her—a curious, concerned expression on his face.

"Do you mind very much, Mother, if I clear the photographs off this table, just for tonight?" Diane called to Mrs. Graham, who was peeling apples for a pie.

"Why, no," her mother replied, although to her the room looked bare without the friendly faces smiling at her.

Finally Diane made an expedition to the garden for some rhododendron branches. These she arranged with artistic care in a silver pitcher and placed them where the photographs had been.

"Well," she sighed, "that's not too bad." She didn't notice her mother wince, stung by something in her daughter's voice that had not been there before Christmas, when for the first time she had gone to a party at the Cooks'.

Diane rubbed at a ring on the coffee table with the corner of her dustcloth and felt unhappily aware of the patch on the corner of the sofa which Honeypot had chewed. Compared with the impressive thirty-foot living room at Toby's, their own looked cluttered and almost disreputably homey. Diane sighed again.

Six o'clock rolled around to the accompaniment of the delicious aroma of the baking pie. One thing that Diane could always count on was her mother's marvelous cooking. As she showered and dressed, Diane hoped that her father wouldn't try to be funny and that he wouldn't fidget if Toby—to whom time meant very little— happened to be late.

One thing you could never be confident about, she decided as she brushed her hair, was what your own parents might do next. Much as she loved and needed them, she was never sure when they might disgrace her. Sometimes they did or said things that seemed to Diane either excessive or even childish. They seemed to have no idea how desperately a girl her age needed a mother and father who were carefully "correct."

At this same moment, downstairs, Marcia Graham was mentioning to her husband, who had just come in, that it would be sporting of him, this evening, to put up with the candles and refrain from comment.

"Umph," he grunted in what could possibly be interpreted as an affirmative. "Who're we entertaining—the Aga Khan?"

Granny was the only person in the house who was unaware that this evening was a special occasion. She had napped through the afternoon and now she appeared on her way downstairs in a cotton house dress.

"Granny!" Diane, who had been seated carefully on the couch, flipping through the pages of *Vogue* with studied absorption, leaped to her feet in dismay.

"Diane," called Mrs Graham at the same moment. "There's the bell!"

"Hello, Toby." Diane stood so that Granny could be only half seen from the door.

"Hi, Diane!"

"Come in, won't you?"

"Sure thing."

"Toby, you've met my father." Mr. Graham, hat on the back of his head, was on his way to the hall closet, where he kept his overcoat.

"You bet. Good evening, sir."

"Hi," Mr. Graham said casually. "How's the creature that you call a dog?"

"Mother—" started Diane.

"Good evening, Toby!" Mrs. Graham, her face flushed from the heat of the oven, looked very young as she came in from the kitchen.

While Toby crossed the living room to shake hands with Mrs. Graham, Granny descended the remaining stairs, taking each step slowly, holding to the banister with trembling hand. Finally, on level floor, she shuffled carefully to her rocker and settled down with a little grunt.

Mr. and Mrs. Graham both waited for Diane to introduce her great-grandmother, but it was Toby who crossed the room and bent to take Granny's gnarled hand. "I'm Toby Cook," he said. "You must be—"

"Oh, I'm sorry," Diane cut in lightly, "Granny Graham."

"Cook—Cook," piped Granny. "Any kin to old Ephraim Cook down Bells Mills way?"

"I'm afraid not," said Toby gently.

"Old Eph was quite a man," continued Granny, uninhibited. "Quite a man! When I was a girl, and that was some sixty-five years ago, Eph used to—"

"Now, Granny!" A film of annoyance coated Diane's voice. "Toby doesn't even know your friend."

"That's so," mumbled Granny. "That's so." She cut her anecdote off and made no further contribution to the conversation.

Mr. Graham dropped into his big chair and looked from his daughter to Toby. Diane is getting too big for her boots, he thought. She had no need to be rude to Granny, and that's what she was—just plain rude. He had an opportunity to bolster his judgment with other incidents at the dinner table. Diane kept up a bright, vivacious line of chatter that excluded Granny completely from the conversation and allowed her parents only a snatched sentence here and there. Toby seemed ill at ease. Whenever Diane gave him a chance, he turned to Granny or to the Grahams with a remark or question nicely calculated to shift the basis of the talk. But Diane would dart in and snatch the conversational ball before any of the older people had a chance.

Diane is nervous, Mrs. Graham told herself. She's trying too hard to make a good impression. Toby is a nice boy; he'll take our family as he finds it. Why can't Diane see that?

Diane could see only details. She could see that her dad completely disregarded his butter knife, that Granny had spilled something down the front of her dress and was dabbing at it with her rumpled napkin, that her mother seemed to be jumping up from the table constantly, and that a piece of evergreen from the centerpiece had spilled into the mashed potatoes.

Finally the meal ended. It ended, to Mrs. Graham's satisfaction, on a hopeful note. Toby, bless his heart, downed two pieces of her outstanding apple pie and looked as though only his conscience kept him from accepting a third.

Diane's father, as usual, was the first to push back his chair. He wanted to get upstairs and find his slippers. Diane could like it or she could dislike it—he didn't intend to sit around all evening in stiff new shoes.

So upstairs he clumped, while Toby escorted Granny to her rocker and Diane helped her mother clear the table. One slipper was in its accustomed place under the bed, but the other was nowhere to be found.

"Honey!" muttered Mr. Graham. "That dog's always going off with my slippers!"

He went from one bedroom to another, one slipper on, one off, switching on lights as he went. Finally he unearthed the shoe in Diane's room, under the desk where she had been working on her paper. With a sigh, he sat down in the desk chair to slip it on. He glanced idly at the sheaf of notes Diane had been making, at the open books spread everywhere. "Lincoln." The name rose from the books and papers and reminded him of Diane's recent tirade. He chuckled. "Why can't you be like Lincoln?" she had asked.

Idly he flipped the pages of the book nearest it. It was a large red volume, entitled *Abraham Lincoln, The Prairie Years* by Carl Sandburg, and on page 388 Gordon Graham read an anecdote that interested him. Mr. Lincoln had just been elected President, and he was besieged by office seekers at his home in Springfield. In the midst of a large gathering of men who had come from far and near to see the new executive, entered another caller, a little old woman.

"Now, Aunt Sally, this is real kind of you to come and see me," Lincoln is reported to have said. "How are you and how's Jake? Come on over here." And he took her to a group of officials and political workers. "Gentlemen, this is a good old friend of mine. She can make the best flapjacks you ever tasted, and she's baked them for me many a time." The old woman handed him a large pair of yarn socks, saying, "Knit 'em myself."

Diane's father reread the paragraph, then read it a third time. He picked up a pencil and drew a light line all the way around it. In the margin he scrawled, ever so carefully, so that it could be erased, this message: "Diane—why can't *you* be like Lincoln?"

She'll see it tomorrow, he thought, and maybe she'll see the parallel—just maybe.

But Diane was to see the note much sooner than her father expected. She raced up the back stairs to powder her nose not long after Mr. Graham had left the room.

"Hurry! Hurry!" she was saying to herself. "Toby's downstairs stuck with Granny, while Mother's in the kitchen, and Daddy is goodness-knows-where."

Then, as she crossed her bedroom she saw the penciled markings on the library book. Never mark up a library book! The life-long warning made her pause to inspect the vandalism, and she read the ringed paragraph and the message in her father's writing. Her face burned with shame.

Dad's right, she thought with sudden insight. He means Granny. It's his way of saying I've been pretty cheap. He's right.

It was ten minutes before Diane came downstairs. She came slowly, her eyes on Granny Graham and Toby, who were over in the corner by the fire, talking. She didn't dash over and interrupt, as she would have done a half hour before. She walked over to them slowly and sat down on a footstool without speaking.

Toby glanced at her and smiled; then his eyes returned to Granny's. The old woman was leaning forward in her chair, engrossed in the story that she was telling. She hadn't yet seen her great-granddaughter.

Then Mr. Graham came into the room and switched on another light. Distracted, Granny raised her eyes and became aware of Diane. In the middle of a sentence she broke off. "You young folks go on, now," she said quickly, a tremulous note in her voice.

"But you're right in the middle of your story," said Toby. "It's interesting. I'd like to hear the end."

"No, that's all, that's all," Granny's eyes were on Diane, expecting disapproval.

Diane hitched the footstool closer and gathered her knees in her arms. "It *is* interesting, Granny; do go on! We have half an hour before we have to leave. And when you've finished this story, there was something else you wanted to tell us—about old Ephraim Cook down Bells Mills way."

"Good girl," Toby whispered softly. Unexpectedly he reached out and covered Diane's hand briefly with his own.

It takes strength and courage
to blaze a lonely trail

Champions
Walk Alone

J. Myron Christy

During the sunless, frost-nipped days of late November, a small airport on the western plains can be a cold and lonely place, especially for a sixteen-year-old girl who is suddenly without friends.

Small, brown-eyed Gina Mack slouched in an ancient leather chair. The end of her spinal column rested precariously on the edge of the worn cushion, and though her stockinged feet curled their toes in unconscious pleasure a few inches from the grumbling stove, her big eyes were clouded unhappily, as she watched an occasional sleet pellet tick against the office window. Outside, an angry wind whistled around the hangar, a sound Gina had known all her life.

The office door opened, admitting a chill blast of air, as Ed, her father's mechanic, came in to warm his hands. "Morning, Miss Gina," he said, giving her a searching look.

"Hi, Ed."

"How come you're hanging around the airport on Saturday morning? Your dad isn't going to give you a flying lesson in this weather."

"I sort of—well!" She studied her toes. "Most all the kids are mad at me," she confessed.

The old man's eyes narrowed. "You tell me about it!" he commanded. He had worked for her dad since before the death of Gina's mother eleven years ago, and he considered himself the equal of an uncle, at least.

"Well," she sighed, "remember that football game I went to last Friday night? Probably you heard that it meant the State championship for Twin Lakes. We won it by one point, you know."

Ed lit his aged pipe and nodded. "Everybody in town is mighty proud of the team," he said.

"I know," Gina said. She tried to swallow the persistent lump in her throat and continued miserably, "I took my camera to the game and snapped a picture of the winning kick after our last touchdown. When the film was developed, it showed that Twin Lakes had twelve men on the field!"

"Well, what's the matter with that?"

"It's one too many!" Gina wailed. "The boy who goes in to kick the extra point replaces our star halfback, Don Carver, but Don didn't get off the field! That's against the rules! The officials didn't see it, but nevertheless, we didn't win fairly!"

"What did you do?"

"I told the coach, some of the kids—lots of people. I thought they would like to know in order to do the right thing, but instead everyone is mad at me   They say that I'm not loyal—and oh, just about everything horrible!"

"How come you noticed this?" Ed inquired. "It seems funny for you to count the people in a picture."

Gina colored slightly. "Well, I was only—I was sort of taking a picture of Don—" she stammered, adding hastily, "After all he's our best player!"

The old man grinned, "Couldn't be that you're a little sweet on this fellow, could it?"

"I hardly know him," Gina protested, but it seemed to Ed that her protest held regret.

"I see," he said. "What happened to the picture?"

"The coach asked for it and the negative, so he could study them. But now he says they got lost somehow."

"Um hmm." Ed puffed slowly on his pipe. "Doesn't this Don fellow know whether he was on the field or not?"

"I suppose so," Gina said resignedly. "I haven't seen him."

"Well, by jingo," Ed said positively, "you did right! And if the others haven't got gumption to admit it, they aren't worth worrying about!"

"But I *like* people," Gina wailed, "and I want them to like me!"

"Of course you do," Ed agreed. "And getting people to like you is easy—if you're willing to compromise a few ideals and be ruled by the prejudices of the crowd! But some folks can't do that, Miss Gina, and that's the reason that some mighty good people often walk alone!"

"I don't know," Gina said doubtfully. "It's the first time that our little town *ever* has won a State championship; it means an awful lot."

"It seems to me," Ed said, knocking his pipe against the stove, "that it takes something to be a champion besides the highest score."

The following week saw little change in the attitude of Gina's fellow students. Most of them cut her dead. And although, covertly, a few whispered that they were "for her," none risked censure from the rest by showing open support. Mostly, she walked alone.

Wednesday afternoon brought the only bright spot in an otherwise dismal week and, though Gina didn't know it then, indirectly forced the final showdown.

When her father picked her up after school for the two-mile drive to the airport, he asked casually, "How do you feel today, Gina?"

"Fine, Dad."

"How many hours of flight instruction do you have in your logbook now?"

"Ten," she said.

Her father nodded, looking very pleased about something. Neither spoke again until they pulled onto the apron in front of the hangar. Then Mr. Mack smiled down at Gina and said, "Ed thinks you're ready to solo."

Gina felt her heart race. The black Stinson monoplane was sitting on the line, with its prop swishing over slowly, grumbling impatiently to itself.

"Of course," her father teased, "I told Ed you'd probably smash up my best airplane, but if you want to try it—" he broke off, grinning broadly.

Gina flung her arms around his neck. "I *know* I can do it, Dad!" she squealed and scooted from the car, racing for the black monoplane.

The old mechanic was standing beside the open cabin door, holding the pillow which enabled Gina's five feet, two-and-a-half inches to reach the rudder pedals.

"Now you just show that dad of yours, Miss Gina!" he encouraged, "Set her down in the first fifty feet of the runway!"

Gina laughed nervously. "I'll probably be lucky to get down right side up!"

"Don't take any chances!" Ed cautioned earnestly, "just solid, good airplane driving, the way you were taught!"

Gina smiled and reached for the throttle.

She took off smoothly and, after circling the field twice at five hundred feet, established a fast glide in the downwind leg of the traffic pattern. She lowered the flaps as she turned into the final approach; then, flaring out about twenty feet above the end of the runway, she touched down as lightly as a gull. Her tires left their marks among the others within fifty feet of the beginning of the runway. These were marks of the professionals, placed there by pilots capable of touching exactly where they wished. So, for the remainder of *that* day, at least, the snubs of Gina's schoolmates were forgotten.

Then, on Friday morning, a situation which Gina had believed was as bad as it possibly could be became worse. When she entered the study hall, Rod Cameron gaped ceilingward with an awed expression and cried, "Is it a bird?"

Someone else took the cue. "No, it's a plane!"

"What do you know!" Rod exclaimed in mock amazement. "It's Supergirl!"

Gina halted in mid-step. Titters swelled into laughter. Gina, her step firm, continued to a corner table, but the pages of her English book were too blurred to be read.

The rest of the morning was pure torture. Everyone seemed suddenly to have fresh resentment against her, but it wasn't until noon that she finally discovered the cause.

It was Elsie who set her straight. Elsie was the plump, blond girl with whom Gina usually shared a table in the cafeteria at lunchtime. "Y'know," Elsie confided between bites, "some of the kids were sort of rooting for you until this morning." Elsie paused for a mouthful of meringue from the top of her pie, then went on,

"But since that item appeared in the paper—well, they're saying that you are just a show-off and you only started all this argument over the game to get into the limelight; that you probably made up the whole thing!"

"What in the world are you talking about?" Gina demanded. "What's in the paper?"

Elsie's mouth closed upon another huge bite of coconut cream pie; then she fished in her purse, finally extracting a piece torn from the front page of the *Twin Lakes Journal*. She thrust it at Gina.

Spread across two columns was the photo of Gina, standing before the Stinson, that her dad had taken a couple of weeks ago. It was captioned: "Gina Mack Flies High." In smaller type, the subtitle proclaimed: "Sixteen-Year-Old Daughter of Local Airport Operator Solos!" The story which followed mentioned that she was a sophomore at Twin Lakes High and a Girl Scout, and that her hobby was rock collecting. It was the final sentence which had caused the damage. "Last week Miss Mack introduced violent controversy into the State football scene with her charge that the Twin Lakes championship was illegally won."

Gina handed the paper back. "They make it sound as if I—" she broke off, concluding dispiritedly, "I only did what I thought was right."

Elsie swished the straws around in her milk carton, and took a last, long draught. Then, she pushed back her chair and said lightly, "Well, if you're telling the truth, all you have to do is show the picture. Nobody can doubt you then!"

"But I don't have it," Gina said in a small voice.

"Oh?" Elsie picked up her purse from the table. "See you," she said and walked off.

Gina sat alone for a few minutes, eyes on her untouched sandwich. She did not notice the couple passing behind her until the girl spoke.

"Do you suppose we could get an autograph from the famous Miss Mack?" The voice was hateful with sarcasm.

"Not a chance," the boy said. "You know how nervous I get talking to 'High Fliers'!"

Gina was on her feet, facing them. Her brown eyes were brimming with tears, but her small fists were clenched defiantly. "Why don't you leave me alone? I'm not bothering you!"

"You're alive, aren't you?" the boy retorted.

"All right!" a masculine voice from behind Gina ordered. "That's enough."

Gina turned quickly and looked straight into the serious blue eyes of Don Carver. His expression and his one-hundred-and-seventy pounds of football-conditioned muscle effectively discouraged argument. The other boy walked away, red-faced.

It had suddenly become very quiet in the cafeteria. Gina looked questioningly at Don.

He placed a reassuring hand on her shoulder, and surveyed the room for a moment in silence. Then he said, "I just want to tell you that during the past three months, when I was out there on the playing field, I've recognized the voice of each of you at some time or other, encouraging me and the other guys on the team. Believe it or not, you gave us a courage and spirit when we needed it—" He paused, meeting their stares unflinchingly. A foot scraped somewhere; there was no other sound. Don straightened his shoulders, and continued, "I also want to tell you, I *was* on the field—just as Gina said." He turned to Gina and somehow managed a smile, "Can I—I mean, may I take your books?"

Gina nodded assent; she didn't trust her voice.

The cafeteria was buzzing with excited conversation as they went out into the autumn sunshine together.

They walked slowly down the hedge-lined walk toward the main building. For a long time, neither spoke; then Don broke the silence. "You must be wondering why I waited so long to speak up."

"I suppose you had your reasons, Don."

"Sure, I did," he agreed bitterly, "I wanted the championship for Twin Lakes!" He grimaced, then added, "I wanted it so hard, I snitched that picture off the coach's desk!"

Gina looked up at him in shocked disbelief.

"I know—I know how it must look to you." Don's handsome features reflected his self-contempt. "But finally," he went on, "I got so disgusted with myself, I mailed the picture to the State Athletic Commission."

"Then—then you *did* show how a real champion plays the game!" she said softly.

"I don't know," Don said humbly. "It—it was watching one small, brown-eyed girl who had the courage to stand up for what she thought was right against almost the whole town."

Gina smiled up at him. "A few minutes ago, you did a pretty good job of that yourself!"

Don grinned back at her. "D'you suppose we have any friends left?"

Gina shrugged. "Oh, I think most people will be for us eventually, once they have a chance really to think this through." She added hopefully, "At least we can be friends to each other!"

"I'd like that," Don said, his blue eyes serious again. "In fact, I'd like to be a very special friend to you."

"I've always liked that word 'special,' " Gina said with a laugh.

"I warn you." Don was grinning again. "I plan to go into the Air Force as a jet pilot, and you're *really* going to have to 'fly high' to keep up with me!"

"Just watch me!" Gina said happily.

And, as if all this were not joy enough, on the following Monday, the Athletic Commission declared Twin Lakes High the State football champions after all—because, they said, Don's offense was clearly unintentional and no infraction of the rules is recognized officially unless noted by the referees during play.

Gina and Don often walk alone, but it's because they prefer it that way.

Two filled a home with happiness
that three found hard to share

The Crowded House

Margaret Goff Clark

D ad has never understood how I feel about writing. When he finds me chewing my pencil over a poem or a story, he says, "Sherry, dear" [my name is Sharon but he always calls me Sherry] "why aren't you out riding? It's too nice a day to be sitting in here alone."

"But, Dad," I explain, "this is what I want to do."

"Oh, well, then. Have fun."

"It isn't *fun*."

"But you just said—" By now Dad is puzzled.

I try to make it clear. "Writing is hard work. Sometimes I'd rather wash dishes—or dust—but I *have* to write."

He goes out, shaking his head. "I guess a mere man should never try to bring up a girl alone."

I run after him and throw my arms around him. "Don't say that!" I tell him. "You're the best father and mother a girl ever had, and I'm completely, absolutely happy!"

And that's the way it was until Dad went to that alumni reunion of his and Mother's college class last spring. He hadn't been back for years, but he had been corresponding with some of his classmates for the past few months and had decided he would like to see them again. I didn't go with him because of school. It was my first year in high and, with exams coming up, I didn't dare be absent, especially since there was still some question whether or not I would pass algebra.

I could count on the fingers of one hand the number of times Dad had gone away without me since Mother died, leaving him with a baby to bring up—me.

"Maybe I'd better get Mrs. Hollis to stay with you," Dad suggested.

She was the woman who used to take care of me when I was little. Now that I was older she came in only to get dinner at night and on Saturdays to clean. The rest of the time I was the housekeeper.

"I don't need anyone," I protested. "I'm no baby." I felt that I would like to be alone for a few days. I would have lots of time to think and write.

"But you might be lonesome."

I shook my head. No one could be lonesome at our house. We live on Long Island, near enough to the south shore so we can hear the waves talking all the time. Besides, our house is in a little town with neighbors nearby. Only three houses away is Mr. Cranby who keeps riding horses. If I am ever lonely for a minute, I go up there and talk to him and Silly, my favorite horse.

Dad was gone only four days and I had a wonderful time. Every day I went riding with some of my friends, and three of the four days I was invited out to dinner.

Even so, I was mighty glad to see Dad. He came in and put his bag down in the hall. He kissed me and asked, "How'd you get along?"

Then he wandered into the living room without taking off his coat and stood by the fireplace, looking around the room as though he's never seen it before. He turned around so the light from the north windows was right in his face, and I was startled by the shining look of happiness in his eyes. Something had happened to Dad while he was away—something wonderful that made him seem far away and out of my reach. I put my arms around him and hung on tight.

"What happened, Dad?"

He patted my shoulder and gave me an absent-minded smile. "Nothing, Sherry, nothing. What's for dinner?"

"Fried shrimp," I said, but I knew he was just changing the subject. Something *had* happened. He wasn't going to tell me yet, but I would watch and listen and pretty soon he would let the cat out of the bag.

Sure enough, it happened at dinner. Mrs. Hollis had gone home. Dad and I were finishing our dessert and he was drinking his coffee. The little table in the dining room is right against the window overlooking the beach. We could sit across from each other and see the waves curling up on the shore and watch the gulls swooping low.

"I met an old friend of your mother's at the reunion," Dad said. "Martha . . . Martha Franklin . . ."

I looked up, alerted by the tone of his voice. He was trying too hard to sound casual. Now his eyes were on the gulls, but I could tell that his mind was far away with this woman . . . this Martha.

"Oh? Was her husband with her?"

Dad's eyes shifted from the gulls to his plate. "Her husband died five years ago. She's alone, like me."

Alone! I did not say it aloud, but I was hurt to the bone. All these years while I had tried to be a companion to Dad, he had thought of himself as being alone. I kept my head down to hide what my eyes would tell him.

But Dad had realized. "She's not so lucky as I am," he added quickly. "She doesn't have any children. You've kept me from being lonely."

That did not help much, but I tried not to let him know. "I guess nothing can take the place of a wife," I said.

Dad looked relieved. He smiled across the table at me, his nice dark-blue eyes crinkled at the corners. "I told Martha you'd understand. You're a very understanding person for your age."

"Understand what?"

"That Martha and I . . ."

I held my voice steady. "Are going to be married?"

"Yes."

I felt as though the room were closing in on me. "When?"

"We thought . . . next month."

This was certainly sudden. But maybe not so sudden as it seemed. Probably Martha was one of those old classmates to whom

Dad had been writing. I had been holding my fork all this time. Now I laid it carefully on my plate. "Congratulations, Dad. I hope you'll be very happy."

Dad reached across the table and put his hand over mine. "You'll like Martha, love her. She's very much like your mother. At your age you need someone to help you with dresses and fixing your hair, and things like that."

I got up from the table and walked up the stairs to my room, not running, not even walking fast. But once inside, I closed my door, sat down on the edge of my bed and cried. A mother! I wasn't getting a mother. I was losing my dad. Now he would love her instead of me. He would walk beside the sea with her. In the evening when we lit the fire he would read to her. We would never, never again have those long intimate talks about life, and things.

Finally I got up and washed my face. I stared into the mirror. What did Dad mean, I'd have someone to help me with dresses and my hair? My hair was all right. It was blond and long and shining clean. I pulled off the ribbon I'd tied around it to keep it out of my eyes. It *was* rather bushy, and the ends were straight as Silly's tail. Well, I wouldn't change it for her! If she didn't like me the way I was, it was just too bad.

Martha lived in Buffalo and that was where the wedding took place. Dad and I drove there. It was a very simple wedding. Martha's brother and I were the only attendants. But there was a big reception so Martha's friends could meet Dad and me. Everyone seemed crazy about Martha. "You lucky girl, to have her for a mother!" I heard that so often I was ready to scream.

Martha stood beside Dad looking stylish and sophisticated in a blue silk dress with a square neckline and a straight, slim skirt— the white orchid Dad had given her perched like a bird on her shoulder.

I felt dowdy next to her. My pink dress was too short in the waist, too tight around the hips, and there were wrinkles across the front where it pulled when I sat down. It was a hot day and my hair felt like a blanket on my shoulders. I thought the reception would never end.

It did end at last. Martha changed into a suit and I put on a skirt and blouse. When we were ready to leave, I climbed into the back seat of the car. "There's plenty of room in the front with us," Martha said.

"No, thank you," I answered. "I think I'll go to sleep." This was where I belonged. It was the back seat for me from now on.

We drove to Rochester where they dropped me off to stay with Aunt Florence, my own mother's sister. Dad and Martha went on for a week's trip together. I had wanted to go home but Dad wouldn't let me. "You'll have a good time with Aunt Florence and your cousins," he said.

I had a miserable time. My four cousins, all younger than I, kept dreaming up things to do like picnics and swimming, things that I usually enjoyed, but I was in no mood for fun. Whenever I had a chance I would escape to my bedroom and try to write, but even my old friends, words, had left me.

I took the train back to Long Island. Dad and Martha met me at the station late Friday afternoon. They looked happy, with an air of belonging together.

Martha had prepared the dinner. Dad must have told her what I liked to eat because she had all my favorite foods. We ate at the little table overlooking the shore. The gulls were circling. Through the open windows I could hear their high voices. Everything was so familiar and yet so different that I could not eat. I just nibbled, pushing the food around on my plate.

"What's the matter?" Dad asked, looking annoyed. "You're hardly eating anything."

"People often don't feel hungry after a train trip," Martha said as she took the plates away.

She needn't make excuses for me, I thought angrily, sitting still while she brought in the dessert, a lemon bisque which I love. I tried desperately to eat it to please Dad, but it was no use; I couldn't swallow. I could see Dad was cross because I had not eaten the dinner his precious Martha had cooked. The shining look had gone from his eyes.

That made me stop and think. If you love someone, you want his happiness more than anything. Dad could not be happy unless Martha and I were friends. All right, I would try—I would make a real effort to be friendly.

Briskly, I stood up. "That was a delicious dinner," I said. "I'm awfully sorry I didn't feel hungry."

"Thank you, Sherry," Martha answered. I could see the pleased smile she and Dad shared, as I trotted to the kitchen with my hands full of dishes.

"Why not let me do the dishes?" I offered, determined to go the whole way. "You two go sit down."

Martha hesitated. "Oh, no. That's not fair. Sometimes when you're rested, but not tonight."

"Martha'll wash and I'll wipe," Dad said.

I took one look at Dad and the dish towel in his hand, ready to help Martha as he had always helped me in the kitchen, and I fled upstairs with my good resolutions crashing around me. I *couldn't* like her! She was pushing me out of my home. Sitting by my window, watching the moon over the water, I wrote a poem about the way I felt.

> There are some houses made for two
> Where three do not belong,
> And when a third comes in the door,
> There seems to be a throng.
> I lived in such a house for years,
> A house beside the sea,
> And when another came to stay
> There was no room for me.

I put it away in the bottom of the box where I kept the things I wrote. No one ever would read this, but it made me feel better to have put it in words.

As soon as Dad left for work Monday morning, I went out, telling Martha over my shoulder that I was going for a ride. Mr. Cranby was in the stable, feeding the horses.

"Hello," I greeted him. "May I take Silly out?"

"Sorry. Silly's not going any place," he said. "She's got a lame leg and she's going to stay in her stall like a good girl and get it strong."

I put my face against Silly's mane and felt like crying. "Poor Silly," I whispered. "You and I are out of luck."

"What's the matter with you, Sherry?" Mr. Cranby asked. "You look as if you'd lost your last friend."

"Maybe I have," I answered shortly, getting away in a hurry.

I went down to the shore and watched the tide coming in. The sky was gray and threatening. Within half an hour great spatters of rain came down. I stood it as long as I could. Then I ran to the house.

The kitchen was empty. The breakfast dishes were washed and there was a fresh rhubarb pie cooling on the shelf. I went into the living room. Yesterday's papers had been picked up and there was a fresh bouquet of roses on the mantel but this room, too, was empty. I took off my wet sandals and stretched out on the daven-port, soaking in the quiet of the house. Maybe Martha had gone shopping. I hoped she'd get wet. Then I heard a faint sound. It came from upstairs, an irregular tap-tap-tap-tap.

Silently I went up the stairs in my bare feet, then stopped in the hall outside Dad's room, now his and Martha's. The door was closed. She must be in there now because the tap-tapping was coming from there. It was the sound of a typewriter. She must be writing letters. I went on down the hall to my room.

Write! I thought. Tell all your friends about your dopey step-daughter who has hair like Medusa and won't eat.

I dug out my poem. It was pretty good, not quite as good as I had thought it the night before, but still probably the best thing I had written.

The tap-tapping came through the two closed doors. What long letters she must write! What was she doing, telling everything that had happened since she got married?

When an hour had passed and the typewriter was still going, I could stand it no longer. I opened the door of my room and went down the hall. I knocked lightly on her door. There was no answer but the tap-tap of the keys. I knocked again, more boldly.

"Come in."

I went into the room. Martha had set up a card table by the window.

"What time is it? I lose track of time when I write," she said apologetically.

"Almost noon," I said. "You must have a lot of letters to write."

"Letters?" Martha looked blank. "Oh, I'm not writing letters. I'm writing a story."

I sat down on the edge of the bed, because my knees gave out suddenly. "A story?"

She smiled at me. "Didn't your father tell you that I'm a writer?"

I shook my head. "A writer? You mean you write and get things published?"

"I'm not exactly famous, but, yes, I get them published." She looked vaguely around the room. "What did I do my with my last book?" She got up, lifted up a couple of magazines on the night table, and pulled a book from beneath them. "Here it is."

I took it. *Late Summer.* I turned to the title page. *By Martha Franklin.*

I was floored. "Dad wouldn't think writing's important enough to mention," I explained. "I write, too, but I don't get mine published."

Martha sat up straighter and looked at me hard. "You do? May I see something you've done?"

I got up slowly. "I wrote a poem last night." I went back to my room and got it.

It was cruel and crazy to show her that poem. It was the last unkind thing I ever did to Martha.

She read it thoughtfully while I stood by the window embarrassed and uncertain. She must have read it twice before she put it down, saying "It's exactly the way I'd have felt, myself."

"It's the wrong way to feel," I burst out, my face hot.

"You're human and you have feelings," said Martha, giving the poem back to me. "Thank you for showing it to me. It's pretty good poetry. I'd like to see more of your work. Maybe we ought to have lunch first, though."

Martha was a writer! She and I shared the same interest. That made her someone I could understand. She was no cruel monster, stealing my Dad from me. She had been kind to me from the very first. All that nonsense about driving me from my home had been my imagination. As she started down the stairs ahead of me, she reached back and took my hand.

Suddenly, as if her touch had opened my mind, I saw Martha through Dad's eyes. No matter how good a companion a daughter might be, she couldn't take the place of a woman his own age—a woman he loved.

I would have to learn to share Dad. That hurt. It would hurt for a long time, but already I was beginning to see that I, too, had gained when he brought Martha home. Dad had a wife, but I had an understanding friend.

Karen could not know that the new boy
would change her life

Joe and I

Margaret Goff Clark

I'm getting a terrific idea," Joe said to me. We were standing on the steps outside Galeton High on one of those golden days in late October. As Joe was two steps above me he could look me in the eye. "Why not let me be your manager? I can practically guarantee you'll soon be pretty, popular, and pursued."

"You sound like a soap commercial," I said.

"It's funny you should say that, because writing soap commercials is pretty close to my aim in life." He was completely serious. "I'm going to be a promotion man. I may be short but I can promote big things."

"Like me."

Which is how little Joe Martel took me—a long, thin caterpillar—and turned me into—well—

The first time I saw Joe I would never have believed he was going to change my life. I had my arms full of books and I was tearing into home room because it was about time for the last bell. Just inside the door I ran into something solid. It was Joe.

He looked up at me—and he had quite a way to look. "My, you're tall," he said.

Of course half the class heard him and began to laugh. Furious, I stalked to my seat without a word. When you are a girl five feet, eleven-and-a-half inches tall, you do not relish remarks like that.

I glanced back to see if Reed Harrington was laughing with the rest. That would be the last straw. But Reed was studying chemistry and did not seem to be aware of anything else. Even if he had heard, I assured myself, he would not have laughed. It would be hard to say why I considered Reed my friend. We hadn't exchanged more than a dozen words in the past year. Maybe just the fact that he was a good two inches taller than I made me feel as if he were an ally. Anyway, every time I blew out my birthday candles or wished on a star, it was a date with Reed Harrington I had in mind.

I came back to earth to see the cocky newcomer standing in front of Miss McCarthy's desk, telling her his name was Joe Martel and that he'd moved to Galeton from New York City.

"Take that seat," Miss McCarthy told Joe, pointing to the only vacant one, in the back of the room. The seats were graduated from from front to back, and when Joe sat down his short legs did not quite touch the floor.

"We'll have to bring you up front," Miss McCarthy said. "Change with Peter Clark."

Joe grinned. "Just give me a couple of dictionaries."

Again the class laughed, but with a difference. Before they had been laughing *at* me. Now they were laughing *with* Joe. He had been here only ten minutes and already he had them on his side. I began to hate him. He had made me look like a fool, and every time I stood beside him I would look like a fool again.

It was bad enough being almost six feet tall without having a smart-alec midget around to make me feel bigger than ever. The last few years hadn't been easy, what with listening to my mother's friends make corny jokes about how they'd have to put a brick on top of my head; and my mother saying things like, "I think ballerina shoes are so becoming to you, dear." Then I would catch her reading articles on "What the Tall Girl Should Wear."

I read those articles, too. And I tried a few ideas of my own, too, like wearing ruffly skirts to make me look wider, and walking with my knees bent. This is the way it was when I met Joe, except for one more sad statistic. At fifteen I had never had a date.

The bell rang for classes, and as I stood up to go I saw Joe coming toward me. I cut through a row to escape him, but he managed to outflank me.

"I'm sorry I embarrassed you," he said.

I looked straight ahead over the top of his tan-colored hair. "That's all right."

"I ought to know better." He was still blocking my way. "What's your name?"

"Karen Forbes."

"You probably heard me say, I'm Joe Martel." He held out his hand. Unwillingly I shook hands with him. He looked up at me seriously with light-blue eyes that were old and wise. "I don't see why you're so touchy."

This time I brushed by him and said as cuttingly as possible, "You wouldn't understand."

He followed me a few steps. "I'm just the one who should understand, Karen," he said. "You and I have a lot in common."

It was the school elections that forced me to think of Joe again. They were held the last part of October. Reed Harrington got the presidency of the sophomore class, as I had hoped, but Joe Martel was elected vice-president.

"How come?" I kept asking myself. "How come this shrimp who's only been in town for a little over a month gets to be so popular?" I had not even been picked to be chairman of a committee. When I was in eighth grade, I had been chosen class president in an almost unanimous vote. What had happened to me in the two years since then? I knew what had happened. I'd grown three inches taller.

Being tall was surely hard on a girl. But being short must be just as bad for a boy. Yet it didn't seem to be bothering Joe. I had to find out why.

So on that perfect October morning I have already mentioned I waylaid Joe and said, point blank, "It doesn't seem to bother you —being short, I mean."

He looked up at me. "Of course I mind being short. I get a stiff neck every day from looking up at people like you. And on elevators I suffocate."

"I might have known I couldn't get a sensible answer from you." I started up the steps.

"Hey, don't go away. Please."

I stopped.

Joe was through kidding. "Sure, it bothers me, being knee-high to a flea. But there's nothing I can do about it. And after all, is it so important? Do you pick your friends by how tall they are?" He gave me a sidelong glance. "Well, yes, I suppose *you* do. But most people don't."

As Joe warmed to his subject I draped myself on the wall beside the steps like a string of ivy.

"When I realized I was going to have to spend my life in this undersized skin," he said, "I decided to make the best of it and concentrate on being myself."

"You seem to get along great," I admitted. "But what about me? No boy wants to date a girl taller than he is."

"The trouble with you is you're afraid to be yourself."

I looked down, way down, at my scuffy, flat-heeled brown shoes. "How would you know if I'm myself?"

"From watching you," he said promptly. "You're smart. And you'd have a good sense of humor if you didn't take yourself so seriously." He stared at me. "Look me in the eye."

I did.

"Um, nice brown eyes," he said. "You could be pretty. In fact, you might be more than pretty."

I felt myself turning red. "Oh, great. Supposing I were, who could see me way up here?"

"Everyone. Don't you see? That's your advantage. No one can overlook you." He had a strange light in his eye. "I'm getting a terrific idea." Right then was when he suggested being my manager.

I was skeptical. "W-e-ll—"

"Look," he said. "First, let your hair grow. That short cut makes you too small on top. And stand up straight." He almost fell off the steps in his eagerness.

"Maybe I don't want to be managed," I said.

"Prize fighters have managers. And movie actresses. Besides, what have you got to lose?"

I shrugged. "Okay. Go ahead."

The first bell rang and we started up the steps with Joe still talking.

"I'll meet you tonight at the Cozy Corner and we'll block out our campaign. I've got a few ideas about how you should dress. Y'know, my dad used to be connected with the garment industry in New York City. Boy, the fashion shows I've watched!" He rolled his eyes and I had to laugh, even though I was busy keeping a step ahead of him so people wouldn't notice the two of us walking together.

"That's it!" he exclaimed. "Laugh. Smile a lot. It's very becoming. And speak to everyone you know."

"Everyone? I'd feel silly."

"Do it anyway. Start now!" It was an order.

I went to the Cozy Corner after school. I don't know why, unless it was because I already had an inkling that Joe knew what he was doing. Even that one thing—saying "Hi!" to everyone—was beginning to get results. No less than two girls had asked me to sit with them at lunch. Joe was waiting for me at a corner table with paper and pencil in hand.

"Get out of those sissy, ruffly things you wear," he said as soon as I sat down. "You're the tailored type. Can you sew?"

"Well, some."

"Learn," he said. "And I'll tell you what to make." He looked me over. "Now, tomorrow wear a sweater and skirt, a single string of pearls, big pearls. And polish those shoes."

By the time we had finished our sodas, he had my new life planned. I was to volunteer to work on the school paper, practise at home walking with a book on my head, make sure I put my lipstick on straight, and go out for dramatics.

"Dramatics!" I protested. "I can't act. And anyway they don't have parts for female giants."

"You won't be alone," he assured me. "I, too, am joining the Dramatics Club."

Four months went by—four months of being a puppet with Joe untiringly pulling the strings.

April came around, which might be called spring, although I felt sorry for any birds who were crazy enough to go by the calendar. In spite of the warmth of my boxy tweed coat, chosen by Joe, I was shivering as we hurried to the Cozy Corner.

"Wait'll I brief you on our next move," he chortled. "This is really the high spot in our campaign."

I failed to get excited. After all, what had he accomplished so far? I looked better with long hair. At least everyone said I did. And I was a lot busier than I used to be. But anyone can be busy who wants to be a slave on the school newspaper and a scene shifter for the Dramatics Club. Then I caught a glimpse of Joe and me reflected in the drugstore window. Four months ago you wouldn't have walked down the street beside him like this, I told myself. In fact, four months ago you couldn't even hold your head up.

In a humbler mood I sat down beside him and listened to his latest brain wave. It seemed my dramatic career was about to burst into flower with the lead part in a play Joe had dug up somewhere about a six-foot model who falls in love with a jockey.

"You, I suppose, are the jockey," I said.

He grinned, so pleased with himself he was bursting.

"No soap," I said. "That story's been done so many times it has lost its humor. The dramatics coach'll never let us put on a play like that."

"That's where you're wrong, Karen," said Joe. "It's all arranged. And you're wrong again. That plot is still funny."

"But I don't want to be funny," I wailed. This would be the worst thing I could do. Reed Harrington hadn't asked me for a date yet, and if he saw me making a clown of myself he never would.

Joe gave me a pleading look. "Karen, I've never asked you for a thing for myself in all this time, have I?"

He hadn't.

"And now, I want you to do this for me. There's a swell part in this play for me. I want to play that jockey as I've never wanted anything in my life. And we can't do this play without you in it."

What could I do? He'd devoted hours—months—to me. I knew it was the most foolish move of my life but I said yes.

I could not put my heart into that play. It was pure nonsense from beginning to end. The tall model and the jockey were in every foolish situation ever invented. There was one small con- solation. As the model, I would wear some beautiful clothes which were being furnished by one of our best department stores. Even my pleasure in that was tempered by the fact that I had to wear high heels so I would tower even higher above Joe.

Joe had a field day at rehearsals. While I slunk disheartedly through my part he rollicked and clowned all over the stage. Every day the director would exhort me to "put some life into it," and every day I tried—but without success.

The night of the play I felt lowest of all. I didn't see how I could go out on that stage and make a laughing stock of myself. My parents were there. How could my poor mother hold her head up after this night? I only hoped something would keep Reed Harrington away, but a quick glance between the curtains revealed his dark head in the fifth row center.

I went back to Joe who was jittering impatiently in the wings. "I can't do it," I wailed.

He reached up and patted me on the back. "Stage fright. All the best actresses have it. You'll be a wow."

I could see he could hardly wait for the curtains to open. His blue eyes, shining with eagerness, looked bluer than ever with the stage make-up. And his hair had a part so neat and straight it reminded me of a canal through a field of tan-colored grass. This was his big chance to be somebody. I had to go through with it for him.

"I'm with you," I said, winking my eyes so I wouldn't cry and smear my mascara, "to the end."

Joe took my hand in both of his. "We'll go to the Cozy Corner and celebrate after the play, hey, Karen?"

I managed to smile down at him. "It's a date." I felt numb.

The orchestra stopped playing. We took our places on the stage and the curtains swished open. The play began.

Joe as the jockey and I, the model, were seated at a table, supposedly in a place like the Cozy Corner. From our conversation the audience could tell we were falling in love. There was no comedy yet. Then as we stood up the awful difference in our size became clear; there was a chuckle all over the auditorium. Joe wanted to kiss me good-by but he couldn't reach my face. I bent over and he stood on tiptoe to give me a peck on the chin. A shout of laughter burst from hundreds of throats.

Where had I heard laughter like that before? It was on the first day Joe came to school when he told the teacher just to give him a couple of dictionaries to sit on. Now they were laughing with me the same way they had laughed with Joe. It was a good feeling.

I walked off the stage with an exaggerated model's walk. More laughter.

From then on I let loose and acted for all I was worth. Joe was even better than at rehearsals, and the rest of the cast reacted to our enthusiasm and the audience's laughter. Again and again we had to hold up our lines.

As the curtains closed at the end of the play Joe threw his arms around my waist. "You were terrific!" he said. "Bend over and I'll give you a kiss." I did, and just then the curtains opened again and we were caught in the act. How the audience loved that!

I don't care if I did make a fool of myself. I'd do it again for Joe, I thought, as he and I took curtain call after curtain call.

But underneath, I was worrying about what Reed Harrington might be thinking.

The house lights went up and people began pouring backstage to congratulate us.

Mother and Dad were flushed and happy looking. "I'm proud of you, dear," Mother said. Dad just looked emotional.

Mobs of my classmates crowded around, but I was looking for one person who would tower above the others. At last he came.

First he stopped to shake hands with Joe, saying, "Joe, you were great." Then he came to me.

"You're a real comedienne," he said taking my hand and looking me straight in the eyes. Then he cleared his throat nervously. "I was wondering—That is, if you haven't something else planned, would you go out with me for something to eat?"

Here it was at last—my chance. I knew Joe would say, "Go ahead." But somehow, now that I had the chance I knew there was something more important than going out with Reed.

"Thank you," I said, smiling at him. Then my eyes wandered over to the greatest little guy in the world. "Some other time I'd love to, but tonight I have a date with Joe."

There is a magic moment when a girl finds
she can be lovely to look at

The Wish

Lois Duncan

Jane slumped on her bed. "Oh," she moaned, "why did I ever say I would go!"

Downstairs she could hear the clatter of supper dishes being washed, her father's radio, her mother and Alice laughing together in the kitchen.

Jane had told them at dinner. Alice had said, "I think I'm going to take a night off and get to bed early for a change," and their mother had answered, "Good for you, dear; you've been out too many nights this week as it is." Their father had nodded.

Jane said, "I have a date tonight."

There was a moment of silence. Everyone stared at her in amazement.

"Well, for heaven's sake," her father said at last, "who?"

"A boy named Kent," replied Jane matter-of-factly, "Kent Browning." She was pleased with herself for the way she said it, calmly, casually, as though she had dates every night, as though it were nothing to become excited about at all.

"Kent Browning," repeated Alice. "I don't believe I know him. Is he in your class?" Now that Alice was in college she no longer knew all the high school boys.

"No," said Jane, "he's here for the summer. He's visiting Ed Morris."

Her mother found her voice at last. "Why, that's lovely, dear. Where are you going?"

"To the country club dance. We're doubling with Ed and Kathy."

The family was still staring at her, dumfounded, when she excused herself to get ready. "Is it all right if I don't help with the dishes tonight."

"Of course!" Her mother rose too. "Can I help you, dear? Is your dress pressed? Do you have a good pair of nylons?"

"What's he like, Jane? Is he nice?" Alice asked.

"I don't know," answered Jane. "I've never met him. Kathy got me the date."

Suddenly the miracle was gone. Her family melted from amazement into understanding. No boy had asked Jane for a date—Kathy had been the one to arrange it. Kathy called herself Ed's girl, but half the boys in school were in love with her, and she encouraged them all. Whenever Ed asked her to get one of his friends a date, Kathy blithely skipped over her own group of friends and chose someone who supplied no competition—usually Jane.

"Oh." Alice got up and started toward the kitchen. "Well, you can take my new evening bag if you like."

"Thanks." Jane went slowly upstairs. The date was no longer a bright, shining opportunity; it was only an evening that would go as flat as any other date evening. The boy would arrive, and he would be good-looking, because all Ed's friends were good-looking; he would look at Jane and try not to appear too disappointed, and they would get into the car with Ed and Kathy, and Kathy would be beautiful. The evening would pass, somehow, and finally Jane would be home again and the date would be over.

In a wave of hopelessness, Jane took her strapless evening gown off its hanger and hauled it unceremoniously over her head. Then she sat down in front of the dressing table to put on her lipstick.

All she could see in the face that looked out at her from the mirror were freckles and a tight-lipped mouth full of braces. "It's your fault," Jane told the face furiously. "Why can't you look like Alice?" It was hard to have a pretty sister, especially when that sister looked so very much like oneself. Feature by feature, Jane was forced to admit that she and Alice were practically identical, and yet not a soul hesitated to call Alice pretty.

"It's not fair," Jane said bitterly. She got up in despair and crossed to the window. The sky was deep and the stars were thick and bright and very near the earth.

Jane chose one, almost without thinking, and said, "Star light, star bright—first star I've seen tonight." The childish words of the old rhyme were familiar and reassuring. How many thousands of times had she wished on stars! First with Alice, and then, when Alice grew older, by herself—always the same wish, but it had never come true.

"I wish," said Jane softly, "that I were beautiful."

The stars seemed to lean nearer the earth, as though to hear her better, and Jane heard her words ringing soft and clear through the night: *"I—wish—that—I—were—beautiful."* The night flowed in through the open window, close and warm and filled with magic. *"Beautiful!"* it echoed, *"I—were beautiful!"* Jane caught her breath.

What would it feel like to be beautiful? How would it feel if, when she looked in the mirror, the familiar freckled face were gone, and in its place there were one she had never seen before? It would be lovely, with deep violet eyes, a flawless complexion, white, even teeth. A sudden warmth and a glow swept over her and she stood there, feeling beauty spreading over her, hardly daring to breathe.

She sat down weakly on the foot of her bed. "I know," she whispered, "I know how it feels to be beautiful! That must have been the right star!"

Downstairs the doorbell rang. There was a rattle of newspapers as her father got up to answer it—the sound of the door opening—voices.

"Jane!" Her father's voice. "Your friends are here."

"Jane!" her father called again.

"Coming!" Jane hesitated, and then turned toward the door. "I won't look," she told herself softly. "I feel beautiful. If I look, I might break the spell!"

Instead she threw open the top bureau drawer and rummaged quickly through it until she found Alice's evening bag, hurriedly transferred her lipstick and comb, and started for the stairs.

Kent was standing in the living room with her father. He was a tall, blond boy with broad shoulders and an easy smile. He smiled now as he saw Jane.

"Hello." He stepped forward to meet her. "I guess you're Jane. I'm Kent Browning."

Jane felt herself begin to freeze, the way she always did when she had to meet new people. She began to draw her lips tightly together to conceal the braces, and then suddenly she remembered. Any boy in the world should be glad to go out with a beautiful girl! The thought was such a new one for her that she laughed despite herself.

"Hello, Kent," she said warmly, taking the hand he offered. "I'm glad to meet you." She glanced sideways at her father's startled face. "I see you've met my father."

"Yes—sure." Kent's eyes did not leave her face.

"Well, we'd better not keep Ed and Kathy waiting. Good night, Daddy; we won't be late."

Kent had the door open, and a moment later they were outside, walking toward Ed's car.

"Here we are," said Kent, opening the back door and helping Jane in.

"Hi, Janie," Ed said, as he started the car, "how you doin'?"

"Fine, thanks, Ed. Hi, Kathy." Kathy turned sideways in the front seat, tossed casually over her shoulder, "Hello, Jane. Sorry we're late; I held things up by taking too long getting dressed. Aren't I terrible?"

"Horrible," agreed Jane pleasantly, "but we'll forgive her, won't we, Kent?"

She heard her own voice, light and teasing and sure of itself. Just the way she had always wanted it to sound. Always before, when she had tried to sound careless and gay, the words stuck in her throat and came out in jerky, self-conscious lumps, but now suddenly it was easy. How could anyone be self-conscious when she felt beautiful!

"Maybe you can forgive her," said Kent, "but I can't. It's made our date fifteen minutes shorter." He laughed, and Jane laughed with him, liking the warmth in his voice.

Kathy turned to them in surprise. "Hey," she said in astonishment, "is this a budding romance?"

Ed said, "You'd better watch that guy, Janie."

Jane had never been to the country club before. She had sometimes passed it at night, driving home from a movie with her family, and heard the music and laughter swelling out into the night. She had daydreamed about it—imagined herself stepping through the door into the fairyland of gaiety within—but the dreams had been tinged with a kind of terror. "What would I do if I were there!" She had imagined herself standing awkwardly in the middle of the dance floor, staring into the unhappy face of her escort, while dozens of beautiful, graceful couples whirled by. But tonight was different. Tonight was a magic night.

When they stepped into the ballroom, Jane gave a little gasp of delight. "Why, it's beautiful!" she exclaimed. "Just the way I imagined it would be!"

"You mean you haven't been here before?" Kent was amazed.

"No, I haven't, but I've always wanted to come."

Kent looked oddly pleased. "I'm kind of glad you haven't. I like being the one to take you for the first time."

Jane smiled at him. "I like it, too."

Kathy, who had been clinging to Ed's arm, turned and looked at Jane. She stood there, watching Jane smile up at Kent, and her eyes grew large with astonishment.

"Jane," she said, "you've changed—"

But Kent was saying, "Would you like to dance?"

"Love to!" Jane said gaily. Then Kent's arm was around her, the music swept over them, and suddenly they were whirling across the floor, leaving Kathy and Ed behind. Jane looked back over Kent's shoulder and laughed at Kathy's amazed face.

"What are you laughing at?"

"Oh, nothing really; just because I'm happy."

Kent said, "I'm happy, too." He tightened his arm, and the music surged wild and sweet all about them. Other couples flew past like blurred figures in a dream.

I'm not dancing! Jane thought, I'm flying! No dancing was ever like this! The music stopped and began again and stopped and began again. Some of the couples left the floor and others appeared.

A dark-haired boy touched Kent's shoulder. "May I cut in?"

Kent said, "Well—"

Jane was dancing with the dark-haired boy.

"I'm Mike Ingram."

"I know. I've been in your chemistry class all year."

The boy shook his head. "You couldn't have been. I'd have known if you were."

"I sit three seats behind you. You should turn around once in a while, Mike."

"Gee, I really should!"

"Cut?"—Another boy. "Hi. I know you, don't I? Girls look so different at dances; you know, all fixed up and shiny."

"I have the locker next to yours," Jane said gaily, "and you've never even said hello in the mornings. I don't know whether I should dance with you or not."

"Well, you never said hello either, then," retorted the boy, "or I would have."

"You're forgiven," said Jane, "and I'm ashamed of myself."

Why, I never *did* speak to him, she thought. I spent the whole year feeling hurt because *he* didn't speak to me!

"Cut!" It was Kent again. "Hey, you might save me a dance."

Jane laughed. "As many as you want."

The music stopped.

"Intermission, I guess. Would you like some punch?"

"Grand!"

He seated her at a table and then stood looking at her for a moment. "You will be here when I come back, won't you?"

She laughed again. "Of course."

"I just want to be sure." He reached over and touched her hand. "Nothing like this ever happened to me on a blind date before. When Kathy told me about you, I never thought you'd be like this."

"Why?"

"Well, she said you were quiet and aloof, but a nice enough kid. When a girl says that, it usually means she can't think of anything better to say."

"May we join you?" It was Kathy and Ed.

Ed looked hard at Jane. "Golly," he said, "Kathy's right. You do seem different tonight, Janie."

Jane looked at Kathy and her heart sank, for Kathy's eyes were hard. On other blind dates Kathy had been sweet—almost too sweet —talking with Ed and the other boy and every now and then speaking gently to Jane, as though she were a child. But, on the other blind dates, Kathy had been the only pretty one. Jane had sat awkwardly apart, not knowing what to say and afraid to call attention to herself by saying anything at all. Never before had Jane's date looked at her the way Kent was looking at her now—never had Ed's eyes wandered from Kathy to focus on Jane. Before Kathy had been a friend, but now suddenly she was a friend no longer.

"I have a cousin," she said coldly, "who has terrible buck teeth like yours, Jane. The dentist thinks she should have braces. You've had braces so many years—do they feel as awkward as they look?"

Jane started to answer, but no words came.

"The poor little thing has freckles, too," Kathy continued. "It does seem a shame, doesn't it? Some people have all the hard luck when it comes to looks!"

Any other night words as cold and cruel as these would have shriveled Jane into a self-conscious heap. She would have turned her face away, wordlessly fighting back the tears. Now she found herself actually smiling. What did it matter how she had looked in the past?

"Oh, most girls have to go through these things," she said as casually as possible. "We all can't be blessed with your looks, Kathy."

Kathy's eyes widened in amazement. She opened her mouth and closed it again. For once in her life she could think of nothing to say.

Kent broke the awkward silence. "I'm getting punch," he said. "Want to come, Ed?"

"Yes," said Ed, "good idea." He got up to follow Kent, and then turned back to Kathy for a moment. "If I'd been Jane," he said quietly, "I wouldn't have been that polite." He turned abruptly away.

Kathy's eyes were blazing. "What are you trying to do?" she demanded accusingly of Jane. "Break Ed and me up? This is the last blind date I'll get for you, I tell you!"

Looking at her, Jane felt a wave of pity. What an unhappy girl she is, she thought in amazement. How unsure of herself she must be if she is afraid to ask anyone attractive to double with her! Why haven't I noticed before! Aloud she said, "Don't be silly, Kathy. You're Ed's girl, and he's always been crazy about you."

Kathy didn't answer. Instead she turned her face sulkily away, and they sat in silence until the boys returned to the table.

"Here it is," said Kent, setting down the glasses. "They call it punch, but I wouldn't advise you to drink any of it—it tastes even worse than it looks."

Jane glanced at the foamy, purple mixture and laughed.

"I think maybe I can survive without it then. How do you feel about it, Kathy?"

Kathy did not answer. Instead she turned pointedly to Ed and asked, "Shall we dance?"

Ed looked at her for a long moment—at the pretty, selfish face, at the pouting mouth, and then he slowly shook his head. "This time," he said quietly, "I'd like to dance with Jane. That is, if you and Kent don't mind."

"Of course not," agreed Kent.

Ed took Jane's arm and steered her out on the dance floor. They danced for a while in silence. Then Ed said, "Until tonight I always thought Kathy was swell—she's so pretty and cute and always seems to know the right thing to say. But after seeing the way she's treating you tonight, I'm not so sure. I never knew there was another side to her."

He sounded young and confused. Jane felt sorry for him.

"Kathy's the same as always," she told him. "Lots of girls forget themselves when the boy they're interested in seems to—to—" She stopped and blushed.

"Seems to be getting interested in somebody else?" Ed finished for her. "Maybe she's right. To tell you the truth, Janie, I wasn't too keen on Kathy's getting you as a date for Kent. I didn't think you'd hit it off together. You've always seemed so quiet and serious and all tied up inside yourself. But tonight—gee, I don't know what the difference is exactly. You just seem to kind of sparkle."

Jane was surprised. "Sparkle? You mean I look different, don't you?"

Ed shook his head. "No, you look the same—very nice—but that's not what I meant. It's something else."

"What?"

Ed shook his head. "Whatever it is, I like it. And so does Kent; here he comes to cut in."

A moment later Jane was looking up into Kent's teasing face. "Hi there, Freckles!"

Jane laughed back at him. She thought: Even if the wish hadn't come true—even if I still did have freckles—I wouldn't mind being teased about them by Kent. He makes freckles sound almost like an accomplishment!

"And all that talk about braces!" Kent was still grinning down at her. "Boy, I used to hate those things, but I'm sure glad now that I wore them."

"You wore braces!" Jane said in astonishment. Somehow she had never imagined the calamity of braces happening to anybody as attractive as Kent.

"Up until this spring," Kent answered without embarrassment. "Then I graduated to a nightly retainer."

The orchestra swung into the last dance. Kent tightened his arm and laid his cheek against Jane's hair. The lights dropped low, and for a moment they were lost in the softly swinging maze of dancers, swept along by the warmth of the music. Then, suddenly, it was over.

"Hey, here we are! Ready to go?" Ed had his hand on Kathy's arm, but his eyes were for Jane. The crowd swept them out the door and they tumbled, laughing, into the car.

It was on the ride home that Kent kissed her—a boy's kiss, shy and awkward and half-afraid.

"Jane," he whispered afterward, "you're not mad, are you?"

"No," Jane whispered back, "I'm not mad."

She felt somehow that she should be—that girls were always angry and injured when they were kissed on a first date—but to-night it was part of the magic.

She leaned her head back against Kent's shoulder. From the car window she could see the night sky, still heavy with stars. She wondered idly which was her star, but they all looked exactly the same, swinging together high over the earth.

And then the ride was over and Kent was opening the car door for her, and she was saying, "Good night, Ed—Kathy—thank you for taking me."

Kathy did not answer, but Ed said "Good night, Janie; I'll be seeing you—soon."

They paused a moment at the front door.

"Good night, Kent," Jane said softly. "It's been the loveliest time I've ever had."

"It has been for me, too." He hesitated. "How about tomorrow? There's bound to be something we can do, even if it's just a movie."

"I'd love to," Jane said. And to herself she thought, how easy it is! There's nothing terrifying or complicated about it; it's the simplest thing in the world.

She went into the house and up the stairs. She could remember other evenings when she had come home from a blind date and crept up the stairs to throw herself miserably on her bed. But that was before, when she had not been beautiful! Tonight was a magic night. She slipped into the room quietly so as not to waken Alice and undressed in the dark. When she lay down on her bed she could still feel the magic, leaping and laughing within her, and when she shut her eyes she could feel the warmth of it all about her.

"Jane!" It seemed only minutes later that her mother's voice called her name. "Jane!"

She answered drowsily, without opening her eyes.

"Jane, telephone!"

Jane opened her eyes. "Why, I just got home a few minutes ago!" Then she saw that the room was flooded with light and Alice's bed was empty.

"Goodness," she said, "I must have slept and slept!" She stretched and yawned and stumbled downstairs to the telephone. "Hello."

"Hello," said Kent's voice on the other end. "I hope you don't mind my calling so early. It's just that it looks like a swell day for the beach, and if we went early we could spend the whole day. Would you like to, Jane?"

Jane smiled at the eagerness in his voice. "Fine," she said. "I can be ready in a jiffy."

"Gee, swell. I'll be right over."

Jane hung up the receiver and was starting for the stairs when she heard her name. She paused and heard her mother's voice in the kitchen.

"It was for Jane!" she was saying. "A boy! Our ugly duckling is blossoming at last!"

"Well, no wonder," replied her father's voice. "When she walked out that door last night, smiling and chatting with that Browning boy, I hardly knew her! It could have been a different girl!"

Jane laughed with delight. It was the star! she thought. Even Daddy noticed the change!

She started upstairs, and came face to face with the hall mirror.

"Hi," Jane whispered happily to the face in the mirror. She started on, then did a double take and turned back again. She stood staring for a long time—at the freckles and the snub nose and the braces. Her heart sank.

"I was fooling myself," she said dully, "all along. I probably knew, deep down inside; that's why I didn't want to look in a mirror. Wishing on a star can't change your looks. I knew it—but I wanted so badly to be beautiful, I made myself believe it!" For a moment her disappointment was more than she could bear.

And then through her misery she heard her mother's voice.

"I know what you mean, dear. But it's not a physical change; it's something deeper than that—a kind of inner glow. A girl can go along for years, and then one day something will happen to give her confidence in herself. Maybe a boy will look at her in a certain way, or smile at her, or kiss her. It happened to Alice—remember?"

To Alice! Jane thought of her lovely sister, and suddenly her mind slipped back to a time when Alice was not beautiful—when Alice had wished on stars, too. Why, it's true! she thought, and wondered briefly what had changed Alice—a look, or a smile, or a kiss. She knew instinctively that Alice would never tell her. It is a very private moment when a girl discovers that she is beautiful.

She looked again at the face in the mirror and smiled. The face smiled back, not its old, tight-lipped grimace, designed to conceal the unconcealable braces, but a slow, easy, happy smile. And it was beautiful!

Jane turned away. "Mother," she called, starting toward the kitchen, "may I borrow your swimming cap?"

Roger had one idea about dating
but Nancy had another

Going Steady

Marjorie Eatock

While she waited for Carolyn, Nancy took a good look at herself in the weight-machine mirror. She looked no different—still cute, taffy-haired, wearing a moss-green sweater.

"My, what big sad eyes you have, Grandma." Carolyn popped her perky face up over Nancy's shoulder. "C'mon, 'Camille,' let's go in. And relax. Larry's not there."

It was a little easier, not to have to enter the maltshop door alone. But Nancy's heart still thudded in her throat, because having Carolyn's company wouldn't change the wretched pattern of the last three weeks. The boys at the counter would still exchange glances. The girls, crammed into one booth, would hesitate in their gay talk just a moment when they saw her; then continue casually, as though someone hadn't whispered: "Here she comes without Larry again. Guess they've broken up for good." "Wonder what happened?" "Well, let's be nice, to her, kids." Then Betts, or Susie, would sing out, "Hi, stranger. Come sit."

The maltshop was the same as always. The boys at the counter nodded. Nancy's brother Griffing, at the far end, waved his hand and bent his blond head again over his math book. Susie scrooged over in the seat to make room for Carolyn, while Nancy sat with Kathy and Betts, facing the mirror that reflected the door. Because, some time soon, he would come in. He always did. And she had promised herself solemnly that this would be her last try.

85

No more sitting down at his study table, to have him speak but eventually get up and move away. No more dropping in at his mother's kitchen, hoping he would be there. Then, when he came, watching him and his mother exchange embarrassed looks. No more walking by his empty, parked car, nor sitting in the movies next to an empty seat. For last night, even Griffing had said, "Wise up, kid. You're bruising no one but yourself."

"Will you look!" Susie was saying. "Here's Nancy without her charm bracelet. Don't you feel naked, doll?"

Nancy felt the color surge into her face. "I can't find it," she mumbled.

But she knew where it was. She had planted it last evening in Larry's empty car. He knew how much it meant to her. Surely he would *have* to return it to her.

Cory, the waitress, was asking, "What'll it be, gals?"

Carolyn was laughing. "One stingy Coke, Cory. I have only four cents."

Betts said, "Here, poor child, I have a penny. How about you, Nan?"

Should she order a Green River? Should she let him see she was drinking Their Drink? Would it help? "Green River," she ordered firmly.

"Speaking of green, that's a real cool sweater." Kathy smiled. "New, I bet."

Nancy nodded. Brand new, for Larry who had always liked her in green. Her taffy hair was curling down her back because Larry didn't like pony tails, and her nails were unlacquered because Larry thought polish looked bloody. The girls were chattering about some new boy in school. Carolyn was saying soulfully, "Isn't he a dreamboat! His eyes just send me, don't they you, Nance?"

"Who?"

"*Who!*" Carolyn fell back in mock collapse. "Roger Corning, nuthead. You know—big and tall like Randolph Scott—"

"But curly hair like Tony Curtis," cut in Kathy.

Nancy said, "Oh." She remembered now. He had come home yesterday with Griff. He walked like Larry. For a moment, glancing up, she had thought it was Larry, and had sat there in a daze of happiness, thinking, "He's come back!" Then, realizing her mistake, she had managed a brief, choked hello, and rushed away to hide tears. "He was at our house last night," she told the girls.

"At your house! May I touch you?"

"Oh, for a brother like Griffing!"

"You threw yourself at his feet, of course."

"Hardly," Nancy said.

She glanced at her watch. Larry had to come in soon; walk casually to the booth, look down at her with level gray eyes, appreciating the smooth hair, the pretty sweater, saying, "Hi, Taffy. Come out to the car a minute. Got something to show you." In the car he would say, "Nan, it's no good. Nothing's fun without you. Let's pair up again—"

Then it would be all over—the loneliness, the insecurity; the kids waiting for her to say his name, yet uneasy when she did; getting together without her because she had had other things to do for so long they had grown out the habit of asking her.

The girls all had their hands spread on the table, admiring nail polish.

Susie giggled. "Boy, look at me; the only gal in town with a two-toned hand. I can't get that golf-glove mark to tan. Can you, Nancy?"

"I haven't played very much for a while." Golf wasn't fun without Larry. She didn't put her hand down with theirs, for she had another mark—the white one where his class ring had been.

The Green River was almost gone when she heard his car outside. Everyone knew Larry's car. One of the boys said, "Well, well, here's the bucko with the Hollywood mufflers. Howdy, hot rod."

Larry was coming in the door, ducking his head because he was so tall. Nancy watched him in the mirror, the sudden radiance on her face fading to blind disbelief. For he was towing little, dainty Ann Mary by the hand. She was laughing, running to keep up with his long stride.

"Look at the half pint I picked up on Third Street!" He called out to the boys. "Hi, gals. Hi, Nan, here's an addition to your party." He pulled a chair over to the booth for Ann Mary, tousled her wind-blown hair, and said to Cory as he went on over to the counter, "I'll pay her tab, my good woman. Hello, Griff. Just the man I wanted to see. How about problem four?

"My soul!" Ann Mary was laughing. "I didn't want to come here —I was going home when that big goof—lemon Coke, Cory, please. Well, what's doing, kids?"

Nancy's hands gripped her empty glass. She felt cold and numb. She didn't look up, so she failed to catch the glance of pity her friends exchanged, nor see Ann Mary's silent but eloquent gesture of helplessness.

Ann Mary's voice was curiously gentle as she said, "Real lush sweater, Nan."

"Don't look now," Kathy said in a trembly voice. "Dreamboat is just walking in."

Nancy saw him in the mirror through a blur: red sweatshirt on a rangy body, a furry crew cut, cleated shoes dangling over one shoulder.

"Horror!" Carolyn moaned. "He's cut off that beautiful hair!"

He walked by the booth, gave them a friendly grin, nodded to Nancy. "Hi, girls."

They chorused, "Hi, Roger."

Ann Mary asked, "How'd practice go?"

"We'll murder 'em." He laughed, and went on to the counter.

Ann Mary rolled her eyes heavenward. "If he doesn't ask me to the mixer I'll just die," she said. "He's in my chem lab, and I'm being so charming you just wouldn't recognize me."

Nancy looked at her incredulously. If Larry was interested in her, what did she want with anyone else? How could she even think about anyone else!

In spite of herself, Nancy's eyes wandered down the counter to the bent brown head, flanked by Griffing's blond one and Roger Corning's very new crew cut. For the thousandth time she asked herself miserably, "What did I do wrong?" First he had stopped calling, then he began to skip picking her up for school. Griff had tried to warn her, saying, "Look, Sis, Larry's going to college next fall, and what guy wants a private-property tag on him among all those new dishes?" But the next day, after seeing him at the movies with a girl she didn't even know he knew, she had charged him with it. He hadn't even been disturbed. What had he said? Just: "You've been a sweet kid, Nan. We've had lots of good times. Now let's call it a day."

"Phone, Nancy." Cory's voice brought her back to the present.

As she talked to her mother, she saw Larry raise his head, look at her. Then he slid off his stool, came up close behind her, so close she could see in the mirror the snag in his pullover where once her charm bracelet had caught. Her voice quavered. "Okay, Mom. I'll be right there."

He slid an empty glass across the counter top.

"Green River, Cory. Nice sweater, Nan."

The words were casual and cheerful. But inconspicuously, his hand came from his pocket, dropped something into her hand. And his voice, low but steady, said in her ear, "Don't do things like that."

He got his drink, went back down the counter.

For a moment Nancy stood like stone. The bracelet burned in her hand. Finally she went back to the booth, paid her bill, said, "See you all; I have to go home."

Griff waved, calling, "Tell Mom I'll be there in half an hour."

As she walked out, she heard again that hesitancy in the conversation. And suddenly she was sick of it all.

Part way down the block, she began to run. She was so absorbed in the sound of feet and her own hard breathing that she failed to hear her name called until a firm hand forced her to a walk, and Roger Corning, panting, said, "All right, all right, Wes Santee. Slow down, for Pete's sake. I go out for football, not the four-minute mile!"

She pushed the long hair off her flushed face. "Lend me the rubber band from your math book." Three quick twists and she had made a pony tail.

"That's lots better," he said, looking down at her critically. "I go for those."

He held out her purse. She looked at it blankly.

"You left it on the counter," he said. "I told Cory I'd catch you."

He must have fairly charged out the door! And he could have given it to Griffing! Her surprise must have shown on her face, because he said, grinning a little, "I wanted to talk to you, anyway."

They walked on in silence for a moment. Nancy's eyes were on her shoes; her heart was thumping. But it wasn't all from running; it was a new feeling welling up inside her. A sudden, clean, washed feeling. Roger Corning was watching his toes too.

"Look," he said hesitantly, "I want to say something—and if

you want to shut me up, okay, it'll be all right." Nancy looked up and caught a level glance from under Roger's knitted brows.

"Go ahead," she said, nodding. She thought, he knows about Larry. Griff must have told him.

"Well—back where I came from—I was going steady, too, Nancy. A real swell girl. When I found out we had to move away, I about flipped. We even talked about running off and getting married." His voice, which had been growing lower and lower, suddenly came out strong, and he looked directly at her. "But here's the thing, Nan. We were lucky. We had time to think it over. And golly—all of a sudden I was scared to death."

"Scared?" She had been nodding her head sympathetically, but being *scared* was not very romantic.

"Purple. At the way I felt. Why, good gosh, kids our age have no business feeling the way I did!"

Nancy looked bewildered. Roger stopped short, jammed his hands deep in his pockets.

"What did I know about Linda?" he demanded. "I mean, *really* know—besides the fact she could dance and was a lot of fun at parties. Nothing! I didn't," he added sheepishly, "even know if she could cook. Besides—there's a pile of things I have to do—college, the Army, you know. That's what I mean, I was scared. We both were. That," he finished, "is what going steady does for you. You get too far ahead too soon."

That is just where I was, Nancy thought, staring at the sidewalk with eyes that didn't see it. Getting too far ahead. Skipping over big chunks of my life, big chunks of—

She was brought back by Roger nervously clearing his throat. "Nancy?"

"Here," she said.

He grinned. "I have a reason for this true confession," he said. "I want you to go to the mixer with me."

That good, cleaning feeling had suddenly gone clear to the top of Nancy's head. At last she realized what it was: a sense of freedom! No more did it matter if she were seen talking to another boy, for now there was no Larry to become jealous and angry. She could talk to the whole wide world if she pleased. And she could wear a pony tail—and eat popcorn in the movies—and wear nail polish—

He said, "Look, woman, I made you an offer!"

"I eat onion on my hamburgers."

"The offer stands."

"I accept."

He laughed, reached out and took her books and jacket, tucking them under his arm.

"Roger," she said hesitantly.

"Ma'am?"

"Thank you for telling me."

"Just so you understood how I feel," he answered quietly. "I mean, about going steady again."

"I know, you're against it."

"Oh, no. No. I'm for it."

"For it?"

"You bet." He grinned. "Steady with one girl one week and another girl the next."

Nancy laughed. "Okay," she said. "Put me down for next week."

Annamarie learned the meaning of artistic integrity the night of the school play

To Play
a Snob

Ina Edmondson

The curtain twitched open slowly, responding in uneven jerks to the muscular heaving of a member of the stage crew. From the stool on which she perched in the wings, Annamarie Wilson watched the oblong patch of darkness beyond the footlights widen and decrease in intensity until vague moons of faces in the front row were visible. She heard the final rustling of programs, saw the bright yellow globes of twin spotlights in the balcony waver a moment before converging on the solitary figure on stage, the maid flicking at the furniture with a feather duster.

Willowtown High's junior play has really begun, Annamarie thought, with a prickling of panic. In the next fifteen minutes before her cue, she had to make her decision.

She hooked her high-button shoes on the lower rung of the stool and straightened the lace cuffs of her black dress. She did not feel like Aunt Agatha, in spite of the grizzled wig she wore, in spite of the glassless spectacles and the wrinkles painted on her face. Was this because she had not yet decided which of the two possible Aunt Agathas would walk on stage in fifteen minutes? She glanced at the boy and girl standing behind her, at Burt Matthews nervously fingering his glued-on mustache and at Dorothy Williams patting her liberally powdered hair. It was easy to see that this was a first play for both of them, and the knowledge that they had leading roles obviously increased their tension. They both smiled at her stiffly through their make-up, and the unspoken question on their faces forced Annamarie to think once more of her own dilemma.

Until three-thirty yesterday afternoon there had been no problem, or at least none demanding immediate solution. Annamarie had even begun to hope that she was making progress in being accepted by her classmates. Knowing that transferring from a large New York school might be considered a strike against her, knowing that her own natural reserve might be taken for snobbishness, she had avoided talking about New York, had spoken enthusiastically of the willow-fringed lake which gave the town its name. She had not mentioned her bit parts in several New York TV programs, feeling sure that they would not have been seen on Midwestern channels.

It was Miss Vinson, the dramatics teacher, who first mentioned Annamarie's acting experience the day she announced the cast for the junior play. Afterward there was no way Annamarie could convince her classmates that her interest was not in past productions but in what could be done with her new role of Aunt Agatha, the crotchety maiden aunt in the play.

Annamarie knew exactly what she would do with the part, just how she would arouse the smoldering fires of hatred in the audience, making them grip their programs in intense, instinctive dislike almost from the first moment she hobbled on stage. From that instant when the faint spark of antagonism flickered into life, until the final exploding impact of their loathing, their reactions would be a direct result of her own planning. And after she squeezed the last drop of fierce rancor from their minds, she would expose the bleeding layers of this bitter spinster's heart to them until they were confronted not only with the festering hatred there, but also with the reflection of their own ugly passion. In that moment of their awareness, when they understood their individual involvement in the hatred in the human heart, Annamarie would taste the triumph of creative acting.

But that vision had been shattered at three-thirty yesterday afternoon.

Annamarie had stopped at the drugstore after her last class to buy a tube of tooth paste. Now, as she watched Burt Matthews brush past her into the bright square of the stage living room, she thought of that moment in the drugstore. She saw herself hand the clerk two quarters, heard the brisk *ding* of the cash register, watched fat pink hands shuffle the coins for a dime and two pennies. She saw her own hand reach out for the change, jingling it a moment as she considered buying a soda before going home. Then from the booth at the rear she heard a harsh explosion of laughter and the sound of her own name. Turning curiously, she saw Dorothy Williams and Burt Matthews leaning toward each other, her blond ponytail a sharp contrast to his dark crew cut. She heard the low protest of Burt's voice and saw the doubtful shake of his head.

"An actress—Annamarie Wilson an actress?" Dorothy's harsh laugh erupted again. "Surely you don't think *that,* just because she had small parts in a couple of TV shows? Listen, if she's such an actress, why did she leave New York and come to a little town like this?" At Burt's murmured protest she shrugged. "Anyway, Miss Vinson just gave her the part of Aunt Agatha because of her remote, distant air. It takes a snob to play a snob."

A light film of perspiration stained the palms of Annamarie's hands, as she remembered those last words. They had echoed in her mind, lurking just below the surface of her thoughts all day in classes, filtering through the excitement of putting on make-up in the dressing room tonight, stalking her with implacable tenacity to the stool where she perched now, watching the action on stage.

In a way, the numbness, the shock of the overheard conversation, had helped her escape through the door of the drugstore. It had held her body stiff with outraged pride as she walked the five blocks of Willowtown's business district on her way home. She was grateful that the town was almost deserted, that there was only the relentless pressure of the prairie wind sweeping along the wide streets, only occasional puffs of dust to contend with along the way. The numbness lasted through the ordeal of answering her mother's sprightly questions about the day, about her progress in making friends, in becoming the popular girl her mother hoped she would be. The anger carried her to the threshold of her own room, to the safety of a closed door behind which she could cry.

And then, when she was free to cry, she found herself incapable of tears. Could what Dorothy had said be true? Her mind tore at the remembered words, worrying them like a ravenous dog with a bone. Out of that mauling came a plan.

If playing the role of a snob successfully was likely to endanger her reputation, why not alter the role? Why not eliminate snobbishness from Aunt Agatha's character?

She picked up her play script and went carefully over her lines, penciling in minor revisions, jotting down notes at the side for changes in interpretation. That night at dress rehearsal she began the subtle modification of Aunt Agatha.

Now, watching the maid come in the side entrance with a telegram for Burt, observing him as he read the news of Aunt Agatha's impending arrival, Annamarie smiled as she thought how easy the alteration had been. By the end of the first act last night Aunt Agatha had lost her original force of single-minded viciousness; by the end of the second act she emerged as a confused, flighty, and misunderstood woman; by the third act not only Aunt Agatha had changed, but the entire cast had begun to change with her. As Aunt Agatha grew weaker, as the stark cutting edge of dramatic tension lessened, the tone of the play lightened. A gaiety flared in the voices of the cast.

Annamarie made few changes in her own lines, taking care that none of these were cue lines for other actors. But the alterations she did make were deliberate, carefully thought through, calculated for their effect. Along with the delicate shifts in words came revisions in interpretation—sly grimaces, a twitch of the lips, a fluttery sigh, or a droll wag of the head at appropriate moments. Played this way, Aunt Agatha had no more force of character than a kitten; no one watching could possibly feel more than a mild disapproval of her antics. There would be no dredging of violent emotion in the minds of the spectators, no centering of frenzied loathing on the slight figure in black. No need for the entire town to agree with Dorothy that only a snob could play a snob.

The results were agreeable and sudden. Dorothy's expression underwent a gradual transition from guarded antagonism to benevolent approval. By the end of rehearsal her smiles were frequent and genial, and even Burt began a series of little friendly quips. Afterward they invited Annamarie to have a soda with them at the drugstore, but Miss Vinson called to her, asking her to stay a moment after the rest of the cast left.

Annamarie watched Dorothy and Burt leave, hearing the last echoes of their cheerful laughter, feeling a thick blanket of silence settle over the empty auditorium. She stood halfway down the long center aisle and watched Miss Vinson move across the stage, straightening props, switching off lights, gathering the voluminous sheaf of notes and the stray pencils which accompanied her to all rehearsals. Watching the lights flick off one by one until a single dim light remained, Annamarie felt a prickle of apprehension about Miss Vinson's reaction to tonight's changes.

Finally Miss Vinson finished gathering and arranging. She walked down the steps into the auditorium with a firm, heavy tread and approached Annamarie. With one pencil-smudged hand she pushed her black-rimmed glasses more securely in place, so that her round brown eyes seemed larger and darker than usual. There was no softness in her expression, no bright flare of pride. Her eyes were bleak and tired as they met Annamarie's blue ones.

"I suppose you had a good reason for what you did tonight," she said quietly.

Annamarie opened her mouth to defend herself and then hesitated, not sure just how much Miss Vinson had seen.

"Yes, I know what you did." Miss Vinson acknowledged the look. "I'm not sure how many others will know, if you play Aunt Agatha that way tomorrow night. It's like a contractor using substandard materials in a building; the layman may not detect the flaws at first, but in time of stress the weakness will be exposed. That's what I'm afraid will happen with this play." She paused until Annamarie slowly, unwillingly, met her eyes. "What you did tonight seriously weakened the foundations of the play. You took away the conflict, and there's an old saying, 'No conflict, no play.' " She hesitated at Annamarie's stubborn, unconvinced expression. "Your reasons for altering the role," she went on, shifting tactics, "are they too personal to talk about?"

Annamarie nodded, not quite meeting Miss Vinson's eyes. She heard the older woman sigh, saw her shove a handful of pencils into a sagging jacket pocket.

"Of course, I could order you to play the part as it's written," she said. "But I couldn't force you to play it as I know you can. It was foolish of me to dream as I did; I thought this time a play could be produced in this town with at least one living, believable character in it." Her eyes looked beyond Annamarie into the darkness at the back of the auditorium. "Instead, it looks as though I'll have to watch a fine role and an equally fine talent being wasted tomorrow night." For a moment she was silent, and then her eyes bored into Annamarie's. "You have a conscience, a sense of integrity. Do you know what this will do to them?"

Annamarie nodded, stubbornly, and Miss Vinson's shoulders sagged. She turned and walked down the aisle and out the back door, not even looking at Annamarie hurrying after her. For a brief moment she halted on the top step outside, lifting her face to the cool night wind.

"So you're going to kill Aunt Agatha—with a powder puff," she said, so softly that Annamarie almost missed the words. Then she clumped down the steps and disappeared into the night, leaving Annamarie staring after her with a keen sense of loss.

Now, on her perch in the wings, Annamarie stirred restlessly, disturbed by the memory of those words. The rustle of Dorothy's taffeta skirt as she approached brought Annamarie back to the present. Dorothy's hand dropped, slim and cold and slightly damp with perspiration, on Annamarie's shoulder.

"You're going to play Aunt Agatha as you did last night, aren't you?" she whispered urgently. "I'll never get through this play, otherwise." Her mouth twitched in a nervous smile; then she stiffened as she heard her cue, her fingers gripping Annamarie's shoulder spasmodically before she walked out into the bright lights.

Annmarie watched Dorothy run across the stage to Burt, too fast for someone who was not supposed to know about the telegram. She's really quite bad as an actress, Annamarie thought critically. And with the thought came the realization that she could help Dorothy appear very good tonight, and that Dorothy knew it too. All she had to do was to play it light, to play it smooth and gay and shallow, and Dorothy would be fervently grateful. Burt would be pleased for Dorothy's sake, and in one night she would have made two good friends. The people of Willowtown would consult their programs for the name of the girl playing the part of the delightful old lady, and a little of the delight would stay in their minds whenever they thought of Annamarie after tonight.

And after all, why shouldn't she? Why should she make enemies among her classmates, just so she could walk home tonight with a clear conscience? There would be many other times to live up to her integrity when she did not have so much at stake. And who would know? Miss Vinson and herself. Two people, pitted against an overwhelming majority who would like the play better as it was in dress rehearsal.

Besides, she really owed it to the cast to do what she could to help them. In a way she owed it to Willowtown. The people could leave the auditorium tonight with the pleasant conviction that they were all right, that the junior class was one of the best, and that what this world needed was more folks like those in Willowtown. No one really wanted to be confronted with his own weakness, to be forced to admit that in his own breast were seeds of all the evil he deplored in the world. Not a person sitting in the audience tonight would thank her for revealing this fact. And certainly her mother—sitting on the edge of her seat with a self-conscious smile for those who recognized her daughter on stage—would be disappointed.

Resolutely Annamarie shut out the memory of Miss Vinson's words. She cleared her mind of the last lingering pride in her acting ability. I'll play it light, she decided with a lift of her chin. I'll be the giddiest powder puff that ever killed a character. She waited for the onslaught of guilt, and was surprised to find only a heady sense of relief at the decision. Perhaps I exaggerated it all, she thought with a slight smile, leaning forward to listen to the dialogue on stage.

"—But Robert, I don't want Aunt Agatha to come here," Dorothy was saying. "She'll upset everything. You know she always does when she comes for a visit."

Annamarie frowned. What was wrong with Dorothy's voice? It sounded flat and hollow; it held no hint of desperation, of impending disaster. Annamarie looked at Burt, fingering the telegram.

"Well, she'll be here at five o'clock, whether we like it or not," he said almost casually. "Please try to be nice to her. Remember she has no one but us." His tone was mild and unconcerned.

Then Dorothy began the speech whose last line was Annamarie's entrance cue. "I don't see why I should be nice to her. She's never been nice to me. I don't care if she does have money. She's nothing but a snob—"

The word flared across Annamarie's mind, blotting out the rest of Dorothy's words. Suddenly there it was—there was the flaw Miss Vinson had warned her about. There was the glaring crack in the foundation. That word—which should have been spoken with all the passion Dorothy could muster, all the overtones of fear of what Aunt Agatha might do—that word had been spoken as though it were a meaningless sound. It had been spoken that way because last night it had become false. None of the cast tonight would be able to act as though it were true.

Annamarie drew in a deep breath. I made a mistake, she thought grimly. I didn't help anyone by changing Aunt Agatha. I made us all puppets mouthing hollow words. I killed Aunt Agatha last night, and now they are burying her in tissue-paper words. By the end of this act the audience will be yawning, wishing that they had brought a good book.

She slid off the stool, hearing Dorothy speak the last phrase of her cue. You may hate me for this, Dorothy Williams, she thought, but you will be wrong. And if the whole town hates me tonight, it will be because I've done justice to Aunt Agatha. Maybe Dorothy is right; maybe I am a snob. If that's true, it's wrong for me, but it's right for Aunt Agatha. And this is her night.

As she hobbled out into the glare of the spotlights there was a moment of intense silence; even the members of the cast grappled with a something in the air, an aura of evil radiating from the slight hunched figure in black approaching them. Annamarie turned from the sight of Dorothy's openmouthed amazement, from Burt's frozen stare. Her eyes flicked over the audience, feeling the first waves of dislike leave the minds of the moon-faces out front and lap silently over the footlights until they reached her feet. A triumphantly bitter, malevolent glare settled over her features. Never had she looked quite so much like Aunt Agatha.

Pam found it easy to get into debt—
but no picnic to climb out

The Circle

Elizabeth Eicher

Clutching her green guest check, Pamela Allenby waited anxiously for Mr. K. to come through the swinging doors at the rear of the Sweet Shop. She had intended to initial the check and charge it, but Arthur, the gangling soda jerker, had frowned and said in a voice so low that only she could hear: "I don't know, Pam. You'd better talk to Mr. K. Go over to the cash register."

She slid out of the booth, murmuring an excuse, and went over to wait for Mr. K. Her friends—Ginny, Chuck, Brenda, and the others—didn't notice. They were listening to Scott hold forth about his wonderful new boat. It was her day to stand treat, so they probably thought she was going to settle the bill.

But she wasn't going to settle the bill. She had sixteen cents left in her billfold, and the guest check was three seventy-five plus tax. Arthur had said she'd better talk to Mr. K.

They called him "Mr. K." because his Greek name was so hard to pronounce. He came through the door and stood there, smoothing his apron. "Yes?"

"You wanted to see me, Mr. K.?" She proffered the check.

His face creased into a worried frown. "Oh, yes. Pamela, the bill, she is—let's see—" He stepped over to turn the pages in a black-bound ledger. "Yes. Nineteen dollars and sixty-three cents."

"I'm sorry, Mr. K., but I don't have that much with me today. If you'll just add this to it—"

100

"But, Pamela," he shook his head in a worried way, "that is twenty-three fifty. Twenty-three fifty on the books!"

"I know," she pleaded. "I know, but, please, Mr. K. It was my turn to treat today. I *had* to, don't you see?"

"But these items: K's delight—forty-five cents. Pecan spree—fifty cents. Things like that, Pamela. You should order something cheaper."

"But—" She gulped. "Mr. K., you *can't* tell people they can't order anything that costs over a dime. They're my friends. Please. I promise I'll pay. Only I can't today."

He sighed, shaking his head again. "Pamela, you make big mistake. Bills—you let them go, they snowball and bury you. I don't want to be mean. I like you kids, all kids. Good friends of mine."

"Please," she begged, and by now she was almost in tears.

He sighed again. "Okay. This *one* more time. But you got to pay on the bill, Pamela. I don't want to go to your father, but . . ."

"Oh, no," she cried. "I'll pay. Honest. Please don't go to Dad, Mr. K. Please! You . . . you just don't understand! Please!"

"Okay. But you do something about the bill, Pamela. You hear?"

She nodded dumbly, her heart hammering. He mustn't go to Dad. She would have to find the money somehow. Only how? Her eyes swung slowly back to the crowd, her friends, four boys and three other girls. They had been nice to her right from the start, including her in their parties, their fun. She couldn't lose them now. Then she would be all alone, with two whole years in Berkshire Heights High to be passed in a succession of endless days.

If only there hadn't been a fire. None of this would have happened but for that. Her thoughts flitted back to the night made hideous by smoke and flames when she and her parents stood shivering and helpless in their night clothing, watching their home burn.

Of course, they were grateful that they had got out safely, but their possessions, rescued by neighbors, made a pitiably small heap. Her father had insurance, of course, but it wasn't nearly enough.

"I never considered the cost of replacing everything we owned," ne said, his face white and drawn. "You don't think of all the thousand and one items you've accumulated bit by bit."

It wasn't as though they were destitute, or needed help from the Red Cross. Her father had a good job. It was just the cost of replacing everything at once. Then had come this opportunity to transfer to Berkshire Heights.

"It's a good suburb," her father said. "Better than this one. Good school, nice people. We can make a down payment on a house with the insurance money. The only trouble is that Berkshire Heights is a suburb of wealthy people. We won't be able to spend money the way they do."

"We know we're not millionaires, Jim," her mother said. "We've never pretended to be."

"I know it. But even with my salary increase, it will mean tightening our belts for a while. We'll be limited to necessities for a year or two, and that's going to make it hard on all of us. As for your allowance, Pam, I'm afraid we'll have to cut it. You see, this affects all of us."

"He doesn't need to worry about us," her mother said, "does he, Pam?"

"Of course not," Pam said fiercely. "I won't mind an allowance cut. Honest. Besides, *everybody* in Berkshire Heights surely can't be a millionaire."

"Of course not. And in a couple of years, things will be easier. It's just this first year or two that will be tough."

They had moved, and everything went better than Pam had expected. She had felt a little shy on her first morning in Berkshire Heights High, but by the next day she was very much at home. Brenda Kirk asked her to join a group in the cafeteria, and Chuck Norman offered to squeeze her into his already overcrowded 1949 Pontiac. They may have been privileged young people, but there wasn't a single snob in the group so far as Pamela could see.

They went to the out-of-town games together, piling up in several of the boys' cars, stopping along the way for a hamburger. It was all Dutch, of course, and she was able to pay her way.

There were the parties at each other's houses. And then they had begun going to Mr. K.'s daily with one or another of them taking the check each time. She had begun to feel a little desperate about the financial situation, trying to push the ugly problem of money into some remote recess of her mind. But now Mr. K. was insistent.

Her throat was suddenly dry and she swallowed convulsively.

She walked woodenly back to the booth. Brenda looked up, smiling. Chuck stood up. "Want to squeeze in?"

"Thanks, I'd better get home."

"We'd all better move," Chuck said. "I've got to walk the dog. My kid sister *had* to have him, but now she's down with some spotty kid's disease, and I'm elected dog-walker!"

They all laughed and there was a general surge toward the door. Murmuring an excuse, Pamela trudged down Main alone. She *had* to find some solution to her problem, and she couldn't think surrounded by chatter.

She was aghast that Mr. K.'s bill was so large. Mr. K. was honest, though. If he said it was twenty-three fifty—she winced— it was. That wasn't the only bill! There were the things she had charged at the Sporting Goods Shop in the shopping center. She had been with Brenda, and Brenda had charged her purchases. Pam had gazed longingly at a racquet and balls and then hurried to the phone.

"A racquet and balls, Dad. Do you mind if I charge them this one time?"

The bill wouldn't come till the first of the month. Pam had thought she could save the money—the first had seemed so far away. Now it was almost here.

Nervously she pushed her hair back from her forehead. She ought to be giving a party for the gang soon. She hadn't had one lately. There would have to be refreshments and other things. Even the simplest party would cost something.

Her fingers began to tremble as she dabbed at her forehead again. She couldn't go to Dad. Her parents were trying hard to make their money stretch this year. She couldn't ask for a larger allowance.

But how could she back out of things now? She couldn't say, no, I don't want to go with you to Mr. K.'s. Or to the out-of-town games, or to all the other places that cost money. They would be surprised, and then perhaps hurt. Or maybe they would just shrug it off. Pam doesn't want to go? Okay, she can stay home. And that would be that. She would lose her friends.

She couldn't tell them she liked them but couldn't afford to treat them. There was always money in their pockets—at least it seemed that way—and they wouldn't be able to understand a girl who had to be careful about spending a dime.

She heard the whir of the borrowed sewing machine as she came into the front hall. Her mother's voice called from upstairs. "Pam? Is that you?"

"Mmm hmm." She went up the stairs.

"Look." Her mother's eyes were bright. "Cushions. Aunt Ann picked up some remnants, and see what we have."

Pam forced a smile. The pillows *were* colorful, but she couldn't be enthusiastic about them now.

"This little one, why don't you take it and buy your own material to cover it?"

"Thanks, but—" she strove for lightness, "I'm flat broke."

Her mother put down the cushion. "Perhaps I could lend you a little money this week, dear."

"No, thanks," she said bravely, "I wasn't hinting for a loan. Only, I wish there were some way to make money."

"There aren't many opportunities here," her mother said. "But cheer up. Maybe next summer you'll find a job."

Pam smiled and went to her room. Next summer! It was true that there weren't many opportunities for part-time jobs in Berkshire Heights. She would have to think hard, read the classifieds, maybe run one herself—a guarded one, so that no one would know. Because *something* had to be done and she couldn't bear the thought of losing all her friends.

It was Thursday when the promotion letter came. Her mother opened it, and left it lying on the table with some other advertising circulars. The folder lay on top. It looked like a bankbook—with $100.00 written on the top line. Pam picked it up, stared at it "What's this?"

"That? Just an advertisement. Drop it in the wastebasket, Pam."

"But a hundred dollars—" Pam was reading the print. "There's a hundred dollars just waiting for your signature at Fairest Family Finance. It says so."

Mrs. Allenby laughed and went on upstairs. "Well, thank goodness I don't need their hundred dollars," she said.

Pam held the folder tightly. Why not consolidate all those

annoying, small bills into one? it said. Why not? Her mother didn't need to, but *she*—she would be free of her immediate worries, and she had three whole months in which to pay back the loan. Come in and see our Mr. Putnam right away, the folder urged.

It was so astounding she could scarcely take it in. Why couldn't she do it? She could tell Mr. K. tomorrow that she'd pay his bill Saturday. It shouldn't take long to get the money—if she had only to sign her name.

She hugged herself happily. It couldn't have come at a time when she needed it more. It was *wonderful!*

Mr. Putnam's office was small, and there were only a couple of girls at work. But then he didn't need a big office just for people to sign their names in. The redheaded girl eyed her oddly when she asked to see Mr. Putnam, looked at the folder with "Mrs. Allenby" on it, and shrugged. Pam sat down confidently.

Five minutes later she was stumbling toward the elevator. Mr. Putnam had explained kindly that they did not lend money to minors. Their letter was not meant to include children. *Children* —that hurt. Mr. Putnam continued in his fatherly way. Didn't she agree that it might be difficult for her to repay the hundred dollars? And then of course there would be the interest. If she needed a few dollars, didn't she think it would be better to talk it over with her father and mother? They could help her—to earn some money perhaps—

Tears stung Pam's eyes. It was true that she hadn't thought about repaying the money, but three months was a long time. She certainly could have thought of something in *that* time. She rode home, feeling numb.

"Pam, you look sick!" her mother cried, and insisted on taking her temperature. She had a time convincing her mother that it was only a headache—and her head *did* ache by then. What should she do? What *could* she do? Mr. K. was expecting his money. The bill for the delights —the sprees—

Her headache kept her home all the rest of Saturday, but of course she had to go to school on Monday. There was no getting out of that. Chuck met her on the front steps and held the big glass doors open for her.

"Hi. Missed you Saturday."

"I had an atrocious headache."

"Tough luck. Okay now?"

"Fine."

"That's good. Say, we're going to Collingsgrove for the game Saturday. Stop at the Red Horse later. My car. I'll put your name down."

"Oh," she said. "I—I don't think I can go."

"Not to Collingsgrove? Why, it's the biggest game of the season!"

"I know—I—" She *couldn't* say she would have a headache again next Saturday.

"Well," he said. There was an odd silence between them. "Well," he said again.

"I'm sorry." It sounded so flat, so unnatural.

"See you," Chuck said, and they separated to end the painful moment.

She made an excuse for not going to Mr. K.'s and saw the blank looks on the faces of her friends. She dragged miserably from class to class, avoiding them, making excuses. She managed to dally so long at noon that all the chairs at their table were taken. Relieved, she carried her tray to one of the side tables. A big girl she vaguely recognized sat at the end. The big girl smiled. "Hello. Lost your place today, didn't you?"

"Yes, I did," Pam said miserably. "I know you're in my English class, but I'm sorry, I forgot your name—"

"Harriet Carroll."

"Hello, Harriet."

"Now that the formalities are over, how come?"

"How come what?" she parried.

"You aren't with your friends."

"I—Well, why aren't you?"

"Me? With your friends? Goodness, I can't afford to run with that crowd. Costs too much. I baby-sit a lot and that cuts into a girl's spare time. But even if I had all the time in the world, 'They're too rich for my blood,' as Dad would say. Not that I don't like them," she added. "But they're out of my class. *Everybody* in Berkshire High isn't rich, you know."

But Pam had heard only one thing. "You *baby-sit?*"

"Sure. What's strange about that?"

Pam clasped her hands. "Do you ever have jobs you can't take?"

"Lots of 'em."

"Would you—would you recommend me?"

"Why, if you're good at it. Of course."

"Oh, Harriet!" she breathed, beaming. "You're wonderful!" Maybe this way she could pay off her debts!

Harriet gave her an address to go to after school for an interview, and as a result she was booked for Thursday and Friday nights. On Saturday she paid Mr. K. two dollars, told the whole sorry story to her parents, and insisted on continuing to earn the money to pay off her debts herself. Their understanding and their pride in her helped and so did the feeling that her feet were set on the road out of the nightmare that had engulfed her.

A few days later, Scott stopped her in the corridor. He looked undecided, then plunged. "How about going with us to the Carnival next Saturday? It's for charity, you know."

Carnival? That would cost money. She looked up, and met his honest, concerned eyes. "I'd like to, Scott, but I can't. I'm booked up. You see—" she swallowed, "I have to work. I am baby-sitting to earn some money."

"Oh, I'm sorry," he said. Then suddenly his face cleared. "Say, is that what you've been doing when you seemed to be avoiding us lately?"

She nodded. Now he would say good-by, and that would be that.

"Well, for Pete's sake, why didn't you say so?"

"You—you don't mind?"

"Mind! Why should I? We'd know you had to work that night, that's all."

"Oh!" She felt lightheaded with relief.

"Hey, fellas." He was calling them over—Brenda, Chuck, the others. "Pam's been baby-sitting; that's why she's been incommunicado the past few days."

In a rush of gratitude she burst out, "Gee, you're tops! I was scared—I want to—listen, I want to give a party!"

"Swell idea."

"That is," she added hastily, "if it's all right with my mother and if you'll settle for soda and popcorn. I can't afford anything else." She waited. Now they would say no, thanks.

"What's wrong with popcorn?" Chuck asked. "Personally, I'm a pretty good hand with the popper. Pete's sake, we don't come to your house just to eat!"

They were laughing and planning. Pam stood in a happy silence. It was all right. They were still her friends. She had worried for nothing. As soon as she was out of debt, she'd—no, sir, no more living beyond her means— But there would still be popcorn parties. She had wonderful, wonderful friends.

The family could not afford college for Hilda,
but she found an answer

The Cost

Elizabeth Eicher

Ed steered the car toward the high, old-fashioned curb and cut the engine. He shifted in his seat to look down at Hilda and his hand rested lightly on hers.

"How about State U., Hilda? Did you send in your application?"

Hilda's gaze dropped. "Not yet." It was almost a whisper. She was silent for a moment. Then she faced around fiercely. "Ed, I've *got* to go. I've just got to. It's the only thing I want to do."

"I thought you wanted to marry me," he teased. "I thought that was the important thing."

She was not to be diverted. "I mean it, Ed. I've got to go to college. All these years the family has praised my art work, but now when I really want to study seriously, they hesitate about college."

"Maybe they don't want you to leave home."

She turned, her eyes picking out the dim bulk of the house through the darkness. "It's late," she said. "I better go in. Dad's still up. His study light is on."

"I'll see you tomorrow?"

"Tomorrow," she agreed. "Good night."

She let herself in the front door and walked softly down the hall to the open door of her father's study.

Her father looked up and smiled. "Come in. Have you been out with Ed?"

She nodded. "He asked me about my application to State, Dad."

Her father cleared his throat. "I wish I didn't have to tell you this, Hilda," he said slowly. "I'm a coward, I guess." He squared his shoulders. "But I've got to face it, I suppose. Better not count on college, honey."

"But I have to go, Dad," she pleaded. "It's the most important thing in—"

"Honey—"

She was unable to choke back the words that came out in a rush. "It's my whole life, Dad. I can't bear to waste it working in the store. I want to be a commercial artist. State has the courses I need."

"I know, honey, I know." He reached a hand out to her, anguish in his eyes, but she was too full of her own despair to realize that his suffering was greater than hers.

"It isn't that Mother and I don't realize what this means to you," he said slowly. "It is just that we simply can't afford the cost."

He remained silent for a moment, staring down at his tightly clenched fists. "Besides, honey," he said after a moment, not looking at her, "I need you in the store."

"But I couldn't be happy in the store, Dad," she protested. "It's all right for Tom. He *likes* to sell hardware and fishing rods. I'd be bored to death."

Her father winced. "I need you both," he said bleakly. "We haven't been doing too well these past few years. There's the mortgage on the house and the store. And Janet and Marcia are coming along. We have to count every penny."

Afraid she would burst into tears, Hilda got up quickly. "It's all right, Dad," she said, above the sob in her throat. "Don't worry; I'll manage somehow."

Later, lying stiff and tense in bed, she thought of the store. To Dad, the hardware store was practically heaven. He loved to putter about among all the knobs and bolts. Tom was just like him. Tom, nineteen, had worked at the store during summers and after school hours. He had jumped at the chance to go into the store. Dad had had a new sign made—J. L. MORROW AND SON—and Tom had been as puffed up as a blowfish over it.

The store was all right for Dad and Tom, but not for her. To sit cooped up in the tiny office typing invoices all the dreary days that stretched ahead—she couldn't do it. It wasn't fair to ask it of her. Let Janet or Marcia go into the store. If either one wanted to, of course.

After their talk, Dad must know she was serious. To be a commercial artist wasn't just a whim. It was her life. Somehow he would help her to manage college.

When she came down for breakfast in the morning, she was surprised to hear a deep voice in the study. "Hasn't Dad gone yet?" she asked her mother.

Mrs. Morrow pressed down the toaster handle. "No. Jam?"

Foreboding swept over Hilda. "He isn't sick, is he? Why is he staying home?"

"He wants to talk to you, Hilda, in the study, after breakfast." There was no smile in her mother's eyes.

"I'm not hungry." Hilda pushed her plate aside. "I don't think I'll ever be hungry again. Mother," she begged, "don't you see—" She stopped.

"Go talk to your father, Hilda. You're only tearing yourself to pieces. And Dad, too. Don't forget that."

In the strong light of the study Dad's face looked almost gray. Hilda closed the door behind her.

"Hilda," he began, "it's no use." She looked away from the pain in his eyes, staring down at the old threadbare rug under his feet. She could see her life there, threadbare—all the brightness, the happiness, gone.

"I wanted to suggest that you get a good paying job somewhere else, save your money, and take night courses. But I just can't. I need you in the store. Hilda. Tom's too new to carry on by himself, and I can't be there all the time."

"All right, Dad," she said flatly.

"The way matters are now— There's only one thing I can promise you, Hilda."

"Yes?"

"Things might change in a year. Try the store for a year. If we can possibly manage next year, we will."

"All right, Dad," she said again in the same hard tone.

"It won't be so bad, honey, you'll see," Dad said, forgetting his own distress in an attempt to comfort her. "Today is Saturday. Why don't you give the store a try?"

She went upstairs, her face tight with the effort not to cry. She pressed her lips together grimly as she pulled off her playsuit, slipped into her plaid cotton dress, and gazed darkly at herself in the mirror. This was the dress she had been saving for an important occasion. Instead, she was wearing it to be buried in a dim, dusty little office.

Tom would be happy, growing fat and good-natured with contentment. Perhaps Janet and Marcia, when they grew up, would have exactly what they wanted. But she, Hilda, was stuck.

Her hands clenched. She felt as though she couldn't breathe. The air was heavy on her chest, the way it had been that day the barometer had registered so low. But the barometer wasn't low now. This feeling was something else, something akin to despair.

She loved her father. She should be glad to help him. But all she could see was the store—the ugly, hated store.

She picked up her purse and went down the stairs. A year, Dad had promised that when the year was up, they'd talk it over again. Maybe things would be different, he'd said. But she could not imagine how they could be different in the small, poorly patronized store.

Things *would* be different next year, she resolved suddenly. What was the matter with her, anyway? She wasn't a baby to expect her parents to do everything for her. She was young and strong. What was wrong with working herself for what she wanted? Yes, things would be different next year. She would make them different. She had promised her father a year in the store. She had a year to think, to plan.

Hilda worked Saturdays during the rest of the spring and five days a week all summer. In September she said good-by to Ed and other friends and saw them off for college.

Early October flamed outdoors, but Hilda was unaware of it back here in the dim office. For her they were days of invoices, of bills.

That morning her father said, "I'll have to help Tom today. He has that new fall stock to arrange." He shook his head, peering into one of the show windows. "Dusty, too. I always change 'em first of the month."

"Let Hilda change the windows," Tom said.

"But I never dressed a window before."

Tom shrugged. "You can find the posters and stuff in the back somewhere."

The posters and advertising material were stacked on a carton in the storeroom. Bored, Hilda turned them over. "What do you want in the window?" she called to Tom.

"Oh, anything," he shouted back. "Ask Dad."

"Whatever you want, Hilda," Dad called from the doorway. "This is an off month. We're not featuring anything special."

"Then we ought to be," she told him. "Stores feature back-to-school clothes, things like that." She stood for a minute, frowning in thought. Why *didn't* they feature something?

She scrambled up into the show window and dusted it thoroughly. People stopped to grin or wave at her occasionally, but she paid little attention. She was thinking, planning. In the storeroom were some big flats she could use for a background. With a brush and a few small cans of paint, she could splash the flats with autumn leaves.

What did people use in autumn? She frowned again in concentration. Leaf rakes, for one thing. She jotted down the items as they occurred to her. From the shelves she helped herself to cans of paint and some brushes. Big, bold, splashy leaves. Maple leaves, small oak leaves. Soon the big flats looked as if a high wind were scattering leaves in a swirl.

At lunchtime she sent out for a sandwich. There was so much to do. The guns—hardware stores in small towns sold everything—had to be chosen carefully. The right kinds of rifles, the right kinds of shells, hunting jackets scattered casually to one side. Then a large cardboard figure of a man, sketched in charcoal, with the rake in his hand, collecting leaves.

She sat back on her heels to rest for a moment when the display was finished, then stood up wearily, suddenly aware that someone was tapping on the glass. She turned and gasped. A crowd had gathered and the man who had tapped was applauding.

When Hilda reached the store next morning, she found her father out front, admiring the window.

"How do you like it?" she asked.

"It looks mighty fine, daughter," he said. "Mighty fine. Entirely different from mine."

She laughed. "I should say so. All that jumble of stuff."

"Will it sell things?" Dad asked mildly, as they went into the store.

As she went through the mail Tom rushed in. "Come out and wait on trade! We're swamped."

"Me? But I don't know—"

"You can help the women buy collars for their dogs or jackets for their husbands."

She was amazed at the number of customers. Dad was busy showing guns. Tom was flying about. She helped an old lady find the right dog collar and then decide on a new coffee percolator. She sold a bride a hunting jacket and a glass baking dish. It went on like that all morning. Her attractive windows made people stop and, while they stood there, they remembered things they had been meaning to buy.

By noon Hilda was almost exhausted. Even Dad sat down heavily, shaking his head. "We've sold more guns in one morning than in a whole week last year," he said.

"More rakes, too," Tom added. "In fact, we're sold out. I had to phone for a rush shipment." His voice was excited. "Every solitary thing in that window of yours, Hilda, has been a good seller."

It was Thanksgiving week end. Ed had come home on Wednesday evening, and Hilda had had dinner with his family. Now she and Ed were walking through the deserted streets.

"Come downtown," she said. "I've something to show you."

Ed grinned. "The jeweler's window? Engagement rings?"

She laughed. "Nothing like that."

"I wish it could be, Hilda," he said, suddenly serious. "When I'm through school, I hope."

"I don't mind waiting," she said happily. "There's so much to do. Look." They had stopped before the store. The four big display windows were brightly lighted. In each one Hilda had featured a different theme, yet there was an over-all tie-in.

Ed whistled. "Why, they're wonderful! Hilda, they're better than Benford's windows with all their high-priced stuff."

"They sell things, too," she told him proudly. "Dad's so pleased and proud."

Ed turned to look down at her. "Hilda," he said, "I bet you'll get to college after all."

She shook her head. "No." She hesitated. "Dad doesn't spend nearly so much time at the store any more. He rests at home."

Ed's face was suddenly concerned. "Anything wrong?"

She nodded. "I just found out last week. I made him tell me. The kids don't know yet. But he'll be better—if he rests more."

"So you can't leave," Ed said slowly.

"No, but that doesn't matter any more."

"Doesn't matter!"

"Honest, cross my heart. Do you know why? I've been going to night school at the Art Institute in the city. It's only twenty-five miles. It may take me years, but, Ed, I'm learning things! I've been helped loads already. Mr. Price—he's one of the instructors—said he knows I'll make my way in commercial art because he says I'm good already."

He seized her hands. "Hilda, that's swell! You're getting what you've always wanted and you're earning it yourself."

She laughed again. It seemed she could never stop laughing. Her voice held laughter now, as she said, "Yes, and it didn't take me a year to find out how to do it. Sometimes," serious now, she looked up into his eyes, "you find out that the way you wanted to do something costs too high a price, so you tackle it another way."

When death threatened her sister,
Jeanne learned the meaning of love

A Party
to Remember

Beverly Conant Fuller

The sun flitted off and on through the dancing elm leaves. Jeanne turned her cheek to let the warm, clean-smelling wind blow against it. A day made to order, she thought. During her sister Kitty's illness, she had missed her special friends, Lynn, Carol, and Sue, her fifth-grade classmates at Webster Hill School. Jeanne had suggested inviting them to a tea party.

Since Kitty's return from the hospital after her operation, her strength seemed to come in waves. When she was excited, her white cheeks bloomed briefly, but her pallor returned as quickly as the wind scatters ripe dandelion heads.

"Jeannie," Kitty called to her now, "I can hardly wait. I haven't seen my friends for so long." Her cheeks were pink with excitement, "Wear your blue dress—we'll be twins."

On a surge of vitality, Kitty went skipping indoors. Jeanne followed and found her fumbling with the buttons of the blue dress. Jeanne knew better than to help her.

"Call me if you want me, Kit."

The worry that always plagued Jeanne when Kit was not around assailed her now. Sorrow in its purity, she told herself, can only purge if we let it; otherwise bitterness corrodes our very being.

Kitty had been so brave at breakfast this morning. From experience, Jeanne could tell that her head was beating like a tom-tom, when she refused to eat her breakfast. Yet later she insisted on helping with the sandwiches for the party. Jeanne suggested that she rest a while, but she begged so hard to be allowed to continue that Jeanne let her do as much as she wished. Only when it came time to frost the cakes, she asked Jeanne to squeeze the initials on each square.

Now Jeanne dressed as carefully as she ever had for her most glamorous date. She smoothed the blue silk carefully over her hips and chose her highest heels, the ones Kitty called her stilts. Perhaps this party would be her only chance to weave a yesterday and a tomorrow that would have to last forever for both of them.

Only the day before, Kitty had whispered to her, "When are you going to get married, Jeanne? I want to be a bridesmaid at your wedding. I'll wear a pink swishing dress and everyone will say, 'There's the bride's sister!' "

Jeanne's lips trembled as she pinned a blue ribbon in her hair. Her sister's thin face, full of suppressed excitement as she imagined herself a bridesmaid, floated before her. Why, oh, why, must Kitty suffer like this? All over again she vowed to make this a happy day for the little girl—a party to remember.

"Ready, Kit?" Jeanne asked at her sister's door. How pretty Kit looked! She had all their mother's best features, oval face, hair that curled naturally, big blue eyes.

"There's the doorbell." Kitty squealed and raced ahead down the stairs. She would pay for this later, Jeanne thought, but for the moment, excitement subdued pain.

Lynn was the first to arrive. She adjusted her many starched petticoats, moving slowly into the living room, very conscious of the billowing effect. "I'm wearing three," she told Kit, "so I have to be careful where I sit."

"Sit here in this big chair, Lynn," Kitty said. "Isn't her dress lovely, Jeanne?"

Jeanne admired the dress and its many petticoats. It was much like one she had worn last night for her date with Tim. "I love you, Jeanne," his words rippled through her again. After the party, he had kissed her, under the full moon. And now he was driving West to summer school. So much could happen between now and September. Good-bys were funny things. One had to say them so many times, but one never really learned how.

After a year away at college, Jeanne was spending the summer at home with Kitty. She kept remembering little things that made her younger sister special. Twelve years ago Jeanne had prayed for a baby sister with long curls, and a year later Kitty had been born. On her second birthday her curls had hung below her shoulders. Before the operation, no child could ride as well as Kitty, and even the boys admired her roller skating.

Like a lusty breeze on a spring day, Sue came in, calling to Kit, "I brought you some mysteries. Mom said you had lots of time to read and these are real good."

"I don't like mysteries," Lynn said with disdain. "I think love stories are more exciting."

The three girls went into giggles. When Kit closed her eyes, Jeanne noticed how dark her lashes were against her cheeks.

While the girls talked and giggled, Jeanne thought about Tim.

"What's on your mind, Jeanne?" he had asked last night as he had so often. She never told him exactly, but he always seemed to know.

"You love Kit and she knows it," he had said. "Don't think. Just have fun together."

Most boys avoid things like sickness and death. The first time Tim had guessed about Kit, Jeanne had been surprised, but now she expected him to know what she was thinking.

Carol the last guest, arrived. Kitty ran to meet her.

Kitty began to serve her guests. When Jeanne offered to help, she said, "No thanks, I'm all right," but Jeanne saw the cup tremble in her shaky hand.

The girls emptied four sandwich plates and sucked the pink ice cubes from their lemonade.

Tomorrow would be Sunday, Jeanne thought, and she dreaded Sundays more than week days. Last year Kitty had won a book for perfect attendance. She had yearned for this year's prize, a week at camp. Though she was struggling to enjoy her guests, Jeanne knew it meant another Sunday-school absence tomorrow.

When Jeanne had cleared and stacked the dishes, she suggested a game. Carol chose a word game which won prompt approval from the other guests.

Jeanne left the four friends kneeling on chairs, chins cupped in their hands, eagerly waiting their turns. She turned on the faucet in the kitchen and the spray poured into the sink and pinpricked her arms. She sneezed twice as she shook in the soap flakes. Three times to kiss a fool—or however it went. Anyway, she didn't know a fool.

The hot water crept up her wrists as she lowered the glasses. Love is a funny thing, she thought. It comes slowly—real love, that is. The kind you feel first for your mother and dad. You take it for granted until your mother saves some money from the groceries for your new dress or until your dad fills the gas tank the night before you are going out with the girls. Once you start noticing, lots of things like this happen. They add up and choke you now and then. You vow, "I'd do anything for them—anything!" That must be love.

It was this way now with Kitty, certainly. Lately she seemed to have grown up in so many ways. She read stories in *The Saturday Evening Post*. She tried to use Jeannie's lipstick without smearing it. Only last week Mother had bought her nylon hose. She was waking up to life only to find it shot through with pain. Yet in spite of the headaches, she and Jeanne did many things together. Jeanne asked herself if she had found a love only to lose it.

The doorbell rang and she went to answer it.

"Sue, your dad's here, to pick you all up."

"Do you *have* to go?" Kitty sighed.

"I had such a good time, Kitty," Sue said. "You must come to my house sometime."

At the door Kitty waved to each friend before she came inside. She threw herself in Jeanne's arms. "Thank you, thank you, Jeanne," she said. "It was a wonderful party. I'll remember it all my life." Against her will, she sagged against her sister. "My head aches," she confessed.

Jeanne helped her to the sofa. "You rest here for a few moments, honey," she said. She covered her sister with a blanket. "See now, you'll be warm and comfortable, and you can think about the party. Later, I'll help you upstairs."

"I didn't want to say anything when my friends were here," Kitty said. "It was such a lovely party, but when we began to play that game, I got dizzy." Her face crumpled into a sob. "Will it ever go away, Jeanne? I want to be well again."

When the long lashes, wet with tears, lay motionless on the pale cheeks, Jeanne walked out into the garden.

"I want to be well again. I want to be well again."

The words said themselves over and over above the dull ache in her heart. Kit had said she would remember the party all her life. Jeanne knew *she* would never, never forget it. The breeze touched her, soft as milkweed-pod seed in July. The elm leaves rustled above her head, and one leaf fluttered to her feet as she stared into the gathering shadows.

Souvenir

Mary E. Gross

When Gilbert had gone, Joyce stood staring after him for a full minute before she moved mechanically toward the chemistry lab and her next class.

It had happened! She had a date for the senior prom.

She had hoped desperately that *someone* would ask her, but as time passed, the hope had grown dim. Now it was only ten days before the dance. That probably meant, she realized, that Gil had asked somebody else and been turned down, but why should she care? She was going to the senior prom!

Gil had caught up with her as she walked out of study hall second period. One minute she had been mulling over an unsolved algebra problem, and the next minute there was Gil beside her, asking the important question.

"Why, thank you, Gil," she had said, trying to be casual and yet not overdo it. "I'd love to."

"That's fine, then." The words were almost brusque, but he was smiling at her. "I'll walk you home after school, and we'll hatch some plans. See you at the west door. 'By now."

Of course Gil Ballard wasn't one of the really big wheels at Windon High. Not like the boys who played football, or Ed Bromley, the basketball star. Or Whit Jones, who was a brain and class president. Gil, Joyce knew, didn't have a lot of money to spend on girls. He dated now and then, and he certainly wasn't considered a creep.

121

He wasn't specially good-looking. He had a square-jawed, earnest sort of face, and a short-short crew cut. Only the occasional smile that lit up his brown eyes could be classed as an asset. That and his nice manners.

He always spoke to Joyce in the hall, and once he had compared papers with her when their algebra test had been returned. He had never before asked her for a date, but then, Joyce hadn't had many dates. Twice she had been on double dates fixed up by Betsy.

"You're too shy with boys," Betsy scolded her. But now Gil Ballard had asked her to the prom!

Joyce dreamed through most of the chem period. Fortunately, the experiment was easy, and her partner enjoyed doing most of the work.

Next came lunch. Joyce could hardly wait to tell her news to Betsy. Only when she reached the lunchroom did she remember that Tuesday was the one day Betsy didn't have the fourth period free.

The conversation at the table brought her down to earth with a jolt. It was the same conversation that had been going on for weeks. The *prom*. Who was taking whom. What each girl was going to wear . . .

Before today, Joyce had only half listened. Now she sat in frightened silence, taking in every word. Mildred Ackers was describing the gown she had bought after visiting a dozen shops. *And* the accessories. A special slip, a wrap, slippers, an evening bag— the list went on and on. The prices Mildred and the other girls quoted made Joyce's head whirl. The whole thing was impossible. She would have to tell Gil that she couldn't go.

Then something within her hardened. She *would not* give up the prom. There must be some way—

Hastily swallowing the rest of her lunch, she ran up the stairs to consult Miss Romney, the class sponsor.

As she went she reviewed her financial situation. It did not look bright. True, she had paid the final installment of her class dues. That would take care of graduation expenses. She had about eight dollars left from her once-a-week baby-sitting job. But she had been saving that money toward a puppy. Ever since she had seen the blond cockers Sally Perkins was trying to sell, she had set her heart on having one. A soft, cuddly puppy. Something to love. Something alive, to belong to her alone. Well, she would have to give up the idea of buying the puppy.

She really could not ask her father for even one cent just now. Only a week out of the hospital, he had taken a new job, at less money than he had earned before. Paying his own board and Joyce's and taking care of other necessities would be all he could manage in the next few months. A luxury such as a prom gown was strictly up to Joyce.

"Miss Romney," she said, bursting unceremoniously into the room where the gray-haired sponsor sat checking accounts, "Miss Romney, I simply have to earn a lot of money right away."

"Sit down and tell me about it," the teacher smiled. "What's the occasion?"

"I'm going to the prom! Remember, we talked about it last week and you said you wished I could go? Well, I'm going. Gil Ballard asked me this morning."

"That's fine, Joyce," Miss Romney said heartily. "How much money will you need?"

Reassured by the matter-of-fact tone, Joyce plunged into a discussion of her needs. Miss Romney made a few suggestions about maximum amounts to be spent. Joyce tried not to be staggered by the totals.

Finally the sponsor made some phone calls, the net result of which was that Joyce had a two-nights-a-week baby-sitting job in addition to her previous one. The proceeds would be used weekly to pay back a loan from Miss Romney which would cover minimum prom expenses.

When Joyce, her eyes shining, had poured out her thanks, she turned t· go, but stopped at the door.

"Miss Romney—"

"Yes, Joyce. What is it?"

"It's so late—only ten days before—I can't help wondering why Gil asked me. If he was turned down by some other girl, I don't mind, but I—I haven't had many dates. I'm so afraid he won't have a good time with me." The last words came out with a rush, and color flamed in Joyce's cheeks.

"Don't worry, Joyce." Miss Romney smiled encouragement.

"Even if Gilbert asked ten girls before you, remember you're the one he's going with. You're a pretty girl as well as a nice one, and you'll find a pretty dress. I'm sure Gilbert will be proud of you and you'll both have a wonderful evening."

By the end of the day, Joyce still hadn't told Betsy. There hadn't been time for confidences. "I have an errand," she said when they met at their lockers. "I'll phone you tonight."

Off she hurried to the west exit before Betsy could protest or ask questions. Would Gil be waiting? Yes, there he was. His friendly smile made her feel more at ease.

They left the building together. Joyce was glad that the west door was less used than the east. Being with a boy was so new to her. She needed time to get accustomed to the idea before anyone saw her with Gil and commented on it.

She wondered how Gil felt. He seemed relaxed, strolling along beside her. And yet, there was something—

"Is there any girl you'd like to double with, Joyce?" he asked. Joyce's ear caught a note of strain. She wished she could tell what he wanted.

"No—no," she faltered. "I guess not." Betsy, she knew, had already arranged a double date, and Joyce had no other really close friend.

"How about you?" she asked timidly. "Is there somebody—" She stopped, noticing with a feeling of panic that his face had darkened.

"No," he said almost roughly, "nobody."

Then, to her relief, his smile reappeared. "We'll make it a twosome, then, shall we? I'll have my brother's sports car, and it's handier for just two. Now, about flowers—do you know what color you're going to wear?"

Of course she didn't know. How could she?

"I don't know yet, Gil," she said, "but I'll let you know in a couple of days. It's sweet of you to ask."

She smiled up at him and was momentarily shaken at seeing a flush mount to his cheeks.

"That's all right," he muttered.

By this time they had reached Mrs. Custer's boarding house, where Joyce had lived since her mother's death three years before.

Achingly Joyce wished for her mother. Mrs. Custer was kind, but she really couldn't be expected to share Joyce's present excitement. There was no one, actually, to be interested in her big news. Even her father could be told only by letter, since his new job had taken him to a large industrial city, ninety miles away. And he might worry about the money. Firmly Joyce decided she would tell him only after the dance was over.

Gil was still standing by the gate. Obviously he was searching for something to say.

"I hear they're getting together some sharp door prizes for the prom," he said after a pause. "I missed the last meeting of the committee, so I don't know what they are. I'm not lucky, though, are you? Ever win anything?"

"Once. At a movie. A bag of popcorn."

They laughed together briefly. More silence.

"I'm looking forward to the prom," Joyce said at last. "It'll be fun."

"Yes," he said, and repeated, "Yes, yes, it will. Thanks for saying you'd go. Good-by, Joyce. See you at school."

The next ten days were the swiftest Joyce had ever known. She saw Gil every day. Twice he walked her home. But they did not seem to have much to talk about. The weather, the basketball season, practical details about the prom. Once Gil said abruptly, "I suppose you want to go to Mildred's party. She's asking everybody. We'll just nip in and nip out on our way to the dance. Will that do?"

"Of course." Joyce reflected that Mildred hadn't really invited her, but she had said breezily at lunch that everybody must come.

Betsy was generously thrilled over Joyce's date. She helped select the all-important gown. A pale-blue nylon net with a bouffant skirt was found to be within the budget. Exactly the thing for Joyce's fair coloring and red-brown hair, the salesgirl assured them. Joyce breathed a sigh of relief when she totaled the amount of money she had spent. With careful management she would be able to pay her debt to Miss Romney before graduation.

In the space of a moment, seemingly, it was the night of the prom. Joyce was radiant in the blue nylon, certainly the most glamorous dress she had ever owned. Gil had sent a wrist corsage of sweetheart roses, and Betsy's mother provided a white wool stole for a wrap. The tiny gold bag Betsy had given Joyce for her birthday added an elegant touch.

Gil arrived on time, looking scrubbed and nervous. He admired the gown, spoke politely to Mrs. Custer, and whisked Joyce out to the waiting car.

For the next hour Joyce floated through a nebulous dream. The visit to Mildred's party was brief indeed. Gil steered her expertly into the press of people around the refreshment table and quickly away again. It was almost as though he couldn't wait to get out of the house.

"I didn't even have a chance to speak to Mildred," Joyce protested.

"You'll see her at the prom," Gil said gruffly. "We don't want to waste any more time. Let's get on, before the floor gets crowded."

Then they were dancing. At first Joyce found it easy to follow. Only gradually did she realize that Gil was holding her stiffly and dancing in silence. Didn't boys talk while they danced?

Gil answered her timid attempts at conversation as briefly as possible. She began to feel more and more ill at ease.

Something was wrong. Gil evidently wasn't having a good time. Maybe he was sorry he had invited her to be his date. Her self-confidence deserted her, and she fled to the powder room, where she spent as much time as she dared re-doing her face. Betsy came into the room, and her exclamation, "Oh, Joyce, you look so pretty," helped. When Betsy was ready, Joyce walked with her back to the ballroom.

At first she could not see Gil. Her heart constricted. Had he tired of waiting and left the dance?

No, there he was, standing near the opposite door with Mildred and Ed Bromley. Threading her way along the edge of the room, Joyce came within earshot just as Mildred said teasingly, "Really, Gil, if you're trying to make me jealous, you'll have to do a little better than Joyce."

Joyce shrank back, grateful that several couples had moved between her and Gil. It was Mildred, then, who had turned him down. How could Joyce hope to compete with a poised and popular girl like her?

Then Gil's voice came to her clearly, in hot protest. "I'm not trying to make anyone jealous. I had to have a date, didn't I? I'm on the prom committee."

Her cheeks burning, Joyce crept back toward the powder room. No, not there, where other girls would see her. She must get away. She would slide out the door and run home as fast as she could. The checkroom—She would have to retrieve the stole Betsy's mother had lent her. But she had to get away from Mildred's scorn. Away from Gil. No wonder he had seemed moody and standoffish. He had hoped to escort Mildred. He really hadn't wanted to come with her at all.

Maybe it had been a bet or a dare. She hadn't minded being second choice, but this was different.

Tears burned Joyce's eyes as she headed for the nearest exit from the ballroom, but she held them back proudly. For a minute she waited for a group of dancers to clear the path to the door. As they moved on, a voice called to her from the bandstand, where the class officers were gathered.

"Joyce Ivers." It was Whit Jones. "We've been hunting for you. Where's Gil?"

Joyce stood still, numbly staring. Whit spoke to the band leader, who obliged with a roll of the drums. The crowd grew silent and Whit's voice boomed through a portable mike, "Gilbert Ballard, please join your partner here at the bandstand to receive your door prize."

Joyce was conscious of myriads of faces turned toward her, of Gil coming across the floor with an anxious look on his face. Then Whit placed a soft furry object in her arms.

She looked down. A honey-colored cocker-spaniel puppy was gazing wistfully up at her, his pink tongue licking her arm.

A sigh of delight rippled through the dancers, as they surged about her.

"Oh, Joyce, isn't he precious? Aren't you lucky? Oh, let me pet him—"

Sally Perkins was beaming. "Joyce, I'm so glad. We finally sold the others, and Mom said we simply couldn't keep this one any longer. I figured any senior would be glad to have him, but it's perfect that he goes to you."

It seemed the entire senior class was milling around Joyce and the puppy. All she could do was stand there, her eyes misting with tears.

Presently Gil led her out of the ballroom to a sofa in a corner. She sat down automatically, raised her eyes from the puppy for the first time, and looked questioningly at her escort.

He dropped to the sofa beside her. "Please, Joyce—"he said. "I know you heard. Mildred saw you running away. I—I'm not sure she didn't intend you to hear. Anyway, when I realized you had heard, I finally woke up. Believe me, I didn't want to hurt you. I know I didn't try hard enough to give you a good time and I am sorry and ashamed about that, but I never meant to hurt you."

"It doesn't matter," Joyce said dully. "I understand about bets and dares. Really I do. You couldn't help it. I—I think I'd like to go home now."

"Please don't go. You must let me explain," Gil urged. "It's bad enough, but it isn't as bad as you think. Please let me explain."

Gil's eyes were as pleading as those of the cocker puppy. Joyce's face softened into a smile. She remembered Miss Romney had said, "You're the one he's going with."

"Gil," she said firmly, standing up. "We're a couple of sillies. You can explain later, tomorrow, any old time, but right now let's go in and dance. We're missing half the prom."

Hope lighted Gil's face. He sprang to his feet and took her arm.

"That's what I call being a real sport," he said, his eyes warm with admiration. "We'll park the pup with the checkroom attendant, and dance every minute till they put us out."

Once again in the ballroom, he looked straight into Joyce's eyes and said rapidly, "I want you to hear this, Joyce. It wasn't a bet or a dare. You've guessed that Mildred turned me down. I—I acted like a fool about that. Now I know she was just stringing me along, using me to hook Ed Bromley, but I didn't understand still tonight. Believe me, I'm cured."

"Well, I *am* on the prom committee, you know, and everybody kept needling me about my date. Then Betsy sort of suggested that I ask you. Joyce, that was a favor I'm just beginning to appreciate— Oh, come on, we're really going to enjoy the rest of this prom."

They danced lightly, happily. They chatted in the easy fashion of two who have known each other for a long time. The dance was what every prom should be, a dream come true. When the band began the final number, "Souvenir," chosen as the senior song, Gil murmured, "Shall we make this our theme song, Joyce?"

To her own surprise, Joyce broke into a merry laugh. "Oh, Gil," she cried. "I didn't mean to spoil a lovely moment. Forgive me. But it just came to me—it's more than our theme song—it's the perfect name for our prize, the cocker puppy." Laughing together this time, they went hand in hand to reclaim their prize.

*Planning to skip Christmas, Marie almost
missed the most meaningful one of her life*

Substitute Mother

Alice Eleanor Jones

Marie stepped out of the hospital into the rainy, winter afternoon, tense with the strain of holding back the tears. Her father
said, touching her arm, "Cry if it helps, Marie."

The call had come at eleven o'clock that Saturday morning. John
Sims had turned from the telephone, his face white. "Your mother's
been hit by a car. I must go right away."

Through her own shock and dread, Marie asked, "Would you
like me to drive?"

He tried to smile at her. "No thanks, but I'd like you to come
with me, if there were someone to stay with the children."

The ten-year-old twins, Jeffrey and Gregory, were in their room
making model planes. Kathy, not quite four, was playing with
her dollhouse.

Marie said, "I'll ask Mrs. Reilly."

Then Marie and her father had driven to the hospital to see
Mama, who had not known them. Marie had not cried in the hospital room. She would not cry now. She said, taking a deep breath
and blinking her eyes, "I'm all right now, Daddy."

As they drove home, he said, "Can you manage the house and
the children? It's a good deal to ask." His kind, fine-drawn face
revealed his concern for her.

"Of course I can manage," she said quickly and proudly. "Don't worry." She was sixteen, and Mama had taught her well. Christmas vacation was coming soon, and she wouldn't have school to take up her time. Christmas—who could think of Christmas without Mama?

John Sims said, "You're a good girl." He looked so pale and worried that Marie had to blink her eyes again.

Mrs. Reilly met them at the door, looked at their faces, and said immediately. "It's bad, isn't it, Mr. Sims?"

He nodded. "Thank you for watching the children. You're very kind."

"Anything I can do—any time," she said, and left, shaking her head sadly.

The twins had hung back, standing close together, a double image of disaster. Now Jeff said in a faint voice, "You said it was bad." And Greg asked quickly, "But she'll be okay, won't she?"

"I don't know," John Sims said. He was always honest with his children.

Jeff asked, "What will they do to him—the driver?"

His father said again, "I don't know. He feels almost as bad as we do. His car skidded in the rain."

"They ought to put him in jail!" Jeff cried, and Greg added fiercely, "For life. Forever."

"No," John Sims said. "No. He couldn't help it."

Marie said as brightly as she could. "I'll get dinner. What would you like?"

Greg said with a jealous look, "M'rie got to see Mama." Jeff added, "And we didn't."

"You have to be twelve," Marie told them kindly, but the memory of seeing Mama almost shattered her precarious composure.

Kathy awoke from her nap and ate her dinner happily enough. Although it was a good dinner, the boys ate little, Marie and her father almost nothing. Kathy asked only, "Where's Mama?" and seemed to accept Marie's "Away. She'll be back." John Sims opened his lips to speak and closed them again. Marie knew that he could not bear to explain it twice.

Kathy was restless all evening, asking again, "Where's Mama?" and then, "Away where?" Their father had gone back to the hospital, so the question was up to Marie. She thought sorrowfully: *I* can't explain it even once. Besides, she's too young to understand. Aloud she said, "On a visit."

At bedtime, Kathy cried. Marie made ineffectual gestures of comfort, murmuring. "Mama will come back," and "Go to sleep," until the child's eyes closed, and she was quiet. Afterward, kneeling by her own bed, Marie prayed, "Please, please, make Mama well, and oh, please help me."

Again and again during the following days, she found herself repeating this prayer. It was not that her problems were insurmountable. She knew how to manage a house, and she found time to do it and her schoolwork, too. Her brothers were good boys, and Kathy, after the first night, no longer cried or gave trouble. Marie thought with relief, she's so young; this can't mean as much to her as it does to us. But there were small, subtle things that weren't right.

Although Kathy did not cry, she moped; it was depressing. Although the boys were good, they were scatterbrained, and they would not always mind. How did Mama get them to obey? Their room, for instance, was always in a mess. They didn't put anything away nor hang anything up, and they could never find anything. When Marie scolded them, Greg said, "Mom doesn't holler." Jeff added, "At us," and the room remained a mess.

They didn't always like her cooking, either. When Marie baked beans, Greg said, "We don't like beans." And Jeff added, "Like this. Mom makes them different."

Marie snapped in desperation, "I'm not Mom," and Greg said, "You're darn right." When his father told him to leave the table, Jeff said defiantly, "I'll go, too." They said afterward, without even being prompted, "We're sorry, Marie," and shyly patted her shoulder, but Marie felt a touch of panic. She was trying to be Mama, but *nobody* could be Mama. Suppose it had to be like this forever?

John Sims continued to look sad and drawn, worrying about his wife, his children, and especially his elder daughter. He said, "The burden's all on your shoulders, Marie, and it shouldn't be. Perhaps if I had a woman come in—" But Marie knew he could not afford to add to the heavy hospital costs, and there were no relatives near enough to be of assistance. He helped when he was at home, and the neighbors helped, especially Mrs. Reilly, but they had their own families to occupy them. Mama still did not recognize anybody, and it was up to Marie to carry on. "It's all right, Daddy," she told him; and he said, as he had that first day, "You're a good girl, Marie."

It was difficult at school. As Christmas vacation approached, things grew more and more festive, and Marie became more and more unhappy. Many things distressed her: the kind inquiries of her friends and her teachers, who had to be answered, "Mama's just the same"; the necessity of curtailing her Coke-and-movie dates with Tommy Graham.

When she said, stumbling over the words, "I don't have time, Tommy. And besides, I can't enjoy myself, when—when Mama—" He answered gently, "Sure, Marie. I know how you feel." So far as she knew, he had not dated another girl. But if he wanted to, he would just have to do it. Nothing really mattered to Marie except Mama.

Giving up her clubs was a minor hurt, but sometimes Marie felt —she groped for the word—confined. She had to hurry home directly after classes, stopping for Kathy at Miss Lucy's nursery school and being sure to be at home when the boys came in. If she were not there to fix their snacks, they would get their own and wreck the kitchen doing it.

They were beginning to adjust to Mama's absence. Marie knew they still worried, but they had always lived in a private world of their own, and they were beginning to find it again. They had their model planes, their stamps, and their television. They went out to play in the sullen winter weather, saying hopefully, "It looks like snow. Maybe it'll snow for Christmas and we'll get a sled."

Marie knew they would. There were two sleds hidden in the attic If Mama had been home, there would have been Christmas cookies and candies and decorations. Marie cried, "How can you even think of presents, when—" and stopped. They were only ten years old, after all.

It took something Miss Lucy said a few days before Christmas vacation to make Marie realize how healthy the boys' adjustment was compared with Kathy's.

Miss Lucy said, "Marie, I'm worried about your sister."

"About Kathy? Why?"

Miss Lucy said quietly, "Look at her," and Marie looked.

Kathy sat in a corner, absolutely still, doing absolutely nothing; a small, forlorn figure with a desolate face. Marie felt a shock that was almost physical. She thought: where were my eyes?

"She sits in that corner all the time now," Miss Lucy said. "She won't play, and if the others try to coax her, she hits them."

"I thought she was too young to understand, or to—to care so much."

Miss Lucy looked at her gravely. "Let me tell you how much she cares. Today she took her doll, laid it in the crib, and then she walked away from it. When I asked her why, she said, 'I don't love her any more.' "

Marie drew in her breath sharply. "Oh, Miss Lucy—"

"Tell her," Miss Lucy said, "tell her exactly what has happened." She added gently, "And love her unusually hard."

Walking home along the quiet, small-town streets, Marie watched her sister. The little girl who used to chatter and skip, now moved quietly, head down. Marie thought, I couldn't explain it even once, and felt her cheeks burn with shame. She could not tell herself that Daddy should have told Kathy. He was beside himself with worry, and anyway he was hardly ever at home. She thought, It was my job, and I didn't do it. "Kathy," she said, "when I see Mama tonight, what shall I tell her for you?" Not that Mama would hear her voice.

Kathy stopped and looked up, her eyes big and dark in her little face. She said in her clear, precise voice, "See Mama?"

Marie knelt and put her hands on the child's shoulders. "I see Mama, you know. Some nights, after you're in bed and Mrs. Reilly comes to sit, I go with Daddy—" She paused, overcome by pity and guilt. Of course Kathy didn't know. Kathy didn't know anything, except that Mama had gone, vanished.

Kneeling beside her sister, Marie said urgently, "Kathy, Mama is sick. A car hit her. She's in the hospital."

Kathy repeated, "Hospital?"

"A place where they make you well. Lou Ann went there when she broke her leg. Don't you remember, everybody in your class made get-well pictures for her, and Miss Lucy signed them all for you?"

"Yes," Kathy said. "Did Mama break her leg?"

Sorrow clutched at Marie's throat and almost made her say, "It's much, much worse than that!" She said truthfully, "Yes, Kathy."

"Why can't I see her?" Kathy asked.

"They don't let little girls in. It's a hospital rule."

Kathy said, "Only big girls?"

"Yes, or big boys. The twins can't see Mama, either."

Kathy was quiet, considering that. Then she said, "Tell Mama to come home."

"I'll tell her you said that," Marie said, "but Mama can't do it, Kathy, till she gets well." Miss Lucy had said, "Tell her exactly," but Marie couldn't say, "*If* she gets well." She said, more urgently still, "Kathy, Mama doesn't like being away, and she'll come home just as soon as—as she can."

"For Christmas?" Kathy asked.

"No, I'm afraid not for Christmas."

Kathy asked unexpectedly, "Will she have a Christmas tree?"

"I'm sure she will." Marie leaned forward impulsively and kissed the little girl's soft cheek. She had seldom kissed Kathy. She said, "Mama loves you. We all love you, baby." She had never called her "baby."

Kathy twisted away from Marie's hands and began to walk on, head down. Marie wondered whether she had understood. Neither spoke again until they had reached their own front gate. Then Kathy said shyly, "I could make a get-well picture for Mama."

Marie stooped again and hugged her. "Yes, baby, you could."

Going up the steps, Kathy volunteered, "Or send her my paper chain."

"Paper chain?"

Kathy almost smiled at such stupidity. "At Miss Lucy's. I didn't have so very much done, but I could do one *home*." She smiled outright. "For Mama's Christmas tree."

That night in bed Marie thought very hard about the two sleds and a paper chain. The next morning she said to Kathy, "I'm going to make cookies."

Kathy's face brightened. "Cookies?"

"Like Mama's." Marie thought of the baked beans and smiled. "I hope."

"Can I help?" Kathy asked. "Mama lets me."

Marie had not counted on a not-quite-four-year-old in the kitchen, but the little girl's face was so eager that she said, "Of course."

Kathy was earnest and surprisingly neat. She sifted flour carefully, spilling hardly any. The boys came in when the cookies were barely begun and asked, "Can we chop nuts?" "Can we put in the raisins?" Marie thought of their tumbled room and had a sudden inspiration. She said, "I might let any boys who cleaned their room chop nuts or put in raisins."

Later when Marie inspected their room, she found it hospital neat. Was that how Mama got them to mind? Perhaps that was partly how. The other part was understanding them—which meant loving them. She thought of Miss Lucy: "Love her unusually hard." A wise woman, Miss Lucy. Marie looked at her brothers' serious, identical faces and thought, I never loved you enough. "Don't eat more than you chop," she said, ruffling their shaggy hair. "And you need haircuts."

Jeff said, "Mom lets us eat more than we chop." Greg added, "And doesn't make us get a haircut," but their eyes twinkled, and Marie laughed. She had not laughed in two weeks. She said— strangely, it did not hurt to say it—"I'm not Mom. I'm your nasty old sister."

Kathy looked up from the mixing bowl and said, "You're not nasty, Marie," Greg said generously, "You're not even old." Jeff contributed, "Twenty-*five* is old."

The last days flew by. Marie bought the stocking presents that Mama had not had time for. She kept the twins and Kathy busy making cookies and candy. She brought home evergreens, and they arranged them together. She asked Dad to bring down the Christmas tree ornaments, because she did not trust the boys in the attic. The house began to look as gay and to smell as delicious as it always did at Christmas. The little ones seemed happy, and Marie was happy—almost. The ache of anxiety grew less sharp whenever she was especially kind to Kathy or joked with the twins, who kept wistfully hoping for snow.

She teased them, "What would you do with snow? You'd take it up to the jungle you call your bedroom and lose it."

They laughed and gave her their highest praise: "You're funny, M'rie."

John Sims said on the second day before Christmas, with the special faculty he had of understanding his daughter, "You are making it almost a happy Christmas, Marie. I'm proud of you."

The next afternoon, to the ecstasy of the twins, it snowed. Marie and her father drove carefully to the hospital, taking with them a small Christmas tree and ornaments, the boys' presents, and Kathy's get-well picture and paper chain, which she had made at home.

The hospital looked festive, and somehow the institutional cheer was not depressing, but hopeful. For no reason—Mama was just the same—Marie felt hopeful. A group of carolers came down the hall singing very softly, almost like an echo. John Sims sat beside his wife, gently holding her hand. Quietly and lovingly, soothed by the music, Marie trimmed the tree.

She was making Christmas for Mama. She had made Christmas for the boys and Kathy, as Mama would have wanted her to. She had made it with love; not with a mother's love, but with a sister's, and a sister's love was worthy. For the first time in three weeks, Marie did not feel like a substitute.

Suddenly her father said, "Anne?" His voice sounded strange— quiet, but breathless, as if he were seeing a miracle. Marie looked quickly toward the bed. Mama's eyes were open, and this time there was recognition in them. Marie said, "Mama—" her voice sounding like Daddy's.

Mama smiled and said, "John. Marie." She closed her eyes again, as if the words had tired her, but she did not stop smiling.

A few minutes later the doctor came in. "She knew us," John Sims said in his shaken voice.

The doctor beamed. "It looks better," he said. "It looks good."

Marie said, "It's going to be all right."

She rode home beside her father in a mood of quiet happiness. She said without words, "Thank You for helping Mama, and thank You for helping me."

The Better Girls

Claire Jones

Lucy watched her father finish a second piece of apple pie. He grinned at her with appreciation. "That was great, kitten; you're almost as good as your mother. I'm beginning to look forward to the Friday nights when you cook."

"Lucy's a good cook," her mother agreed with a smile. "And she's quick, too. Why, she had the whole dinner ready almost before I knew she was in the kitchen."

"That's just because I was in a hurry," Lucy confessed. "I didn't want to be late getting away tonight."

"What's on for tonight?" her father asked. "I was just about to ask my two favorite cooks to go to the movies with me. There's a good picture at the Centre, and the maker of such a pie should be rewarded."

"Oh, Daddy!" Lucy was reproachful. "You know it's BGC meeting tonight."

"You couldn't miss it, I suppose?" he asked, and then, hurriedly, seeing Lucy's face. "Of course you couldn't. Nothing comes before the BVD meeting."

"BGC, Daddy; you never get it right." Lucy was smiling. Dad liked to tease her, but he knew how important the meeting was to her. She had missed only one since her initiation six months before, and that was because she'd had flu. Dad was always making fun of the name of the club and trying to get her to tell him what the initials stood for, but she wouldn't. Not even your parents were supposed to know that the letters meant Better Girls Club.

The kids at school who weren't members made up all sorts of names to fit the initials, but many of them, she knew, were envious because they didn't belong. It was "the" club at school. All the most popular and sophisticated girls belonged.

Lucy still could scarcely believe that she was a member. She wasn't especially pretty, not breath-taking and blonde like Roz Jackson, nor sleek and theatrical-looking like Kay Lindsey. She was just average—brown hair, brown eyes, shy smile. And while she had many friends at school, she certainly wasn't what you'd call a popular girl with real dates, and boys crowding around her locker to invite her to have a soda or to go riding after school. She was shy and quiet and not really talented at anything, although she did make good grades.

But that certainly was no reason for an invitation to join BGC. She knew if she hadn't been sponsored by Sue Clayton, she would never have made it. Sue's mother and Lucy's were best friends—had been for years—and she and Lucy had known each other since they were big enough to talk. Sue was one of the most popular girls. She was too busy to have much time for Lucy, but they were still good friends, and Sue had lots of influence in the BGC. She must have needed it to get me in, Lucy thought wryly.

She knew how hard it was to make the club. Two votes against you were enough to keep you out. She had seen several girls turned down during the months she had been a member—prettier and more talented girls than she was. But she had never voted against anyone. She couldn't, knowing how much she had wanted a bid.

Mother volunteered to do the dishes for her, but Lucy had time, so she shooed her parents off to the movies. Dad rumpled her hair affectionately. "Have fun, kitten. And give the girls my love."

After they had gone, she hurried through the cleaning up. It would take her a while to dress, and she had to call Doris before she left. They were going to take their lunch and hike out to the lake tomorrow. She was looking forward to it. Doris was fun and her best friend. After Lucy had been elected to membership in the club, she had suggested timidly to Sue that she would like to have

Doris invited to join, but Sue had groaned. "Gosh, Lucy, she's just not the type. She's a nice girl, and all that but—well, you need more than she's got to make BGC."

Doris was smart and fun and loyal and a wonderful friend. It seemed to Lucy that she "had" a lot. But Lucy hadn't pushed for it. She herself was still too much on the fringes. She could imagine Roz Jackson's—Roz was president—blank look if she had had the temerity to nominate Doris for membership. She had never had that much nerve and she couldn't have endured having Doris discussed and criticized the way the candidates always were. I'm glad I don't know what they said about me when Sue presented my name for membership, she thought ruefully.

Well, anyway, she was in, and if she wasn't an important member, at least she was a member. And Doris was still her best friend, even though Sue had said one day, after a meeting, "Really, Lucy, it looks a little disloyal to the BGC for you to spend so much time with Doris."

Lucy hadn't said that she felt more at ease with Doris than she did with most of the club members, but she had gone right on being best friends with Doris. She couldn't turn off friendship just because she was in and Doris was out. She wouldn't want to, even if she could.

She left the house in plenty of time to walk to the meeting. It was to be at Roz's tonight, and the Jacksons lived just a few blocks away. The soft spring twilight was lovely. The lilacs were in bloom, and Lucy found herself smiling as she walked along. Such a nice night!

When she rounded the corner into Second Street, she saw Rosemary Parker come down the steps of her house. Lucy stopped to wait for her.

Rosemary was new in school this semester. She was one of the prettiest girls Lucy had ever seen. She had soft, black hair; wide, blue eyes; and a sweet, shy smile. She had had her choice of dates from the first day. And when her name had been put up for membership in the club three weeks ago, she had been pledged right away. In spite of being so pretty and popular, Rosemary seemed a little shy, a little unsure of herself, a little too anxious to please, and Lucy felt a kinship with her. She remembered how nervous and eager to please she had been when she was a pledge.

"Is it all right," Rosemary asked anxiously, "for a pledge to walk to the meeting with a member?"

Lucy smiled. "I don't know any rule against it."

"It's just that I wouldn't want to do anything wrong." They walked on together. Then Rosemary said a little hesitantly, "I wonder if you'd mind—Roz assigned my pledge duties for the week, and one of the assignments was to choose the adjective that best fitted each one of the members. I'm not sure I've chosen good ones. Would it be all right if you looked at the list to see what you think?"

"I'd be glad to." Lucy remembered when Roz had assigned that task to her and how hard it had been to find suitable flattering adjectives. Any other than a flattering one would bring the wrath of a member down on the poor pledge's head. It had seemed a rather silly assignment to Lucy—many of the pledge assignments did—but Sue said you could tell what kind of a member a girl would make by the way she cooperated on the assignments. Lucy privately suspected that Roz assigned this type of thing so that she might hear nice things about herself.

She glanced down the neatly written list. "Roz—glamorous," "Kay—sultry." She grinned. Kay considered herself something of a *femme fatale;* she would love that adjective. "Sue—vivacious." She glanced on down the list. When she came to her name, she smiled a little wistfully. "Lucy—kind." It seemed a pretty tame adjective compared to all the others. It sounded colorless and unexciting. Well, she thought, I'm certainly not glamorous or sultry. She handed the list back to Rosemary. "It's fine. Just right. They'll eat it up."

Rosemary breathed a sigh of relief. "I'm so glad. You know, I get absolutely panicky in pledge court. Last meeting it was so bad, I was afraid I was going to be sick right in the middle of it."

Lucy knew what she meant. She, too, had dreaded the pledge court when she was a pledge, and she didn't like them. It seemed to her that some of the members were unnecessarily hard on the pledges. Sometimes they made the girls cry. Roz could be terribly sarcastic when she wanted to. That was one part of the meetings Lucy never enjoyed.

Rosemary was saying, "You know, Lucy, I was scared when I came here. My brother and I hated to leave Center City. We were afraid we wouldn't be accepted and all—but we have been, and I'm so glad."

"Well, why shouldn't you be?"

Rosemary's pretty face flushed. She looked away from Lucy. "Oh, I don't know. I just didn't expect to be happy, but I am." They were at Roz's now. Lucy went on into the living room where there was the excited buzz of voices. Rosemary vanished into the back of the house where the pledges waited anxiously until summoned before the regular members for the ritual of pledge court. Roz was just calling the meeting to order. Lucy slipped into a chair in the corner.

Sue smiled and waved a lazy hand from the floor across the room. While the opening formalities were going on—roll call, reading of the minutes, report of the spring party committee—Lucy looked around the room at the girls and felt the usual pride of belonging to the club. They were such nice-looking girls—well-dressed, well-groomed, poised, and sure of themselves. Any girl would be proud to be a member.

She brought her thoughts back to the meeting. Roz was saying dramatically, "And now, girls, I have the most awful thing to tell you." There was a hush. The girls waited eagerly. Roz's meetings were never dull.

"I've just found out," she continued, "that we made a mistake, a big mistake, in pledging one of our new girls." She waited a moment to get the full effect of her announcement. "Rosemary Parker!"

There was an excited babble. "Rosemary?" "But why?" "What?"

"Girls! Girls!" Roz pounded her gavel. "I'm going to tell you. Rosemary's father is in *prison!* Now what do you think of that! That's why they had to move from Center City! That's why they came here after the semester had started. Rosemary's father is a *criminal!* And she has the absolute nerve to apply for membership in the BGC. Why, it's a disgrace!"

There was another buzz, this time variously shocked, pleased, excited—depending on each girl's reaction to the announcement.

Lucy thought with dismay: poor Rosemary. That's what was wrong.

Roz rapped again for order.

"There's only one thing to do. During pledge court we'll tell her we *know* and that we don't want her in the club. Who does she think she is?"

Kay rose importantly. "I move that we tell Rosemary Parker she is no longer considered a suitable member for the BGC."

Someone seconded the motion. And then Lucy heard her own voice saying, "Wait a minute, girls. Belonging to the BGC means a lot to Rosemary. It will hurt her cruelly if we put her out now."

Roz and the others turned to look at Lucy in amazement. I'm as surprised as they are to hear myself speaking out, Lucy thought. It's the first time I've ever said anything at meetings except to answer the roll. But she stood her ground.

"Even if it is true that her father is in prison, it isn't her fault. You said three weeks ago when we pledged her that she was a lovely girl and had everything it would take to make a good member. She's just the same now as she was then." She finished with a breathless rush of words. "I think we should let her stay."

Roz's glare was icy. "But her father is in *prison*, Lucy! It's true. My father checked the whole thing for me. You surely don't want a girl like that in the club if the club means anything to you."

Lucy had never imagined herself standing up to Roz, but she persisted. "But think how bad she must feel already. About her father, I mean. We can't make it worse. She needs us."

Roz laughed—a brittle, scornful laugh. "Really, Lucy, we aren't a charity organization. And we *do* have a motion before the house." She dismissed Lucy as being of no further importance. "Shall we vote? All in favor of dropping Rosemary at once?" There was a show of hands. One by one all the hands except Lucy's went up. Sue glanced uneasily at Lucy, but put up her hand in time to be counted.

Lucy sat numbly in her corner, her face hot. When Roz said, "All opposed?" she raised her hand high. Roz glanced at her briefly and said, "Motion carried. Bring in the pledges."

The four girls, big-eyed and solemn, came stiffly into the room. They stood together in the center regarding the members warily. Sometimes, if a member had it in for a pledge, it could be unpleasant. Rosemary clutched her list.

Roz began the attack, "Rosemary," she said sweetly, "What do you think of our club?"

Rosemary cleared her throat. "Why, I—I—it's the best club in school. I'm proud to be a pledge."

Roz looked at the others significantly. "You think it's the best club in school? What kind of girls do you think should belong to the best club in school?"

"I—I don't know." Rosemary's face was pale. "The girls other members think should belong, I guess."

"But what *kind* of girls?" Roz persisted.

"The best girls, I guess."

"I see." Roz was heavily sarcastic now. "And do you consider yourself to be one of the best girls?"

Rosemary mumbled, "I don't know."

Lucy wanted to cry out, "Oh, stop it. Stop it. Let her alone. Can't you see she's miserable?"

But Roz was in top form now. Why, Lucy thought with wonder, she's enjoying this.

Roz said, "So you don't know whether you are one of the best girls or not. Maybe we'd better help you decide. Personally, I feel—and the others feel—you're not." She waited a minute. Rosemary said nothing. She looked as though she were trying hard not to cry.

Roz went on. "We think a girl whose father is in *prison*—whose father is a *criminal*—has a lot of nerve putting in her application for BGC. We've voted to drop you. Did you really think we wouldn't find out about it?"

Rosemary lifted her head and straightened her shoulders. Two bright spots of color burned in her cheeks. She said quietly, "I thought you knew. I thought you all knew and were too kind to mention it to me."

Roz laughed lightly, a little at a loss. She said, a little uncertainly, "You, too, seem to have the mistaken idea that we are a charity organization given to doing noble deeds."

Rosemary rushed on. "And my father is *not* a criminal. He's in prison. That's true. He made a mistake—a big one—and he's paying for it. But he's sorry for it, and he's . . . he's my father and I love him." The tears were very close now, but her head was still high. She turned quickly and went out of the room. They heard the front door close after her and her quick footsteps going down the walk.

There was silence in the room. Roz broke it. "Well," she said, "that's over."

Lucy stood up. Her legs were trembling and her face felt as

though it were on fire, but her voice was surprisingly steady. "No it isn't, Roz. Not quite. Some of you know how much being a member of BGC meant to me. I was proud to be a member of the club. I'm not proud now. I could never be proud again. It's— it's sort of like finding out that something you thought was fine and worth-while turned out to be shoddy and second-rate. I'm resigning from the club."

"Oh, no, Lucy," Sue protested. "You can't resign. No one has ever resigned from the club. Why, none of the members would ever speak to you again."

Roz's voice was scornful. "Let her go. Who cares! She wasn't much of a member anyway."

Lucy walked to the door. She turned to look back at them. She said softly, "Maybe I wasn't much of a member, but I loved the club. I guess I loved it for what I thought it was—not for what it is." She took off her pin and laid it on the table by the door. Then she followed Rosemary out the door.

She hurried down the steps and up the street in the direction of Rosemary's house. She must catch up with her—to tell her that everyone didn't feel the way Roz and the others did; to show her that she still had a friend. As she hurried along, she thought, I was so happy walking over here tonight. Now she didn't know whether she felt glad or sorry. She only knew that she had had to say what she did. Imagine *me,* she thought, making a speech in front of the club.

She was so engrossed in her own thoughts that she almost missed the huddled figure of Rosemary sitting on the steps of her house, a figure of misery in the gathering darkness. Lucy sat down beside her and Rosemary lifted a tear-streaked face.

"Oh, Lucy," she sobbed.

"Don't mind it so much, Rosemary. Please don't mind it so much. They aren't the only girls in school."

"Oh, but Lucy," Rosemary's voice was tragic, "they'll tell everyone. They'll make it sound so—so awful. I won't have any friends. It will be just as I was afraid it would be."

"No, it won't. There are plenty of kids who will like you for what you are—no matter what your father did. I tell you, I know it. I like you, Rosemary, and I won't be the only one."

A little hope crept into Rosemary's voice. "Do you really think so, Lucy?"

"I know so." Lucy's mind was busy. There was Doris—she'd be on Rosemary's side. And Jan Rogers, who was always fair. And Nancy. And Virginia. Now that she thought of it, there were a lot of talented and pretty girls who were not members of the club. Nice girls, too. It would be good to have more time to spend with them.

Rosemary said timidly, "About my father."

"You don't have to tell me about it."

"But I want to. My father . . ." she stumbled over the words. "They said he 'mishandled' the funds of the city office he held. He'll be in prison for two years. He's always been wonderful to us— to Bud and Mother and me. I'm ashamed of what he did, but I love him. Can you understand that?"

"Of course I can." She thought of Dad—big, laughing, kind Dad. No matter what he did she would love him. But how deep the hurt would be! Rosemary would need a lot of understanding and friendship to make up for it.

"I'll tell you what, Rosemary. Doris Lee and I are going for a hike tomorrow out to the lake. We're going to take our lunch and spend most of the day. Come with us. You'll have fun."

"You really want me?"

"Of course we do." She could speak for Doris. Doris would be just as eager as she was to make it up to Rosemary. Doris was one of the *best* girls—*really* one of the best.

"Thank you, Lucy," Rosemary said shyly. "I'd love to go. And you know what? That adjective—the one on the list I picked for you—it's true. You are kind. *Really* kind."

And the way Rosemary said it, it didn't sound colorless or unexciting at all. It sounded as though it was a pretty good thing to be.

To Marcia, Commencement had an
unexpected significance

Graduation Day

Miriam F. Lander

Standing nervously by the door of the auditorium, Marcia saw the chairman of the Class Day dance committee coming toward her. Smiling timidly, she said in greeting, "Hello, Adele, how lovely you look."

Ignoring Marcia, Adele continued on her way across the dance floor. Marcia's face burned. She sat down in a straight, uncomfortable chair against the wall and looked around, admiring the decorations. Inside her a familiar knot of embarrassment was forming, but she ignored it, firmly resolved to stay until the end. This would be her only Class Day, tomorrow her only graduation.

She arranged her face in the expression of one who is thoroughly enjoying herself and lacks a partner only to share her fun, needing no one to add to it.

Across the floor she accidentally caught Jerry Beecham's eye and he smiled. She turned her head, wanting to ignore him as Adele had ignored her. He was definitely outside the senior crowd. His behavior and even his looks were different from theirs. He was tall and lean, with a stern, bony face. He seemed both older and younger than the rest of the class. When he was hurrying through the corridors, his hair rumpled, books piled carelessly on his arm, black-rimmed glasses falling down his nose, he was almost a caricature. He was shunned by those bright, laughing boys and girls who whispered of plans in class and met for sodas afterward, the crowd who had gaily decorated the auditorium this afternoon so they could dance even more gaily in it tonight. Marcia could not admit that she, too, was outside the circle. She would not admit that she and Jerry were lumped together by the others.

She turned her head away from his stare, but the inner longing to dance, to laugh and talk with a boy here, tonight, to join the circling couples and feel a part of her class, made her eyes linger even as she turned. She saw him start across the hall and realized with mixed dismay and excitement that he had interpreted her look as an invitation. In the short time it took him to come up to her she had decided it would be better to sit all night on the side lines than to dance with him.

"Hi, Marcia," Jerry said. He stood shyly before her, in his neat blue suit, his sandy hair carefully slicked back.

Somehow she could not stop smiling, and her "Hi, Jerry," was more cordial than she intended.

"Would you like to dance?" he asked. "The band is very good."

"Why—I'd love to," she heard herself say, and rose almost automatically.

When they were on the floor, silence grew between them. Marcia blushed hotly for no reason and felt her hands grow damp. The aroma of shaving lotion and hair tonic prickled her nostrils and she felt another blush color her face as the first subsided.

Jerry cleared his throat. "Where will you be this summer, Marcia?"

She recognized the stock question of one senior to another. She compared his polite, stilted tone with the easy, happy chatter of the others about summer plans for camp and picnics and swimming parties.

"Just loafing at home," she said. There seemed no way to escape saying the expected. Just as formally as he, she asked, "What will you be doing?"

He steered her carefully past the row of teachers, turned her around the corner and back again into the middle of the floor before he answered. "I'm staying home, too. I've a lot of experiments planned."

She felt her interest in him stir. She seemed to be outside of herself, watching them dance together, hearing the words they spoke. This outside self floated somewhere between the ceiling and the festoons of crepe paper, looking approvingly at this young couple getting to know each other—talking, dancing. Yet at the same time she was herself, dancing in uneasy embarrassment with Jerry Beecham.

"What kind of experiments?" she asked.

The music ended, and Marcia felt as if she had been pulled up short. She wanted very much to hear Jerry's answer.

He walked with her back to her chair. Off the dance floor he was silent again. His silence communicated itself to Marcia. He thanked her smilingly for the dance and went back across the floor. She watched him from her seat as he asked another girl to dance.

She flushed, suddenly angry, as she realized he must be asking a different girl for each dance. She had merely been one of those on his list. Even *Jerry Beecham* had treated her as if she didn't matter.

She stood up as the music ended and almost ran to the classroom where the coats were hung. She was determined to go home. She snatched her jacket off the hanger, buttoning it with hurried, fumbling fingers. How dare he! She had almost been enjoying herself, while to him she was no one! To Jerry Beecham!

"Going so soon?" He was standing in the doorway.

"Yes." She smiled nervously. "Tomorrow's a big day." She waited uncertainly as Jerry made no move to leave.

"It is exciting, isn't it?" he said. "It's the first—well—big thing to happen to us."

"I suppose it is." She wondered why he stayed. He looked strange to her as he leaned against the door. Different from the Jerry who moved quickly through the halls, talking only to a few. Seen unfamiliarly alone, he was pleasant and almost handsome. She wondered what he was really like, how he talked, what he did. He seemed to be a new person, someone she had just met.

"You said you had planned experiments for the summer," she began haltingly.

He came into the room then, and sat companionably on a desk. "Yes, I did," he began eagerly. "I have a fish tank at home—to watch, you know—" he broke off, his animation dying. "You don't want to hear about my fish," he said. "Won't you come back to dance again?"

He had become the old Jerry Beecham. Marcia could think of nothing to say but, "No, thank you, I don't think so. Good night." She went out.

"See you tomorrow," he called after her.

When she was in her room at last, she dropped down on her bed. She knew her parents must have wondered why she was home so early. She half wanted to tell them about it, but instead she had said good night and come upstairs.

Then for no apparent reason she began to cry. The tears kept coming until finally she cried herself to sleep.

On graduation morning the sun shone down on the line of girls in fresh white organdy outside the auditorium. Marcia stood in the thin gray shadow cast by the building. The heat thickened the air and made her forehead damp.

"Listen," Marcia could hear Adele behind her, whispering urgently to the girl next to her. "Listen, we'll meet right out front afterward. Okay?"

"Okay," the girl answered, turning to pass along the message.

"Girls, girls, it's almost time!" Miss Bush was nervous, her voice shrill with excitement.

The organ sounded a single, throbbing chord. Miss Bush rushed to open the big door to the auditorium. The first girl stepped into the darkness, then the second. Marcia felt herself move slowly and smoothly, mechanically fitting her steps to those of the girl before her. As she entered the door she saw the boys in navy blue suits, white shirts, and dark ties filing in from the other side. The blue line and the white line advanced slowly to the front.

The auditorium was full of heat, perfume, rustling dresses. "There she is, Sam!" "Here's Sue!" "Betty's on the left." Marcia heard the excited whispers. She moved her eyes without turning her head, looking for her parents, but when finally she came to her row, she hadn't seen them. She stood tall, feeling each chord of the organ as a weight, impressing on her that this was the last time she would belong here. "Pomp and Circumstance" faded away and the graduates began to sing the high school alma mater song. A wave of sadness swept over Marcia and she felt a lump rise in her throat.

When they stopped singing, the auditorium was quiet. Mr. Howard, the principal, motioned them to be seated. He cleared his throat and began to speak.

"Members of the graduating class of Holbrook High School, I am happy, as I am every year, to extend my good wishes to a group of young people who are now going out into the world . . ."

The lump in Marcia's throat swelled and her throat hurt all over. She thought back over the four years of high school: the clang of locker doors; the shuffle of feet in the long bare halls, cut off sharply by the sound of the bell; German 109, Physics 304, Geometry 102; chipped desks with carved initials; the hand on the wall clock clicking as it jumped the minutes.

Applause startled her. Mr. Howard drew forward the little table piled with diplomas and began to call out the names. Marcia took a deep breath and the hurt in her throat lessened. Slowly each graduate mounted the platform, took the diploma with his left hand, shook hands with his right.

"Marcia Roberts." Marcia rose and walked carefully toward the steps. Her knees felt weak, her palms cold. She walked across the stage, shook Mr. Howard's hand, felt the smooth white roll of her diploma. As she went back down the steps to her seat, an enormous exultation filled her and she smiled happily, gaily.

The rest was a blur. At the end, she rose with the others and filed slowly out. The lawn was crowded. She stood alone, looking anxiously for her family in the milling crowd of beaming fathers and mothers.

"Well, congratulations," Jerry said, suddenly beside her. He was grinning as widely and as happily as she had been a moment before.

She said gaily, "Congratulations to you, too." The exultation, still with her, died slowly as he said, "Well—uh—got to get back to the folks," and walked away.

Her parents came up beside her.

"What a lovely graduation." Her mother was smiling. She kissed Marcia affectionately.

"Congratulations, honey." Her father, deep-voiced and beaming, kissed her too.

"Thank you," she said tremulously. They were excited and proud and happy, but she didn't feel any of those things now. "It was nice, wasn't it?" she forced herself to say.

"Well, where shall we go to celebrate?" her father was saying. He put her arm in his, and the three of them walked toward the car, leaving the noise and the heat and the chattering people behind on the sunny lawn.

During dinner and the drive by the shore, a usual part of family celebrations, Marcia kept thinking of Jerry. She tried to recall the new impression she had formed of him at the dance, the pride and gladness of the morning, but she felt dull and tired and flat. It was over and she was still the same Marcia. No miracle had happened at all.

Finally alone in her room, her parents settled on the porch out back, she unzipped her dress and slipped it over her head. As she shook it out, she saw herself reflected in the mirror. For a moment, she seemed to have no connection with that bright-faced image. The girl in the mirror was almost pretty, with soft, shining brown hair and grave eyes and a mouth that looked ready to smile. This girl in the mirror looked as if she might be fun to know.

But even as she looked, Marcia realized that it was herself, and the prettiness faded, the face became uninteresting. But still—she studied herself thoughtfully—if, in an unguarded moment, she looked as she had just seen herself—maybe there was another Marcia, hidden, perhaps, most of the time, but there all the same. She would have to remember that mirrored Marcia and try to make her real.

It was easy to make this decision in her room, but she knew that outside, with other people, she would still be afraid to reveal her hidden self.

The phone rang. "I'll get it," she called downstairs. "Hello?"

"Hello, Marcia, this is Jerry Beecham."

"Hello, Jerry." She felt as if something inside her had been satisfied. It was as if all day she had expected him to call.

"I hope you weren't just about to go somewhere," he said, his voice formal and stiff.

"No, I wasn't." She waited, feeling a little thrill of excitement begin inside her.

"I was wondering if you'd like to go out tonight," he said, "—to celebrate graduation."

"I'd love to." It was as unreal as if she were reading the lines of a play.

"Swell! Shall I call for you about eight o'clock?"

"Fine," she said. "Do you know where I live?"

As she told him, she had a sudden vivid picture of him, still in his graduation suit, standing there talking on the phone, his long-fingered hands holding the receiver, his glasses low on his nose.

"See you, then," he said and hung up.

A tingling aliveness took hold of her and made her run downstairs to her parents. "I'm going out tonight," she said, strangely casual.

"How lovely, dear," her mother said.

"That's nice," said her father. "With whom?"

"Jerry Beecham—a boy in my class," she said.

"Beecham—Beecham?" Her father tried to place the name.

"A tall boy, sandy hair, nice-looking," her mother prompted.

"Why, how do you know?" Marcia asked in surprise.

"He spoke to our club last fall about—oh, yes—'Science and You.' He's a most intelligent young man."

Marcia was pleased, as if somehow she were included in her mother's praise. She would tell Jerry about it when she saw him. The excitement within her glowed in the bright smile she gave her parents as she went up to dress.

It lasted until she saw Jerry actually standing at the door. Then it faded as he greeted her and her parents. She and Jerry went silently down the steps together. The awkward silence continued until they were driving along the parkway.

He cleared his throat. "Wasn't it a nice graduation?"

"I—yes, it was."

"It's a little sad, though, in a way," he said. "You know, leaving everyone and everything."

"Oh, did you feel that way too?" she asked eagerly.

"Why, of course. Everyone does," he said in mild surprise.

"I suppose so," she said, feeling stupid.

They were in the city now and he concentrated on maneuvering the car through the heavy traffic.

"Where would you like to go?" he asked when they stopped for a light.

"I don't care. Anywhere you say." The evening seemed dull now, something to be lived through and forgotten.

"Chinatown?"

The light turned green and he started the car again. The sun was beginning to go down and the neon lights glowed on Washington Street.

"No, not Chinatown," Marcia said. She knew that was where everyone went, to roam along the winding streets and peer into the musty shops, filled with figurines and little ivory idols.

"All right. How about walking through the Public Gardens and the Commons? And a swan-boat ride?"

"What a wonderful idea!" Marcia said. It was the right, the perfect place to go on a summer night like this one. She was pleased and surprised that he had thought of it. Yet, she knew no one at school would walk in the Commons. She wondered why they didn't, why she had never heard anyone speak of going there in giggling Monday morning locker-room conversations.

He put the car in a parking lot and they walked together through the Commons, breathing deeply of the June air scented with new grass.

"I love Boston," she said impulsively, feeling suddenly gay and free in the summer dusk. "The houses on Beacon Hill, the State House, Tremont Street stores."

He nodded without speaking and abruptly her gaiety died. As the silence lengthened, she sought desperately for something to say. "My mother heard you speak, last fall, at her club."

"Oh, that," he said disparagingly.

"I didn't know you did things like that."

"Well, you see, it's very important that everyone should realize—" he broke off with a deprecatory laugh. "Don't let me get started. I'll talk all night."

His face had suddenly come alive for a moment, and then the animation faded. She wanted to bring that glow of interest back; she wanted to know more about him.

"Please, tell me what you were going to say."

"Don't say I didn't warn you," he said, and they laughed together. They walked slowly through the pleasant evening, and he began to talk. "I think people should learn to appreciate the marvels and beauties around them and get over the idea that science means just the atomic bomb. There are other fields— biology, botany, astronomy—that teach you to enjoy little every-day things, make you a part of the rhythm of the whole universe."

"I like that—rhythm of the universe."

He smiled at her, and she felt a moment of closeness with him. "Go on," she said.

He talked on, explaining and describing. She asked him a question now and then, laughed once, and realized she was enjoying this very much. She felt that she was seeing him as he really was, and she wondered that he was so different from the boy in school.

"I wanted to ask you for a date before," he said suddenly. "But you always seemed so—I don't know—so different from the others."

"Did I?" She felt herself blushing and was glad of the darkness.

"I mean—you never seemed like the other girls," he said earnestly. His brow wrinkled in concentration. "I always thought we could be friends, but I never found a way to talk to you."

"Oh," she said lamely. There was an awkward silence. "I'm glad you told me about—science—and everything," she said.

"I'm glad you enjoyed it," he said politely.

There was another pause.

"I didn't mean to embarrass you," he said softly.

"You didn't, really you didn't," she protested quickly. "It's just that I'm not what you think I am—different or anything. I *want* to be like everyone else." She stopped, suddenly ashamed.

"But you're not, so why should you try to be," he said. "Everyone is different in his own way. All anybody has to do is find out how he's different, and then—well, *be* it."

In the darkness she could believe him. She sat thinking for a long time: of Adele and the others at school; of the first glimpse she had had of Jerry last night at the dance; and most of all, of the mirrored girl she had seen in her room. She knew she had been that girl tonight.

At last she said softly, "I'm glad we came here tonight. I don't feel sad about graduating any more, not the way I did this morning. It seems as if it happened a long time ago."

"I know." He reached over and took her hand. "We're going to have a wonderful time this summer, Marcia," he said.

They smiled at each other in a moment full of promise of things to come, of a close happiness that was warm and eager.

Florence Nightingale's light can be
heavy in a girl's hand

Hold High the Lamp

Eliza Ledford

The big clock on the wall above the nurse's desk said five minutes after four. The afternoon shift had already begun to shake down thermometers when Marcia remembered the letter, and turned back. She had promised to buy hand lotion and stationery for two patients, and to mail a letter for Mr. Wiggins so that it would leave by the five o'clock plane. Wigge smiled at her as she entered his room. "I knew you wouldn't forget, Miss Hunt. You're one nurse I can always depend on."

"This is the letter, isn't it? Anything else I can do for you in town?"

"Nothing in town, thanks, but perhaps you wouldn't mind putting a blanket on me, I can feel myself beginning to chill. There's one in the closet." He was having a transfusion to boost his blood count so a stomach operation could be performed.

"I'll get one from the warming closet. Be right back." She dashed out, smiling as she considered the small, gray, henpecked man, knowing him to be an expert patient, skilled in getting maximum attention from every nurse with minimum effort. In a moment she was back tucking the warm, soft blanket around him.

"You're wonderful," he said with a teasing smile, as she turned toward the door. "I feel better already."

I'll have to report this, Marcia thought as she started down the hall. Charlotte Crawford was alone at the desk. The senior nurse must be in the kitchen with the dietitian, the others in the utility room.

"I just put a blanket on Wigge, Crawford," Marcia tried to sound friendly.

"Maybe you had better chart it; he's beginning to react a little to that transfusion—said he felt chilly."

"Oh?" Crawford said haughtily. "Why didn't he put on his light?"

"I had to go back to his room to get a letter I had promised to mail for him, so I just went ahead and put the blanket on him." Marcia stopped because Crawford had already started turning the pages of the chart, completely ignoring her.

Marcia sighed. It was impossible to get along with Charlotte Crawford. They had both entered training the same day and as classmates they should have been friends. But Charlotte would never forget that Frank Gowers had stopped seeing and telephoning her and started dating Marcia instead. In the nurses' home she was openly hostile, but while on duty the nurses had to maintain a certain degree of cooperation. Marcia told herself there was no use worrying about Crawford.

Thinking of her errands, she hurried out of the hospital eager to get her shopping done for the patients. Having finished her transactions early, she was back on the campus in time to eat supper in the hospital cafeteria. As she was leaving, one of the orderlies called her. "Hey, good-looking, wait a minute." He joined her, saying, "A letter from the warden for you," and dropped a white envelope as if it were contaminated into her hand.

"From Garver?" Marcia gasped, taking the letter dubiously. In the upper left-hand corner was the official *Bradley Hospital School of Nursing, Supervisor of Nurses, Miss C. Garver*. "What in the world for? Well, thanks anyway, Jimmy."

Fear touched Marcia's heart. A student nurse didn't get a letter from the supervisor unless she were in some sort of trouble. She racked her brain for a possible reason, but could think of none.

Finding a secluded spot, she opened the letter slowly. The brief note said, "This is to inform you that until further notice you are not to leave the campus on any condition. Please report to the supervisor's office tomorrow at five o'clock." It was signed, "C. Garver."

There was no reason given, no explanation, nothing. Just the worst punishment a student could get, short of being actually expelled. Campused! Again and again she read the cold note. A deep-down, furious rage possessed her at being treated in this high-handed way. The dance tomorrow night! What if she couldn't go to the dance! By the time she reached her room, her mind was made up. She would leave this place. She would quit. They couldn't treat her this way!

Luckily, her usually crowded room was deserted except for her roommate, Cleo Cane, better known as Candy, a pretty girl, with a sense of humor, but much too fat. Candy had never had a real boy friend and she was fascinated by Marcia's expert juggling of boys, dates, compliments, and complications. Now surprise and anxiety filled her eyes as she noticed Marcia's flushed, angry face.

"This is a communication from the Dalai Lama," Marcia said furiously, as she flourished the note under Candy's nose. "And I might add, the last one she will have a chance to send me."

Candy took the note and read it. "Oh, Marcia, what does it mean? What are you going to do?"

"I'm going home," Marcia said grimly. "But first I'm going to that dance tomorrow night. Neither she nor anyone else is going to stop me."

"But there must be some reason for this." Candy waved the note in the air. "Garver doesn't hand these out to just everyone you know."

"Don't you think I'd know if I'd done anything terrible enough to warrant this? Why, you'd have to poison a couple of patients to be campused indefinitely, beside having to go see the old monster. I've planned for this week end so long." Marcia flung herself face downward on the bed and began to sob into her pillow.

"Oh, honey, don't cry. No dance in the world is that important." Candy began to pat her roommate with motherly concern.

But Marcia only cried harder than ever. "Frank will never get to see me in my new dress and he'll probably ask Crawford to go to the dance with him. I hate this hospital!"

"For goodness' sake, Marcia, he isn't the only engineer at

Bradley University. Certainly, Frank doesn't mean *that* much to you." Then, as Marcia gave her an indignant look, she added, "I mean you wouldn't quit nursing just so you could flaunt a new dress and a new boy friend."

Marcia jerked upright. All the bottled resentment of her first fifteen weeks away from home and family, burst forth in a torrent of words. "That's just the latest reason in a long, long list! I've never worked so hard in my life merely to be slapped in the face for my pains. That's what all this superregimentation amounts to. I hate this place and everything about it from the food to the philosophy—everything!"

"Do you even hate me?" Candy asked in a meek little voice.

"Oh, Candy," Marcia said remorsefully, "you've been a life-saver, and you know it. All the kids in the class have been swell, except Crawford. I can't stand her."

"I know how you feel, Marcia dear. I've threatened to quit a dozen times; we all have. Just don't do anything drastic without thinking it over."

"I've thought about it more than you realize, Candy," Marcia said seriously. "Frankly I'm not sure nursing is for me. I wanted to help humanity; I was a Florence Nightingale going out to do my bit. But what have I done? Emptied bedpans and passed orange juice! I'm sick of it. I'm going home and do my bit for humanity in a nice comfortable welfare office, where at least I'll be appreciated."

Candy stood up. "I've got to go. I'm the play lady tonight. Why don't you talk this over with Harbin? That's what a counselor is for. She likes you and I'm sure she would help you if she could."

"I don't want to talk to Harbin. I'm too mad at the whole hospital setup."

"All right. Just let me take one parting shot. Then I'll leave you in peace. If you had received this note and there were no dance, no party plans for tomorrow night, would you still be mad enough to quit? Think it over," she said softly as she closed the door.

Marcia felt herself getting angry all over again. It's true I want to go to the dance, she admitted, but the dance really isn't influencing me at all as far as my decision to quit is concerned. That ridiculous little note simply made me realize how tired and disgusted I am with the kind of life I've been living here at the hospital. Her thoughts went round and round. Why does Garver want to see me? What on earth have I done? Most of the night she spent trying to answer questions for which there were no answers.

Next morning she felt weary and apprehensive. With plucky resolution she somehow managed to get through the classes that occupied most of the day. Thirty more minutes of floor duty and she would be through! MacGuire, the senior nurse in charge of the floor, asked her to pass the afternoon nourishments for the west hall. Quickly arranging the glasses on a large tray and filling each one with ice, then orange juice, she was soon ready to begin her small mission.

Mr. Wiggins' room, 204, was the first stop. Expertly opening the door with her shoulder, she called out gaily, "Mr. Wigwam, how about a little O. J.? Awfully good for you; tones up the whole system." She rattled on, imitating a popular testimonial heard over the radio. "I've been using it for fifty years myself." Then, in exasperation, "Wake up, Wigge!"

He opened his eyes and said goodnaturedly, "I've never seen such a place; you can't have a minute's peace. If it isn't orange juice, it's milk of magnesia."

To please him she pretended anger. "No wisecracks, young man. You drink your juice and then turn over and go back to sleep."

As she left the room she nearly collided with Miss Harbin, who was making her rounds. Marcia continued doggedly cheerful, determined not to burden the patients with her troubles. The patient in 206 was sleeping, and 208 was in X ray. Mrs. Wentworth in 210, was a plump society matron who, though snobbish outside the hospital, was a friendly and goodnatured patient.

The rest of the rooms on that side of the corridor were closets and interns' laboratories. Marcia started up the other side, intending to skip the room on the end because the patient, a young girl with a lung disease in an advanced state, was in an oxygen tent and was not expected to live. It was tragic that she had been brought to the hospital too late to be helped much. Now her sister came hurrying toward Marcia, a distressed look on her face. She was thin, mousy, and bedraggled looking from her night-and-day vigil beside her dying sister.

"Nurse," she said meekly, "I wonder if you would please check just once more on the oxygen tank. I know it's probably all right or the water would stop bubbling, but my sister keeps complaining of not getting enough air. Could you please just look at it?"

Marcia didn't know what to do. First-year nurses were not supposed to tamper with the oxygen apparatus, and as long as the water was bubbling, there was probably nothing wrong. But MacGuire, the senior nurse, had little time or patience with importunate relatives and probably wouldn't bother to reassure this girl. "Why certainly," Marcia said, "I'll be glad to."

Immediately on entering the room she saw that the tank was working perfectly. With her body hiding what she was doing from the sister, she pretended to check the tank. "I believe it's all right now," she said with a smile as she left the room.

The sister followed her out. "Thank you, thank you so much I do hate to bother you, but I want to do everything possible to make her comfortable." It was such a little thing, the girl's gratitude made Marcia feel uncomfortable.

Thank goodness, she thought, only a few more rooms. Passing two rooms with fresh operatives, she continued down the hall, finally knocked on Dr. Lucas' door. He was a heart case, a general practitioner from a small upstate community.

She chatted cheerily with him for a few minutes, and was hurrying down the hall when she saw Candy.

"Don't wait for me, Marcy, I have some gloves in the sterilizer, so I'll be a little late." Candy gave Marcia a little hug. "Don't be afraid, honey. After all, even a supervisor is human. If you explain everything to her, she will understand."

"Sure," Marcia said, "she has all the sympathy of a Puritan on a witchhunt. 'By."

I can at least look the part of a nurse, Marcia reasoned as she bathed and put on her last clean uniform. This was the only way she knew to prepare for the interview. Now, walking the last few steps across the campus to the supervisor's office, she felt a reckless wave of courage. I don't care what happens, she thought, she can't eat me. With false bravado, she stepped into the busy reception room. Although she was a little early, the secretary motioned for her to go on in to Miss Garver's office.

Knocking gently on the inner sanctum, Marcia heard a voice say quite naturally, "Yes, come in." Miss Garver was a gray-haired woman with black brows and black eyes that seemed sometimes to turn green as they penetrated your unspoken thoughts. All aspects of her job were important to her.

She continued writing, as she said without looking up, "Please sit down, Miss Hunt."

After a moment or two she looked up and began to talk rapidly in her deep, mannish voice. "I imagine you're wondering why I sent you that note. I didn't know if you'd be gone for the week end or not. I wanted this cleared up at once since Dr. North raised so much fuss. Miss Hunt, did you go into Mr. Wiggins' room around four o'clock yesterday?"

"Yes, Miss Garver, you see—"

The supervisor stopped her with a quick motion of her hand. "No explanations now. Just answer questions. He was having a transfusion. Did he complain of a chill and ask you to get him a blanket?"

"Yes, Miss Garver."

"Are you aware that that is an important symptom, especially during a transfusion?"

"Yes, Miss Garver."

"Then why didn't you report it? Dr. North made rounds about fifteen minutes after you left and found Mr. Wiggins in the throes of a severe chill. The girls on duty had not had a chance to make rounds because of an emergency with the thyroid case at the other end of the hall. When questioned, Mr. Wiggins said he had reported this situation to you and he thought the nurses were too busy to check again on his condition. That's the confidence he has in the nurses and you, Miss Hunt."

Marcia began to see through the whole mix-up. Either Charlotte Crawford had been too busy at first to chart the blanket and too cowardly later to admit her fault, or else she had omitted it purposely to get Marcia in trouble.

Near tears, she strove for control as she said. "Earlier in the day Mr. Wiggins had asked me to mail a letter for him and I remembered it just as I was leaving the floor. When I went back to his room for the letter, he mentioned he was beginning to chill and I got him the blanket."

"But why didn't you report this?"

Marcia hesitated. It was an unwritten rule never to involve another student in trouble. Ordinarily, it would never have entered her mind to break this code, yet it was not fair for her to have to uphold it under these circumstances. Glancing up, she saw Garver regarding her doubtfully. Indignation flooded Marcia! *She thinks I'm lying and I can't think of an excuse.* Taking a deep breath Marcia answered in a calm, positive voice. "The report had been given and the morning shift had been relieved. I was off duty when I went back after the letter. I was doing Mr. Wiggins a favor as a friend."

"Miss Hunt," Miss Garver's words rang with icy sharpness, "a nurse doesn't shed her duty as she does her cap simply because the clock says she has stayed a minute overtime. You have already admitted you knew that Mr. Wiggins' chill was an important symptom of a serious condition. Many times a human life is saved or lost, depending upon the degree of responsibility a nurse takes. Or is taught to take," she added pointedly.

Miss Garver ruffled through the stack of papers on her desk. "Since you do not have any other detentions on your record, Miss Hunt, you'll be campused only two weeks. This could be a very valuable lesson, although it should be an unnecessary one. Good day, Miss Hunt."

Marcia went blindly through the office, the tears flowing unchecked. Seeking solitude, she headed for the nurses' lounge, which she knew would be empty at this hour. It was all so terribly unfair! Why, of all the nurses in the class, did it fall to Marcia to shield Charlotte Crawford? She had been a fool to trust the charting to Crawford. And now Dr. North, whom she respected more than anyone else in the whole hospital world, would always remember her as the dumbest, most thoughtless nurse in the hospital.

But she wouldn't be in the hospital, she remembered. She was going to the dance with Frank and then home for good. Suddenly she felt unbearably weary!

She dried her eyes, slipped on her jacket, and started across the campus. It was especially beautiful this time of year, and the quiet peacefulness soothed her. The bells from the carillon began to peal and a heavy sense of nostalgia overcame her. How could she think of giving up, of leaving because of the first unpleasant happening? Being part of this great university medical school and hospital had given her a sense of contributing to something worthwhile. Thinking of the useless, carefree days at home, she suddenly knew without a doubt that her place was here. For her nothing could take the place of nursing. As little as she had actually done here for humanity as yet, still the effort had made her happier than anything else she had ever done. Besides, now that she knew Garver's reason for sending her the note, she wanted to stay to prove her integrity.

Returning to the dorm, she felt relaxed for the first time in twenty-four hours, and knew her decision had been the right one.

Candy came in, calling out, "Marcy, Harbin wants to see you. She called the floor just after you had left."

"Oh, heavens," Marcia said wearily, "How many times today am I going to be bawled out?"

The preparations for her second interview were much more simple. She smoothed her uniform and combed her hair. "I had changed my mind about leaving, Candy," she said, "but if Dr. North wasn't satisfied with the explanations, it could be this is to tell me reluctantly to please leave."

Miss Harbin had been such an understanding friend, it would be hard to know she was disappointed in Marcia. Last night Marcia had decided to quit because she was angry and dissatisfied with the hospital. It had never entered her mind she might be quitting today because the hospital was angry and dissatisfied with her.

The door of the counselor's office was open and Miss Harbin said in her friendly voice, "Hello, Marcia, come in and sit down."

This eased Marcia's doubts a little, but as Miss Harbin went over and firmly closed the door, her heart sank. Here it comes, she thought.

But when Miss Harbin turned to face her, she was positively beaming. "Marcia," she said, sincerely, "I want to congratulate you. I think you're a fine nurse."

Marcia burst into tears. "Miss Harbin, you don't need to baby me," she wailed. "I know I've been stupid and unreliable, but I didn't do it on purpose."

"Marcia, I heard about yesterday's uncomfortable episode and I'm sorry I couldn't have handled it instead of Miss Garver. You must realize there is probably some such incident at least once in the life of every student nurse. What happened to you is not as important as the way you have reacted to it. As you know, I was making my weekly rounds this afternoon, and the patients in every room in which you had been were helped by your sympathy and understanding. Only a few nurses have the ability to subjugate completely their own personalities, their own affairs—worries, trouble, even personal joys—to their duty, as you did today."

Marcia could only stare in amazement, as Miss Harbin continued, "I know this is the first time you've been away from home. This battle of yours to overcome by yourself the problems you find here is probably one of the most difficult you will ever have because it's the first." She stood up and smiled.

"Dr. North is a fine surgeon, but he expects the whole world to be as efficient as his operating room. Isn't it a blessing we nurses understand him. I guess that's all, dear. Good-by."

Marcia moved out of the room in a trance. When she recalled the dance and the beautiful dress, she heaved only one small sad sigh of resignation.

She knew that Crawford would never be blamed or punished for her deception, but still Marcia felt good! For the first time in her life she tasted a deep, peaceful sense of satisfaction.

Once outside, she turned to look back at the big bleak building and she knew that her interest, her duty, and much of her happiness lay within its walls.

Betty had to decide where
to give her first allegiance

A Question
of Loyalty

Ada Lefkowith

A hush spread tensely over the 12B assembly while Miss Arnold was speaking. Betty stared straight ahead, not responding to Terry's whisper.

"I'm sorry it is necessary to take this action," concluded Miss Arnold, "but you have given me no choice. The stolen articles will be paid for with the money set aside for the senior prom. There will be no social activities for this year's graduating class. I am deeply troubled that the school has so seriously failed."

She hates to have to go through with it, thought Betty. She's still hoping that the girls who took the stuff will own up. But they won't—they're scared stiff.

A crisp "Dismissed" broke into Betty's thoughts. When the crowd of girls reached the hall, the silence burst in a storm of protest.

Grimly, Betty wove her way past a tangle of cries. "Betty, what will we *do?* . . ." "It isn't fair! . . ." To go to school for twelve years just for a senior prom and then bang—no prom" . . . and so on until she reached her first period class.

The morning seemed endless. It was almost impossible to pay attention. But if winning a scholarship was your only means of getting to college, you had to pay attention, you just had to. Miss

Bollen was putting down a mark in her little black book for everyone she called on. Betty could hear the zeros dropping like bombs.

The grumbling went on between classes. But somehow lunch period came at last. Terry was waiting outside the door. "Hey, you look pooped," she said. "Don't be so glum. We're going to have a meeting at lunch to see if we can't fix Miss A. She can't *do* this to us."

Betty looked questioningly at Terry. "Look, Terry," she said, "the tail's wagging the dog. This is serious. Remember, twenty dollars' worth of stuff was stolen on our class trip. If only the girls who took the things had brought them in as I asked them to last week, there'd be no trouble."

"What's got into you, Betty?" Terry sounded angry. "Everybody takes souvenirs from hotels—oh, all right, we should pay the bill—but gee, we're not criminals."

Betty shook her head miserably, but she pushed past the lump in her throat and continued. "I'm sorry, but I do see Miss Arnold's point. Before we went on that trip, you remember, she talked to us about hotel conduct. And honesty is honesty. Maybe there's no other way to get those girls to come clean."

"Well!" said Terry. "What do you know!" She pulled away from Betty and walked ahead to the lunchroom.

Excited seniors made a place for them at the long upper-class table. Betty, seating herself next to Sue Morrell, the class treasurer, looked over Sue's shoulder at the class account book. "Look, Betty," Sue said, "right now we're forty dollars to the good. We could pay the old bill and still have the prom by raising a little more money—that is, if we settled for having it in the gym."

An angry muttering swelled around Betty. I'm so mixed up. I don't know where I stand, she thought. But though she knew the girls would not like what she was about to say, she had to speak. "Let's get this straight," she said. "Miss Arnold isn't just interested in our paying for the articles; she wants them returned. She wants the girls who took them to accept the responsibility. *Everybody's* suspect until that happens."

Betty could feel the chill all around her. Terry got up and walked to the window. A few girls nodded reluctant agreement. "Maybe you have something, Betty," admitted Sue, closing the account book. "But why in heck must you sound just like Miss Arnold?"

This time Betty knew she'd have to make it perfectly clear. "All right, I'll tell you. Yesterday in Miss Arnold's office I agreed that this was the only way—and I still think so! Go ahead and blame me. I can't help it."

Grabbing her books, she rushed into the hall. If she could only get away before the tears came. A fine president she was! Now everybody would hate her. She would never forget the words that followed her—"Well, that's *one* way of winning the character scholarship!"

All afternoon in class Betty alternately wondered why she had told the girls—and was glad she had. Miss Arnold hadn't mentioned Betty's name in assembly, but the idea had been hers. In Miss Arnold's office, it had seemed so terribly important to get at the bottom of the scandal—for the honor of the class, for the honor of the school. Betty had thought that the guilty ones would have to own up if the whole class were threatened with the loss of their cherished prom.

The three o'clock bell always had meant fun—the crowd walking home together, first down Broad Street to get a Coke, then going their separate ways. Even though you had to hurry afterward, it was worth it—to stop and compare notes and plan senior fun. But today was different. Betty grabbed her books and hurried out of the room alone. She slipped out the side door, hoping she wouldn't meet anyone. She wanted to get home to think this thing through, away from everyone. But when she turned off Broad to Passyunk, a breathless Terry and Sue caught up with her.

"Hey, Greta Garbo, what gives?" scolded Sue. "How come you didn't wait for us?"

Betty didn't answer. She wished she had managed to get away—or did she?

"You wanted to be an old martyr, didn't you? Like that silly Griselda in Chaucer. Well, we won't let you," said Terry, as she linked her arm in Betty's. "Look, there's the house we lived in when you called for me on our way to Thomas in first grade. Long time, huh—with no break?"

The three walked on in silence. They had reached the big house on the corner where Terry's family lived, now that her father was so successful in politics.

"Come in," invited Terry. "I'll see if there's some Coke."

No one was home. The two girls followed Terry out to the kitchen and sat around the table drinking their Cokes.

"Got one for me," a male voice called. "I'm ready to cave in after that last exam. Don't let anyone tell you Temple's easy—not unless you're a Brain like that Angus McCormick of yours, Betty."

Betty's heart missed a beat as Terry's brother Mike sat down with them. No use kidding herself—Mike had been her secret dream for a long time. But of course Mike preferred girls more dashing than quiet Betty, his younger sister's friend. Betty admired his dark hair which waved instead of curling as Terry's did, and his great bigness—like a young Clark Gable. Angus was—well, Angus—not glamorous or anything.

"What's cooking at your jail?" Mike grinned. "Hear the warden won't let you have a prom." He opened his dark eyes wide in mock horror.

"How'd you hear so soon?" asked Sue. "But it's no joke, really." She outlined the latest events. "A lot of us agree with Betty that the guilty ones ought to speak up. I've a suspicion it's that Connie and her crowd—they come from a pretty rough section down near Front Street—and there was that time with the gym shoes when we were freshmen, remember?"

"You can't start blaming Connie or anybody else without proof," Terry broke in quickly. "That's not fair!"

Mike took a long drink. "That Front Street gang would steal a fellow from under his hat." He reached over and pulled Terry's hair. "Why don't you kids forget about the whole thing? Call it an unsolved crime and pay the money. Maybe Pop can fix it with Miss Arnold. So long! And stop worrying."

Betty watched Mike bound down the steps to the yard. She rose to go. "Poor Connie," she said slowly. "She hasn't done a wrong thing since her freshman year, but just because of that one time, she's blamed for everything that's stolen. I was so glad she could go on the trip—and now this—"

Terry said nothing, but Betty could not help noticing the strange expression on her face.

She picked up her books. "So long! You'll see I'm right. Detective Sue Holmes."

As Betty rounded the corner, she saw her ten-year old sister Peggy waiting on the porch. "You're late," Peggy cried reproachfully.

Betty put her arm around her sister. "Sorry! Let's dash to get the work done before Mommy and Dad get home."

The kitchen clock looked accusingly at Betty as she put on her apron. Peggy hurried upstairs to give the dusting and bedmaking a hit-and-run treatment. With Mommy nursing again, since Dad's failure and the accident, everyone had to pitch in. There was hardly a minute to think of school troubles at this point, but Betty kept hearing the disappointment in Miss Arnold's voice; Sue saying shrilly, "It's Connie and her crowd"; and seeing the funny look in Terry's eyes.

She mixed the meat loaf carefully, throwing in two eggs with reckless abandon. She was grimly conscious that at home, at least, she could do things right. Everyone would eat this dinner with relish —or else! She shoved the loaf into the oven and began to peel the potatoes.

Peggy came down to set the table. "Mmmm, smells good," she said. "Could I use a linen tablecloth, Betty, the one with the roses?"

"Okay," Betty replied absent-mindedly. She noticed her hands— roughened from housework in spite of rubber gloves and all her care. I hate it when people look at my hands, these days, she thought. Then she made a face. That's the trouble with me. I care too much what others think of me. I'm not Betty at all—just what I think others want me to be.

She walked to the door and looked out at the tiny square garden.

Angus McCormick, a long coil of boy topped off with red hair, unwound himself from the back porch next door. "Hi, Betty," he called, and sauntered into her yard. "Mike's been telling me about the Wilson High stew. You mean I'm not going to get to a prom with you?"

Angus was grinning, but his eyes were kind. He followed Betty into the kitchen. She took a quick survey of the progress of dinner before replying. "I'm getting so I don't care a Mexican peso about the prom," she said. "I just want everything cleared up. Angus, I keep feeling to blame because I don't know what I ought to do. Now I'm not sure I should have suggested that prom deal to Miss Arnold. Some of the kids are so mad they're beginning to blame one of the girls—without any evidence! I think Miss Arnold will be pretty disgusted with me. I made a mistake and started something we can't finish."

"Sounds a little like Lidice," Angus said, "punishing a whole group for a few. You think it out, Betty, and decide what's right— for you. Nothing's important, Betty, except that you do what you think is right."

Later when she sat with her family around the table, Betty's depression began to fade a little in the cushion of family love. It was a Howell rule that nobody should talk about anything trouble-some until after dinner. It was good to have everyone enjoy her cooking, to hear her father say, "Betty, you're a great cook!"

But after dinner when they all were doing a whirlwind cleanup job, Betty brought her family up to date on school events. As her father hung up the last towel, he looked at Betty thoughtfully. "I'm wondering if you aren't worrying about one aspect of this affair you haven't admitted even to yourself. Are you, too, guessing who might have taken the stuff? And you don't think it's Connie, do you?"

Her father's question brought out the nagging doubt that had been troubling Betty. The ring of the doorbell saved her from answering. Connie was at the door—a bedraggled Connie, the remains of hastily washed-away tears streaking her face. Somehow Betty wasn't surprised to see her, though Connie had been there only once before—the time she had brought the tennis shoes and Betty had helped her—but that was a long time ago.

"Betty, I didn't do it," Connie burst out, her words mixed with little gasps. "Sue came to our house and tried to make me say I had taken the stuff. I wouldn't steal—not ever again. Why, Miss Arnold paid my way so I could go on this trip. She said we'd keep it a secret and that I could help her in the office to make up the money if I wanted to. Oh, Betty, I feel so awful."

Betty pulled out a tissue from her apron pocket and handed it to Connie. "Come in and sit down," she said, pulling the weeping girl down on the couch. "Sue shouldn't have done that, and I know you didn't steal anything. We'll find the culprit, I promise you."

After a moment Connie's sobs grew less.

"Want to stay and do homework with me?" Betty asked, but Connie shook her head.

It was hard to get down to homework. Betty sharpened her pencils, filled her fountain pen, while her mother looked questioningly over her sewing, and her father rattled the newspaper quizzically. Somehow Betty got started, although gnawing questions were right below the surface. Which was most important—loyalty to her school or to an old friend? What about Connie, who was already unjustly suspected? Halfway through her grammar assignment, something clicked. She was diagraming a sentence: "This above all: to thine own self be true." Betty closed her book.

"Okay if I go out for a bit, Mummy?" she asked. "Just over to Terry's for a minute?" She was out of the house before her mother's nod was completed, and ran all the way until she was in front of Terry's big house. It was dreadful to accuse anyone—look at how Silas Marner's life had been almost ruined by a false accusation. And Terry had been her friend for so many years. Wasn't Betty just as bad as Sue with Connie if she asked Terry the same question?

She marched up the steps, rang the bell and walked right in, up to Terry's bedroom, the way she always did. Terry was lying on the bed, face down. When she saw Betty, she jumped up.

"All right," she burst out angrily, "I'm the thief, but it was just a stunt to pay back that mean old Gulch for not giving us the decent food our contract called for. Go ahead and tell Miss A. She'll expel me sure."

Betty sat down on the bed next to Terry. She was worried and unhappy, but somehow relieved. "Why don't you tell Miss Arnold, Terry?" she pleaded. "She'll understand, and think how much better you'll feel."

"It was only a stunt," Terry repeated. "We—I—didn't want their old bath mats and towels and things. The kids in last year's class took their share of souvenirs. Why should I be made to feel like a criminal? I'll never give Miss A. that satisfaction."

"Do you think it's fair for the whole class to lose its senior prom for something you did?" Betty persisted. "And what about Connie?"

"Oh, we'll—I'll see that no one really suspects Connie. I'll talk to Sue tomorrow. But I'm not going to go to Miss Arnold!"

"Can you locate all the stuff, Terry," Betty asked quietly, "tonight, if possible?"

Terry went to the closet and yanked out a suitcase jammed full. She flung it in front of Betty. "We were going to put it in the office, but we got cold feet. Betty, you won't tell?"

Without answering, Betty picked up the suitcase, walked quickly down the stairs, out of the house, through the street, up her own steps, and into her room. As she deposited the case in the corner, she felt its weight for the first time, and her arm ached. She was glad her family never asked questions.

At breakfast there were no questions either, "I'll drive you to school, Betty," her father said, and put the suitcase in the back of his car.

Betty reached Miss Arnold's office so early there was no one around. She waited wearily. She was well aware of Miss Arnold's ideas of maturity—and of right and wrong. If you were really adult—how often Miss Arnold had told them—the honor of the group became more important than protecting a guilty individual, no matter how fond you were of her.

When Miss Arnold entered the office, Betty felt a stab. There were circles of tiredness under the principal's eyes.

Betty rose, remaining standing even when Miss Arnold mentioned for her to be seated. She would get this over with quickly. "I am returning all the missing articles," she said, "I can't say any more."

"You mean you won't say any more, Betty, don't you?" Miss Arnold asked in a tired, disappointed way. "You will be graduating soon. Would you carry this idea of loyalty into your role as a citizen?"

"I don't know, Miss Arnold," Betty answered miserably. "I just know what I have to do."

Miss Arnold put her arm on Betty's shoulder. "Suppose we close this unpleasant episode then. Tell the girls to go ahead with their prom preparations. I think I'm a bit to blame, too. I've handled this badly by expecting too much even of seniors. You can only do what seems right to you."

It was over and Betty went to her classroom. There was a bitter taste in her mouth, and she knew the joy had gone out of all senior activities—for her anyhow. To the question in Terry's eyes, Betty shook her head reassuringly and found herself hating the relief in Terry's sigh. She caught Sue, told her that the pilfered articles had been returned, that Connie had had nothing to do with it, and suggested an apology was in order. Sue, overjoyed that the prom was safe and ashamed of her suspicions, apologized handsomely and even invited Connie to eat with the crowd.

The buzz at lunch was a gay one. Most of the girls didn't care two pretzels who had been guilty, just so they got to the prom. They talked dates and dresses. Terry wasn't there. Someone hazarded a guess that she had gone to the typing room for extra practice.

On her way out of school that afternoon, Betty was passing the office just as Terry and her three trip roommates came out. Terry rushed over to put her arm through Betty's.

"We just told Miss Arnold," she said, "and she's as pleased as if we'd all made the honor society. Gal, do I feel relieved! You were swell not to tell, Betty—we're glad we had the backbone to do it ourselves."

"What did Miss Arnold say—will you be able to go to the prom?"

Terry nodded, wrinkling her nose in a wide grin. "Miss A. said she felt that owning up voluntarily indicated that we had learned a lesson, and that living with ourselves these past weeks had probably been punishment enough. She's dead right and she was pretty swell!"

As the gang walked up Broad Street together, Betty felt happy all over.

*Fran and Sheila had come to that new world
which needs a private place for its dreams*

My Heart My Own

Catherine Marshall

Fran Avery had no intention of going to the picnic. None whatsoever. But in the morning, her firm resolution wavered. It began with the smell of honeysuckle, the sound of bird song, and the sun, warm on her skin and brilliant against her eyelids, pulling them open to a bright blue day. Summer! Summer at last! The heaviness that had weighed on her was suddenly lifted, and she sprang out of bed. Minutes later, light brown curls still tousled, she appeared in the kitchen and announced her change of plan.

Her mother was pleased. "I bought your hamburgers yesterday, just in case," she said. "Fran, honey, I *know* you'll have a good time."

Fran felt the letdown begin. Her mother's encouragement was based on the knowledge that Fran might not have a good time at all. Somehow this understanding did not help. It was—well, a sort of invasion of privacy.

From the dinette table, Bobby taunted, "Honey! What's the matter, honey? Afraid to go to the picnic without darling Sheila?"

Fran whirled toward her younger brother, but her mother intercepted her angry retort. "Of course she's not afraid, Bobby. When girls grow up, they don't need to be together every single minute."

Her mother exchanged a between-us-grownups look with Fran that enabled her to answer Bobby with some disdain. "Would I be going if I needed Sheila? She has a date for the picnic."

"Dates! Mush!" But Fran hardly heard Bobby, for her words, so bravely spoken, had sent the pain welling up inside her again as she sat down opposite her brother. It was not that she was jealous of Sheila or minded her having a boy friend. Wasn't this what they had both longed for, dreamed of, talked about, for endless hours?

No, the hurt came from Sheila's withdrawal. Fran had expected Sheila to tell her all about her dates with Larry—exactly what Sheila had done to spark his interest, what they talked about together, if the first date had been scary— Oh, why hadn't Sheila told her these things? Were they not best friends any more? How could Sheila leave her behind like this?

Bobby, not at all squelched, eyed her with speculation. "I suppose you'll be having dates next."

"Could be," Fran said. But would she? Would a boy ever choose her and would she know what to say if he did?

"Not me." Bobby shook his head. "Not ever. Girls are a pain in the neck."

Mrs. Avery had poured herself a cup of coffee, and now as she slid onto the dinette bench next to Fran, she smiled at Bobby. "You'll change your mind one of these days," she said. "Wait and see."

Her mother's remark was another invasion of privacy, Fran thought, Bobby's privacy this time. It sent Fran into a quick shift of alliance. "Maybe he won't, Mother," she said indignantly. "Lots of boys don't date."

Why did Mother always have to predict this way? Fran and Bobby probably had the nicest parents in the world—much nicer than Sheila's, for instance—but why couldn't they let their children go along at their own pace, find their own way?

Fran pushed back her plate and excused herself as her mother twisted around on the bench to let her pass. She hurried up the stairs to her room, then completely forgot there was such a thing as a ten o'clock bus to be caught.

Unlocking the drawer of her desk, she took out the loose-leaf notebook thick with Sheila's letters and settled down on her bed. Sheila had a similar notebook filled with letters from Fran. Before Larry, just being together had not been enough. They had written to each other nightly, filling pages and pages with deep confidences, recording every secret thought and feeling. It had been a kind of mutual diary.

Fran turned to one of the last letters in the book, the last good one, really, written less than a month ago.

Dearest Fran,

I can't tell you how wonderful I felt after our walk today and our talk. You made me feel as if I was—well, I don't know—good, sort of, and I went back to the apartment determined not to let anything spoil it.

My mother had one of her headaches and right away began to scold. It seemed to her that when she was feeling so miserable, I might have been considerate enough to stay with her instead of gallivanting all afternoon.

I was simply not going to lose that good feeling, and so I said I was sorry and offered to get her some aspirin. Then Pop came out from behind his Sunday paper, practically barking. "Oh, leave her alone. She enjoys suffering."

Honestly, Fran, your parents may baby you, but at least they don't bicker all the time.

I went all out to get them a good supper—waffles and bacon, tossed salad, and some ice cream we had left from dinner. I thought it would be nice to set up the table in the living room with candles and all, but my mother said, "Oh, Sheila. Don't *fuss* tonight." So we ate in the kitchen, as usual.

And a gruesome meal it was! Pop hardly said a word, and Mother kept up a running line of complaint. I couldn't talk, Fran. I just couldn't. So then my mother asked if I acted this way with you or did I save my sulks for my family. Honestly! It was a relief when the dishes were done and I could escape to my room.

I'm embarrassed to tell even you what I did there, but we have promised to have no secrets from each other, so here goes. I took off my dress, yanked the elastic from my ponytail, and brushed and brushed and *brushed* my hair. Then I stood in front of the mirror in my slip with my hair all soft on my shoulders and kept saying over and over, "You're lovely, Sheila. Lovely, lovely, lovely."

I know it sounds silly, but it worked because when I went to bed with my hair still down, I felt as if I really was lovely.

Oh, Fran, do you think I'm completely crazy?

Love, Sheila

Perhaps Sheila had not been crazy. Perhaps her feeling of loveliness had persisted, communicating itself to others, for almost immediately she had attracted Larry's attention, and the daily letters had stopped.

Hearing her mother's footsteps on the stairs, Fran thrust the notebook under the blanket and jumped up from the bed. She didn't want to read any more letters anyway, especially the last one, the one that said, "Don't be silly—of course I'm still your best friend. I just don't feel like writing letters any more, that's all." But why? *Why?* What had Fran done to deserve this desertion?

"Fran," Mrs. Avery spoke from the doorway, "I'll drive you to—Frances Avery, what *have* you been doing?"

"Be ready in a sec, Mom. There's time."

Fran was right about the time. When they drove up to the meeting place, though the boys and girls were assembled, their chartered bus had not yet arrived. Fran stood on one foot and then the other, wondering whether she ought to go over and talk to Sheila and Larry. If only they were still Intermediates instead of Senior Scouts! In those happy Intermediate days, there had been none of this business of joint picnics with Boy Scout Explorers.

"Hiya, Fran." Eleanor Rogers came up from behind and gave Fran a thump on the back. Standing on one foot, Fran was caught off balance and dropped her lunch.

"Oh, sorry. I'll get it," Eleanor said, but Fran had already stooped down, as much to hide her red face as to retrieve her lunch bag.

As she reached for the bag another hand stretched toward it, a hand bigger than hers and definitely male. The hands touched, were both snatched back. Redder than ever, Fran looked up into the laughing, very blue eyes of Doug Follett, and without conscious direction, her own eyes responded with a smile.

"Shall we toss for it?" Doug asked.

"Oh, I'll get it, thanks." Fran picked up the bag and straightened up.

Doug stood up, too, a full head taller than Fran, and now his smile was one of discovery.

"Hey, I've seen you around school. You're Frances Avery, aren't you?"

Fran nodded. "I've seen you, too," she said, and for one unprecedented moment of delight, there was no Sheila, no Larry, no Eleanor Rogers, no anybody in the world but this handsome blond boy and herself. The bus pulled in. Everyone began to move toward it. Someone yelled, "Hey, Follet. Let's go."

Doug waved a hand, but did not turn away until he had said, "I'll see you later."

From a high, high peak, Fran watched him go. So this was how it was. One look, a few words, and you were off.

"You comin', Fran?" Eleanor Rogers, who had so nearly knocked Fran off her feet, now pushed her from her blissful heights, and the descent was filled with despair. Oh, she had done everything all wrong! She should have let Doug pick up her bag. He'd think she hadn't been around at all. *I'll see you later.* That was really a brush-off sentence. She would never see him again, in the same close way.

And indeed, when they reached the picnic grounds Doug seemed to have forgotten all about her. Once, in the rough and tumble of the games, they had a brief encounter, and Doug's "Hiya" had an intimate, old-friend quality that raised Fran's hopes. But the next minute he was off with his friends to go rowing.

"You on the food patrol?" Eleanor asked.

"I'm not on any patrol. I—well, I wasn't sure I could come today."

"Be on food then. That way we'll get lunch ready quicker."

"Okay." Eleanor, outsized and awkward, had always gotten on Fran's nerves. Still, there was no one else to whom she could turn. Her exclusive friendship with Sheila had cut her off from other girls.

But Sheila was still her friend, after all. Fran heard the familiar voice at her side. "Scoop." It was their word. It meant, "Break away. I have something to tell you." Flooded with gladness, Fran followed Sheila to the fireplace where the pooled hamburgers sizzled.

"What I wanted to say was, why don't you eat with Larry and me?" Sheila said.

"Thanks. Are you sure it will be all right?"

"Of course. I mean, it may not be much fun for you, but anything's better than Eleanor."

But Sheila's rescue effort had been in vain, for Eleanor appeared now at the fireplace flashing a toothy grin. "Oh, there you are," she said happily. "Let's go."

Eleanor's voice, Sheila's nudge, were lost to Fran. The rowers were returning!

"Chow!" Like the twist of a kaleidoscope, the pattern on the picnic grounds changed as clusters of people shifted into one long line.

Now Fran became two people, the one going through the motions of a picnic, the other taut as a bowstring in awareness of Doug. Chatting with Sheila and Eleanor, she took her place in line. Doug was somewhere behind her. A heaped plate in her hand, she settled down under a tree with Eleanor, Sheila, and Larry. Doug was on the opposite side of the fireplace.

Once she caught his stare and knew, with a kind of knowledge she had never hoped to possess, that she could make Doug her friend.

But how was it done? Sheila! Sheila! You should have told me. A long-forgotten scene flashed across Fran's mind. She and her mother had been on the back terrace; Diana Best and a bevy of young men in the yard next door. Her mother had admonished, "I hope *you'll* never chase boys, Fran."

"Fran!" Eleanor shrilled. "Didn't you hear me?"

"You'd think she was in love," Sheila said but her laughter denied the possibility. Sheila, all out of touch again!

Fran thrust her plate aside, jumped up. "I'm going for a walk." She called back a belated, "Excuse me," to the startled group behind her and went off among the trees.

Deep in the wods she found a path, its shade not yet reached by summer's warmth. The earth was soggy beneath her tread, and its coolness spread up over her bare legs. As she walked along, the picnic voices gradually faded away, leaving her alone in the silence. She was alone and glad of her aloneness, for now she could be just one Fran.

Then, far-off and dim, voices came to her again; the path grew brighter until, unexpectedly, Fran squinted against the glare of sun-bright water. The path had circled around to the edge of the pond.

How long before she heard footsteps? How long before, turning, she found herself face to face with Doug? She was surprised, yet not surprised. Her heart seemed to pound right through her ribs, but though her voice held a strange new timbre, it sounded calm. "Hi."

"Hi," Doug said. There was a short silence. Then, "Want to go for a row?"

"I'd love to."

"They're kind of wet. The boats, I mean."

"Who cares about that?" Fran said.

What did you talk about to a boy? How many times had she and Sheila asked each other that question? Yet how easy it was, there in the enchanted little world of a leaky rowboat!

Make them talk about themselves. That was one of the rules, but Doug, pulling at the unwieldy oars, needed no prodding. He loved the water and boats, he said. He had a sailboat of his own at his family's summer place on Greenley Lake. Next week end he planned to go up and start the scraping and painting.

Fran said she liked the water too, but mostly for swimming. She had never sailed. Her kid brother, though, was nuts about boats. He was twelve years old and an awful tease.

On the bus trip home, although Fran and Doug were one of the few pairs, the magic was dissipated. The excitement was there still, but Fran was back in her own world now, and worldly elements entered in. Pride, for instance, and self-consciousness. And toward the end, anxiety. Would this be all?

It was not all. Doug walked her home, then stood there, fidgeting nervously, shifting his weight from foot to foot.

"Good picnic," he said.

"Yes. Thanks for taking me rowing."

"That's okay. Listen, Fran. Do your folks let you go the movies at night? With a fellow, I mean?"

"I—I—" Would they? *Would* they? Oh, they must! "Why sure they do," Fran said.

"Want to go some time?" Doug leaned toward her. "Hey! How about tonight?"

"Well—fine!" A little prayer formed in Fran's mind. *Please make them let me go!*

"Then I'll see you about—is seven too early?"

"Oh, no!" So Doug had a curfew, too. It brought him closer. " 'By for now, then."

" 'By."

They flew apart, flying toward their next meeting.

But in the kitchen, her mother stopped Fran's flight. "It sounds like fun," she said. "Only who *is* this boy?"

It was Dad who saved the day. Wonderful, wonderful luck! He knew Doug's father.

"Lives up on Latten Drive," he told them. "Nice family."

"Well, all right then." Mother beamed as brightly as Fran. "And I won't need any help with dinner. You get yourself ready."

Fran soared up the stairs. In her room she stopped short, staring at the lump in her hastily made bed. Sheila's letters. Slowly she pulled the notebook from under the covers, able now to read the last letter.

Why of course Sheila had not felt like writing! For how could any girl describe the fragile wonder of a boy's first attentions? The shining afternoon on the pond, Doug's fumbling and hers as they made their first date, the joyousness of anticipation, these things Fran could never share with Sheila or anyone else. Certainly she and Sheila would always be friends. But now they had come to another world, wider in its loyalties, yet needing a private place for its dreams.

Fran tossed the notebook on her desk just as Bobby appeared at her door.

"Honey!" he said. "Hey, honey dear! I hear you've got a date for tonight."

"Oh, Bobby, yes! You just wait till you—" Fran clapped one hand over her mouth. Bobby, too, was entitled to privacy.

Sally felt that she was an intruder
in her own family

Eldest Daughter

Emily Rebecca Page

Sally stood in the empty schoolroom, looking down at the white arm band with its blue "S. C." for Student Council. The other bands, hanging on the rack near the door, were blue. They belonged to the regular council members, but the white band signified the president, and today's election had suddenly made it Sally's.

Slowly she removed the band and moved toward the rack to hang it with the others; then she stopped abruptly and refastened it about her arm. She would wear it home to show her family. When her parents saw it and realized that she was the Student Council president, perhaps they would think of her as a real person, instead of a convenient baby-sitter for the younger children. For once, their attention would be on her. Maybe now they would realize that at school she was really somebody.

Suddenly anxious to get home with her news, Sally snatched up her books and hurried from the room. Once outside the building, she fairly flew along the sidewalk. It was idiotic to keep grinning, all by herself, but her lips just wouldn't stay in a straight line.

She bounded up the porch steps and burst through the front door. Her mother looked up with a smile from where she sat in the living room, but Sally's own smile faded as she saw Mrs. Bates. With her there, the news would have to wait. No one else had a chance to talk when Mrs. Bates had the floor. Sally dropped her books on a table and greeted her mother and her guest politely.

Mrs. Bates nodded absent-mindedly and continued, "I'm so proud of John. He's doing very well in high school."

Sally brightened. Perhaps John had already told his mother about the election. Maybe Mrs. Bates would speak of it now, and Mother would realize, better than if Sally told the news herself, that she had a daughter of some importance at school, however much she was overlooked at home.

But Mrs. Bates went on, "John got B in advanced algebra this term."

"I understand how proud you must be," Sally's mother said. Sally held her breath, waiting to hear Mother boast right back about her daughter. Though she didn't yet know about the Student Council election, she could say that Sally had received an A in algebra. And in Latin, too.

But her mother continued, "I know what pleasure I take in Jane's arithmetic papers when they show a good mark."

Sally stared at her mother. Jane's papers! Wasn't Sally's mark in advanced algebra more important than Jane's little fifth-grade papers?

She slumped back in her chair, suddenly feeling as let down as if an elevator had dropped her from the tenth floor to the basement. After a moment, she got to her feet and stumbled from the room.

"Oh, Sally," her mother called after her, "will you get the baby? He's been awake for some time."

Sally climbed the stairs blindly. Here goes the baby-sitter again, she thought bitterly. At school, people elected her council president, but at home her own mother treated her like a Cinderella.

As she opened the door to the baby's room, he crowed delightedly. Sally bent over the crib and blew in his fat neck. He gurgled with laughter. "I was elected a president, today," Sally whispered in his ear. The baby's chubby arms shot out on either side, as if in amazement. At least someone in this house appreciates me, Sally thought, even if it is only a baby who can't even talk.

Downstairs, the front door was closing after Mrs. Bates. Sally picked up the baby and carried him down to the kitchen. Her mother took him from her arms and sat him in the high chair. As she turned toward the stove, where the baby's food was warming, she patted Sally's arm. Sally caught her breath. Now was the moment! In another second, her mother would look back at the arm she had just patted, belatedly conscious of the woolly felt she had touched.

But her mother set the dish of mashed carrots on the high-chair tray and gave all her attention to the baby. Sally couldn't help noticing the fond way her mother smiled at him. She seemed to have forgotten all about Sally; she hadn't even noticed the arm band or inquired about her eldest daughter's day at school.

Watching the loving smile on her mother's face, Sally could imagine it still there, in years to come, when the baby was a high school boy, like John Bates. No doubt her mother would boast about her son then, just as Mrs. Bates had done. But she never boasted about her eldest daughter, who was in high school right now. Maybe I'm not really her child at all, Sally thought. Maybe I'm just the child some friend or relative left for Mother and Dad to bring up.

"Patty won't sleep tonight if she doesn't wake up now," her mother said. "Be a dear, Sally, will you, and get her up from her nap?"

Sally turned from the room without answering. First the baby, now Patty. It was plain her mother thought of Sally only to order her to do something for the little ones. But what else could a Cinderella expect?

As she approached Patty's room, Sally was scowling, but she had to laugh at the sight of her little sister. Patty was already up and dressed, but not in her own clothes. She looked so adorable, Sally couldn't be cross.

"Hey, that's my good plaid skirt you're dragging on the floor!" she protested. "I hope you didn't get any lipstick on it!"

Patty hitched up the skirt, and her brightly painted lips curved in a smile. "I'm Mrs. Bates," she said, "and I was just coming to call on you and tell you all about John's report card."

"You've been listening on the stairs," Sally accused. "Well, come on. Let's show Mother how you've dressed up." She picked up the hem of the plaid skirt and snapped it against Patty's legs. Patty shrieked happily and galloped from the room, a runaway pony with Sally as driver.

"Whoa!" Sally ordered, at the kitchen doorway. "Oh, Mother!" she trilled. "Mrs. Bates is here again!"

"What!" Her mother's head turned sharply. Then she laughed. "Oh, it's Patty!" She exchanged a smiling glance with Sally. "That's just the way you used to dress up, when you were little, Sally," she said. "Watching Patty and Jane is like having you all over again."

Only better, Sally thought bitterly, because they're your own children. She felt tears stinging her eyes and looked away quickly, but her mother had turned toward the back door, as Jane burst in.

Jane was all smiles. She threw her jacket on a chair and stood in the middle of the kitchen, looking about expectantly.

"Hang up your jacket, Jane," her mother said automatically.

Jane scowled and pushed out her lower lip. "Don't you notice anything?" she wailed.

Jane sees what it's like to come home from school and find Mother too busy to listen, Sally thought sympathetically.

Her mother scraped up the last of the baby's carrots. "Why don't you dress up like Patty?" she suggested absent-mindedly.

Jane's face brightened and she dashed for the stairs, with Patty after her, tripping over the long skirt. Already Jane was absorbed in the idea of the game her mother had suggested. She never had to worry about being left out of things. She wasn't the uninteresting, eldest daughter.

Maybe Dad would listen to her news when he came home. It would seem much more important anyway, announced at the dinner table.

But at dinnertime, there was still no chance to talk. Patty clamored to have her meat cut up; Jane had to tell about the trip her class had taken to the airport.

Sally bit her lip as she watched the attentive way her mother and father bent toward the younger children, with as much interest as if they really had something important to say. They wouldn't listen to her like that, Sally thought forlornly, even if she told them about being elected president of the Student Council.

When her father passed her the dish of mashed potatoes, he looked right at her. But he never noticed the arm band. He only smiled, indifferently it seemed to Sally, and turned to ask Jane about the weather station at the airport.

Sally wanted none of the potatoes. She couldn't get the food she already had on her plate past the lump in her throat. She passed the dish to her mother.

"Well, Sally, what happened in school today?" her mother asked.

Sally's lips parted eagerly, but her mother had turned to steady the glass of milk Patty had almost spilled. Sally closed her lips tightly. Mother needn't try to be polite. Sally knew she wasn't really interested in anything her eldest daughter might say. All Mother seemed to care about was the little children.

The best way to get attention in this house, Sally thought, nursing her misery, was to be helpless or gurgle baby talk.

As she watched Patty, her little sister's rosy face blurred, but Sally did not wipe away the tears that clouded her vision. No one would bother to notice them.

When she had been small and curly-headed like Patty, her parents probably had thought her pretty special. But now she was no longer a cute little thing, and the others had taken her place. Hadn't Mother said this very afternoon that each new baby was like having Sally a baby all over again? Wasn't that proof that Sally herself had grown beyond the age when her mother cared about her?

Blindly she picked up her plate and carried it to the kitchen. Then, as her mother cleared the table, Sally stacked the dishes and began to fill the dishpan.

"There's still dessert," her mother reminded her.

"I don't want any."

"Oh, dear, you aren't going to be sick, are you?"

Now she's thinking about what a nuisance it would be if I got sick, Sally thought. She doesn't really care at all how I feel.

All by herself, she washed the dishes, listening to the voices of the rest of the family, lingering over their dessert in the dining room. Then there was the sound of chairs scraping when everyone left the table. She heard her mother talking to the baby as she carried him up to bed. No one came into the kitchen.

Sally finished clearing the dining-room table. Jane was supposed to help with the dishes, but she had followed her mother upstairs, and Sally would have bitten out her tongue before she called her.

If her parents didn't care enough about Sally to see that Jane did her share of the work, Sally wasn't going to remind them.

She was putting the last dish in the china closet when her mother came downstairs. "Oh, Sally, why didn't you call Jane? She should have helped you."

Her mother put an arm about her. Sally held herself straight and stiff. Her mother was probably just glad to find the dishes all done. Sally would show her that Cinderella knew how to keep her place.

With a little sigh, her mother dropped her arm and went into the living room. Sally spread her books on the dining-room table and sat down to her homework. From the other room, came her mother's quiet voice, reading a story to Patty and Jane. The little girls kept interrupting. Their mother listened with pleasure to their chatter.

Why shouldn't she listen, Sally thought; she's interested in them. But she doesn't listen to me when I try to tell her anything.

She saw Patty run to the big leather chair where her father sat reading and squeeze her small self in beside him. He smiled as he moved to make room for her.

Watching the cozy group from another room was like being at a play. Sally was the audience, isolated from the actors. If I were an actress, she thought, I'd have a place on the stage. Then the family would be the ones to sit in the audience and watch me.

She saw herself—beautiful, admired, in a lovely off-the-shoulder gown—standing in the blaze of footlights on a huge stage, bowing regally to the thunderous applause from the darkened house.

She pushed her homework aside. What was the use of bothering with school? It was time to get out in the world. Her parents would be glad to get rid of her. With the seventy-five dollars in her bank account, she could go to New York and take a room in some theatrical boardinghouse. She had read about such places.

Oh, she knew very well that she couldn't become an actress the moment she decided on it. But that was all the more reason to start right away. Of course, her teachers and her friends wouldn't approve of her leaving school to go on the stage, just when she had been elected council president. But they couldn't know how unimportant that honor had become. It had seemed a big thing at first, but it meant nothing now, since her family didn't care to hear about it.

Sally looked down at the band on her left arm. How happily she had worn it home from school, just this afternoon! A tear rolled down her cheek as she wondered who would wear it next, when she had gone off to her career on the stage.

Slowly she pulled the band from her arm and dropped it on the table. She went quietly into the living room, opened the center drawer of the desk in the corner, and pulled out her bankbook. Her mother glanced up casually as Sally left the room with the bankbook, but her eyes dropped again to the storybook and her voice never faltered in her reading.

Let them live their own lives, Sally thought; she'd get out of their way. This time tomorrow, she would be walking along a New York street, looking for a place to live. Tomorrow, when they sat down to dinner, her place at the table would be empty. Would anyone care?

But, oh, she cared! How could she bear to live in New York, far from Mother and Dad! And Jane and Patty and the baby!

The bankbook dropped to the floor, as she pressed her hands over her face. "I can't do it!" she whispered. "Maybe they don't care about me, but I can't leave them. I love them too much!"

She opened her eyes to look again at the dear people in the living room.

Jane was standing in the middle of the floor wailing, "Nobody noticed! Nobody noticed! You didn't notice when I got home from school, and now you just send me off to bed without even noticing!"

"What didn't we notice?" asked her mother. "Tell us, Jane."

"The stars pasted on my collar! One on each side!"

"Why so there are stars on your collar! Imagine my not seeing them! I must need glasses!"

"What are they for, Jane?" her father asked.

Jane's tear-wet face broke into smiles. "They mean I got one hundred in arithmetic all week," she announced proudly.

Wasn't that just like Jane, Sally thought in affectionate amusement, feeling her small affairs were so important and expecting the family to notice a pair of tiny stars!

She turned to pick up the arm band. Realization stabbed her swiftly. To Jane, it probably seemed as though those little stars flashed like a neon sign, just as the band on Sally's arm had seemed to flash. She had been just like Jane, wearing the band home to show it off, instead of hanging it on the rack in the Student-Council room, where it belonged. And then crying because it wasn't noticed—maybe not out loud the way Jane had done, but just like her, really.

Sally went into the living room and knelt down beside her little sister. "Janie, I'm so sorry I didn't notice your stars, dear. You should have told me about them." She looked around the room. "What this family needs is a time for special announcements. Let's have it every night, just before storytime. You begin now, Jane, with your announcement, and then I have one, too."

Jane looked pleased but, more important, Sally could see how proudly her mother and father were watching her. Their affection showed in their smiles. Sally blushed to remember that she had thought of running away to become an actress.

Jane was tugging at her sleeve. "What shall I do, Sally?"

"Just say, 'Are there any announcements tonight?' "

Jane looked around the room importantly, as she asked her question and then answered herself quickly, "I got two stars on my collar for hundreds in arithmetic."

Sally joined in the congratulations that were showered on Jane all over again.

"Now ask for other announcements," her father reminded Jane.

Sally held her breath for a moment, as her turn came. She was grateful she had something special to say, something to justify the pride in her that she could see shining in both her father's and her mother's eyes.

"I haven't any stars," Sally said, smiling at Jane, "but I have this arm band to show that I'm president of the Student Council."

"President of the Student Council?" Her father stood up quickly and strode across the room to shake Sally's hand. "Why, Sally, that's a great honor! I'm proud to be the father of such an important person!"

The storybook dropped from her mother's lap, as she got hurriedly to her feet and kissed Sally.

"That's simply wonderful, dear! When did it happen?"

"This morning."

"And you're only just telling us now!"

"Oh, I was acting Janie's age, and you seemed so busy with the baby and the others."

Her mother hugged her tightly. "Don't ever think I'm too busy to want to hear from my eldest daughter."

"Maybe we do neglect her," her father said remorsefully. "She's been pretty quiet lately, and I'm afraid we've been too preoccupied to notice."

"Of course you don't neglect me!" Sally defended them. "It's up to me to speak up for myself."

Jane interrupted anxiously, "Stars are good, too!"

"Of course!" Sally said. "Stars are very important."

Her mother laughed as she patted Jane's head, but her other arm was still around Sally, and Sally felt it tighten firmly.

Her father was bending down to Jane. "Here's a nickel for each star." As he straightened, he winked at Sally in mature and companionable understanding.

Sally smiled at him, treasuring the wink and the feel of her mother's arm about her—rewards she was beginning to understand, far more satisfying than Jane's nickels.

Patty, too-long unnoticed, began to turn somersaults. Sally laughed with her father and mother. But, though it was fun to have an amusing little sister, Sally wouldn't trade places with her. It was good to be the eldest daughter.

Polly was ashamed of Kim and his hobby,
until Hurricane Hepsibah struck

The Ham
and I

Ethelyn M. Parkinson

Incredibly, the other members of the Conway family were not one bit excited that morning. Daddy was reading the morning paper. Kim had a book propped against the sirup pitcher. Mother had the ringside seat beside the window and seemed completely devoted to her electric waffle iron.

However, Mom was on her toes. "Polly, here they come!" she announced suddenly.

I jumped up. "Oh, let me look! Is he with them? Daddy, aren't you going to look? Kim? Oh, of course not," I moaned. "Naturally Kim Conway, W9JEF, the forever ham, isn't going to drag himself away from a radio amateur's handbook just for a look at new neighbors."

They went quickly up their walk and disappeared into the house next door. I walked back to my chair in a rosy daze.

"Well, Polly, can we keep up with them?" Daddy murmured, one eye on the sports page. "How do they look?"

"Sane and casual, naturally!" I said. "Tall, dark, very handsome. In fact, fabulous. A doll!"

Kim whistled. "Who's all this? Mrs. Silvercup?"

"No, no—Sidney!" I said. "You remember we met him when the Silvercups were looking over the house before they bought it. You saw Sidney's picture in the paper last week." I reached in the pocket of my favorite pastel tweed skirt. "Here in my wallet. Here's the clipping. 'Silvercup Family Moving Here.' It tells all about Mr. Silvercup's association with a big manufacturing company." I read aloud: " 'They are pictured here with their son Sidney and daughter Diana, who will attend Franklin School.' "

"Sounds keen," Kim muttered. "Pass the butter, please. Dad, I wonder if I could take the car for about an hour tonight?"

"You can have it all evening," Daddy offered.

"An hour is plenty," Kim said. "I might buy a jalopy. I'm going to look one over."

"Kimmy!" I breathed. "That's the first sane and casual sentence you've uttered in simply years! Ever since you became a radio ham. Kim, buy a lush color! Remember, Sidney Silvercup is going to live next door. Get white sidewalls!"

At first I thought Kim didn't hear me. But then—as usual—he began to take the pauper's oath. "For seventy-five bucks, I'll be thankful for four wheels! Listen, kid—"

"Spare me!" I moaned. "I know! You just want a heap that will transport you to ham meetings. You're willing to push it back."

Kim grinned and addressed Daddy, not me. "I want to install a mobile unit, Dad. It's good experience. I'll learn a lot."

Daddy nodded. "Can't think of a better project."

"Well, I can!" I declared. "I think it would be just perfectly lovely for Mr. Kim Conway to act human and have some sane and casual friends who think in words instead of code, and who have names, instead of numbers. As, for instance, Sidney Silvercup and Diana. I think *that* would be good experience and he would learn a lot!"

"Now, look," Kim began. "Not that I'm antisocial, but time permits only—"

"Spare me! I've heard it ten thousand times!" I wailed. "Anyway, I'll never know the Silvercups, with our back yard all strung up with wires the way it is, and with everyone telling them that my brother is a queer recluse!"

Kim beamed. Confidentially, he's cute, with blue eyes, a blond butch, a sense of humor, and plenty of personality. All, all wasted!

"Well," he said, "it should be my sister's duty to say good things about me."

"Name three!" I challenged.

"Well, I'm pretty. I have a nice attitude toward other humans. Live and let live! And—"

Right then a horn sounded, and Kim pricked up his ears. Some ham was outside, sounding his call letters in code.

"Excuse me, Mom," he said. "See you tonight."

He was gone—the forever ham!

I went upstairs to get ready for school. I wore my new blue sweater. For blonds with blue eyes, blue definitely does the most.

"Polly!" Mother called. "Diana's on her porch, dressed for school. I think she's looking for you."

I hurried down. "I'm afraid she's looking at something very different," I sighed. "Kim's antennas would make any sane and casual person stare." I kissed Mom good-by and went outside.

Diana was walking down her porch steps. I smiled at her.

"Hi!" I called. "I'm Pamela Conway. Call me Polly. I go to Franklin."

"I'm Diana Silvercup," she said. "I'm waiting for Sidney. Tell me, what in the world are all those gruesome wires in your back yard? Is your father a mad inventor or a wizard or something?"

I practically expired of humiliation. But I remembered a joke of Daddy's.

"Oh," I said airily, "those wires? They're guaranteed to keep giraffes out of the yard."

"They are?" Diana stared.

I was stunned. Could she think I was serious? While I was deciding what to say next, she changed the subject.

"What's your brother like, Polly?"

"Well," I said, "Kim's something of a recluse."

"Recluse!" she gasped.

Serious again! But before I could utter a word, Sidney came out. Sidney was a doll—a living doll.

"I'm glad you Conways are next door," he said. "I hope we'll be friends."

"Thank you!" I breathed, glad I'd remembered to pin flowers around my pony tail.

Sidney went on. "I missed Kim this morning."

I explained. "Kim's science class is having two all-day out-of-town field trips. He left early." I tried to say something good about Kim. "He's an A student, you know."

"Oh," Diana murmured. "Well, that's nice."

She said it exactly as if I'd bragged, "He doesn't have horns." Things were certainly going badly.

I was glad when we met Bill Knight and Mary Milburn and heard about their party.

"It's at our house tomorrow night," Bill said. "Everyone's invited. Polly, you tell Kim."

"I'll tell him," I moaned. "But I can't promise he'll come."

I had band practice that afternoon, so I got home late. There, under the giraffe fence in our back yard, stood Kim's alleged car. Kim was there, too. I could see his legs. Before I could plan an appropriate remark, I heard a voice.

"Hey! Any salvage value?"

It was Sidney Silvercup, grinning at me. He was just getting home with an armload of books. I almost perished with embarrassment. I gave him a feeble wave.

Kim, with his head out of sight under the raised hood, had not heard.

But when Sidney had disappeared into his house, the ham and I had a few words.

"Kim Conway," I began, "our back yard looks like a barbed-wire entanglement. And that tumble-down crate! What do you suppose the Silvercups think of us?"

Kim was tinkering now with the instrument panel. Without turning, he said, "No doubt they think we run a junk yard."

"Very funny!" I said. "Just ducky!"

"What's wrong with a junk yard?" Kim demanded. "It's a very profitable business! Know what this little radio cost me—out of a wreck at Sam's Junk and Salvage?"

"Skip it!" I moaned. Then I remembered the party. "Not that it means anything to you, but there's a simply fabulous party coming up at Bill Knight's tomorrow night."

"Keen," Kim said. Then he turned. "Tomorrow night? Sorry! I've got a date with a hurricane, Polly."

"A hurricane?" I gasped.

He nodded. "Hurricane Hepsibah. She's going to hit hard."

"She's not going to hit us!"

"We hope!" Kim told me. "However, warnings are out for Pulcifer, Bonduel, and Tigerton, and it's probably going to knock out communications. I'm standing by. That's what we hams are for."

"You want me to tell Bill that a hurricane is more important than his party?"

"That's right," Kim said cheerfully.

"And you don't care what the Silvercups think of you?"

"Sure I do," Kim said. "I want them to think I'm an honorable guy and a conscientious ham. What's more, if you were a ham—"

"Spare me!" I said, and walked into the house. It was bad enough to have a disgraceful back yard and an antisocial brother to blight my life. But to be a ham—spare me!

Kim ate his dinner seventy-eight r.p.m., which is nothing new. With one hand he passed his plate for seconds, while with the other he reached for another hot roll.

"Too bad you haven't three hands," I said.

"Do you have a schedule?" Daddy asked him. A schedule is simply an appointment to talk with some other ham over the rigs.

Kim nodded. "We're mobilizing emergency gear. We're going to work things out tonight for greatest efficiency when the hurricane hits."

Hurricane, hurricane!

I had to go to the library that night, and whom should I meet between the history bookcases but Diana Silvercup?

"Hi," she whispered. "Going to Bill's party?"

"Naturally," I said.

"Is your brother going?"

"No." I sighed. "Kim's getting ready for a hurricane." Diana stared. I guessed it was my cue to change the subject. "Is Sidney going?" I whispered.

"Oh, sure," she said. "He asked about Kim."

The librarian shook her head at us, and we had to stop talking. Diana ran out of note paper, and when I looked for some, something fell out of my notebook.

"Oh," I said, "it's just Kim's QSL card."

"QSL card?" She looked bewildered.

"Um-huh," I said. "He has his wall practically papered with QSL cards."

"Kim—has papered a wall—with cards like this?"

"It's only his shack."

"A shack—papered with these cards?"

"Oh, Kim's very proud of them." I pointed to the letters W.A.S. "You see, he has worked all states."

"Worked all states?" she repeated.

I was amazed at my feeling of annoyance. But this wasn't the time or place to explain that a ham's shack is his radio room, and that Kim's is an oversize closet, or that QSL cards are sent to other hams to verify contacts, and that it's an honor to have contacted at least one ham in every state in the union.

Thank goodness, a bell sounded. "That's the warning!" I whispered. "We have to be out of the library in five minutes."

Kim was at his rig until midnight. The next night he was late to dinner and very excited.

"Hepsibah is worse than first expected," he announced. "Also, there's a ham convention upstate, and all the older hams who are out of school are there. There are only a few of us on the job, and mine is the best rig. There'll be telephone calls. I tried to get a tape recorder but—" He shrugged. "It's going to be rugged. Mom, I know you and Dad can't back out of your date, but—" He turned to me. "Polly, there will be other parties."

"A nice try," I said. "However, I hope *I* care what people think of me."

You can't insult Amateur Radio Operator W9JEF. "Okay," he said. "I'll get along."

At eight o'clock I was skittering downstairs, dressed for the party, feeling gay and frothy, when the telephone rang.

Kim called from his radio shack upstairs, "Hey, Polly! Will you get it, please?"

"Okay," I moaned.

I took up the phone and immediately heard a voice. "It's Hank Sheldon. Does Kim know Hepsibah just struck Lena?"

I was shocked. I was sure the storm hadn't been expected to strike as close as Lena.

I called upstairs. "Kim! Kim!" He didn't answer. l knew he had his earphones on and hadn't heard me. "Just a jiff, Hank!" I said.

I flew upstairs. "Kim, Hank's phoning. The storm struck Lena—"

"I know. I've got W9JDG," Kim said. "Polly, tell Hank they

need another ambulance. Wait! Tell him to phone the Red Cross! Wait! There's a message for the Tylor family. Bud's been hurt—" He turned and saw my dress. "Oh!" He sounded suddenly tired. "Well, you'd better go on to your party."

"Kim Conway, what kind of girl do you think I am? With lives in danger and kids like Bud maybe bleeding to death unless they get help fast, my social life can wait!"

I don't know how many phone calls I had taken and made, or how many times I had run up and down the stairs, when the front door opened and there stood Sidney Silvercup!

The party! I thought, in a panic. He wonders where our manners are!

But Sidney smiled. "Hi, Polly! Say, tell Kim I came to help."

"To help!"

He nodded. "I brought my tape recorder. I heard Kim was trying to borrow one. Give it to him, will you? I'll take over the phone. You stay at the head of the stairs where Kim can hear you from his shack and you can hear me."

"Aye, aye, sir," I said.

The phone rang, and Sidney took over.

There was plenty of work for all of us. Messages came thick and fast, relayed through other hams or directly from hams in the stricken towns who had acquired emergency generators in preparation for the catastrophe.

We helped call for ambulances and doctors. We sent messages to and for the Red Cross. We relayed messages between members of families. We communicated with linemen and other repair crews, telling them where they were needed most.

When things slowed up and I looked at the clock, it was midnight. "Sidney!" I gasped. "You forgot the party!"

"Not me!" He smiled. "I sent regrets, if Diana remembers to convey them."

Mother had come home. She brought a lunch upstairs, and we all sat in Kim's shack to eat it. Kim said, "It's certainly keen having your help, Sidney. How did it happen?"

Sidney explained. "When I heard this hurricane was scheduled, I wanted to help in some way. Then," he reached in his pocket, "the kid sister brought me this."

"My QSL card!" Kim marveled.

Sidney laughed. "Diana didn't know what it was, but for me it explained a lot of things. For instance, I knew you weren't a bewhiskered recluse with a giraffe phobia, who put up wires to protect himself from the beasts, and who lived in a shack that he'd papered with queer post cards."

Kim eyed me. "Polly Conway—"

"I'm innocent!" I wailed. "Well, almost. I didn't dream Diana would take it for straight!"

Sidney smiled and shook his head. "When Diana's fairy god-mother passed out gifts, she forgot to include a sense of humor! Sis is a great gal, though, even if she is completely literal and matter-of-fact." He reached to touch Kim's rig. "I've been looking for a ham friend, Kim. I'd like to be a ham, too."

"It's funny Diana didn't know that!" I said.

"I've told her but she hasn't paid much attention," Sidney said. "She thinks it's wild, I guess. Kim, you're lucky to have a sister who turns down a party to lend a hand."

I know I blushed.

But Kim smiled at me. "I think so, too," he said. "I'm lucky—and proud!"

I didn't know then that our pictures were going to be in the paper—Kim at his rig, and Sidney and I right there on the job. I didn't know about the headline: "LOCAL HAM CREDITED WITH SAVING LIVES."

I didn't know the story would start: "Pictured above is Kim Con-way, young amateur radio operator of this city, who, with the help of his sister Pamela (Polly) and their neighbor and friend, Sidney Silvercup, played an important part in directing rescue activi-ties . . ."

I didn't know Kim would be on TV, or that there would be a special party for us, or that the mayor would personally congratu-late Kim.

I didn't know all that. When Kim smiled at me and said to Sidney, "I'm lucky—and proud!" that was my happiest moment.

"I'm lucky and proud, too," I said, and meant it, "having Kim for a brother."

Sidney smiled at me. "Include me, please!" he said. "I'm proud and lucky to have two such keen new friends. Diana will feel the same when we carefully explain all this."

We laughed together—and there's nothing like a good laugh together to make a friendship grow.

*Delightful Maggie Renleigh discovered
something not found in her college texts*

"I'm Nobody!"

Herndon Rion

The four-o'clock bell rang, and Maggie Renleigh, clutching a stack of books, edged through the horde of students pouring out of Old Main. Turning left at Chatworth, she used the basement entrance and, once out of the mainstream of chattering students, flew past the empty practice rooms to her favorite retreat. The record room, she had discovered in her first hectic weeks at Carlton University, was deserted at this hour of the day. Most of the students were on campus, strolling in pairs, clustering in close-knit groups around the stone benches, or packed into The Hole for Coke dates. Some of the serious students—graduates, eggheads, brains, or, Maggie thought bitterly, lumping herself with that group, the "squares"—were in seminars or conferences. However it was, blessedly she had the comfortable, shabby room, with its great cases of records and its wonderful machine, to herself; and before the student assistant arrived to check the records and lock the door, she had an hour to listen to the music imprisoned on the black discs. It was enough to wash away the frustrations and agonies of being an outsider and misfit in this new world, peopled with thousands of teen-agers who thought her strange and negligible. This world was so different from her wandering, casual life with her quiet under-standing father and all the people of all stations and nations who

202

accepted the gypsy Renleighs as unquestioningly as the Renleighs accepted them.

Maggie was used to being accepted for what she was and left alone to do what she chose. It was increasingly appalling to her to be regarded as an outcast and an eccentric and to be criticized for studying and going for walks, for talking to odd individuals— doing what to her came naturally. Her roommate Sandi—glamorous, synthetic Sandi Walker—nagged her or twitted her about her lack of dates and boy friends. Maggie didn't particularly like Sandi, but she had to room with her and, putting it practically, preferred to get along with her. Maggie was much too modest to recognize that Sandi was reacting jealously out of concern for her position as the best-dressed, most popular girl at Carlton U. Maggie didn't know that she was strangely appealing—with her long-lashed brown eyes, her ivory skin, and her tawny brown hair. She wore her clothes with simple distinction and, since she was Phillip Renleigh's daughter, she was unconscious of whether she wore a Paris model or a cotton skirt from a Guatemalan market shop. It never entered her head to want to be the most popular, or most anything, but she did wish one of the thousands of young males she saw striding about would notice her. She *liked* boys, and besides, who wanted to be a pariah? Since she was new to all schools, she could not know that the crowd of flip young sophisticates Sandi had gathered about her was far from typical at Carlton. She knew only that she was not happy and not welcome with them, and she quietly withdrew to the fringes.

Today had been especially bad. Arriving early at chemistry class, she had heaved a sigh of relief and taken a front-row seat, because with her scant five feet, she had been having trouble seeing and hearing from the back row. She was greeted by a pained, "Oh, brother!" from the great Wilson Devlin, then an annoyed, "Look, miss—uh, this is Sandi Walker's seat." Sandi, arriving, had glared at her, not realizing or caring that from her submerged position at the back, Maggie could scarcely have known who sat where in front.

She had tried to rise and awkwardly had knocked her stacked books to the floor. Into her agonized reflection that only a grind, only a square, only a drip, would have so many books anyway, dropped the cool, clipped tones of Dr. Travis, striding to the desk at the front of the class. "Stay where you are, Miss Renleigh; that will be fine." While she subsided, unable to speak, he had added the final words—damning words, Maggie felt, from the cool silence.

"It will be pleasant to have at least one interested face in view. Mr. Devlin, if you feel you *must* sit by Miss Walker, you may find seats in the rear. I believe you'll learn as much chemistry one place as another."

Then there had been lunch. Passing Sandi and her crowd, Maggie had attempted to explain the seating fiasco, and been ignored. Home-coming Ball with all its attendant festivities was approaching, and Sandi was a candidate for queen. That was all that really concerned Sandi, Maggie realized, as she started with her inevitable book to a single table. But Carol Gage, a gay, attractive redhead Maggie hadn't met before, drew her along with them.

"Come along, Maggie," she invited. "Let Sandi pout. I've seen you in chem before today and wanted to know you. We'll have to get together sometime for some lab work. Chemistry is my favorite subject, and maybe I could help you. You *are* new, aren't you?"

Maggie and Carol had got along famously. Maggie had been offering to help Carol with her English—Carol had the campus terror, Dr. Jackson, for a prof—when the PA called for quiet to announce the Homecoming queen.

Sandi had straightened and smiled self-consciously, then reddened painfully when the impersonal voice on the loud-speaker had continued: "For queen, Miss Carol Gage." She had smiled with tense stiffness when the voice continued, "For senior princess, Miss Sandi Walker."

Maggie had turned to her new friend with astonished pleasure, "Why, you're queen! How wonderful!"

Then she fought her way through the bedlam to offer Sandi congratulations. Sandi said coolly, "Probably all the new people identified me with my eager-beaver roommate—and voted for someone else!"

Thinking of all these things as she entered the record room, Maggie quickly dropped her books on the nearest chair and hurried to the record cabinet. She selected the *Emperor Concerto,* slipped the record beneath the needle, and with a grateful sigh, curled herself into her favorite leather chair. As always, she closed her eyes when the music started, and almost perceptibly she relaxed as the majestic chords filled the room. Suddenly a loud crash cut across the music. Maggie had stacked her books too carelessly when she dropped them near the door. She cowered deeper into her chair, and then leaped to her feet as a deep voice spoke her name.

"Miss Renleigh? Maggie Renleigh?" She looked up to see a lithe, tweedy figure advancing toward her with books stacked neatly in his arms. Dark eyes under heavy eyebrows were glinting at her in friendly merriment, and a tiny scar at the corner of his mouth twitched as he said easily, "So! Maggie Renleigh! Let's put them on the floor so I won't knock them over again. This concerto always gets me excited, and I'm likely to flail around."

As she stared at him in amazement, he held up her folded math paper, pointing to the *Maggie Renleigh* lettered neatly at the top. "My name is Carter Jackson," he offered, as he stowed the books at her side. "Do you know Phillip Renleigh, in fact or in fiction?"

"Phillip Renleigh is my dad," she said, with a flash of pure satisfaction that someone in this strange world knew her father, or at least knew his books.

"Well, then, no wonder you like to come here every afternoon for the music," Carter Jackson said matter-of-factly, pulling a chair around beside her. "I look in on you almost every day, you know, but you're always mesmerized, and it never has been necessary to disturb you. You choose very good things, very good. I've never had to quarrel with you. Today, for instance, I didn't know it, but I had been wanting to hear some Beethoven."

"Imagine!" Maggie said. "I didn't even hear you. I thought I was always alone—"

"Oh, I stood in the doorway," he said easily. "But I'm rather glad the books fell today. I've been 'curiouser and curiouser' about who you are. Look—" He rose and lifted the needle. "We should start this again, you know. But tell me, when did you come to Carlton, and where have you been keeping yourself? I never see you except here."

Maggie chuckled. "I'm one of those who crawl back into the

woodwork—after class, that is. I never go anywhere. I'm a square."

He regarded her gravely. "What classes do you go to, then? I stay around the English department myself."

Maggie told him how Phillip Renleigh and she had decided that she needed to know some math and science. "There's a yawning chasm in what I know, Dad says, and how true, how true! Dad thought I should come to college anyway—know some American young people my own age. Only sometimes they're harder to know than math or chemistry." She added a little about her first weeks at Carlton and, vaguely, about Sandi, her popular roommate.

"All very different from wherever it was you were," Carter Jackson commented. "Where were you anyway? Renleigh's last book had an American setting."

"We've lived in Spain," Maggie said, "since I can remember—since Mother died, really. But we were in Arizona when Dad wrote *Beyond a Near Horizon.*"

"Do you write him that you are something less than entranced with American college life?"

Maggie searched the dark, quiet face. There was no disdain there, no concern, only a listening look. Why, I could tell him how completely I'm out of things, Maggie thought, and he would understand and not be afraid of me. He's really interested. He *cares* what I say.

Suddenly she laughed, the clear peal that used to make Phillip Renleigh look up from his typewriter and smile.

"I feel," she said, "like the pig. You know Lewis Carroll's pig? 'By day and night he made his moan: It would have stirred a heart of stone . . . Because he could not jump.' I'm perfectly willing to jump, but I can't tell how to, or when to, or even where to!"

Jackson grinned delightedly.

"How do you like it here," Maggie asked, "and are you going to the Homecoming Ball? Everybody is, you know."

"So I understand," he murmured, still grinning. "But then, I'm nobody. And so, you say, are you. That makes two of us, as Miss Dickinson would have noted. And if you would consider going with me—"

"Heavens!" Maggie gasped. "I was fishing for a date, like Sandi. Let's play Beethoven."

Eyes closed, listening to the music, Maggie recognized a deep, warm happiness. Why, I *like* talking to him, she thought. He knows what I mean, and I know what he means, and he's comfortable. Then she sat up with a shock and her eyes flew wide open. Maybe he's faculty! she thought, remembering that it was teen-agers who baffled and rejected her. Looking at him, with his head thrown back against the red leather chair, his feet propped up on another chair, she thought. He does seem older, but he certainly doesn't act like faculty. I'll ask him, when this is over.

But when the music ended, he spoke first. "Look, Miss Renleigh —Maggie—how about that Homecoming Ball?"

"No," Maggie said, "I certainly didn't mean to put you on the spot about that. And now it's time for me to crawl back into the wormwood. Supper in twenty minutes."

"Then let me walk you to your dormitory," Carter Jackson said. "This pile of books must get heavy late in the day."

Leaving her at the front door of Memorial, he said, "See you in the record room, I hope? Let me know if you want to go to Homecoming."

I wonder who he is, Maggie thought, as she approached Room 219, hers and Sandi's. I'll ask—no, I won't ask Sandi, but maybe I'll ask Carol.

Sandi's voice reached her through the open transom. ". . . and I'll wear green. I'll buy a new dress and borrow Maggie's jade. She won't be going, of course; she never goes anywhere except to classes—and the library on a big night!"

There was a little silence. Maggie stood by the door, frozen.

"What will you wear, Carol?" Sandi's voice went on. "Of course, you'll have to wear white. Have you ordered your dress yet?"

Carol's voice spoke lightly. "I phoned Mother this afternoon, and she's sending me a dress."

"Oh, how sweet!" Sandi's voice was smooth. "I suppose she will make your queen's gown, just as she made your prom dress last spring?"

Carol spoke flatly. "Yes, Mother will make my dress. That's the only way I could have one. She will work late at night for hours and hours, and it won't look any better than my dress did last spring." Her voice broke, and she finished wildly, "I'm thrilled they want me to be queen, but I didn't dream I would be. And if every-one—if you all—if I'm not going to look right, I'm sure I could arrange to be sick. In fact, I'm definitely getting sick of it all right now."

"Oh, dear!" Sandi spoke silkily. "Don't have such a fit, Carol. Of course you'll look fine."

In the dark hall, Maggie shuddered. How could she have been such a fool? How could she have thought that Sandi and her stupid snobbery mattered? She thought of Carter Jackson, leather patches on his tweed elbows, saying easily, "I'm nobody . . . That makes two of us." And suddenly she wanted very much to go to Home-coming with him. Just as suddenly, she stopped being Sandi Walker's awed little roommate. She *did* know how to jump, she realized, and when and where and how far, as least just as well as Sandi knew. And she would, she determined, see Carol Gage crowned queen.

Quickly she opened the door, swirled in, and flung her books on the desk.

"Really, Maggie," Sandi spoke imperiously. "The court is meet-ing!"

"Oh? Well, hi, everyone!" Maggie responded blithely. "I'm so glad. I was looking for Carol. Carol, can you possibly . . .? I have a message for you." And the heretofore timid Maggie swept Carol along with her to the hall.

"Now, where is your room?" she whispered, laughing. "Before I lose control and go back and *hit* Sandi!" As she rushed Carol along, she went on, "Carol, don't you dare resign and let Sandi be queen! Why that would be lese majesty! But don't you let your mother slave over your dress either. You're going to wear a Paris creation, as they say in the fashion sheets. Come in here—" as they reached Room 340—"and let's plot."

During the supper hour, Maggie and Carol descended to the basement and took from Maggie's trunk a froth of white ruffles and a crimson velvet wrap. In the room of the dean of women, Carol stood before a long mirror and gasped with delight as she looked at the graceful ruffles billowing from a tiny bodice, outlined at the neck and waist with seed pearls and rhinestones. The dean, Mrs.

Russell, rummaged in a drawer and brought out a dazzling rhinestone necklace and a bracelet to match.

"It's perfect," Carol whispered. "Maggie, you absolutely must see me crowned."

"Perhaps I will, Carol; that is, if I can pick up a rain check. But tell me, who is Carter Jackson? I think I'd like to go with him."

Carol and Mrs. Russell exchanged glances. "Dr. Jackson is the Llewellyn Professor of English, Maggie dear," Mrs. Russell, explained. "He's quite the youngest man we've ever had on the faculty, and possibly the most brilliant. But he never goes out, except to the president's reception."

"And to the record room," Maggie added. "He carried my books!"

Back in Room 219, Carol greeted Sandi and the others on their return from supper. "Everything is fine now about my dress."

"Oh," said Sandi. "So that was the message?" She turned to Maggie, "You won't mind, Maggie, if I wear your jade, will you?"

"You may wear it, Sandi, unless Nobody wants me to wear it."

"Whatever do you mean, Maggie? *You're* the good English student; you ought to speak more clearly than that!"

The next day Carol kept Maggie a few moments after chemistry class to introduce her to Hugh Taylor, who was to be her escort and Homecoming king. "If we could get Maggie to speak for us, Hugh," she said, "I believe we might persuade Dr. Jackson to crown us."

"Spare the guy," Hugh said. "Or rather, spare us. With Jackson on the floor, none of us would rate."

Carol said, "Maggie would look after him."

Maggie muttered, "Don't you *dare!*"

When Maggie reached the record room, the red chair was waiting; an album stood open on the floor, and Carter Jackson unfolded his length from his chair nearby.

"I was afraid you weren't coming," he said accusingly. "I was afraid you'd found out who I am and wouldn't ever come any more. Maybe I should have told you. Only I did, remember?'

"Maybe I should have known, Dr. Jackson. Probably everyone else at Carlton does."

"I'm nobody," he insisted.

"You're *not* nobody. I did know that. And then I knew, of course, that you are nobody. And I am. And everybody is nobody. It's comfy that way."

"Yes, isn't it?" he said gratefully. "I'm glad you don't mind if I'm a teacher. Now what shall we play? That's the *Jupiter* on the floor."

"The *Emperor,* the *Jupiter.* We're quite imperial," Maggie said. "And all this royalty reminds me. I would like to go to Homecoming, if I may, just to see the court presented. All right?"

"All right, Maggie Renleigh. Only I should like to waltz you around once or twice, madam."

"That," she said, "would be nice. Incidentally, do you like jade?"

"Not much," he admitted hesitantly.

"Good," she said. "I really don't care too much for it myself."

Raynelle found that an ending can sometimes mean an exciting beginning

The Slamming Door

Janet Roberts

The minute she stepped into her home room, Raynelle Hughes saw the girls grouped around Cleo Parkinson, her best friend. She was disappointed because she wanted to talk to Cleo alone and get her advice about Hal's not yet having asked her to the dance.

Then, ". . . will Raynelle say?" she heard clearly.

Cleo laughed lightly. "What *can* she say? Hal has a right to date anyone he pleases, and he's asked *me* to the dance. He told me that Raynelle is just too, too sweet. Hal likes girls to be more—mature."

One of the girls began to laugh and then stopped short as she saw Raynelle.

"Cleo!" she warned sharply.

Raynelle turned and stumbled blindly to her desk. Her knees felt too wobbly to hold her up. When the bell rang, she automatically opened her books.

This was the reason Hal Mead, her steady date for the past six months, hadn't asked her to the Spring Formal. This was why he hadn't called her for two nights. This was why he had ignored her in the hall a few minutes ago.

Cleo—her best friend, who gave her advice, double-dated with her constantly, giggled with her over the same jokes, ate with her every noon, confided in her, and listened eagerly to her confidence— Cleo was going to the dance with Hal, and she had laughed with him about Raynelle behind her back! It was like a door slamming hard in her face.

"Too, too sweet!" "Wanted a girl who was more mature!" The print on the book danced before her eyes. She reached for her hand-kerchief and pretended to blow her nose, as she secretly wiped away tears. If only she could go home—but there was that test in history, and the quiz in algebra.

When Cleo tried to talk to her later, Raynelle walked away. She didn't want to speak to Cleo again, ever. Cleo shrugged, and at noon Raynelle saw her laughing and talking to that silly Marcia Smith. Cleo, with her slick short hair, her black blouse and plaid skirt, her amused sophisticated air that all the girls envied.

She wasn't pretty, Raynelle thought for the hundredth time, but there really was something very smooth about her.

Hal had always liked double-dating with Cleo and anyone she wanted to date. Now that Raynelle thought about it, she began to see that often she had been stuck with Cleo's date, while Hal and Cleo danced, or talked, or strolled off together. And yet Cleo had made fun of Hal behind his back to Raynelle, and laughed when Raynelle had defended him.

"Big football blond," Cleo had scoffed. "All brawn and no brains. What do you see in him?"

By evening Raynelle was so angry and unhappy, she was plan-ning all kinds of revenge. She would date the handsomest boy in school—ask her mother to buy her a daring red formal—cut her long curly blond hair to a smooth slick boy cut, even shorter than Cleo's. She would wear her mother's long earrings, and put on heavier make-up. She would show them! Hal would come begging to her—he would never want anything to do with Cleo again. He would say, "I didn't realize how mature you are, Raynelle!"

That night at dinner her mother was troubled. "Raynelle, what-ever is the matter with you?"

"I'm all right," Raynelle answered, not touching her favorite Dutch apple pie.

"Let her alone," advised her father sensibly.

"Aren't you going to the Dixieland?" her mother asked later. The Dixieland was the place where the high school kids gathered when they had nothing more important to do.

"Not tonight. I have homework."

Raynelle went up to her room. She sat for a long time in her window seat, looking down the shadowed street toward town. At the Dixieland, Cleo was probably meeting Hal. The kids would notice and whisper, "Wonder what happened to Raynelle? Hal throw her over? Too bad. Poor kid, she's a little young, don't you think? Too young . . . too young . . . not very mature . . ."

She bit her lips against the sobs that wanted to come. She stared out at the garden and saw the gang at the Dixieland, laughing and talking and having fun. No more of that for her.

She had dated Hal this whole junior year—ever since Hal's terrific one-man triumph in the first football game of the season. Hal and Cleo and her date had come over that evening to Raynelle's to celebrate. They had never laughed so much, they said afterwards.

She and Cleo, Cleo and Raynelle, all winter. And Raynelle and Hal, Hal and Raynelle, dating almost steadily. One night, coming back from ice skating, she and Hal had been talking about the future. He had stopped her, pulled her around to face him, and said earnestly, "I want to be in your future, Raynelle. Do you mind?"

"I don't mind," she had answered, lifting her face up to look at him.

He had kissed her then—a quick, shy kiss. Remembering that kiss, and then thinking of the way he had avoided her for the past three days, Raynelle bent her head down to her knees. She could no longer keep from crying.

The next day was terrible and the following day was worse. Only two more days to the Spring Formal!

In class she looked over the boys, trying to get up courage to ask one of them to take her to the dance. But they were probably all dated by now, and even if they weren't—she cringed at the thought of how they would look at her! A girl didn't ask a boy to the Spring Formal. She just didn't.

Jim O'Connor was nice, though he was the class cutup. But she knew he was going with Sally Davis. She might ask Ben or Burt. They wouldn't laugh—but they might talk about it afterwards.

There was Dick Webber who had just started to school in January. He was quiet and brainy, not handsome, but he was very polite, and he had a wonderful smile that flashed quickly and was gone. She almost asked Dick when he grinned at her in history class one morning. He sat next to her, so it wouldn't have been too hard to slip him a note. But something held her hand, and the moment was gone.

Everybody knew by now that Hal had dated Cleo Patterson for the Spring Formal. Raynelle avoided them all, sitting by herself in the cafeteria at noon, pretending she had to study. She didn't need to; she had been staying home and studying every evening. She thought she might never go out again. She would stay in and study, become a brain, go on to college and a university, get a Ph.D., become—maybe a woman doctor or something like that. Maybe someday Cleo would come to her with some terrible disease, or a horribly broken leg, and cry and beg her forgiveness. "Of course I forgive you," she would say magnanimously. "Hal really meant nothing to me; you were quite welcome to him. My career came first with me, always." And she would heal Cleo and send her on her way, not even asking her to pay because by that time Cleo was terribly poor.

Her parents kept trying to get her to go out with them. "Don't you want to go with me to the church supper?" her mother asked.

"No, not tonight. I have a big test in English tomorrow."

Her dad suggested, "How about that baseball game at State on Saturday? Since you're not going to the Formal, we could stay in the city for dinner. You name the place."

It would have been tempting back in her childhood, thought Raynelle, but it meant little now. "No, Dad, you go ahead with Uncle Jim. I have some sewing to do."

On Saturday she rushed from one thing to another—sewing, cooking lunch for her mother, washing the car, raking the leaves around the tulip bed, keeping furiously busy so she wouldn't think about how the other girls were taking beauty naps, trying on make-up, and comparing formals. But by the middle of the afternoon she had run out of things to do. She went to her room and picked up a book she had wanted to read for a long time. It was good, and it finally captured her attention. When she finished, she heard voices downstairs, and realized her dad was back from the baseball game.

Mom would be having supper soon; she could smell the meat cooking.

She slid to her feet, combed back her hair without looking at it, and started for the stairs. Then she heard her name and paused. Was *everybody* talking about her behind her back—even her own parents?

". . . so moody and unhappy. Oh, I could just kill that Cleo! I knew she was bad for Raynelle, acting so sophisticated and silly. But I never dreamed she'd take Hal away. I thought she really liked Raynelle."

"Oh, she probably did," said Raynelle's father. "But that kind of girl thinks first of herself. Mark my word, Hal will soon drop her. Her own pleasure will always come first. But don't worry about Raynelle. Our daughter is a smart girl. She'll figure out the right answer. Just give her time."

"You're probably right, dear," her mother agreed more serenely.

Raynelle stood still at the top of the stairs. The right answer? What was the right answer, the right thing to do, when your best friend walked off with your boy friend? And not only that, but acted so callous and hateful about it, as though she had never cared for you?

It wasn't just the loss of Hal that had upset her so. It was that Cleo was no longer there to talk to, to laugh with, to plan things with, to sit with in the Dixieland and compare ideas, talk about the future. Where would she find another girl to be her best friend?

She didn't want another. One was quite enough. And since that one had betrayed her—

She went down to supper when her mother called, but she couldn't eat much. Her father described the baseball game, and kept up the conversation with them till the meal was over. Silently, she helped her mother with the dishes, then went back up to her room.

Once again she sat huddled in the window seat. All over town girls were dressing for the Formal. In her closet hung the dress she would have worn, the pink net with little golden butterflies sprinkled over it. Hal would have sent her pink roses. What would he send to Cleo? Orchids?

Her father's words bothered her. "She'll figure out the right answer." What was the right answer?

Down at the Dixieland she supposed there would be a few kids who hadn't gone to the Formal. If she went down, it would be very obvious that *she* hadn't gone to the Formal. Very obvious. And people would ask her, "Where's Hal? Break his leg?"

The right answer? She couldn't stay in seclusion the rest of her life. She couldn't hide in her room or in her books at school. She had to face her schoolmates sometime. Might as well get it over with.

She turned on the lights and looked at herself in the mirror. She didn't look happy, but her cheeks were pink as ever. Not mature, not smart, not chic—just sweet.

"Okay!" she said, savagely, out loud. "That's what I am. They can laugh all they want."

She went to the closet, and after much deliberation she picked out a pink plaid dress. Her father liked the dress very much, had often said it was just right with her blond hair and brown eyes.

She bathed and dressed, brushing her hair till it shone. The spring evening was cool, so she wore her light coat and took a scarf along. As she came down the stairs, her parents looked up from their chairs in the living room.

"Raynelle?" Her mother looked startled.

Her father grinned at her. "You're looking very pretty."

"Thank you, Dad." The word "pretty" hurt, but she forced a smile for him. "I thought I'd go to the Dixieland for a while. I'll be home by eleven."

"All right, dear," said her mother.

She walked out the door alone. She wouldn't be stopping at Cleo's so they could go to Dixieland together. They wouldn't pick out a small table at one side, and order "Two Cokes with lemon," and sit and talk all evening.

She wouldn't go to a table at all. She would go to the fountain, sit on a stool, and drink a Coke very, very slowly.

It was just about the hardest thing she had ever done to walk down the lighted main street, pause at the door of the Dixieland, take a deep breath, then push open the door and walk in.

All the faces seemed to turn toward her; the unexpectedly large crowd appeared strange and completely unfamiliar. She smiled blindly, not seeing anyone clearly, and walked toward the soda fountain.

She sat on a stool, taking a deep breath, looking unseeingly toward Gus. "One Coke with lemon," she said in a voice that sounded squeaky in her ears.

"Raynelle?" said a pleasant, deep voice behind her. She turned so quickly the stool tipped, but she kept her balance somehow.

"Oh—hello, Dick."

"Alicia and Bunny and the rest said to come on over with us."

"All—all right." She even managed to smile back at him. He did have a nice smile, quick and friendly and warm. She liked his dark eyes, his black hair that somehow fell over his forehead. She took her Coke from Gus and slid down from the stool.

He stood aside to let her walk in front of him toward the large table where two girls were waving at them.

"Hello, Alicia; hi, Bunny; hi, Ben; hi, Burt." She sank down in the chair Dick held for her, and wondered. Why aren't they at the dance? Why isn't Alicia with Martin, and Bunny with Scott? And why hadn't Ben and Burt and Dick gone to the dance? She had thought everybody was going.

She caught the drift of the conversation. ". . . in a summer theater," Dick was saying. "There's lots of talent here. Why, Alicia, the way you played Catherine in the junior play was great."

"Thanks," Alicia smiled. She was tall, blond-haired, interested in music. Raynelle had never felt she really knew Alicia. "I like acting, and I think it's a swell idea to form a summer theater group here. Raynelle, you've done some acting, haven't you?"

"A little—I always enjoyed it." Raynelle didn't try to join in the conversation very much. She sipped her Coke, and listened to the eager talk, and smiled at them when they looked at her.

No one mentioned the Formal. No one asked about Hal or Cleo.

"—place to perform," Dick was saying. "Back home we had the plays in a big barn. Fixed up the floor, turned the stalls into dressing rooms. It was as much fun doing that as giving the plays."

Raynelle woke up. "We have a perfectly mammoth barn," she heard herself saying. "Dad keeps the car in it; otherwise it's just going to waste. Our place was a farm not long ago, you know."

"Oh, Raynelle, that would be perfect!" cried Alicia. She turned eagerly to the others. "I've seen it. It's just huge. And if your folks don't mind, we could start right in fixing it up. Do you think they'd mind?"

"I don't think so, but I'll ask tonight. I'll let you know Monday.

Or—what about my calling you tomorrow afternoon? It's Sunday. Why don't you all come over and look at the barn, and see what can be done? Then next Saturday, we could start working."

"Swell. Wonderful!" "Paint? Whitewash?" "I'm handy with tools if I do say so myself." "Chairs? Benches? Curtains?"

"I can sew and we have a sewing machine," said Raynelle. She leaned forward, put her elbows on the table and cupped her chin in her hands, to listen intently. Ben was talking about the lights; Burt chimed in about the background scenery. "Dad could give us advice about that," Raynelle put in. "He's an artist." It was such a fascinating new idea that it put Cleo and Hal and the Formal completely out of her head.

Bunny drawled something funny, and they all laughed. Raynelle was still smiling when she looked over at Dick and caught him staring at her. His dark eyes were serious and intent, almost wondering. Then as they gazed at each other, he smiled, this time slowly, warmly.

She flushed, and finally looked away, a strange feeling tingling through her. They went on with their plans for the next day, and had talked for a long time when Raynelle finally said, "I have to leave. I told Mom I'd be home about eleven."

When she stood up, the boys stood up too. "We might as well all go. We live along the same way," said Alicia. So all of them walked down the street together.

Raynelle found herself between Ben and Dick, who were still talking about lights. "This is it," she said. "This is where I live."

They stopped. "Good night. See you tomorrow." "Good night, Raynelle."

"Good night!" She turned and ran up the steps and into the house. She heard their laughter fading away down the street.

Her parents looked up at her expectantly when she came in. Her mother asked anxiously, "Did you have a good time, dear?"

"Wonderful," said Raynelle, gaily. She leaned against the back of a chair and smiled at them. Sometimes, she was thinking, you imagine a door is slamming in your face. And all the time it's just a new door opening so fast and so wide that it hits you in the nose.

New York seemed alien and cold until
Meli met the boy from Finland

Foreigners

Bernice A. Stevens

The subway train gave a sickening lurch as it shrieked around a curve. Melisand gritted her teeth and closed her eyes as she swayed helplessly against the bodies packed so tightly against her own. Well, at least you couldn't *fall* in a subway! Not possibly! There just wasn't room!

Suddenly, unbidden, a vision floated behind her closed lids: a vision of a peaceful, tree-lined, mountain-shadowed Carolina walk. Last year, and for many years before, that walk had been her route to school. Homesickness welled up, to be followed quickly by futile anger. This eternal noise and bustle were just too much! She muttered a word she had heard her gentle father say once or twice under extreme provocation. And then, in horror at herself, she opened her eyes wide.

"Not as bad as that, surely!" shouted an amused voice close to her ear, and Meli found herself looking into blue eyes as amused as the voice. He must have read her lips!

Meli was pink with shame. But above her shame rose rebellious exasperation, for here it was again! A voice with something strange in it. English words said by an un-English, quite un-American tongue. This one was not Spanish or Italian or French. Her quick ear knew that, just as her eyes knew that the south of Europe had never produced those teasing blue eyes. What *was* that accent? Not Irish, not Scotch, not German. She thought she had learned to catalog them all during her one month in a New York school!

As if he could read her mind as well as her lips, the boy spoke again. "Finland," he said. The one word, shouted above the howl of the train, sounded proud, and somehow gallant.

Melisand frowned in concentration over a mental map of Europe.

"You do not like Finland?" Again the voice was amused.

Meli opened her mouth to explain. At that moment the train gathered speed and went shrieking around another curve. She gave up, shaking her head hopelessly.

"Never mind!" Evidently the boy was used to the noise, for he yelled competently above it. "You can tell me later!"

Meli looked away. Small chance that she would ever tell this young man anything. At home if you saw a boy you didn't know, and he looked as interesting as this one, with his plain, alive face and his merry eyes—well, it couldn't possibly take more than a couple of days to find someone who knew him, and then you could get introduced and that would be that. But here—small chance that she would ever see him after she got off at the next station. Even her classmates at school were people that she knew for only a few hours each day.

The train slowed, and Meli, completely absorbed in the intricate problems of battling her way off the train, through the turnstile, and up the right stairs, forgot all about her recent neighbor.

Oh, dear, raining again! Resignedly, she pulled her raincoat closer and opened her red umbrella. The wind caught it and she gasped, trying to hold it steady. Suddenly a strong hand gripped the handle and tilted the umbrella against the wind. She looked up, but not too far up, into the eyes of her subway acquaintance.

"Now!" The voice was gay. "What is this that you have against subways, or the Finns, or whatever?"

Meli, gratefully relinquishing the umbrella, felt her irritation slipping away. She smiled up at the boy. He wasn't very tall, she reflected, but he was older than he had seemed at first—older than her own sixteen years; nineteen, maybe!

"I didn't mean to be rude," she apologized. "I don't like subways much, or going to school in New York. I never knew a Finn, so I can't dislike them. It's just that, here in New York, all voices sound—" She stopped in embarrassment.

"Foreign, I'll bet!"

"Yes." Her agreement was hesitant.

"And you'd like New York to sound just like the place you're used to?" There was a question in his voice that wasn't in his words. She answered that first.

"North Carolina," she said, and went on, "Oh, I don't know. Maybe I would. I just can't seem to get used to hearing so much Italian and Chinese and French and Spanish! Even English doesn't sound like English!"

But the boy's interest had been caught by her first words.

"North Carolina! I *thought* you had a foreign accent—foreign to New York, that is!"

At the thought of her own accent as foreign, Meli giggled. Their eyes met and suddenly they were both laughing.

"Now tell me all about it," invited the young man.

"There's not much to tell, really," protested Meli. "I guess I'm being childish. But I thought it would be such fun to spend a year in New York. Daddy had told me such wonderful things about it. I do love the big stores and the shows and the museums. But Daddy has so little time to take us around. And riding the subway to school, and forever hearing voices that sound as if they belong someplace else! Almost all the kids at school, even some of the teachers, speak with accents. Even the real New Yorkers sound strange to me!"

"I expect you don't sound too familiar to most of them," commented her companion drily. "What else?"

"I guess I miss the mountains. And I don't like pushy crowds of strange people."

"Where are you living?"

"Oh, we're lucky enough to live right in Manhattan." Melisand gave her address.

"Why, that's only a short bus ride and a few subway stops from my studio!" He sounded pleased. Then he snapped his fingers and exclaimed, "Do you know, we haven't even introduced ourselves? I'm Finn Grotell; Finn's my real name."

"I'm Meli—Melisand Mitchell."

"You know, Meli, I've an idea!" Finn grinned companionably as he used the nickname. "I think you need to get better acquainted with New York. Why don't you come over to the studio Saturday

afternoon? Maybe I can show you a few things about the place you
don't know. I'm starting a new class, and that's always fun. Here—"
He fumbled in his pocket and brought out a card.

"Class? Studio?" Meli stared at him stupidly without looking
at the card.

"Right here, ma'am," Finn pointed to the card. *"Rikki's Studio
of the Dance.* You see, I teach dancing."

"Dancing!"

"Yes—ever hear of it?"

"Oh, of course, but—"

"Ever been to the ballet?"

"No, but Daddy's promised to take us. He loves it."

"Good. When you come to the studio maybe you'll see Rikki.
I think Rikki's the best dancer in New York and he's with one of
the big ballet troupes, besides having this studio of his own where
I teach. Well, I leave you here. Think you can manage that umbrella? And how about coming over Saturday afternoon at three?"

"Well, I don't know, I'd like to, but Dad and Mother—"

Finn's walk slowed and so did Meli's. "Tell you what! Why don't
I drop in this evening and ask your parents about it?"

Privately, Meli was appalled. A perfect stranger—a New York
stranger—a Finnish stranger—how would her family take it? But
Meli had been brought up in the Southern tradition of hospitality,
and she was afraid that her manners so far had been less than perfect.

"Of course!" she exclaimed. "Just the thing! Do come!"

"See you then!" With a nod, Finn was gone.

All day at school, while her ears were bombarded with strange
foreign voices and her eyes traveled anxiously over Chinese, Spanish, Italian faces, Meli thought of Finn and worried about the
evening to come.

She must tell Dad and Mother about him right away, at dinner.
What would they say? They had always been so definite about
the perils of taking up with strangers!

But Mother had gone shopping when Meli reached home after
school. Much later, her parents arrived together, Father carrying
an assortment of bundles with exaggerated care. When one of the
bundles proved to hold a new sweater and skirt for Meli, she forgot
all about Finn. Unheralded, he arrived at seven.

Meli looked stricken when Dad opened the door and she saw

her friend of the subway standing there, a small box held unobtrusively under his arm.

"Oh, Dad, Mother, I forgot to tell you! This is Finn—Finn Grotell. I met him this morning on the subway."

"Come in." Father's soft Southern voice was hospitable, but Meli heard the doubtful note in it. Quickly, she made a more complete explanation, and everyone sat down. Meli saw Finn lay his package on the end table.

"When I talked to your daughter today, sir, ma'am," Finn looked from Dad to Mother, and the merry look that Meli had liked was in his eyes, "she seemed a bit confused by New York. I thought maybe I could help her get acquainted with my favorite city. I invited her to my studio, but I guess you've brought her up pretty carefully. She didn't think you would approve."

"Studio!" Meli could see Mother having visions of easels, canvas, paint, and models, probably nude. She giggled in spite of herself.

Gravely, Finn arose and gave one of his cards to each of her parents. "Rikki's dance studio," he said proudly.

"Rikki!" Father's voice was awestruck.

"Rikki! We saw him dance in the International Ballet five years ago! He's the best male dancer I've ever seen!" Mother's voice was ecstatic. "You work with Rikki!"

"Only in the studio, teaching," answered Finn modestly. "Though I hope to have a small part in the ballet next season if it doesn't interfere with the college work I hope to be taking."

As the three others fell to discussing ballet, Meli felt left out, for she had never seen a ballet and had not known that her parents had enjoyed so many in their younger days. She listened closely, but it was like hearing another foreign language.

At last Finn flashed her a warm smile and said, "Then Meli may visit the studio next Saturday afternoon?"

"Indeed she may." Father's voice was hearty. "Now, let's see. That's down in the Village where I lived in my student days. She'll take a crosstown bus, and the subway—"

After Finn was gone, Mother discovered the small box he had left behind the lamp. "Oh, dear," she said. "He's forgotten something!"

Father laughed. "I'm afraid you don't know your Scandinavians," he said. "That's the usual hostess gift. A box of candy, I imagine.

No Scandinavian would think of paying a call without a gift. And he probably received a very bad impression of our hospitality. We didn't even offer him a cup of coffee."

"Dear me! I was so excited I never thought!" Mother looked so upset that Dad hastened to reassure her.

"Never mind! We'll have him over for one of your wonderful dinners and make amends."

When Saturday afternoon came, Meli's excitement was almost uncontrollable. She kept thinking what her classmates back home would have said at the idea of her visiting a real dance studio in fabulous Greenwich Village, the section of New York so famous for its artists in all fields.

"You will be in historic territory today," Father had told her. "Edgar Allan Poe lived down there, and Washington Irving and, more recently, John Sloan."

Meli was much too excited over her visit to think about the rest of the Village and its history. She hardly looked at the old buildings as she sped along the street, seeing only the numbers over the doors.

When she found the right place, she came out of her daze with a jerk. What a building! Why, it must be hundreds of years old! It looked as if it would tumble down any minute! Only the memory of her father's reverence for the Village and for Rikki gave her courage to open the door.

Inside, it was even worse. Meli walked fearfully into the dark, narrow hallway and peered up the dim, steep stairs. Nervously, she retreated to the doorway. Her eye fell upon some bells and above one was Rikki's name. She touched it gingerly.

"Come up!" called Finn's voice from above.

It seemed to Meli that she would never get to the top of those steep stairs. When she finally stood in the dark, narrow upper hall, with Finn greeting her, she looked back down the long flights and thought perhaps it would be best to go right back down again.

But Finn opened the door. A cone of light lay about them, and a hubbub of voices greeted them. Meli looked into an enormous, cheery room, with sunshine pouring gaily through windows and skylights. Around the edge of the polished floor and pushed up against the light-painted walls were comfortable chairs.

The voices that poured out at them belonged to boys and girls of all ages, from people in her own age group down to youngsters of nine or ten. Everyone was milling about; everyone was chattering, and in the babel Meli caught the usual accents of Italian and German and Chinese and French, as well as pure New York.

"Come!" Finn caught her hand and drew her in. "I was just ready to begin. Sit here, please."

Meli dropped into a chair. Finn clapped his hands for silence.

"This is a dancing class," he said pleasantly when everyone had settled down. "You are probably here because you love movement and rhythm and want to become a part of it. For the first few lessons, I'll teach all of you a little about rhythm and movement. Then you'll be divided into groups according to your age and size. Later," Finn's voice held a quality of hushed eagerness and promise, "later, Rikki will come to see how you are getting along and to teach you, too."

Meli was surprised to see awe and pleasure in the children's eyes, and to hear the longdrawn "O-o-oh!" from some of the older ones. Their reaction reminded her of the light in her parents' eyes when Finn had mentioned Rikki.

"Dancing is wonderful," Finn went on, "but it's not all just play and fun. It is also hard work and discipline. Some of you will drop out of the class, but those of you who really love dancing will keep on and on.

"First," Finn's expressive voice became gay, "before we are dancers, we are people. All different kinds of people, no two alike. For instance, how many of you were born in this country?" About half the young people raised their hands. "And how many of your parents were born here?" Only a few hands went up this time. "How many of you know something about the country from which you or your parents came?" Every hand went up this time and faces were bright.

"Tell you what let's do," Finn said, as if he had just thought of the idea. "Let's each tell something about ourselves and our backgrounds, so we can get acquainted. I'll start. I'm Finn, and that's funny, because it's both my name and my original nationality. When the war was over, I had no relatives except an uncle, here in New York. He brought me here, gave me dancing lessons, and sent me to school. Next year I hope to start to college and someday I hope to be in Rikki's ballet. Now, who wants to go on?"

A Japanese girl arose shyly. "I just came to America last year," she said, with Nippon on her tongue. "I want to learn to dance. My mother loves the ballet, and she takes me whenever she can save enough money out of her pay check. She has showed me the old Japanese dances, without much action, but with every gesture and movement meaning something. They are beautiful, but I want to learn ballet."

Looking at the Oriental girl's slight, graceful body and her bright eyes, Meli forgot to be disturbed by her strange speech.

"My father came from Italy." A small dark boy had leaped to his feet. "He's a musician, but I like the things his music makes me do!" Humming a little tune, he leaped into the air, clicked his heels together, and sat down again. Everyone laughed.

A tall, blonde girl about Meli's age rose. "My name is Helga and I am from Sweden." Her voice was deep and warm. For the first time Meli was not annoyed by the fact that her "Sweden" sounded like "Sveden." "My people have always had many dances that everyone loved. I love them, too, but I want to learn many, many more dances."

"We're New Yorkers, my brother and I." A wiry, red-haired boy gestured toward a carbon copy of himself who still sat on the floor. "Grandpa was a vaudeville star, and he shows us steps. Pop bought us a television set and we watch the musical shows and stuff like that, but my sister always wants to turn on the love stories!" His look was so disgusted that the older students snickered.

"I am an Indian." The stolid face of a fourteen-year-old boy broke into a grin. "At least, my mother is. Last summer she took me down to Cherokee to see the Cherokee Drama, and I got the Eagle Dancer's autograph. See! Here it is!" He held out a little book, but before anyone could look at it Meli jumped up.

"Cherokee, North Carolina?" she cried.

"Of course."

"That's near where I come from!"

"You sure can tell you're *some* sort of a foreigner!" exclaimed a small boy. "Do they really talk like that in North Carolina?" His voice took on an exaggerated drawl. "Good mawnin', suh! Ah'm from Nowth Caholina!"

The Indian boy was grinning broadly. The others tried hard to be polite, but when Finn shouted with laughter, everyone joined in, even Meli herself.

When things were a little quieter, Meli felt someone move closer to her and heard a shy voice say, "I love the way you talk." Startled, Meli looked down into the wide gray eyes and small freckled face of a girl about her own age. "I try not to use the Irish brogue I hear at home," the girl continued, "but New Yorkers sound so harsh! I—I like *your* way!"

The early dark was falling when Finn locked the door after the last student and followed Meli down the stairs.

"I'll see that you get home safely," he said.

They walked to the subway in companionable silence. Again Meli found herself shoved and jostled. Foreign voices clattered and called around her until the train hit top speed and drowned everything with its wild clanking and shrieking. But this evening nothing seemed to annoy Meli. As the train lurched, she caught hold of Finn's arm to steady herself and smiled.

"See?" he asked silently with his lips. Meli nodded, not even trying to answer.

When they had pushed their way up to the street, Finn had a suggestion. "Feel like walking? It's only seven or eight blocks to your place."

"I'd like it," agreed the girl. "Finn, your class was swell."

"Nice kids, " agreed Finn. "I love a beginning class—every kid so different. You never know when you'll discover a Pavlova—or a Rikki!"

"This Rikki," said Meli thoughtfully. "Where is he from?"

"Czechoslovakia. He came here just before the war. He has some long, unpronounceable name, so he just took two syllables out of it and called himself Rikki. He speaks with a strong accent." Finn looked sideways at Meli.

She giggled. "You know," she said, "I'm beginning to *like* accents!"

"Pretty soon," laughed Finn, "all you'll miss will be your mountains!"

"My mountains!" Meli's voice became nostalgic. "I'll never stop missing my mountains."

"Nor I my homeland," agreed Finn soberly.

Soon they neared Meli's New York home, passing the tall, seemingly endless apartment buildings of the immense housing project where she lived. Lighted windows here and there emphasized the straight, towering heights. Meli started toward her own door.

"Not that way," said Finn. "I found another way the other evening. Come!"

Wondering, Meli followed him up a short flight of stairs that she had not noticed before, and along a walk into a grassy court encircled by tall buildings. Near a little pool of water with an idle fountain at its center, Finn stopped and caught her hand.

"Look up!" he said. "Look up and all around!"

Meli did. How small she felt as she looked up at the soaring height of the buildings and saw the jagged, beautiful pattern of their tops against the evening sky.

"Remind you of anything?" asked Finn.

"My mountains!" breathed Meli. "It's like being in one of the deep coves of the Smokies, with mountains all around!"

For a few minutes Finn said nothing, while Meli stood lost in contemplation. Then he laughed softly.

"Man-made mountains," he said. "You'll be all right now, Meli. Like most of us, you'll be right at home—a foreigner at home in New York!"

More fragile than steel, person-to-person contacts can span two worlds

Build Me a Bridge

Marjorie Vetter

For well over a hundred years, six generations to be precise, there had been a Sarah in the family. The present-day Sarah hated her name and lopped off the "h" whenever she could.

"At least it doesn't look so old-fashioned spelled this way," she said, offending her mother, the Sarah next in line, who cherished her name as part of prized family tradition.

Sara, minus the "h," stood now at the living-room window, gazing glumly down at the necklace of lights that outlined the parkway curving below. She was behaving badly, she knew. She ought at least to try to entertain the Sarah, older by two generations, who sat across the room leafing idly through a magazine.

But what in the world did a fourteen-year-old have to talk about that would interest a strange grandmother of sixty? Maybe Sarah the fourth would go to bed soon and Sara could go back to her book. The trip by air from California yesterday must certainly have exhausted a woman of her age.

She did not look tired, yet she seemed ill at ease, putting down one magazine, picking up another. The thought flashed through Sara's mind that the fourth Sarah appeared as uncomfortable as she herself was, but she dismissed it instantly as ridiculous.

She studied the fourth Sarah covertly as she looked over the fashion photographs in *Vogue*. Her grandmother's dark brown hair was only lightly streaked with silver. The trim little suit she was wearing could not be larger than size fourteen. And she filled it with curves in just the right places. Sara glanced down at her own flat bean-pole length and sighed.

It was hard enough to have to miss the Spring Frolic because of a cold, but if she hadn't had to baby-sit with her grandmother, she might at least be enjoying herself with Betty Cavanna, her favorite author, and *The Boy Next Door*.

The boy next door. There was no boy next door to Sara. In fact, there was no boy her age on the whole hill. Sara frowned at the reflection of her face in the black windowpane—a thin, white face, with a wide mouth and enormous, black-lashed, gray eyes. She wondered why she had protested so vehemently to her mother about missing the party tonight. Her temperature had been normal since morning, and she had argued valiantly to be permitted to go to the dance, as usual, with Mary Kay. Her mother had been adamant, repeating the doctor's instructions not to allow Sara to go out of the house until her temperature had been normal for twenty-four hours.

Sara had protested that she felt as good as new, that it would be unfair to Mary Kay who, abandoned like this, would never take her solitary way to the party on her own. Mary Kay was Sara's dearest friend. Together they had faithfully attended school parties all year. They had never yet had a good time.

Sara might as well face it. There was more agony than pleasure in sitting on the side lines pretending, wildly hilarious, to be having fun with Mary Kay and others (whom Sara had christened "the unclaimed"), smiling from time to time at her more fortunate classmates, as they whirled by with the boys they had somehow managed to attract. It was even worse to stumble around the floor with Mary Kay or another of the "unclaimed," with a silly, set smile on her aching face.

To be strictly honest, Sara had to admit she enjoyed herself a good deal more at home reading about Jane and Ken and their adventures in *The Boy Next Door*. Then why had she battled so hard to be allowed to go tonight in spite of her cold? The reason, of course, was that somehow she kept on hoping that next time would be different. Whoever said "hope springs eternal" knew what he was talking about, she thought wryly.

But hope was a lying cheat, a cynical deceiver. Just suppose a boy did ask her to dance—she might as well make the boy Billy Rhodes while she was about it. Billy was a blond upper-class boy who danced like a professional. Sara and Mary Kay gazed wide-eyed as he clearly outperformed all the others in the Lindy or the Charleston. Just suppose by some miracle Billy should walk across the dance floor and—ignoring the fawning circle of the most important and popular girls at William C. Marshall High—ask Sara to dance. What would she do? She could hardly circle the room once with Mary Kay without stepping on her own or her partner's feet. She had never danced the Charleston in her life. At the moment a revival of the Charleston was the thing at Marshall, and Billy Rhodes was by all odds its leading exponent.

Unconsciously Sara sighed again. She ought really to make an effort to talk to her grandmother.

Her mother had said: "I'm sorry you have to miss the Frolic because of your cold, but it's lucky for us that you'll be here to keep your grandmother company. I'd hate to leave her all alone the second night of her visit, but we simply can't break our date with the Frys at the last minute. He's a client of your father, and we can't afford to offend them. We had no idea your grandmother's office would ask her to take her vacation a week earlier like this."

"You aren't going to leave me alone with her," Sara had wailed in protest. "I've only seen her once before when I was too young to remember it. What'll I do with her?"

Her mother had looked annoyed. "Why, visit with her, of course. Get to know her. She's a lot of fun. You'll enjoy her when you have a chance really to talk with her."

Talk with her. What about? An elderly lady certainly wouldn't be interested in school or movies or dances.

Sara moved away from the window and sat down gingerly on the edge of the chair by the coffee table. She had only to reach out a hand to pick up her book. Her grandmother was looking at a magazine. Surely it would be all right for Sara to go on with her reading. But her mother had been so emphatic about leaving Grandmother in Sara's care.

Desperately, Sara searched for a subject that would appeal to a woman who had already lived three times Sara's whole lifetime even before Sara was born. What did elderly people think about? Church, maybe? God? Religion? Would it be tactless or a kindness to bring up these subjects with someone so near the end of life?

Nervously, Sara shifted her position, curling her feet under her in the big chair. She sighed softly again and looked up into the troubled gray eyes of the woman across the table.

"School," her grandmother said in a sort of hurried, breathless way. "How do you like your school?"

Sara said fine; her grandmother asked what subjects she studied; Sara told her and that was that. The minutes passed. Sara squirmed in her chair. Her grandmother fidgeted in hers. The rumble of the oil burner sounded loud in the quiet room.

"Your mother used to like to play cassino," Sarah the fourth said at last on a note of desperation. "Would you like to play?"

Sara said no thank you, she didn't know how. She searched wildly for something to talk about. She couldn't let her grandmother make all the effort.

"There was a party at school tonight—a dance called the Spring Frolic. Mary Kay and I sold tickets," she babbled on. "I planned to go with Mary Kay until I caught this cold."

"What a shame to miss a party! Spring Frolic sounds so carefree and gay."

Carefree and gay! About the last words, Sara thought wryly, in which to describe the worry and misery of a school dance for girls like herself and Mary Kay. "School parties would be a lot more gay and carefree for Mary Kay and me," she said wistfully, "if we could really dance so the boys would ask us. Boys like Billy Rhodes, I mean. You ought to see Billy do the Charleston!"

"The Charleston!" Sarah the fourth's voice was shrill with amazement. "You mean to say you youngsters do the Charleston?"

Sara nodded. "Billy's really good," she boasted. "Of course, he only picks out girls like Wilma Harris and Nancy Block. He never dances with Mary Kay or me. We're not very good," she admitted, "and we can't do the Charleston at all."

"You can't?" Sarah the fourth said briskly. "Well, something ought to be done about that. How would you like to learn tonight?"

Sara's big eyes opened wide. "How could I learn tonight?"

Sarah the fourth got up from her chair. She had lost her nervousness, Sara noticed, and her eyes were sparkling as if she might be going to enjoy this evening after all. "Have you any Charleston records?"

"Down in the playroom, but what—"

"Come on then, honey, let's not waste time. I used to be the Charleston expert of my day and I still keep my foot in, so to speak."

Two hours later, when Sara's parents returned, they found two flushed, disheveled people having a snack at the kitchen table. They were laughing and talking together as companionably as if Sarah the fourth were Mary Kay.

"You ought to get to bed, Sara," her mother said after an exchange of greetings. "Rest is the best medicine for a cold."

Sara said good night, giving Sarah the fourth an extra hug as she murmured, "Thanks, loads." When she was halfway upstairs, she heard her grandmother say to her mother, "You probably won't believe it, Sal, but honestly I was scared to death when you asked me to stay home with Sara this evening. It worked out just fine though. We had a wonderful time."

Sara began to laugh as she went on upstairs. Just who had been baby-sitting with whom? What an amazing evening! Never had she had such a shock as when, to the rhythm of the record on the hi-fi, her grandmother began to dance the Charleston. She was good, too. Even better than Billy Rhodes. Sara was still smiling when she went into her room. Look out, she thought triumphantly, look out, Billy Rhodes, here I come—me—Sarah Allen. She hardly realized that unconsciously she had put back the "h" on her name.

Incident on
a Train

Mabel Cleland Widdemer

Annette Marie, on the way home to spend the summer holidays
with her parents, followed the porter along the gray concrete platform. It was a nuisance having to change from the through express
to the meandering Southern local.

She wasn't paying much attention to the porter. She was thinking
of the days ahead. Life was going to seem different and strange
back home. It had not been easy for a girl who had received all
her training in small Negro schools to make a place for herself in
a large Eastern college. Gradually she had lost much of the shyness and worry that had handicapped her during the first weeks of
her freshman year. The memory of the things the dean and the
girls had said to her when she had won the intercollegiate debate
for her class still glowed in her heart. Now she felt assured and
properly dressed and as if she belonged. Perhaps her clothes weren't
as expensive as some of her new friends; but they were *right*, and
that meant everything.

She climbed the train steps behind the porter. But the minute
she stepped into the coach and started down the aisle, she remembered where she was and knew the porter had made a mistake in
bringing her into this car.

"Just a minute, porter," she began. But he had already swung

234

her bags into the overhead rack and was holding out his hand for the expected tip. Suddenly the old timidity, the old, shy uncertainty came flooding back; she decided in panic that it was too late to ask to be taken to a rear car. She knew she was a coward, but she couldn't face that long, humiliating walk down the aisle.

She gave him the tip and sank down next to the window. She felt people staring at her, even though after a few seconds their inquisitive eyes roamed elsewhere. She told herself they looked at her only as they had looked at others, out of idle curiosity. She tried to hold on to her recently acquired pride and self-assurance. But the old feeling of inferiority she had struggled so hard to overcome came creeping back.

She had had her hair done recently and it lay soft and wavy under her pert little hat, cocked at just the angle approved by her college friends. She knew her well-tailored suit and spotless blouse and gloves were right for traveling.

Protective coloring, she thought grimly, disparaging the feeling of comfort they gave her.

If she tried to be as inconspicuous as possible, and paid no attention to anyone, perhaps the others, like the porter, would not realize she was in the wrong car. She opened a magazine and began to read, but her eyes kept wandering from the pages.

Four other girls had boarded the train at the junction. She hadn't paid much attention to them at first. But now she saw they had chosen seats across the aisle and just a little ahead of where she sat. They had turned over one seat to face the other so that their knees touched companionably. They were babbling about their plans for the coming holidays.

Three of the girls were brunettes. One of them had skin and hair and eyes almost as dark as Annette Marie's. The fourth, who sat facing Annette Marie, was small and blond.

"Let's have some bridge," one of the girls suggested, and beckoned to the conductor to ask him for a lapboard. He chuckled as he placed it across their waiting knees.

"Seems sort of like old times, doesn't it?" he said. "When you all used to come home from Miss Damen's school for the holidays and wanted a lapboard so you could play Old Maid. Now you're all grown-up young ladies. Time certainly flies. Take it easy, Miss

Betty," he smiled at the small, blond girl. "Don't do any wild bidding unless you've got the cards to back it up."

Annette Marie returned to her magazine. But she couldn't keep her mind on the story. She kept glancing across at the group of girls. How wonderful it must be to be as gay and self-assured as they were. How easy it must be for them, knowing that wherever they went they were welcome. They could demand the best seats in any theater; they could walk into any restaurant or hotel with their heads held high and no fear that someone would turn them away with that polite phrase: "Sorry, no seats, no vacancy."

It was evident that Betty wasn't playing a very good game of bridge. Her mind seemed to be on other things. Her friends kept telling her that she wasn't paying attention. Finally, when Betty had trumped her ace, Betty's partner threw down her cards with a sharp exclamation.

"Betty Munroe, you're impossible! You simply won't put your mind on the game! Let's play Canasta. Even a child or—"

She broke off, and Betty, grinning, supplied the word.

"A fool!" she laughed. Catching Annette Marie's dark eyes over the top of her magazine, she smiled and winked drolly.

Annette Marie forgot that she wanted to remain inconspicuous behind her magazine until it was time for her to get off the train, and answered the friendly smile with a flash of her white teeth.

The lonely whistle of the train approaching a crossing brought her back to the present with a heart-stabbing clearness, reminding her that she was in the wrong car of a Southern local.

It was ridiculous, she told herself, what the rule about separate cars for Negroes and whites and the porter's mistake had done to her. With each revolution of the wheels carrying her away from college, she seemed to be shedding more of her newly won feeling of adequacy and courage. With each racing mile she was falling back to the old mistaken feeling of inferiority. Making herself as small as she could, she hid behind her magazine again.

She tried to read, but a nagging worry pricked at her. She had been conscious for some time of a tall, angular woman seated across the aisle. She had been one of the people who had stared when Annette Marie entered the car.

The troubled feeling persisted. At last Annette Marie could

stand it no longer. She turned and faced the small, gray eyes of the woman across the aisle. For a moment their glances met and locked, then Annette Marie's dark eyes dropped and she turned with a little shiver back to her magazine.

She was furious with herself for not being able to hold those sharp, prejudiced eyes longer. How could all that she had gained since she had entered college last fall desert her so quickly? Where was that newly won self-assurance—the pride in herself and her people which had been building up inside her? What had happened to all the high-sounding phrases she had cherished so proudly in her heart? The things she had been taught of civic rights and equality for all Americans which had been the subject of the debate she had won for her college? Where was her pride? Her courage?

Scold herself as she would she could not bring herself again to meet those cold gray eyes across the aisle. Emotions bred of generations of discrimination came flooding back to make her supinely willing to accept this feeling of inferiority again.

"Honestly, Betty, you're awful!" The half-angry voice rang through the train. "Can't you *try* to keep your mind on the game? You've been wool-gathering ever since we changed trains."

"I'm sorry," Betty said contritely. "I'll drop out. You don't need me. I've tried your patience enough."

The conductor opened the door of the car, letting in a whiff of sweet-smelling air.

"All tickets, please," he said, shutting out the welcome freshness before he started down the aisle.

Annette Marie nervously opened her purse. Her gloved hands made it awkward for her to get the ticket out of the small zippered pocket. The conductor was coming nearer. She mustn't keep him waiting. She must do nothing to focus any special attention on herself. She ripped the glove from her right hand, groped again in her bag for the ticket, and slipped it under the velvet cording on the seat ahead of her. The conductor was joking with the girls across the aisle.

Annette Marie became conscious that the tall, thin woman was staring at her again. Annette Marie's breath caught in her throat. Suddenly she was sure the woman *knew*. And she was going to do something about it. She had risen from her seat.

Annette Marie, watching out of the corners of her eyes, saw her step out into the aisle. Then she crossed and began talking to the women behind Annette Marie. They spoke in low, excited whispers, but Annette Marie couldn't hear what they said.

Her hands tightened on the magazine. Although she couldn't *hear* what the women were saying, she *knew* what it was—as if they were speaking in clarion tones that echoed down the dusty car.

"Trying to pass herself off for white! Well, we don't have to stand for it—"

The conductor, having collected all the tickets, had taken a seat in the forward part of the car, where he was sorting and counting the colored bits of pasteboard. The tall, angular woman, clutching at the backs of the seats to steady herself, was weaving down the aisle toward him.

"It won't be long now," Annette Marie told herself grimly. He and the woman would come bearing down upon her in what they considered righteous indignation. They would tell her she was in the wrong car. She should know better than to try to pass herself off as white.

Annette Marie braced herslf for what was to come. She, who had followed the porter carrying her bags down the aisle, was now going to be forced to scramble up on the seat, haul down the luggage, and carry it as best she could as she stumbled through the swaying cars to the rear one.

The woman with the cold gray eyes was speaking rapidly. The conductor, first looking surprised, then reluctant, and at last resigned, got to his feet. They started up the aisle. The two women behind Annette Marie were whispering excitedly.

Annette Marie laid the magazine on the seat beside her. No use to hide behind it anymore. She fastened the jacket of her suit, brushed an imaginary piece of lint from her skirt, smoothed it over her knees. Any minute now—any minute—

The angry woman and the conductor were only a few feet away. Any moment the deep, flooding humiliation would be upon her, engulfing her, pushing her back completely into the old shyness and fear, wiping out the last vestige of the self-assurance she had worked so hard to gain.

An excited squeal jerked Annette Marie upright. Betty was

coming toward her with outstretched hands, dropping down on the seat beside her, not even bothering to move the magazine.

"How are you?" Betty was asking. "When did you get on the train? I didn't see you— Play up!" she hissed, as she took Annette Marie's cold hands in her own warm ones. "To think you were on the train and I didn't know it!" Betty's excited voice was raised, for the woman and the conductor were very close now.

They stopped beside the seat. Betty looked up inquiringly. "What is it, Mr. Quimbly? Did I forget to give you my ticket? I'm such a scatterbrain!"

"I've got your ticket all right, Miss Betty," Mr. Quimbly said awkwardly. "It's this young lady—"

"You mean my friend?" Betty squeezed Annette Marie's hands. "Didn't you give Mr. Quimbly your ticket, honey?"

"So the young lady is a friend of yours, Miss Betty," Mr. Quimbly said, not trying to disguise the relief in his voice.

"Of course," Betty said sweetly.

Mr. Quimbly turned coldly to the woman. "I guess that makes it all right, Madam. Miss Betty's father is governor of this state. She's been traveling back and forth with me since she was in pigtails. Maybe you'd like to apologize to the other young lady."

"Apologize? Whatever for?" Betty's blue-eyed innocence was disarming. "What's the trouble?"

The woman's face was scarlet. "Everyone makes mistakes," she blustered. "Nothing has been said or done that needs an apology."

Annette Marie jerked her hands away from Betty's and got to her feet. She controlled her voice as well as she could, but her lips twitched nervously.

"There is no mistake," she said. "I am a Negro and I am proud of it, but I shouldn't have stayed in this car when the porter through error left me here. I should have obeyed the regulation. I thought I couldn't face having to follow him to a rear car with all of you staring and whispering, but now I know I could not remain in this car and keep my self-respect."

She began to pull the bags down from the overhead rack.

"Here! I'll help!" Betty's voice was warm.

Together, amid a dead silence, the girls carried the luggage down the aisle, past the staring people, to the rear car. People stared here, too, but not unkindly. Betty and Annette Marie found a vacant seat.

"Thank you," Annette Marie said huskily. "I'll never forget."

"You don't remember me," Betty said quietly, "but I know you. You're a freshman in my college. You won the debate for your class this spring. I recognized you when I got on the train. I thought at first that everything was going to be all right. Then I saw those women whispering, and I knew one of them was going to make trouble. I didn't want you to be hurt. I tried to help. You could have stayed, you know. Why did you do what you did?"

"Because——" Annette Marie began. She hoped Betty would understand.

In her mind's eye, as she talked, she was seeing again the president of the Eastern college standing on the platform of the big auditorium, about to begin his welcoming speech. Annette Marie, self-conscious because she was the only Negro in the audience, thought that, as his blue eyes traveled over the sea of young faces before him, he had singled her out when he said:

"Many of you before me are of different nationalities and races. I want you to remember that it will be up to you to make others respect and admire you. Not only you, as an individual, but the nationality or race which you represent.

"It isn't always going to be easy for you. You will meet with old prejudices. Sometime you may find yourself in a situation where it might be easier to repudiate your nationality or race. Never do this. We, in this college, want and hope to build in you a pride in yourself as an individual, and a pride and deep respect for your people. We want you always to remember that you are their representative. It is a heavy burden to place upon your shoulders. We hope that you will make yourselves worthy to carry it . . ."

Annette Marie felt Betty's hand close over hers again.

"So now you know why I had to leave the car," Annette Marie ended simply. "Suddenly, I hated myself for being weak and letting the old feeling engulf me again. I hated myself for being a coward and not admitting at once to the porter that I was a Negro and under present regulations didn't belong in that car. But when that woman came with the conductor, something snapped inside of me. And I knew that, if I stayed, what I had said, and meant with all my heart in the debate I won, would have been false. I am a Negro, but as a good representative of my race I should abide by the rules. They may be changed someday, but until they are, I shall obey them."

"They will be changed," Betty assured her warmly. "People like you will help to change them. What you did was a fine thing. Prexy will be proud of you."

She went back to her friends and Annette Marie settled down for the few stations left of her short journey.

As the train pulled away, Annette Marie stood watching the rapidly passing windows. Betty was there, waving, her face pressed against the dusty pane. Annette Marie smiled and waved back, and turned to meet her parents.

Problem Pounds

Frances Fitzpatrick Wright

Dearest Janie:

This is a deep, dark secret, so don't breathe it. Since last Christmas I have gained ten pounds, which makes the terrible total a hundred and thirty! Isn't that repulsive? What makes it worse is that today Lucy Ellen gave me her white-and-silver evening dress. I have been racking my brains about what to wear at Mrs. Catagna's recital. You remember I have been taking voice lessons from her all winter. She was born in Italy and is a wonderful teacher, but her figure is long gone.

She told me the other day that I am to sing *"Après le Jour"* at the recital. That means "After the Day" and I love it. Besides, it's a great honor to sing at one of Catagna's recitals. I could just see myself on the stage of the Women's Club with the spotlight striking silver gleams from the white dress.

Sandy hasn't been over much lately. Last week I heard he took Lillian Davis to the movies. You know what a featherweight she is. All I could think of was the impression I'd make on him when he saw me as a slim prima donna in the white and silver.

But when I tried on the dress Lucy Ellen laughed and said, "You'll have to get rid of the extra tonnage, Pat." And when she said it, she was eating chocolate cake with icing an inch thick. It burns me up for her to eat anything and everything she likes and remain a size twelve.

242

I am *determined* to reduce. The clipping about the de Milo reducing plan is from *Mode Magazine*. The girl in the "before" picture is fatter than I am by far, but there is a resemblance and I take it as a grim warning. But isn't she adorable in the "after" picture? I cut out the coupon to send for particulars.

I showed Sandy the advertisement, but didn't mention that I had any idea of reducing. He looked at me suspiciously and said, "Don't tell me you are going in for a diet of fruit juice and raw carrots." Of course, I told him not to be silly. He then went into a speech about the Venus de Milo.

"Take it from me," he said, "she was no sylph. Remember those copies of Greek statues we saw in Nashville? The reason people love the Greek statues after all these centuries is because they are beautiful. The human body at its best. Neither thin nor fat." He looked at me accusingly and said that the women and men in those statues have power, grace, symmetry, and repose. Modern women, he added, lack repose, are forever trying to change their figures, hairdos, nails, and clothing to conform to someone else's idea of how they should look. Honestly, he sounded like Father.

"You have a strong, athletic build, Pat," he said, "and excellent health. You're full of life and fun. Why in heck do you want to shrink yourself to a pallid, bony clothes-horse like this gal?"

I asked him if he had ever thought of syndicating a column of advice to women. But he needn't think he can change my mind. Especially now that I know about Lillian Davis.

Boys really aren't half as smart as they think they are, don't you agree? I'll let you know all about the de Milo plan when I get the answer to the coupon.

Your ever-loving friend,
Pat Downing

Dearest Janie:

Thanks so much for your darling letter. I knew you would be sympathetic. I enclose the letter I got from the de Milo people. I think it sounds wonderfully easy and effective, don't you? But twenty dollars! That's pretty steep, it seems to me, when all you get is menus. They don't send you any food. Of course, they tell you what exercises to do. I guess it's like a lawyer's fee. You are paying for expert advice. But where in the world will I get twenty dollars?

I couldn't ask Father for the money. He would simply rave. He highly disapproves of almost everything people do to improve their looks. He says you never see an unspoiled, natural-looking beauty these days; that dieting and beauty parlors are destroying nature's handiwork.

I haven't dared mention the de Milo plan to Mother either. You know Mother and how she dotes on feeding people. She thinks a schoolgirl's breakfast should be fruit, cereal, bacon, eggs, toast, jam, milk, and to leave out anything is dangerous.

Agnes Regan is willing to share the lessons with me and pay half the cost. She, too, is worried about her weight. But baby-sitting at forty cents an hour, I could never earn even ten dollars in time. The recital's only six weeks off and I should think it would take all of that to lose fifteen pounds, wouldn't you?

We'll just have to go it alone. Agnes is going to try it with me. I made a set of menus for us, mostly fruit juice and vegetables. We are resolved no sweets or starches shall pass our lips. If I stick to it and take plenty of exercise, in six weeks I ought to be able not only to wear the dress but to give Lillian Davis a run for her money, don't you think? I'll have my picture taken and send it to you.

Your ever-loving friend,
Pat Downing

Dearest Janie:

I've lost three pounds! I think I am beginning to look a little pale and interesting. This is what I ate today: For breakfast I had a grapefruit and hot tea without sugar. For lunch two crackers and a glass of orange juice. For supper spinach with lemon juice on it. a slice of broiled fish, and a pear.

Mother knows that I adore steamed chocolate pudding with caramel sauce, so she had it for supper tonight. I am proud to say I didn't weaken. I excused myself when dessert was served. Father muttered that experience keeps an expensive school, but fools will learn in no other. Mother just sighed—

Sandy came over this evening to invite me to play table tennis at his house. You know how I love to play and how good I usually am. You won't believe me when I tell you that Sandy beat me three games straight.

I felt so tired it seemed like work instead of fun. I wasn't having a good time and I had the awful feeling that Sandy was bored.

"What's the matter, Pat?" he asked. "You sick or something? You're about as much fun as a funeral."

If he hadn't made me so mad, I would have burst into tears. I felt like it. He took me home a few minutes later. I couldn't help thinking that he was glad to get rid of me. It made me more determined than ever to dazzle him with my beautiful new figure at the recital.

Write when you can. I need cheering.

Your ever-loving friend,
Pat Downing

Dearest Janie:

If you notice any difference in my handwriting, it is due to weakness and hunger. *Honestly.* Unbuttered toast, poached egg, and tea with lemon juice have their place, but to call them dinner is an exaggeration. Tonight Mother served Idaho potatoes, baked and dripping with butter, homemade rolls that smelled better to me than the perfumes of Araby, and chocolate pie. I chewed away on my raw carrots and celery stalks, and for dessert I had four stewed prunes.

I am not suffering in vain, though, dear Janie, I have lost seven pounds. But I certainly get no sympathy or help. Sandy quarrels with me; Mother tries to tempt me beyond endurance; Father berates me.

"You can't tamper with the laws of nature," he booms, "and escape punishment."

Mrs. Catagna is against me, too. As I told you, she is huge. She collects cookbooks and eats her way through them. Today she offered me some cake made by an old family recipe. I steeled myself to say no, thank you. When she insisted, I told her, in a burst of confidence, about the diet. She shook her head and said I was a foolish, deluded child.

"Besides," she added, "are you not pleased with the way the dear God made you?"

I told her that, meaning no disrespect to God, I felt I could look a lot better a few pounds lighter. Then I explained about the dress and how much I wanted to wear it at the recital. She threw up her hands, rolled her eyes and wailed.

"Dress! Who cares how pretty the dress, if the voice is thin and weak! A strong, vital body, a big chest, this gives to the voice beauty and resonance. Who wants a little pip-squeak voice?"

With that she got to her feet, opened her mouth and sang "*Après le Jour*" in a way to make your spine tingle. But she is too old to care how she looks. And she has already had years of success. It's different with me. But I didn't say a word. I just looked at her and the cake and began to cry. The worst of this dieting is it makes me so emotional. I am embarrassed to think a mere stomach can dominate my life.

I know you are bored stiff, darling Janie, with a pound-by-pound account of my battle of the bulges, but you are the only one who fully understands. Agnes has quit! She said she wouldn't go on like this if it made her look like Elizabeth Taylor's twin! So I am going it alone.

Your ever-loving friend,
Pat Downing

Dearest Janie:

Thanks a million for your funny letter. How grand that you were chosen queen of the fiesta!

As for me, I am weak and wan, but I have shed twelve pounds. I can wear the dress without sucking in! No one is pleased but Lucy Ellen and me. Mother says I have dark circles under my eyes. Sandy says I'm as touchy as a yellow jacket and he's keeping out of my way. Father said if I will give the dress back to Lucy Ellen he will buy me one for the recital. This is really touching when you consider that as a rule Father vetoes new evening dresses automatically.

But with only ten more days to go, I am not going to weaken. My will is steadfast, even though I'm hungry a lot. Today at my music lesson, chocolate cakes and lemon pies were floating in front of my eyes. Mrs. Catagna stopped the lesson and scolded me roundly. She said:

"Patricia, I am disappointed. I thought you loved music enough to work hard. I had even the hope for you to win the Grace Moore Scholarship next year, when you are a senior. I think to recommend you for it, but now I have the doubt."

The idea that I might have missed such a thrilling chance made me feel worse. It's a wonderful scholarship. Only one high school senior can compete from west Tennessee, one from middle and one from east Tennessee. It's a real honor and it would make it possible for me to go to the University of Tennessee if I won. You know Grace Moore was born in east Tennessee.

In weepy tones, I said that I do love music, and, like the three little kittens who lost their mittens, I began to cry again.

Mrs. Catagna looked at me unsympathetically. "So you love music?" she said with sarcasm. "But you love better to starve yourself and look fashionable and wear the glittering dress. Now you have no energy left for singing." She stamped her foot and the floor trembled. But not as much as I did. "Foolish one!" she shouted. "What is a dress if the voice is not fit for singing? What is a dress compared to a scholarship?"

She raved on that music has to bubble up like water from a fountain, that it has to come from great vitality, a great enjoyment of life, or it is a poor, mechanical thing. And then she waved her hands as if to brush me and my diet into oblivion. She is the *temper*mental type, but she is a fine teacher, and I respect her.

Dear Janie, how I wish you were here. I never dreamed (a) how hard it is to lose fifteen pounds, or (b) how many people would make it their business to prevent my losing it. It really burns me up. I'm not Eisenhower, or even Mamie. It would seem a plain, private citizen, who never will be President, could eat as she pleased. Far from it. Even Doctor Malone wagged his finger at me yesterday in the drugstore. He offered to buy me some ice cream but I asked for a lemonade without sugar instead. He warned me that proper dieting under your doctor's supervision is all right up to a point, but I must be sure the diet is right for me and I must not carry it too far. He added that women can ruin their health with foolish dieting.

If I have a nervous breakdown, dear Janie, it will be from too much advice rather than not enough food. I am really worried. But if I have lost the opportunity to try for the Grace Moore Scholarship, no silver dress, no size-twelve figure would be worth it.

Your worn-to-a-frazzle friend,

Pat Downing

Dearest Janie:

"If you have tears, prepare to shed them now." Nothing is going my way. But listen to this. Mrs. Catagna, to everyone's joy, announced that she is having a supper dance after the recital. Very ultra. Each girl may invite her escort.

So, natch, I invited Sandy. He stalled, saying he might have to be in Knoxville and could he let me know in a couple of days! Can you imagine? So I said never mind, skip it, and walked off in a huff to invite Tim Tresslar. He is no Adonis, but he sings in the choir with me, and he is a nice boy. He said he would be delighted. So there! I was sure the Knoxville business was a mere excuse, that Sandy wanted to wait and see if Lillian would ask him. And then who do you think he took to the ball game last Saturday? Agnes! Agnes Regan. They sat and ate peanuts and hot dogs all afternoon. Tim told me Sandy said he had a wonderful time.

Tim is a nice boy and knows how to appreciate an invitation. My one regret, and it certainly is a bitter one after all I've been through, is that Sandy won't even see me in the white and silver!

Your ever-loving friend,

Pat Downing

Dearest Janie:

How melodramatic can you get? I mean can I get? (You never are melodramatic.) But this is what happened to me last night. There are only two more rehearsals before the recital so we are using the auditorium at the Women's Club where I think I told you the affair is to be held. I was walking to the rehearsal when I met Sandy. It gave me a turn, as I hadn't seen him since the day I invited him to the dance. He walked along with me and sat down in the back of the auditorium among the escorts and parents.

But later, when I was standing in the wings waiting to go on for my number, I saw him laughing and talking with Agnes, who sings a duet with Peter Foster in the second half of the program.

I was already upset because just as I was leaving home Father said that my new figure might be fashionable but that to him I looked like the last rose of summer. I was so hungry and nervous and unhappy, I had a small tantrum and went out the door with a bang.

I have to admit I was in no state to sing my best to win a chance to compete for a scholarship. And now here was Sandy, who had been so queer and moody with me all these weeks, apparently having a fine time with Agnes Regan. Maybe she asked him to the recital, and not Lillian Davis after all! Suddenly I was sick of feeling half-starved, tired of not having pep enough to enjoy life, weary of quarreling with Sandy and fighting my family. Maybe it was meant for Lillian to be fragile and willowy and for me to be strong and athletic-looking, as Sandy had tried to tell me. He seemed to be having as much fun with plump, good-natured Agnes as he ever had with the ethereal Lillian.

I was so deep in thought Madame had to call me twice when my turn came to sing. I walked out on the stage and in the moment before the spotlight picked me up, I saw Sandy and Agnes still talking halfway down the auditorium. Then, in the glare of the spotlight, I couldn't see anything, but I imagined I could hear them laughing. They weren't even going to bother listening to me. Suddenly the auditorium seemed to be swimming under water. The notes of my song stuck in my throat. I couldn't sing; I couldn't breathe. I thought bitterly, I hope I'm satisfied. I've lost the scholarship! I've lost Sandy! I'll never wear the silver dress now!

The next thing I knew I was on the sagging couch in the dressing room and Sandy was rubbing my hands. Pretty soon Mrs. Catagna came in with a man-sized dose of spirits of ammonia and poured it down me.

I asked what had happened and Sandy said I had fainted, but now I was going to be all right. I started to sit up and Mrs. C. gently pushed me back. She said it was not the time to scold but that if I wanted to be in the recital, I must do as she said.

"I know," I said. "I'll never be so foolish again. I'll never diet unless my doctor tells me to and then only under his direction."

She looked from me to Sandy and began to laugh so that her big body shook like jelly.

"No," she said, "I think you will not be the foolish girl any longer."

She gave me careful directions for what I should eat for the next three days and said she hoped I hadn't lost my chance for the scholarships tryouts because of my foolishness.

But when I got up to go, holding on to Sandy's arm, she kissed me and said: "You must thank the dear God for health, and show your gratitude to him by singing like a lark at the recital."

On the way home, Sandy was tactful. When we arrived, he said, "Look, Pat, I'm going to be in town the night of the recital after all. I know you're dated up, but Mrs. Catagna says I may come to her party as a stag."

So after all he will see me in the dress. Tim is a nice boy, more deserving than most, but strictly between us, there's just one Sandy.

When he was gone, I went in, much abashed, and apologized to my dear, long-suffering parents and told them I was not going to live on lettuce any longer. They were sweet to me and very relieved to learn the dieting was over. And I bet you, too, my darling Janie, will be overjoyed to hear the last of it.

Your happy, contented, and well-fed friend,

Pat Downing

Cara found to her delight that
a loss can sometimes mean a gain

A Little Less
of Cara

Evelyn Z. Zagami

Cara anointed her features liberally with the cream and regarded the result in the mirror of the medicine cabinet. My face, she thought miserably, looks like a baking-powder biscuit.

This harsh criticism was not entirely untrue. Her skin did have the heavy tone of biscuit dough, and her face was beginning to look moonlike. Lying around with the feet up, reading romantic novels, may be relaxing, but it does not promote a slim figure or a radiant glow.

"I used to think teen-agers had dates all the time," observed Cara's sister Linda, not yet quite in the magic span at twelve.

Cara looked pained. "Who wants to waste time with high school kids?" she countered loftily.

This was crying wolf. As a freshman she had been pursued by a young man with an unhappy habit of telling everybody how to do things. Cara, too kind to snub, had eventually been coupled with this admirer and ignored by the other boys.

"Books are much more interesting," she told Linda.

"Ye gods!" her sister explaimed indignantly, "what kind of a reputation will the name of Carmody have by the time *I'm* in high school?" And in her apprehension she added, "Look at you, Cara Carmody, you're getting fat!"

Cara, scrutinizing her eyebrows, did not deign to reply, but before retiring she climbed up on the slipper chair and inspected the half of herself which was not usually reflected in the hanging mirror over the dressing table. Linda's shot had not been a blank. The figure in the pink robe was definitely not Hollywood material.

"Mom, I'm going on a diet," Cara instructed her mother at breakfast. "Tonight I'd like just steak and salad."

"Oh, *just* steak and salad. You don't think you're going to have *that* every night, do you?" Mrs. Carmody inquired with some irony.

"Well, maybe not every night," Cara conceded. "That's what the movie stars eat, though. This morning I'll have just a piece of dry toast and an orange, please."

Her mother did not argue. She had learned long since that nature balanced most things. This morning she filled her daughter's order and, when Cara left for school, slipped an extra dime in with her lunch money.

"You should have given her a dollar," Ted Carmody, age seventeen, complained later. "She had the regular thirty-cent lunch, and a pie besides. Then, when I was sitting with some senior big wheels, she came over and asked me for a quarter. A quarter!"

"She ate two candy bars with my money," he added bitterly, "and you know what I had for dessert? Some cookies Shirley Wegman made in eleven o'clock cooking class. She forgot to put in the sugar."

Cara's diet was tacitly ignored for the rest of the week. When her skin erupted from too many sweets, she counterattacked with a white clay pack.

"What would your wonderful Rock Hudson think if he saw you now?" Linda, the agitator, inquired, walking in on this ritual.

Cara considered herself in the mirror. Two large dark eyes gazed gloomily back from the ghastly mask topped by a Hottentot arrangement of curlers. "He'd run for his life," she admitted forlornly.

Linda laughed, then became serious as she studied her sister. "You really are pretty, Car," she said judicially. "It's just that you eat too much and don't move around enough. It makes you look— oh, kind of dumpy. But you *are* pretty."

It was somewhat in the nature of an atomic blast, then, when

Cara announced one Friday that she had been invited to a Y.M.I. dance, and that her blue taffeta would have to be let out.

"Who you going with?" Ted demanded, fearing disgrace.

"Nobody you know," Cara said defensively. "He's in my Spanish class, and his name is John Walsh."

"Cara says he's a very nice boy," Mrs. Carmody added, fixing her son with a stern eye.

"If he's so nice, why do I have to meet him?" Mr. Carmody demanded on the crucial evening. "He's just asking for Cara's company for a few hours, isn't he? Surely he's not going to ask my permission to marry her?"

"It gives a girl background—value—if her escort sees her in the midst of her devoted family," his wife told him imperturbably.

"Mama, for goodness sake, say 'date,' not 'escort,' " Linda begged.

"I look simply frightful," wailed Cara, frantically redoing her hair at the hall mirror. It fell into place unexpectedly, framing her face in loose, dark waves.

The doorbell rang. It was Cara's date, and the uncomfortable introductions were made, Mr. Carmody doing his best to act up to his assigned role of fond but exacting father.

"Whew!" he sighed with relief when the young couple had been speeded on their way, the boy's gardenia fastened to Cara's velvet coat. "Nice boy," he said. "Sort of impressive somehow."

"That is character," Mrs. Carmody explained to him.

"Oh—well, since you're such a psychologist, what was it that was wrong with Cara?"

Linda, who had been pondering, suddenly laughed. "She looked like that cooky jar Grandma used to have," she giggled. "You know, the Dutch girl with all the petticoats. Only with Cara it wasn't petticoats."

"What's the matter with La Cara?" Mr. Carmody wanted to know the next night at dinner, when his eldest daughter dreamily refused the homemade orange cake and asked to be excused.

"I think she's in love," Mrs. Carmody confided, *sotto voce*. "Her thoughts are miles away, and she sort of smiles all the time. I'm sure dating John has buoyed her up."

Ted gave a hoot. "The way she looked in that dress last night she could have floated alone," he said.

"Ted, that will be just e—"

"It isn't John Walsh," Linda put in mildly, folding her napkin and placing it in the silver ring marked *Baby*. "It's Jerome Hoberg —a boy from Phoenix who has just moved here. He has golden hair and sea-blue eyes."

"How do you know?" Mrs. Carmody demanded.

"I just happened to hear Cara talking to Kathy on the phone," Linda explained.

"Just happened," Mr. Carmody said. "I bet. Golden hair and sky-blue eyes, eh?"

"*Sea*-blue eyes, Daddy."

"Hah! Now I suppose I'll have to sit around and supply a background for Cara while *this* one gets introduced."

But Mr. Carmody was wrong. The young god from Phoenix never appeared.

Mrs. Carmody got a glimpse of him, though, from the bay window while she was enjoying her afternoon cup of coffee. Cara, the golden-haired boy, and a fluffy little blonde who clung to his arm possessively stood talking for a minute at the end of the path, evidently having walked down from the school bus together.

Then Cara turned toward the house. Unaware of Mrs. Carmody's gaze, the pretty blonde reached up to whisper something in the boy's ear as they walked away. Then they both turned to look back at Cara, mounting the steps heavily. When their laughter had subsided, they went on again, absorbed in each other.

The heart of Cara's mother was hot within her, but her voice was composed as she greeted her daughter and suggested an afternoon snack.

"Oh, Mama, you know I shouldn't," Cara said reproachfully. "I'm so fat. But I'm so hungry, too! I try and try, but it doesn't do any good at all." Her voice was despairing.

Mrs. Carmody sipped her coffee. "In my day," she said, "we tried every crazy diet under the sun, and a lot of us nearly ruined our health. We were the pioneers. Now any girl can go to her doctor for advice and a safe diet, instead of behaving like the reckless flappers we were."

Cara giggled. "You a flapper!" She stared at her mother, trying vainly to envision her in a Charleston contest, the ruffle of a sack-like dress flipping above her knees. When she gave this up as impossible, she returned to the subject at hand. "But Mother, I *do* know how to diet," she said.

She repeated this confident statement to the doctor a few days later.

"Everybody says that," he told her, recording her blood pressure, "but hardly anybody knows what he—or mostly she—is talking about. For instance," ticking off one finger, "do you know what foods refine your skin and beautify your eyes, and also satisfy that craving for sugar which is the downfall of most hit-or-miss diets?"

Cara opened her mouth in a guess, but he was already ticking off the second finger.

"How about vitality food?" he asked. "And what would you eat to build up all the muscles that makes the difference between litheness and just plain jelly? And which exercises would help?"

"You mean I can do all that just by what I *eat* and how I exercise?" Cara said, charmed.

"All that and more," he assured her. "*But,* you have to work at it, Cara. It's a test of character to change bad habits to good. You'll have to take one day at a time, and master that day as well as you can."

Cara stopped on the way home to buy a day-at-a-time calendar pad, and before she went to bed that night she wrote, under the next day's date: "Ten deep knee-bends," and "Stay away from snack shop!"

It was a beginning. After that the struggle was on. The autumn days invited brisk walking, but on the other hand they stimulated appetite. Cara said "just this once" quite a few times at first and went with the other girls to have a chocolate double-decker or a piece of fudge cake in the Hi Snack Shop across from the campus. The food still tasted as delicious as ever, but the pleasure lasted so short a time, and Cara's conscience bothered her all the rest of the day. It took a lot of days before Cara realized it wasn't worth it.

Then there were the knee-bends and the toe touching; the imaginary bike riding and the waist twisting. The first week of her new way of living, Cara stretched her muscles into a system of perpendicular and horizontal aches and pains. For the next week she avoided using a single unnecessary muscle. Then the seniors put on their Seniorpheum, and the Carmody family went in a body to see Ted, in a stupendous false nose, do a parody of *Cyrano de Bergerac*. Act Three of the show turned out to be Jerome Hoberg, doing a tango with Ninette Spilman, who could bend backward until her hair touched the stage.

Cara got up twenty minutes earlier the next morning and bent backward, forward, and sideways. But when the fillip was gone, it was sheer struggle again. To hear the winter rain slashing against the window, while she lay snug and warm in bed, had been one of the high points of living for Cara. Now she closed her eyes tightly, threw the covers back, and jumped out into the cold to swing a make-believe ax.

Slowly but surely her waist measurement declined. By the end of the term the boys were beginning to discover Cara. Her little desk calendor bore such memos as "Kent: picnic. Bring hot dogs." And: "Alan: Square dance. Wear hair ribbon and L's pink pinafore."

The initials J.W. on two or three pages testified to John Walsh's constancy.

"Funny, everything goes right when he's my date," Cara told Linda over a Saturday midnight snack of skimmed milk and celery. "Like tonight. It makes me feel—well, cool."

"Maybe he's your affinity," Linda suggested.

"My *what?*"

"It's like if you were born in Scorpio and he was born in Pisces; you'd be ideally mated."

"How crazy can you get? He's the last boy in the world I'd go for. He's too—too sensible!"

That can be another word for maturity. But Cara wanted glamour, or the boy from far away places. And she finally got him.

It might have been the bathing suit that did it. The brown-and-gold-brocade lastex suit was enormously becoming to Cara's dark eyes and hair, and to the satin skin that was her reward for careful eating and plenty of soap and water.

"I swore I'd never go swimming again, after the way I looked in that old green suit last summer," Cara confided to Linda, as they crossed the boardwalk leading from the bathhouses. "And oh, how I love the beach!"

There were shouts of greeting from here and there on the sand, and a couple of admiring whistles, as the two girls made their way to a sheltered spot against the pavilion wall.

"Aren't you going to ask who whistled?" Linda wanted to know when they were finally settled with blankets, radio, sun-tan lotion.

"You're not supposed to look," Cara admonished. "Who was it?"

"One was your dreamboat."

"Jerome?"

"Yep. And he's coming right over."

"Oh!" Cara, who had been casually applying lotion to her legs, began rubbing it in as though her life depended on it.

"Well, hello there!" The sea-blue eyes looked confidently down into Cara's. "It's about time we got together, don't you think?" He sat down close to her, his back to Linda.

"Say, your hairdo's real George," he said. "It makes you look like Elaine Stewart."

Cara gave him an arch smile but fluttered nervously as he moved in a little. Seen so close, he was not quite as godlike as she had pictured him in her dreams. His romanticized eyes had a bold stare she found new in her experience.

"It's hot, isn't it," she said quaveringly.

"Sure is." Jerome leaned back on his elbows to see behind them. "You girls bring any eats?"

"Just apples." Cara produced one from the pocket of her jacket and held it out to him. Linda took a bite of hers to insure its safety.

"Better than nothing," the golden boy said, demolishing Cara's.

"Anybody here like hot dogs?" John Walsh vaulted over the railing from the refreshment counter into their midst and handed each girl a roll. "Oh, hi, Hoberg. I didn't know you were here. Have a hot dog."

Cara watched her Ideal reach out and grasp the third and last roll. Her eyes went to John's face, apologizing for Jerome. John's eyes flashed her an understanding look and he smiled.

"Cara, I think you're even prettier than the first time we danced together," he said.

Linda gave a snort and swallowed the wrong way, so that she had to be whacked on the back.

"Man, what do you use for eyes?" Jerome asked incredulously. "The first time I saw you with Cara she was *fat*."

"Was she?" John asked laconically. "Are you going in, Cara?" he asked.

Jerome continued to eat his hot dog. "Not now, Walsh," he said.

Shackled by many week of hero worship, Cara shook her head and stayed where she was.

"Come on, then, Linda. I'll race you across the pool."

John held out his hand and they ran across the sand together and up the stairs to a group that was diving and splashing around at the upper end of the plunge.

Cara watched them pensively. It seemed to her that they were having a great deal of fun. Linda took her turn on the springboard and did a header with legs in every direction. John followed her, cleaving the water like an arrow. Cara had never seen him in the water before, and she was impressed. He climbed out, and Linda could be seen urging him to climb the diving standard. He mounted to the first platform and looked down. Linda and several more languorous older girls shook their heads and pointed higher. He climbed again, coming out on the small platform at the top. Poised there against the blue sky, he was a John Walsh Cara had never seen before. Then he stretched his arms wide, tensed himself, and soared downward in a very effective swan dive.

Cara breathed a sigh of ecstasy. She rose from the sand and brushed herself off.

Jerome twisted around, his brow expressing displeasure. "Relax," he drawled.

Cara gave him the same kind of look she would have given Ted.

"I see somebody I want to say hello to," she told him with gentle pity and, turning the back of the flippant little brown-and-gold suit upon him, ran as fast as she could across the sunny beach to the pool.

Ellie learned that too much glamour
can be a boomerang

Sophisticated Lady

Evelyn K. Zagami

Ellie sawed furiously at the nail of her right little finger, first one side and then the other, trying to make it even. She always had trouble with that nail because it was the last one to be manicured. It was like having just a little milk left in the bottle and pouring it out to get rid of it, but slopping it all over the glass because you were anxious to get on to the next thing.

The next thing at the moment was putting on her nylons. With the clock at twenty after seven she was beginning to get butter-flies. Hermione Schultz, next door in her upstairs bedroom, was practicing Gounod's "Ave Maria" on the violin. Hermione had begun her musical studies at the age of ten, and now at twelve she still showed no sign of genius. Confronted by bar after bar of slow, sustained notes, her juvenile bow rasped up and down. Open windows on this summerlike evening in late spring brought the unobstructed sound directly to Ellie's tense ears. Ellie, who had had excellent musical training and possessed a fine ear, played the piano in the school orchestra.

"Oh, *scream! Scream!*" she cried now, and clapped her hands over her ears, shutting her eyes tight.

"Eleanor, did you say that boy was coming for you at eight o'clock?" Mrs. Harper stuck her head in to ask.

"*Yes,* Mother. Why do you insist on calling him 'that boy'?" Ellie demanded quiveringly. "His name is Randy. I should think that would be easy enough to remember!"

Randy. As she said it she felt herself stricken by a sort of vertigo, as though transfixed by spiritual lightning. How could anyone forget the name of Randy?

"Randy. If he's coming at eight, you'd better let me help you. That dress of yours may need some fixing." Mrs. Harper, glaring at it where it hung, pristine, from the closet door, allowed herself an audible "*tst.*"

Ellie set her teeth. "I have to put my stockings on first," she said as calmly as possible. "I'll call you, okay?"

She opened the small drawer of her dressing table, took out a pair of short gloves, and put them on. Then she picked up one of the sheer stockings beside her on the bed and began carefully drawing it on. It was no time to take up arms again over the dress for which she had already done battle.

"Well, if you honestly feel that nothing else in life will ever measure up to this date," her father had conceded finally, "I suppose you had better be suitably attired. Up to fourteen dollars and ninety-five cents, that is. And it has to last for five or ten years!"

Mrs. Harper had added, "Don't you dare come home with a black dress, Eleanor!"

It was a maddening thing about shopping, that when you had absolutely no hope of buying anything, you saw the most irresistible dresses for eight or nine dollars, but when you had cash in hand for a special purchase, you couldn't find anything you would be caught dead in for under twenty-five dollars. Take her dress for tonight. She had had a picture in her mind of something sleek and supersophisticated. The salesday had shown her some frilly pinks and blues, and a white—with ruffles, for Pete's sake! She wasn't having any of that, and she told the clerk so.

"I'm looking for something more mature," she said. "Something tight, and as dark as possible without being black."

The result was hanging there on the door. She took it down and slipped it carefully over her head, making herself concave so that the seams wouldn't burst. She could zip it up in back by herself because the zipper ended not far above her waistline, after which there was nothing. The dress was the latest thing, of course, but it presented her with a problem. Her bra kept creeping up above its extreme décolletage. After all she had gone through for this moment, her mirror reflection was disappointing.

"I look more like a floor lamp than a voluptuous siren," she informed her facsimile in the tube of purple satin.

Hermione played B-flat instead of B-natural, going back over the phrase three times, as if to make sure she had it wrong. Ellie shuddered and then caught her breath as the doorbell rang.

If it had been just any date—Bob Tennier for the movies, or Lefty Meade for softball—she would have finished her dressing and gone to meet him in calm self-possession.

With Randy this was impossible. When you had seen him, with an injured knee, carry the ball sixty yards to a touchdown in the last five minutes of play with the score twelve to seven in favor of the other team. . . When you had heard him sing the "Serenade" in Central High's presentation of *The Student Prince* . . . "Oh, hear my longing cry . . . Oh, love me or I die . . ." When you . . . Well, it was impossible, that was all. And almost as impossible that she had been included in the bunch that went uptown in a burst of camaraderie and mutual congratulation between the orchestra and the cast after the same operetta. Somehow she had ended up with Randy and this incredible invitation to the High Hop.

"Hop is about all you'll be able to do in that concoction," Mrs. Harper said, bringing official news of Randy's arrival. She stuffed the lace edge of the evening bra down into concealment.

It certainly was not a dress for freedom of movement, Ellie realized belatedly as Randy helped her into his highly polished 1941 sports car. In order to get in she had to sort of lie down on the seat and hoist her legs in together. It was very unglamorous.

"Have you been doing any singing lately?" she asked brightly as they spurted off up the street.

"H'm?" He was still wrapped up in the car's mechanism. "Oh. No, nothing but shower solos."

"Wasn't it fun? The operetta, I mean."

"H'm? Oh, yeah. Big stuff."

It was clearly ancient history to him now, two weeks later. What else was there to talk about? Football? That was out of season, too. Ellie gave it a try anyway.

"That was a wonderful touchdown you made in the Piedmont game," she said.

"Thanks." He blasted the horn at a stationary dog in the road. "Dumb dog," he muttered.

Ellie shrank a little, as though he really might have had her in mind.

It should have been pure triumph to walk into the ballroom at Randy's side, but somehow it wasn't. Ellie was too aware of her recklessly bare back and of the periodic ascension of that glaring line of white above the purple satin. The band was playing "Love Me Tender" while she primped in the cloakroom, and the spell the first music of a dance always cast made her glow as she came out into the hall where Randy was waiting. Just for a minute she was the Ellie who could still put away six hot cakes with bacon for breakfast, who laughed a good, appreciative ha-ha-ha when anything was funny, who got up early Sunday morning to get first chance at the funnies. In short, the real Ellie.

"Hi, Ellie!" Randy said, as though he were greeting her for the first time that evening.

The two boys talking with him said "Hi," too, and asked for dances.

"Love Me Tender" finished sweetly, leaving a vast silence, empty of ideas, as she and Randy walked down the corridor and made their entrance into the auditorium. Then, as if on signal, the drummer leaped up shaking a pair of maracas and the room sprang into agitated life.

Ellie was a good dancer. There wasn't anybody she couldn't follow, nor any step she couldn't do. But she had never tried to rumba in a skirt that hobbled her around the knees. Instead of swinging about with South American dips and bends, she had to confine herself to a sort of stiff-kneed, point-the-toe maneuver like an eighteenth-century minuet.

Her cheeks were crimson with mortification as she and Randy slowly advanced down one side of the ballroom. Linda Tarvell,

Randy's date for last year's prom, passed them twice, her red calypso skirt swirling around her knees.

"Isn't Linda's dress pretty?" Ellie asked gaily, determined to be generous if she couldn't be graceful.

Randy turned, caught Linda's eye, which had been on him for some time, and jerked his head in response to her enthusiastic greeting. He and Ellie traversed another few feet of floor space.

"Didn't you think her dress was pretty?" Ellie insisted.

"Tell the truth, I didn't notice. She's a good dancer, though!"

"Isn't she!" Ellie's heart was plutonium.

Wayne Beasley cut in, full of bounce. His legs were a mile long, and when he danced he carried his partner along like a leaf in the breeze. Or the side of a barn in a hurricane. Ellie almost split her purple skirt.

"Come on, doll! Come *on,* let's move!" he exhorted her, trying to beat the field to the far end of the auditorium.

Ellie minced along as fast as she could.

"What're you dancing that way for?" he demanded loudly. "What's the matter? You losing something?"

"No!" Ellie stepped on his foot. "Can't you see my skirt's too tight to go crashing around like this?"

"Crashing! Well, how d'ya like that!"

"Oh, I didn't mean it that way. I *like* to dance with you, Wayne, only can't you take shorter steps?"

They minced along together for the rest of the dance. Wayne's expression was one of acute suffering. Linda passed them again and again, dancing with Randy.

When Ellie hurried out to the cloakroom during intermission she found her worst fears realized. A good half inch of bra was showing.

Things did not improve. Even though she had two or three good partners, the stigma of defeat was on her and she felt hopelessly dull and unattractive.

The last dance—with Randy, of course—was a waltz. The music was melting, and conversation was unnecessary. But the evening was so nearly over, her chance so nearly gone, that Ellie made one more try.

"Do you like to read?" she asked with a spurious, desperate vivacity. And then memory smote her. In an old TV movie, the heroine, striving to make interesting conversation under identical conditions, had asked the same question: "Do you like to read?" Her partner, a caddish type, had looked down at her without emotion and replied, "Not while dancing."

Randy was no cad. He talked books, sometimes letting a sentence go unfinished to hum a bar or two of the music. Then it was all over. The illuminated moon and palm tree and the legend *Monahan's Moonlighters* on the bass drum went dark. Somebody from the dance floor banged out "Good Evening, Frie-e-ends" on the abandoned piano. There was a stampede for the cloakroom. The caretaker stood by the doorway as a reminder that life was not all frivolity.

Thirteen minutes later Ellie had been returned to her doorstep.

"Thank you for a nice evening," Randy said, balancing on the top step.

"I enjoyed it," Ellie returned, per the etiquette book.

There was silence.

"Well, I'll see you at school Monday," she said, opened the door, and went in quickly.

When she had shut it, she leaned against it, pressing her face against the unyielding wood. After the last echo of Randy's departure had died away, she took off her coat and her shoes and went to bathe her eyes. Then she unzipped the purple dress, yanked it down off her arms, stepped out of it, and gave it a good kick.

Later, she got out of bed, hung it dutifully on a hanger, and stuffed it out of sight in the back of the closet.

Monday she and Randy exchanged smiles in English 3-B. Student-to-student smiles. The same thing happened on Tuesday. Wednesday they passed in the upper hall between classes. Randy said, "What d'you say?" and was halfway down the hall before she got out, "Nothing much, Randy." Friday night nobody phoned. Saturday night Ellie waited until eight o'clock and then went to the movies with Hermione's sister Margaret.

The purple dress remained in the back of the closet. Even if it had been her favorite dress, instead of her life's greatest disaster, she couldn't have worn it skating at the roller rink or to the neighborhood theater. Then in a burst of untypical behavior, Mr. Harper bought tickets for the family to see a revival of *The Desert Song* at the opera house, and out came the backless creation.

"I only hope the minister doesn't sit behind us," Mrs. Harper said, basting Ellie's bra securely to the back of the dress, where it would presently overpower the spineless satin and draw it up in a pucker above Ellie's waist. This, however, was not discovered until the second-act intermission, and before that Ellie had fallen in love with the *Red Shadow,* thus regaining an interest in what she had felt was a hopelessly blighted life.

Although the final curtain inevitably fell, it was not the end of the play for Ellie. She herself became *Margot Bonvalet,* somewhat to her father's mystification. Sometimes she trailed about in her dressing gown—utilitarian, but long and sweeping because it was a hand-me-down from her Cousin Barbara who was much taller—singing snatches of "Romance" as she set the dinner table. Sometimes she was the chic Parisienne just arrived in Algiers, replete with salutations and exclamations culled from her French grammar. *Bon Soir* and *Bonne Nuit* and *Alors!* and *Mon Dieu!* And of course *Merci.*

She bought the record, "Medley from *The Desert Song,*" and played it at night in her room, wearing the purple dress and enormous spray earrings with rhinestones that had been on special sale at the Little Gem Novelty Store.

It took almost three weeks for reaction to set in; for Ellie to realize that *Captain Gallant* was probably the closest she would ever get to the Foreign Legion; for the purple dress to return to its exile in the back of the closet. Then it happened—zing!—one warm Saturday morning. Ellie woke brimful of unromantic energy; ate three eggs for breakfast, with toast and jam; got into her old paint-stained, faded jeans; and dragged hoe and rake, trowel and fertilizer, around to the plot against the back fence that was known as Eleanor's Experiment.

There were weeds up and down the neat rows, and her lovely green lettuce plants were drooping in the hot sun, though someone had done enough watering to keep things alive. She got down on her knees with the trowel and worked the crusted earth carefully around each wilting head, then brought the hose and let it trickle down the row as she tackled the weeds vying with the lacy carrot tops. For almost two hours she worked, creating order and beauty.

Next door Hermione vented her creative spirit on "Don't Be Cruel," almost certainly not her lesson for the week. It somehow fitted into the scheme of the sunny Saturday morning—the scheme of home and neighbors and rewarding effort. Ellie felt a positive sense of kinship with Hermione.

For the first time in many weeks, she felt satisfied and proud as she hoisted herself on the fence post and surveyed the result of her work. The lettuce plants were crisp-leaved bouquets now, and the carrot tops waved gracefully alone. String beans, as glamorous as any ornamental vine, reared themselves skyward on crisscross poles.

"Hey, that's all right!"

Ellie did not fall off the fence post because she was leaning on the hoe. She clung to it firmly as she looked down over her shoulder at Randy in the Butterfields' adjoining yard.

"Well, hi!" she said, merely being neighborly. "I never expected to find *you* on the other side of my back fence."

"I was trying to help Stan Butterfield fix his TV set," he said, coming over to rest his chin on a picket. "No fooling, you didn't do all that yourself, did you?"

Ellie posed with thumbs in armpits. "Yup," she said.

"Aw, go on. Girls never get straight, even rows like that."

She laughed. "I learned from a good teacher. When I was in the sixth grade we had to make little gardens. There used to be a big lot where we worked, across from Washington School. I was awful. Couldn't raise a thing. But one of the boys whose father was a truck farmer helped me."

"Uh-huh. You were his type, I suppose?"

Her laugh intimated that such might be the case, but she said, "Maybe he just liked gardening. Anyway, I had sense enough to remember what he taught me, and I'm glad."

"You really like it, huh?"

"Love it."

"I wonder—" She could feel him looking up at her flushed face and wind-blown hair. "Would you help me with my 4-H garden?"

"Of course."

"You would?" He straightened up. "I don't suppose—I mean, you're probably pretty tired for one day, aren't you?"

"Not me!" She used the hoe handle to vault off the fencepost and wiped her hands on her jeans. "I'm starving, though."

"Oh. How long'll it take you to eat?"

"About twenty minutes. Just sandwiches and things."

"I'll wait for you."

"Why don't you come on in and have a sandwich, too?" she asked, as calmly as though he were Hermione's sister Margaret.

"You bet!"

He maneuvered himself over the fence and walked beside her through the green garden. A little breeze blew the scent of talisman roses toward them from the climber over the back porch, mixed with the fragrance of Mrs. Harper's Saturday morning baking.

Randy filled his lungs. "What a day!" he said.

"Isn't it?" Ellie held the screen door open for him to follow her into the kitchen.

About the Authors

LAURA NELSON BAKER is a former newspaper editor and library assistant who now devotes all her time to writing, mostly for young people. Her son and two granddaughters are responsible for many of the insights which make her work so readable. The heroine of "There's Always a Price Tag" is, in fact, named for her older grandchild, Laurie Sue.

Mrs. Baker lives near San Francisco, in a country home surrounded by douglas fir, madrona and bay trees. She is the author of a number of books and numerous short stories and articles which have appeared in many leading publications, including *Woman's Day, Seventeen, Co-ed, The Christian Science Monitor,* and *The American Girl.*

SKULDA BANER has pursued her dream of becoming a successful writer through a host of byways without once losing sight of her goal. Following graduation from high school in Ironwood, Michigan, where she was born, she took various extension courses to study English literature, writing, art and music. She taught school, took a business course, went into advertising, became a radio writer and announcer in Milwaukee, edited a house organ, and turned again to advertising, writing fashion copy.

In 1939 she spent the summer visiting Sweden, her parents' homeland, and returned just before the outbreak of World War II to become involved in a battle of her own—against glaucoma. A final operation in 1940 left her permanently blind.

A year later, with the help of her sister Nana, and as a kind of memory visit with the people of her childhood, she began to work out the stories which became "Latchstring Out," published by Houghton Mifflin. Since then she has written short stories and articles for *The American Girl, Ladies Home Journal,* and other periodicals, as well as several novels and television scripts. The author of "Operation Snow Lift" lives with her sister, Nana, and her husband, Burke W. Taylor, in Los Angeles. Her constant canine companion is her Labrador, Madame Wriggle-Breeches.

BETTY CAVANNA, widely known and frequently honored for her outstanding contribution to juvenile literature, grew up in Haddonfield, New Jersey. She majored in journalism at the New Jersey College for Women (now Douglass College). While working for the Presbyterian Board of Christian Education, she became interested in writing for young people. Since 1940, she has written fifteen books which have delighted teen-age girls throughout this country and in many foreign lands. She is represented in this collection by "The Girl Who Had Everything" and "Mr. Lincoln Lends A Hand." In private life she is Mrs. George Russel Harrison, wife of the dean of science at the Massachusetts Institute of Technology. She and her husband and her teen-age son live in Belmont, Massachusetts.

JOE CHRISTY was in high school in Lawton, Oklahoma when his father's business failed. Joe went to work in a service station, but several years later went back to high school, and continued his education through University of Kansas extension courses. With money saved, Joe started his own auto supply business, then took various jobs. He wound up driving racing cars in Oklahoma and Texas; an accident in a new, unpaid-for foreign car put an end to this career.

Throughout his teens, Christy had spent much of his spare time at a one-hangar, three-airplane, local airport. The airport operator occasionally allowed him to fill an empty seat on a short hop. The field and its owner were inspiration for Christy's first short stories, several of which have been published in *The American Girl,* among them, "Champions Walk Alone." Mr. Christy's first book is a manual for beginners and prospective flyers, but he has gone on to write novels as well.

MARGARET GOFF CLARK began to write poetry when she was nine years old, barely five years after her family moved to New York State from Oklahoma City where she was born. Margaret studied at Buffalo State Teachers College, took summer courses in writing at Columbia University and attended various writers' conferences. For six years she taught in elementary school, then married Mr. Clark, also a teacher.

When her son and daughter were still youngsters, Mrs. Clark met a group of women who shared her interest in writing. They formed the "Deadliners," sworn to produce one completed manuscript per month or pay a dollar. No one wanted to part with a dollar; all have since become published writers. Mrs. Clark has published more than two hundred short stories, of which two, "The Crowded House" and "Joe and I," are presented here, and twenty-five plays as well as a number of poems. She writes from nine to twelve, every day, if possible, at her desk in the Clarks' hundred-year-old house outside Niagara Falls, N. Y.

LOIS DUNCAN sold her first story when she was thirteen. She recalls vividly the excitement of receiving her first check, for $25.00. Lois kept writing through her high school years; by graduation she had a long list of sales to young people's magazines and the *Saturday Evening Post.* She had also taken prizes in three of *Seventeen* magazine's annual short-story contests.

From high school in Sarasota, Florida, Lois entered Duke University where she met and married Joseph (Buzz) Cardozo, who entered the Air Force upon graduation. Later the Cardozos settled in St. Petersburg, Florida. Buzz entered law school and Lois was kept busy with her little girls, Robin and Kerry. Like many another young couple, the Cardozos tried to stretch their GI checks; Lois turned back to writing to help pay the bills. More short stories appeared in magazines. Her first book, DEBUTANTE HILL, was written as follows: "I decided to try a book soon after Kerry was born," she says. "Kerry awakened at five each morning. To keep her quiet so the rest of the family could sleep, I got up with her. Since I was up anyway, I thought I might as well spend the quiet hours at a definite project." To her amazement, DEBUTANTE HILL won Dodd, Mead & Company's "Seventeenth Summer Literary Competition." It was published in 1958.

The Cardozos now live in Sarasota, Florida. Lois Duncan has had stories in many magazines including *The American Girl, Compact, Chatelaine, McCall's, Reader's Digest, Seventeen,* and *Woman's Day,* and is the author of five books for young people. Her story presented here is "The Wish."

MARJORIE EATOCK was seven years old when she began to haunt the library of the Iowa town where her family lived. When she was seventeen, since she seemed to be spending most of her time there anyway, the library hired her for summer work. After junior college and some time at Drake University, she began to teach in her home-town schools. During the next few years she taught gym and history, chaperoned the cheerleaders, took over the school library, and married a former baseball player who is in the poultry business. Together, she reports, they own a conglomerate of fishing tackle, an old automobile and a small son. Her story here is "Going Steady."

INA EDMONDSON's friends and relatives were so enthusiastic over her first story, written when she was in the fifth grade, in Oklahoma, that she was smitten with the writing fever from that day on. In the seventh grade, she began to play the bassoon. These twin hobbies, writing and music, continue to occupy her spare time. She was graduated from the Oklahoma College for Women with a bachelor of arts in English and an increasing enthusiasm for reading. This makes writers, she says, for it breeds the desire to write your own books.

In private life, she is Mrs. Louis Schowengerdt. The Schowengerdts have two sons, Allen and Glenn. She writes at night, and at other times plays the bassoon in the St. Joseph Symphony Orchestra, an amateur organization of sixty-five musicians, and teaches Sunday School. Her selected story is "To Play A Snob."

ELIZABETH EICHER composed her own stories even before she learned to read, running from room to room to tell them to anyone who would listen. This ceased when she was in her teens, she says, only because she was too winded to continue. Born in Ohio, she received her bachelor's and master's degrees in art from Ohio State University. After teaching for three years, she joined a government personnel testing unit, only to be interrupted by a long illness.

During the financially lean years of teaching, she had been writing to augment her income. Now she began again to write, at first for an hour a day, in bed. The following year she decided to make writing her vocation, and it has been her full-time work ever since. Mostly she writes for pre-teen and teen-age readers. She is represented here by "The Circle" and "The Cost."

BEVERLY CONANT FULLER, born in Grand Rapids, Michigan, is a graduate of Wheaton College in Illinois, where she majored in English literature and took part in many college activities. She has written for and edited a small newspaper for the Philalethean Literary Society and has worked on *Woman's Day* as a reader for all non-fiction material. She and her husband, John Arthur Berman, a lawyer, live in West Hartford, Connecticut. Her story, "A Party To Remember," is presented here.

MARY E. GROSS, who was born in Doylestown, Pa., of Pennsylvania Dutch parents, has lived most of her life in the suburbs of Philadelphia. She credits an exceptional teacher of English at Tredyffrin-Easttown High School in Berwyn with influencing her to prepare to teach English. She received her bachelor of arts degree from Ursinus College in Pennsylvania and her master's degree from Middlebury College in Vermont.

During her years of teaching English at West Philadelphia High School in Philadelphia, she has acted as faculty sponsor of the two-a-year yearbooks. In this work, as in her teaching, she has been associated with hundreds of fine teenagers—an association which, she feels, has enriched her life. Although she has always wanted to write, and made some early sporadic attempts at it, she did not write seriously for publication until 1953. Since then she has published some twenty-five short pieces, mostly juvenile fiction. Her story, "Souvenir," was selected for this collection.

ALICE ELEANOR JONES first published (under compulsion and at her own expense) the thesis for her doctorate, and remembers wishing she could write something for which people would pay her. She finally succeeded. Even as a child in Philadelphia, where she was born, she had wanted to write. The neighborhood children used to come to Alice's house and ask her to tell them a story. Sometimes she kept a serial going for weeks, making it up as she went along. In high school and college, she took creative writing courses and submitted occasional manuscripts to magazines without making a sale. After her graduation from the University of Pennsylvania with teaching, master's and doctor's degrees, she taught English for four years at a private school for girls. Teaching and writing both stopped when she married Homer Nearing, Jr., because keeping house and caring for her two sons took all her time.

When the younger boy was old enough to go to school, Alice Eleanor Jones began again to write. She started with science fiction. She has been published since in *The American Girl, Redbook, Good Housekeeping, Saturday Evening Post, Ladies Home Journal, Woman's Day,* and some British magazines. Between stories, she does psychological testing. "Substitute Mother" is her story presented here.

CLAIRE JONES, born in St. Louis, Missouri, was graduated from Oklahoma City University with a major in speech and drama. The following week she and Robert Lee Jones were married. They spent the next four years in Dallas, Texas, where her husband received a bachelor of divinity degree from Southern Methodist University and Claire earned her master's in religious literature from the same university.

After two years at a small church in Oklahoma, they went to St. Andrews, Scotland, for two years while Robert did his residence work for his doctor's degree. It was there that Claire wrote her first story and sold it to the British magazine, *Home Notes.* Since their return to Oklahoma, Dr. Jones has been on the faculty of Oklahoma City University in the department of religion. Mrs. Jones has taught speech classes at the University, taken active part in Little Theater and radio drama, and sold a number of stories. Music, travel, gardening, reading, knitting and a small red-headed daughter are her hobbies. Her story, "The Better Girls," is in this volume.

MIRIAM F. LANDER belonged for three years to a writers' workshop, while studying at Brandeis University in Massachusetts where she received her B.A. degree. A short story or part of one was required to be turned in at every meeting. During her sophomore year, Miriam sold one of these stories, "Reunion of Strangers." As student assistant in the public affairs office, she wrote publicity, was in charge of home-town newspaper features, and reported campus news for a national Anglo-Jewish newspaper. Miriam was born in Boston. She spent some time in Virginia while her husband was in service.

The Landers now live in New York City. They have one child. Frank Lander is an actor appearing in off-Broadway productions. She continues to write short stories which have been published in *Family Weekly, Co-ed* and *The American Girl,* and *Sub-Deb Scoop,* a supplement of *Ladies Home Journal.* One of these, "Graduation Day," appears here.

ELIZA LEDFORD was sitting one day at her desk, where she keeps accounts for a prosperous business firm, when an elderly man came in and asked her if he might rest for a moment. Noticing a pair of crutches leaning against the wall, he said, "I wonder what tall drink of water those belong too?"

"To me," she answered.

"Oh no," he chuckled. "Anyone can see you are not that tall."

She stood up and used her crutches. It has never seemed reasonable to many people that such a tall, healthy-looking girl should use crutches. But they are a necessity for Eliza Ledford, as a result of a fifteen-year battle with arthritis which has left her considerably handicapped.

In Amarillo, Texas where she was born and lives, Miss Ledford is a member of the Junior League, the Forty Niners Club (three dances a year plus a New Year's Special), and a citizens' committee for services to the indigent. A decade or so ago while she was a patient in various hospitals in Tucson, Hot Springs, Arkansas and Ann Arbor, Michigan, she began to collect material for such stories as "Hold High The Lamp," in this collection.

ADA LEFKOWITH cannot recall a period in her life when she did not want to be a school teacher. Her father's illness made it necessary for her to work her way through college. She has degrees from the University of Pennsylvania and Temple University and teaches at the Philadelphia High School for Girls. She was born and grew up in Mahoney City, in the coal-mining region of Pennsylvania, where as she says, children of many national origins became Americans together. For many years, she taught at the South Philadelphia School for Girls, the Wilson High of her stories. Here, where her pupils came from homes of many different national backgrounds, she continued in the United Nations aura of her childhood. With illness at home, there was little time at first for writing, but in recent years she has written numerous articles, poems, stories and a book for girls. "A Question of Loyalty" is her story selected here.

CATHERINE MARSHALL was good enough as an eighth grade student to win an essay contest, but this was her last attempt at authorship for many a year. Later she was graduated from Mount Holyoke College, where she majored in psychology, and from a secretarial school in New York City. She began her business life at the start of the depression.

So many of her employers went out of business that she became more expert at job hunting than at actual work. Eventually she went into the publishing field, where she did textbook advertising and promotion. This sparked her old ambition to be an author.

After several of her short stories had been published, she decided to concentrate on writing. For a short period, she gave her whole time to it, but now she combines it with a position in the Public Library of Yonkers, New York, the city in which she was born and where she grew up. She is the author of many short stories for young people and of two teen-age novels, THE UNWILLING HEART and JULIE'S HERITAGE. "My Heart My Own" is her story in this collection.

EMILY R. PAGE, native of New England, has spent all her life near Boston. She now lives in Lincoln, Mass., situated between historic Concord and Lexington. When her only child was a Girl Scout, Mrs. Page became a Girl Scout leader. She enjoyed this association with young people so much, she began to think of teaching. When her daughter entered high school, Mrs. Page embarked on a teaching career. Then her daughter entered Smith College, and Mrs. Page gave up teaching to study library work at Simmons College in Boston. In their correspondence that year, mother and daughter commiserated with each other over the trials of exams and source themes.

Mrs. Page's first position after graduating was as assistant librarian in the Boston University School of Education library, where she was attracted to the work of school librarian. Now she is involved in the library of a new junior high school in Lexington where, she says, it is a daily thrill to see the girls and boys pounce eagerly on the books as soon as she puts them on the shelves. Mrs. Page's story here is "Eldest Daughter."

ETHELYN PARKINSON has always lived in Wisconsin where she was born. She grew up in the country, was graduated from a county normal school and later from the Bellin Memorial School of Nursing in Green Bay. An early success in writing turned her to a new career. She began with poetry and plays, then turned to syndicated newspaper fiction and to fiction for teenagers. She now writes for three age groups and has lost count of her published short stories. She also has written full-length books for young people.

Miss Parkinson classes her nephews and nieces who live nearby, as her first hobby, coming before her interest in music, nature study or cooking. By reading to them, she learned what children like in stories. Somewhere along the line, she says, the children began to do more for her than she did for them, for they became an inexhaustible source of fiction plots. Their grade school, high school, college and job adventures keep her constantly supplied. Her nieces' hilarious junior high adventures practically write themselves, she says. But her young relatives are not the only children the writer enjoys, for she also has done a great deal of youth counseling. "The Ham and I" is Miss Parkinson's story.

JANET LOUISE ROBERTS was born in New Britain, Connecticut, but spent the first five years of her life in the Philippine Islands with her missionary parents. She received her early education in Connecticut and Ohio and her bachelor of arts from Otterbein College in Ohio. She has held various secretarial jobs while writing in her spare time. Her stories and articles have been published in *The American Girl, Junior Catholic Messenger, Young Catholic Messenger, Treasure Chest, Twelve/Fifteen, Wee Wisdom,* and *Seventeen.* Her hobbies are reading and travelling. "The Slamming Door" was selected for this collection.

HERNDON RION grew up in Dublin, a small town in west Texas. After trying various jobs—weekly newspapers, social agencies, bookmobile libraries, she seemed always to wind up in schools, the Dublin schools and Tarleton State College, either teaching or studying. She now lives on a Virginia farm with her husband, daughter and son. Around the north field winds the historic Bull Run, forming, at the foot of the orchard, Catfish Hole, where oddly enough the neighborhood fishermen catch bass. In the fields are three horses and one pony and, at various seasons, meadow larks, indigo hunting, robins and goldfinch. There are also wild raspberries, Japanese beetles and occasionally deer. There is a haystack which sometimes has boys climbing it and a pond, which often has one boy, Jim, one dog and one cat floating about on it in a boat called a pram. From this quiet spot, the family rushes off each day in all directions to school—Herndon to teach English, her husband to teach math, and the children to learn in someone else's classes. "I'm Nobody" is the author's story selected for this volume.

BERNICE STEVENS lives in a charming modern house, Skyhigh, atop a mountain six miles outside of Gatlinburg, Tennessee. With the building of Skyhigh, she fulfilled a principal ambition, to have a permanent home in the mountains. Other ambitions are to visit at some time, practically every part of the world, except very cold places, to work with crafts and craftsmen, and to write much more than she has yet had time to do.

Miss Stevens was born in Evansville, Indiana, where she went to school and college and where she later taught, first in elementary schools, later in high school and for the last ten years in Evansville College. Her chief teaching field has been arts and crafts, with emphasis on jewelry making. She received her master's degree in crafts from the University of Tennessee. In her work, she went to Gatlinburg, on leave of absence from Evansville College and the Evansville public schools, to complete a survey of crafts in the mountain area. Before she finished the survey, she was offered the position of director of education of the Southern Highland Handicraft Guild. She accepted the job and now works and travels in the mountain areas of eight states. "Foreigners" is Miss Stevens' story presented here.

MARJORIE VETTER is both an outstanding editor and author. Her mother and maternal grandfather were born in her great-grandfather's house in what is now Greenwich Village, New York City. By the time Marjorie put in her appearance in her grandfather's house, the family had moved to Brooklyn. Here, as Marjorie Meyn, she graduated from Packer Collegiate Institute. An inveterate reader, with an urge to try her hand at material of her own, she wrote poems, articles and stories for the school paper. An equally inveterate talker, she captained the debating team and took leading parts in the plays. Later, she acted with a little theater group in Larchmont, New York, with the courage even to attempt Shakespeare.

When she was sixteen she met Carlos Cinta y Calderon, a handsome student from Cuba. The year after her graduation she and Carlos were married. They spent the next decade wintering in Cuba and summering in Vermont on Lake Champlain. Some years after the death of her first husband, Marjorie Cinta married Joseph Vetter. In the meantime Marjorie had joined the staff of *The American Girl* Magazine where she is fiction and book review editor. Occasionally she has written stories with Cuba or Vermont backgrounds. She has authored two novels, CARGO FOR JENNIFER and CHAMPLAIN SUMMER, edited a number of anthologies and collaborated with Laura Vitray on a book for girls, THE QUESTIONS GIRLS ASK. Her story, "Build Me A Bridge," is presented here.

MABEL CLELAND WIDDEMER, if she chose to do so, probably would be able to wear the satin slippers she cherishes because her great-great grandmother wore them when Alexander Hamilton complimented her on "the prettiest feet in town." She herself is a small woman with blue eyes, brown hair and an outgoing personality. An authentic New Yorker, she was educated at Miss Reid's Academy and Notre Dame Academy. She is married to Kenneth W. Widdemer, retired publicity director and brother of the well-known poet and novelist, Margaret Widdemer. The Widdemers have one son, John, and two small granddaughters, who inherit their grandmother's charm. They now live in Gloversville, New York, though they usually spend their winters traveling in this country or abroad and their summers at their Adirondack camp. Mrs. Widdemer is the author of *Souvenir*, a volume of poems which have appeared in many magazines, including *The Saturday Evening Post*, a number of popular books for girls, and a half dozen biographies. "Incident On A Train" is Mrs. Widdemer's selected story.

FRANCES FITZPATRICK WRIGHT has spent most of her life on or near her grandfather's farm near Gallatin, Tennessee, where she was born. She married the year she finished high school and now has five grandchildren, three boys and two girls, the children of her son and two daughters. She lives on the edge of Gallatin at Faraway Hills, an eighteen-acre farm with a charming view of distant highlands. Part of her house is more than a hundred years old. After private lessons in English literature and study of the Bible and related literature, she was for many years a lesson writer for a religious publishing house. Reading has always been her favorite pastime.

She loves old houses and interior decorating, but dislikes a "decorator look" because she believes a house should express the personality and taste of its owner. She is fond of boys and girls and often speaks to

young audiences. She also likes to travel. Her humorous writing style
and her affectionate, sensitive understanding of young people have made
her for many years one of the most popular authors to appear in
The American Girl. Believing the Girl Scout Movement to be a creative,
constructive program much needed in today's "synthetic" civilization,
she is assistant leader of a Girl Scout troop. "Problem Pounds" is Mrs.
Wright's selected story.

EVELYN ZAGAMI is a native Californian. Her English grandfather established a resort hotel in Bolinas on the old stagecoach run to
Sacramento during the gold rush. About the same time, her German
grandfather, a sea captain of a clipper ship, also settled in California.
Evelyn was born and educated in Alamedo. She learned to swim at the
age of five and to play the violin at eleven. She began a stenographic
career with a California oil company, but being too busy dancing half
the night to be an efficient stenographer by day, she lost her job. Having learned her lesson, she made a success of her next job with an insurance company. Later she tried her hand at radio work in Oakland.
After her marriage, she traveled about the country trying to establish
homes away from home for her husband in service. In every town in
which they lived she worked at least part time as a stenographer. Her
advice to girls is to learn shorthand no matter what their choice of
career. The Zagamis have two children, both of whom play the violin.
They live in a house where they view daily the ocean in San Diego, a
pleasure which Mrs. Zagami interrupts to do occasional writing for
television. Her stories selected for this volume are "A Little Less of
Cara" and "Sophisticated Lady."